The Anatomy
of Utopia

CRITICAL EXPLORATIONS IN SCIENCE FICTION AND FANTASY
(a series edited by Donald E. Palumbo and C.W. Sullivan III)

1. *Worlds Apart? Dualism and Transgression
in Contemporary Female Dystopias* (Dunja M. Mohr, 2005)

2. *Tolkien and Shakespeare: Essays on
Shared Themes and Language* (ed. Janet Brennan Croft, 2007)

3. *Culture, Identities and Technology in the* Star Wars *Films: Essays on
the Two Trilogies* (ed. Carl Silvio and Tony M. Vinci, 2007)

4. *The Influence of* Star Trek *on Television, Film and Culture* (ed. Lincoln Geraghty, 2008)

5. *Hugo Gernsback and the Century of Science Fiction* (Gary Westfahl, 2007)

6. *One Earth, One People: The Mythopoeic Fantasy Series of Ursula K. Le Guin,
Lloyd Alexander, Madeleine L'Engle and Orson Scott Card* (Marek Oziewicz, 2008)

7. *The Evolution of Tolkien's Mythology: A Study
of the History of Middle-earth* (Elizabeth A. Whittingham, 2008)

8. *H. Beam Piper: A Biography* (John F. Carr, 2008)

9. *Dreams and Nightmares: Science and Technology in Myth and Fiction* (Mordecai Roshwald, 2008)

10. Lilith *in a New Light: Essays on the
George MacDonald Fantasy Novel* (ed. Lucas H. Harriman, 2008)

11. *Feminist Narrative and the Supernatural: The Function of
Fantastic Devices in Seven Recent Novels* (Katherine J. Weese, 2008)

12. *The Science of Fiction and the Fiction of Science: Collected Essays on SF Storytelling
and the Gnostic Imagination* (Frank McConnell, ed. Gary Westfahl, 2009)

13. *Kim Stanley Robinson Maps the Unimaginable: Critical Essays* (ed. William J. Burling, 2009)

14. *The Inter-Galactic Playground: A Critical Study
of Children's and Teens' Science Fiction* (Farah Mendlesohn, 2009)

15. *Science Fiction from Québec: A Postcolonial Study* (Amy J. Ransom, 2009)

16. *Science Fiction and the Two Cultures: Essays on Bridging the Gap Between
the Sciences and the Humanities* (ed. Gary Westfahl and George Slusser, 2009)

17. *Stephen R. Donaldson and the Modern Epic Vision: A Critical Study
of the "Chronicles of Thomas Covenant" Novels* (Christine Barkley, 2009)

18. *Ursula K. Le Guin's Journey to Post-Feminism* (Amy M. Clarke, 2010)

19. *Portals of Power: Magical Agency and Transformation in Literary Fantasy* (Lori M. Campbell, 2010)

20. *The Animal Fable in Science Fiction and Fantasy* (Bruce Shaw, 2010)

21. *Illuminating Torchwood: Essays on Narrative, Character and Sexuality
in the BBC Series* (ed. Andrew Ireland, 2010)

22. *Comics as a Nexus of Cultures: Essays on the Interplay of Media, Disciplines and
International Perspectives* (ed. Mark Berninger, Jochen Ecke and Gideon Haberkorn, 2010)

23. *The Anatomy of Utopia: Narration, Estrangement and Ambiguity in
More, Wells, Huxley and Clarke* (Károly Pintér, 2010)

# The Anatomy of Utopia

*Narration, Estrangement
and Ambiguity
in More, Wells, Huxley and Clarke*

KÁROLY PINTÉR

*Foreword by Patrick Parrinder*

CRITICAL EXPLORATIONS IN
SCIENCE FICTION AND FANTASY, 23

Donald E. Palumbo *and* C.W. Sullivan III, *series editors*

McFarland & Company, Inc., Publishers
*Jefferson, North Carolina, and London*

LIBRARY OF CONGRESS CATALOGUING-IN-PUBLICATION DATA

Pintér, Károly, 1970–
    The anatomy of utopia: narration, estrangement and ambiguity
in More, Wells, Huxley and Clarke / Károly Pintér ; foreword by
Patrick Parrinder.
    [Donald Palumbo and C.W. Sullivan III, series editors]
        p.      cm. — (Critical explorations in science fiction
    and fantasy ; 23)
    Includes bibliographical references and index.

    ISBN 978-0-7864-4036-8
    softcover : 50# alkaline paper ∞

    1. Utopias in literature.    2. Science fiction, English —
History and criticism.    3. Utopias — Philosophy.    I. Title.
PR830.U7P56    2010
820.9'372 — dc22                                        2010016091

British Library cataloguing data are available

Digital illustration ©2010 Blend Images

Manufactured in the United States of America

*McFarland & Company, Inc., Publishers
    Box 611, Jefferson, North Carolina 28640
    www.mcfarlandpub.com*

# Contents

| | |
|---|---|
| *Acknowledgments* | ix |
| *Foreword by Patrick Parrinder* | 1 |
| *Introduction* | 3 |
| 1. Utopia the Protean Concept | 11 |
| 2. Encounters with a Stranger | 45 |
| 3. Glimpses of a Moving Picture | 97 |
| 4. After Utopia? Anti-Utopia and Science Fiction in the 20th Century | 136 |
| *Conclusion* | 192 |
| *Chapter Notes* | 197 |
| *Bibliography* | 215 |
| *Index* | 227 |

"If anything is in doubt, I'd rather make an honest mistake than say what I don't believe" (More 1989, 5).

# Acknowledgments

This book has emerged after more than a decade of working on various aspects of literary utopias and utopianism, and it is certainly far from complete. During such a long time, I have naturally incurred a lot of debts, and I can only hope I am not forgetting anybody of those who have offered me their help along this long and bumpy road.

The core of this book was written as my doctoral dissertation. I would like to thank all the lecturers of the Modern English Literature Doctoral Program of Eötvös Loránd University (ELTE) Budapest, and especially Dr. Péter Dávidházi for his inspiring course on the history of Anglo-American literary criticism and his personal help in a particularly difficult period of work. Professor Aladár Sarbu, head of the program and the supervisor of this dissertation, not only carefully read and commented on every essay and chapter portion that I presented over the years, but also displayed an incredible amount of patience and understanding in the face of several missed deadlines and a variety of excuses.

I first had an opportunity to delve into More's *Utopia* and utopian theory during a nine-month research scholarship at the Katholieke Universiteit Leuven in 1994–1995, granted by the Soros Foundation. I received a much-needed introduction to the philosophical background of utopian thinking from Professor André Van de Putte, who also read and commented on my first draft of what would become chapter 1. Professor Guido Latré and Dr. Ortwin de Graef offered valuable advice and moral support.

My home institution, the Institute of English and American Studies at Pázmány Péter Catholic University (PPKE), provided me with an opportunity for sustained and uninterrupted work by relieving me of all teaching duties in the fall semester of 2000. I would like to thank the chair of the institute, Dr. Katalin Halácsy, and the dean of the Faculty of Humanities, Professor Ida Fröhlich, for their generous help.

I presented portions of chapter 2 to the Renaissance Research Center at PPKE, whose members — Professor Tibor Fabiny, Dr. Péter Benedek Tóta and Dr. Zsolt Almási — offered a lot of valuable comments. My ideas on More and his *Utopia* have been considerably shaped by Dr. Tóta's unique studies on various aspects of More's oeuvre. Dr. Almási carefully revised and commented on an earlier version of chapter 1, for which I am particularly grateful.

Dr. László Takács, associate professor at the Institute of Classics and Medieval Studies at PPKE, was always ready to help interpret several problematic passages of the original Latin text of More's *Utopia,* for which I remain thankful.

A portion of chapter 3 was presented at HUSSE 2003 in Debrecen, where Professor Zoltán Abádi Nagy directed me to unfamiliar critical literature. I would like to gratefully acknowledge his generous help.

My doctoral dissertation was refereed by Dr. Ferenc Takács from ELTE and Professor Donald Morse from Debrecen University. Both of them provided me with thorough and penetrating critiques, and especially the tough but constructive criticism of Professor Morse gave a whole new direction to my work and decisively shaped the general outlook of chapters 1 to 3. He pointed out both the strengths and the defects of my text and, above all, gave me the courage to pare it down by jettisoning a lot of superfluous material. Without his generous help, this book would certainly display less focus and clarity.

Finally, I would like to say thanks to three people without whom this book could have never been completed. I learned my first English words from Anna Demény, who devoted almost superhuman care and attention to my language education during my secondary school years. Had it not been for her selfless work and insistent encouragement, I would have never had the confidence to apply to a university English program.

My ideas on literature and the purpose of university studies in general were completely transformed by Professor István Géher, head of the Anglo-American Studies Workshop in Eötvös József College. He carefully and patiently guided my first steps in literary studies, in translation and editing, supervised my MA thesis on Anthony Burgess, and suggested the core idea of my dissertation. Had it not been for his admirable skills as a teacher, scholar and psychologist, I would have never ended up as a university lecturer and a doctoral student.

Last but not least, I would like to say thanks to my wife, Vera Benczik, who has not only endured my unceasing complaints and recurring bouts of desperation, and tolerated the several missed holidays and the countless hours spent over books and in front of the computer, but also read almost the whole of my work and offered brilliant insights to help me overcome certain difficulties. Had it not been for her understanding, patience, and love, I could have never brought this book even to a temporary conclusion.

Certain parts of this book have been published before in various essay collections. An earlier version of chapter 2's The Stranger appeared as "Encounter with a Stranger — Introducing Hythloday in More's *Utopia*," in *Elaborate Trifles: Studies for Kálmán G. Ruttkay on his 80th birthday* edited by Gábor Ittzés and András Kiséry, and published by Pázmány Péter Catholic University in 2002; a shorter version of chapter 4's Caliban Stranded in Civilization saw print as "'A Sea-Change into Something Rich and Strange': Aldous Huxley's *Brave New World* in the light of Shakespeare's *The Tempest*," in *What, Then, Is Time? Responses in English and American Literature,* edited by Tibor Fabiny, and published by Pázmány Péter Catholic University in 2001. Both texts are used with the kind permission of the publisher. A significantly abridged version of Chapter 3 was published as "'The Shock of Dysrecognition': Narrative Estrangement, Science Fiction, and Utopia in H.G. Wells' *A Modern Utopia*" in *Anatomy of Science Fiction*, edited by Donald E. Morse and published by Cambridge Scholars Publishing in 2006, and is used with the kind permission of the editor and is published with the permission of Cambridge Scholars Publishing.

Budapest • 2010

# Foreword

With a few exceptions, literary scholars have taken a back seat to sociologists, philosophers, and political scientists in the multidisciplinary project that is modern Utopian Studies. The crucial distinction between utopia as social vision and utopia as text has too often been forgotten. Károly Pintér's perceptive and beautifully written study of four representative literary utopias is, therefore, all the more welcome. Pintér's concern is with the activity of reading utopias, an activity that is, as he shows, less a process of ethical or political content-analysis than of sustained imaginative encounter. Engaging with theorists such as Ernst Bloch, Michael Holquist, and Darko Suvin, Pintér argues in his Introduction that all utopias contain satirical elements and that they should be approached as "literary and intellectual games": "The quality of a utopia is ultimately determined by how challenging and entertaining a game it proves to be." Perhaps the same thing applies to reading about utopias? If so, Pintér's lively and sometimes strikingly original discussion proves his contention to the utmost.

Patrick Parrinder
University of Reading, England

# Introduction

Utopia is a Janus-faced concept in many ways. In everyday use, the word carries a distinctly negative overtone, usually applied to flights of fancy that are impractical at best, irresponsible and potentially dangerous at worst. In this sense, "utopia" is usually contrasted to "reality," "practicability," "sobriety," and the adjective "utopian" is the opposite of "sensible," "realistic," "workable." When applied to people (more often as an epithet attached to someone else rather than a self-proclaimed identity), "utopian" may express a wide range of negative opinions, ranging from condescending derision to outright hostility. Yet the same name is habitually applied to a significant body of fiction, which supposedly constitutes a whole genre of its own and looks back upon a tradition of at least 500 years. Several representatives of this genre are famous and popular books, which seems to contradict the commonly held low opinion about the value of "utopia."

A similar paradox is revealed by the very etymology of the word itself. A Greek neologism coined by Thomas More in 1516, utopia literally means "no-place" or, properly, "nowhere."[1] This "nowhere," however, is described in great detail in More's book, and most subsequent utopias provide a graphic description of their imaginary lands. Utopias are explicitly non-existent, yet they have the power to impress themselves upon the imagination of many readers specifically by their quasi-empirical presence in fiction. Of course, in our postmodern age, when demands of verisimilitude on novels have long passed out of fashion and the "fictionality" of fiction is taken for granted, one may question the relevance of distinguishing between self-identified "nowheres" and other fictional places presented as supposedly real. More's utopia is indeed a purely verbal construction,

similar to Defoe's island, Hardy's Wessex or Dickens's London. But utopias
have a far more ambivalent relationship to contemporary reality than most
novels. Each utopia inevitably emerges from some sort of dissatisfaction
with existing conditions; the author perceives certain problems or defects
in his or her own society, and sets out to picture an alternative society,
which may represent its author's idea of a qualitatively better arrangement,
or may serve as a satirical ploy to ridicule contemporary deficiencies. These
fantastic alternative places are invariably constructed from modified or
inverted elements of the author's contemporary physical and social reality, therefore each and every utopia is connected in intricate ways to a contemporary *topos* (place), resulting in extraordinary combinations of mimesis
and fantasy.

The authorial intent is a major problem for the critical interpretation
of most utopias. Utopia often embodies a social ideal for its author, and
as such, it is highly serious. But it also employs irony and mockery to
expose faults and abuses, and as such, it is satirical and comic. Seriousness and comedy create an odd mixture in most utopias, with the exact
ratio of the two elements varying in each work. It often becomes highly
problematic to discern if the "nowhere" presented in the book is meant as
an ideal to admire, an example to follow, a thought experiment to contemplate or a joke to laugh at — or perhaps all of these at the same time?
Such interpretative decisions are crucial when reading a utopia: the reader
cannot avoid taking at least a provisional stand or else they risk utter confusion and bewilderment as the story unfolds. One might even reach the
conclusion that a given text is not a utopia at all in the sense of presenting a positive ideal, but rather a utopian satire, a parody of utopian ideas
and ambitions — an inverted image of utopia, which is commonly called
"dystopia" in English, or "anti-utopia" in several other languages; perhaps
the term "negative utopia" captures best the essential qualities of this subgenre.

Besides the fascination provided by its imaginary world, utopias tend
to offer something of interest for a number of different scholarly disciplines,
and yet the genre (if it is a genre) cuts across the boundaries of these disciplines, fitting none of their categories clearly. At its heart lies a speculation about the criteria of the good life, which has been one of the
fundamental concerns of philosophy at least since Plato. Such a speculation can hardly take off without postulating certain fundamental premises about what constitutes human happiness and satisfaction, a crucial
question of modern psychology. Such a speculation usually sketches up

alternative ways to organize and govern society, and thus trespasses the terrains of anthropology, sociology and political theory. But "proper" utopias couch their speculation in a fictional form, which assimilates them to literature. It is equally valid to approach them with a predominantly philosophical, anthropological, psychological, theological, sociological, political or literary interest, but none of these approaches seem to do justice to the complexity of the phenomenon.

So far, I have used the term "utopia" in its original or traditional meaning, referring to a literary text bearing certain distinctive characteristics. It should be pointed out, however, that the modern understanding of the term carries a wide range of connotations, several of which are partly or entirely independent of the ancestral literary meaning. The term has had a distinctive career in political ideology and pamphleteering, with various parties and authors hurling it as an abusive epithet at their opponents. Perhaps the most famous, but far from exclusive, example of such demeaning is the way Marx and Engels lumped together three very different early–19th-century Socialist authors and labeled them "utopian Socialists"—with the obvious implication that their own theory represents a new and qualitatively better version of Socialism. Such argumentative and derogatory applications of "utopia" have decisively shaped the predominant understanding of the word in everyday usage.

In contrast to the widespread use of "utopia" and especially "utopian" as a term of mild abuse or mockery, a distinct critical school emerged in the second half of the 20th century that deliberately set out to reinstate the term to its original rights and reinvest it with an overall positive connotation. The representatives of this school are predominantly Western neo–Marxist thinkers who have been inspired by an unorthodox Marxist author, Ernst Bloch, and his massive study, *Das Prinzip Hoffnung* (1953–1959), in which he thoroughly reinterpreted the term "utopia" and made it a central concept of his peculiar theory and criticism of modern human culture. In his wake, a distinct critical approach emerged under the title of utopian studies, which—although Bloch himself was not particularly concerned with literature—eventually branched out into literary criticism as well. Their use of the term "utopia," however, deliberately differs from the original reference to the literary genre originating from More's book; their interest was primarily focused on certain science fiction (SF) authors, whose works were interpreted as critical reflections on contemporary social and cultural problems.

This brief and sketchy introduction can do no more than shed some

temporary light on the multiplicity of interpretations and the diversity of
meaning surrounding the contemporary use of the term "utopia." However, a scholarly approach cannot progress without defining itself vis-à-
vis the current trends of utopian theory, in order to be able to construct
a critical approach that is suitable for a discussion of utopian fiction as a
literary genre. Eventually, my investigation crystallized around three crucial issues: an argument with the currently dominant Marxist critical idiom
of utopian studies, an examination of More's *Utopia* as the generic archetype of literary utopias, and the critical analysis of H.G. Wells' utopian
*oeuvre*, a reference point for most subsequent utopian and dystopian texts.

In chapter 1, I propose to examine the historical evolution of the
meaning and some of the critical interpretations of the term "utopia,"
starting with a semantic analysis and continuing with a brief survey of the
main currents of 20th century critical literature on utopia. I am going to
argue that, as a result of historical changes in the understanding of the
term "utopia" during the 19th century, it received an overwhelmingly ideological overtone, which greatly hindered the emergence of a depoliticized
literary criticism of utopian fiction. Due to the decisive influence of the
Marxist philosopher Ernst Bloch, the critical framework of utopian studies has been defined by a circle of Marxist literary critics, who employ
"utopia" as a hermeneutical method to uncover layers of contemporary
social-cultural critique from literary texts in general, and from modern science fiction in particular, while remaining relatively uninterested in literary utopias. I am going to subject the theoretical writings of the most
influential Marxist literary critic, Darko Suvin, to a critical analysis to find
out if his crucial concepts, cognitive estrangement and the *novum*, relieved
of their ideological ballast, could be employed in the service of a new critical approach to literary utopias. I am going to utilize fundamental generic
insights of Northrop Frye as well as the cultural game theory of Johan
Huizinga to argue in favor of a way of reading that is applicable specifically to the genre of utopian fiction, and which reveals the intrinsic, gener-
ically determined ambiguity of utopian texts. The ambiguity is produced
primarily by the conflicting narrative demands of the utopian genre, generating contradictory currents of meaning in the text, at the same time
reinforcing and subverting the fictional credibility of the utopian vision.
I propose to call this phenomenon — which can be a conscious narrative
strategy of the author as well as an effect produced by the text itself—"narrative estrangement" due to its effect on readers.

In chapter 2, I am going to test my critical approach on the "archetype" of modern utopias, Thomas More's *Utopia*, which — although it was neither written in English nor first published in England — in English translation became a popular and influential part of English literature and provided an inspiring influence for the extraordinary richness of the utopian tradition in English. This wealth is witnessed by several bulky bibliographies of English and American utopian literature, as well as the enduring popular and critical interest in several books of English literature commonly classified as utopian or dystopian, including Francis Bacon's *New Atlantis* (1626), Jonathan Swift's *Gulliver's Travels* (1726), Samuel Butler's *Erewhon* (1872), William Morris's *News from Nowhere* (1890), several novels by H. G. Wells, Olaf Stapledon's *Last and First Men* (1930), Aldous Huxley's *Brave New World* (1932) and George Orwell's *Nineteen Eighty-Four* (1949).

In my examination of More's *Utopia*, I am primarily interested in those qualities of the book by virtue of which it could become the model for a distinct genre of fiction and the archetype of a utopian tradition in English and European literature. I intend to demonstrate that the book established a rich, complex and ambiguous model for the genre with its particular blend of mimesis and fantasy, seriousness and irony, social criticism and mocking satire. To identify some of the historical reasons for this complexity, I am going to begin with a brief survey of the history of the interpretative conflicts around *Utopia*, which are almost invariably rooted in discrepant images of its author, and exhibit a strong tendency toward the intentional fallacy. In my reading of *Utopia*, I am going to focus on the character of the stranger who has brought news about Utopia, the traveler Raphael Hythloday. He is the sole source of our knowledge, and therefore his credibility is crucial to an interpretation of the text. Hythloday is given an ambiguous introduction in Book I and in the accompanying material, and his criticism of contemporary European conditions is debated in Book I by a literary *persona* of More himself, presenting both participants in a dubious moral light, and estranging readers from both narrator and visitor. My concluding argument is that the integrity and credibility of Hythloday as a traveler, philosopher, political reformer, and reporter is inconspicuously but steadily eroded by the undercurrent of the narrative, and by the end his presentation of the alternative community proves not to be an example for the reform of Europe, but an explicitly fictitious construction which reflects an overarching desire to force the variety and complexity of human social institutions into the same strictly rational mould.

The classic literary model of utopia, established by More's *Utopia*, despite its popularity, has been exhausted by the late 19th century, mainly because static visions of ordered and self-sufficient agrarian communities have lost all credibility in the wake of the sweeping economic and social transformation brought about by industrial technology and modern science. A significant part of the literary output of H. G. Wells, the most prolific and persistent author of utopias in the English language, can be broadly interpreted as a series of attempts to find a new model for utopia and lend a new kind of dynamism to the form. In chapter 3, I first examine the young Wells' transformation from an author of scientific romances to the tiresome prophet of the World State, and argue that what most critics consider his decline as an imaginative writer by the 1920s is rooted primarily in a failure to recognize his strength as a satirical writer and to continue to experiment with the genre of the anatomy.

Out of Wells' rich utopian-dystopian oeuvre, I have chosen to examine *A Modern Utopia* (1905), his earliest and in several ways most complete presentation of a new utopian model. The special significance of the book lies in its ambition to present a "meta-utopian" reflection on the crucial issues utopias have to tackle and the characteristic problems the genre has so far failed to overcome. In order to carry out this ambition, Wells proposes a complex and powerfully ironic method of narration, a conscious employment of cognitive and narrative estrangement, which allows him to shift freely between the discourses of fiction and essay, as well as adopting the roles of both omniscient narrator and participant character. His slow and tentative discovery of his modern utopia gradually becomes the allegory of composing a utopia, and his theoretical difficulties are presented as fictional conflicts within the story. My argument is that the eventual failure of the narrator to bring his narrative to a successful conclusion symbolizes the ultimate impossibility of utopia to be invested with sufficient credibility and authority. Despite its inconsistencies and occasional weaknesses, Wells' text is not only a brilliant demonstration of the problems of utopia writing, but the most sophisticated reflection on the inherent ambiguity between social reality and social idealism.

In chapter 4, I propose to cast a long glance on the 20th century, which is commonly seen as an age of the crisis and decline of the utopian genre. While the classic utopian narrative form has been indeed emptied of its potential, two relatively untapped and closely related genres have taken its place: dystopia and science fiction. Although their origins are different, they have been welded into a combined form by H. G. Wells, who is the founding father of both science fiction and dystopia, and he utilized science fiction narrative conventions to present his dystopian visions of future humanity. It is deeply ironic that some of the most vehement critics of the Wellsian utopia, including the authors of the two most successful dystopias, Aldous Huxley (*Brave New World*, 1932), and George Orwell (*Nineteen Eighty-Four*, 1949), were all fundamentally influenced by Wellsian utopian and dystopian visions, and often turned his own weapons against him by presenting nightmare societies in a science fiction genre convention.

I have selected two works for a deeper analysis out of many potential candidates: Huxley's *Brave New World*, which is in my opinion the most ambiguous dystopia of the century, and Arthur C. Clarke's *The City and the Stars* (1953), which I consider to be a representative science fiction treatment of the utopian theme. These two novels provide good examples of how the Wellsian model of evolutionary utopia directly or indirectly shaped and influenced English fantastic fiction well into the second half of the 20th century.

# Chapter 1

# Utopia the Protean Concept

The paradox inherent in any attempt at defining utopia — in fact, in any attempt at defining any concept — was aptly formulated by J.C. Davis: "In order to study what utopias are, it is necessary to know what they are" (*Ideal Society* 12). That is, one is unable to approach the problem itself without first having a prior concept of what "utopia" means. This concept may be derived from the so-called "common understanding" (whatever that means) of the term, or from some sort of familiarity with the more or less clearly defined historical canon of writings called "The Utopian Tradition"; or, in a more fortunate case, from both. Any interpretative attempt must determine its position vis-à-vis this tradition as well as the overtones the term has gained in common use. One of the greatest contemporary authorities in English-language utopian studies, Lyman Tower Sargent, in the introduction to his bibliography of British and American utopian fiction, distinguishes two major problems concerning a working definition of utopias: one is that most scholars have not been familiar with the "vast bulk of the literature," only the "mainstream" of the genre, and the other is that utopian literature, utopian thought and utopian communities are confused in everyday usage (*Bibliography* x). He attempts to clear up at least some of the mess by arguing that a definition should be "usable as a discriminating tool in the analysis of a body of literature," and as such, it should clearly distinguish between utopian fiction proper and various manifestations of utopian thought by an examination of form and purpose of individual books. He obviously dislikes broad definitions that concentrate only on the intellectual attitude of a given work: "If a utopia can take any form, we would have to include virtually all works of political philosophy, most suggestions for reform, and perhaps even all attempts at city planning" (xii). He cites as examples for such a mistaken definition of utopia the inclusion of Hobbes's *Leviathan*, Kropotkin's *Mutual Aid*, and Rousseau's *Contrat Social*, into the canon of the utopian tradition.

What Sargent perceives as a liability, other authors see as an asset. Frank and Fritzie Manuel, authors of a massive study on Western utopian thought, see no practical way of disentangling the different threads of utopianism:

> In the course of time, "proper" utopias, discussions of utopian thought, and portrayals of utopian states of consciousness have so interpenetrated that the perimeters of the concept of utopia have to be left hazy.... A fluid identity will have to suffice, for our primary purpose is to dwell on the multifarious changes of utopian experience through the centuries, and, as Nietzsche taught, only that which has no history can be defined [Manuel and Manuel 5].

They include in their investigation of utopian thought visions of an ancient Golden Age, millenarian prophesies, extraordinary voyages, ideal constitutions, advice to rulers on good government, architectural plans for ideal cities, and the like. They draw the line only at private fantasies with too much idiosyncrasy to have any general relevance, and political reform ideas that are too small-scale or trivial to represent a significant alteration of existing conditions. They themselves describe their concept of utopia as "latitudinarian and ecumenical" (7). Perhaps the only agreement between them and Sargent is that they both exclude from consideration historical attempts to put utopian ideas into practice, in other words, utopian communities. As the Manuels put it, "It would be valid to distinguish between theoretical utopistics and applied utopistics" (9), and their book is an exercise of the first kind of inquiry.

These two examples typify two characteristic positions toward the problems involved in the scholarly application of the term "utopia." Perhaps the most spectacular illustration of the bewildering variety of possible approaches to utopia is the collection of essays edited by Frank Manuel entitled *Utopias and Utopian Thought*. The editor obviously intended to illustrate his own thesis of the protean nature of utopia by bringing together a wide variety of authors and essays in this volume: the illustrious list includes cultural historians, literary scholars, political philosophers, sociologists, evolutionary biologists, a communications specialist, a Protestant theologian, a religious historian, and an economist who was also a member of the French government. They all contribute intelligent and thought-provoking essays on various aspects of "utopianism" (applied as a catch-all term for all the various manifestations of utopian imagination), but it would be hard to find any single issue in which they share a universal agreement, let alone a shared assumption on what constitutes "utopia." Urban historian Lewis Mumford argues that the very idea of utopia derives from the ancient Hellenistic city as idealized by Plato in *Republic*; Frank Manuel identifies a deep unconscious longing for a better life behind every utopian idea; Judith Shklar attributes the post–World War II decline of utopian imagination to a crisis of contemporary political philosophy; religious historian Mircea Eliade links utopian imagination to the quest for an earthly paradise; theologian Paul Tillich examines the transcendental nature of utopia; biologists Paul B. Sears and John Maynard Smith warn against the dystopian prospects of the destruction of the natural environment and the explosion of world population; politicians François Bloch-Lainé, Bertrand de Jouvenel and Frederik L. Polak argue for the practical usefulness of utopian ideas for reforming contemporary society and politics; and so forth. The majority of essays give the impression that utopia functions like a magic mirror: everybody sees in it what they desire to see. Such an eclectic collection obviously benefits an anthology that wants to illustrate the length and breadth of a certain field of interest, but it offers no firm ground for starting a single inquiry.

In an attempt to fathom the source of all this disagreement and confusion, it seems reasonable to turn back to the term itself: I propose to analyze the normative definitions provided by the dictionary to see if it is possible to reconstruct from them a broad interpretative framework based on the most common notions about utopia, with a descriptive rather than a prescriptive intention.

## Dissection of a Word

In order to describe the common uses and understanding of a word, there is hardly a better starting point than the definitions of the dictionary. The *Oxford English Dictionary*[1] provides us with the following:

> Utopia [mod.L. (More, 1516), f. Gr. οὐ not + τόπ-ος a place: see–ia[1], and cf. Eutopia. Hence It., Sp., Pg. *Utopia*, F. *Utopie*.]
>
> 1. An imaginary island, depicted by Sir Thomas More as enjoying a perfect social, legal, and political system....
>
> b. *transf.* Any imaginary or indefinitely-remote region, country, or locality....

2. A place, state, or condition ideally perfect in respect of politics, laws, customs, and conditions....

b. An impossibly ideal scheme, esp. for social improvement....

3. Comb., as Utopia-maker, -monger....

All the circumscriptions above are illustrated with several examples taken from various texts from the 16th to the late 19th centuries, therefore we may accept them as valid and descriptive of the evolving understanding of the term in English. From the examples it also becomes clear that the definitions are arranged in the probable chronological order of the emergence of each distinct meaning. 1a obviously differs from the other circumscriptions as it explains the historical genesis of the word, rather than the meanings it subsequently acquired in common use, but the affinity between 1a and 1b is evidently close in the sense that both uses refer to Utopia as specific place even though its reality or location may be uncertain; hence the capitalized form is retained. A typical illustration for 1b goes as follows: "Ignorant where this River rises, ... whether in Asia, in Africa, or in Utopia" (1684). Utopia in the sense of 1a and 1b still occupies a place on the mental map of contemporaries, similar to Atlantis or the Fortunate Isles of St. Brendan, but it is remarkable that the compilers of the dictionary cite no further example of the use 1b of after 1779, which may be evidence for the decline of the frequency of this use.

The vital transference of meaning from this capitalized, specific place called "Utopia" to the more generic use of "utopia," signifying a disembodied idea and/or a certain kind of narrative, began already in the 17th century: the dictionary quotes the phrase "an Vtopia" from as early as 1613 and "an ... imaginary Vtopia" from 1691. Although the spelling is still capitalized, preserving the origin of the word as a place name, the usage is clearly that of a common noun, standing in general for the qualities associated with it. The earliest cited use of the plural form dates from 1734: "Young men ... create Utopias in their own imagination." The capital U apparently disappeared from the English spelling only in the mid–19th century,[2] recognizing the — by that time clearly well-established — division in meaning between "Utopia" and "utopia": "These are not the wild utopias of a heated imagination" (1843); "the artificial construction of hypothetical utopias" (1871).

From the dictionary entry, the outlines of a historical evolution — at least in the English language — can be discerned. The brainchild of Thomas More first became a generalized term for an imagined faraway place, and then its reference was gradually transferred to the conception of such ideal localities as well as the verbal embodiment of these ideas: utopian thought and utopian fiction. The new meanings have been acquired while the earlier ones have also been retained, which resulted in a complex intermingling of connotations and associations in usage. A closer examination of the individual dictionary definitions may help unfold the diversity of the field of reference associated with the notion "utopia."

*An Island Nowhere:* Definition 1a links the word to its origin, the name of the perfect island coined by Thomas More in 1516. It is crucial to bear in mind that at the root of the word there is a *spatial concept,* a place, a τόπος in the original Greek sense. Utopia is an imaginary place but nonetheless has a certain concreteness and solidity, which is a qualitative difference from an abstract philosophical treatise or a mere discussion of ideas to improve existing conditions.

Definition 1b shifts the emphasis on the peculiar *locality* of the concept: Utopia is a place that is always *somewhere else,* removed from the author's empirical reality in space,[3] and this other locality is either inadequately defined or explicitly placed in the realm of the imagination. This is expressed by the (better-known) etymology of the word "Utopia" itself, cited also by the dictionary entry, which is a Latinized form of a Greek compound, meaning "no-place, not-a-place."[4] The name of the island thus suggests that Utopia and by extension all utopias are *located nowhere,* that is, they are products of human fantasy, *constructed by a creative imagination.* This constitutive metaphor at the heart of the concept firmly places utopias within the bounds of *literature.*[5]

*Community:* Definition 2a focuses on the *social or communal element* of the meaning. Although the phrasing is somewhat unfortunate (or perhaps deliberately vague) because a place can be a locality in nature uninhabited by humans and "state or condition" may refer to a single individual as well as a human community, nevertheless "politics, laws, customs" are all social institutions that regulate the life of a certain group of people. Utopia is associated with a *model community* and focuses attention on the welfare of this community as a whole rather than one or a few of its members, characteristically by an examination of the above-mentioned social institutions. Thus utopias share some of the concerns of *social theory.*

*Ideal:* Definition 2a contains one more crucial element: the model community described in utopias is not merely different from what is "ordinary" or "real" for the author; the model is meant to be an improved or perfected image of social reality, a *positive ideal* held up for contemplation and edification. This aspect is also brilliantly contained in the word itself (overlooked by some) because there is a hidden pun in the name of "Utopia': the Latinized prefix *u-* can stand for the Greek εὐ- *as well as* οὐ- and thus "utopia" can also mean "good-place."[6] Therefore the social aspect of utopias is closely connected to a *moral objective*: to show the ideal society in motion. Utopias can be therefore considered statements in *social ethics*.

*Criticism:* Definition 2b brings into focus yet another aspect closely related to the ambition of a utopia to present an ideal society: the demonstration of the superiority of an imaginary community is inseparable from the *criticism of the existing social conditions*. The moral intent inevitably manifests itself in the explicit or the implicit castigation of what the author perceives as defects in their contemporary social reality, and strong emphasis is placed on how such defects are overcome in the utopian community. The form of this criticism depends on the authorial intent: in the more explicit manner, it tends to become a direct and rather tiresome moral exhortation, with the author adopting the pose of a preacher or a prophet. In the more implicit manner, it tends to take the form of *social satire*, which criticizes by presenting people and institutions and ridiculing them as stupid, unreasonable, incongruous, or grotesque. The stronger the presence of the satirical element, the more pronounced the literary quality of the utopia becomes.

*Reform:* Definition 2b introduces a new problem in connection to the concept of utopia: the question of *practicability*. Social criticism combined with the description of alternative arrangements strongly suggests a reforming intent, a desire to change existing conditions along the lines proposed by the author, although such a suggestion is not necessarily explicit within a utopia. This is perhaps the most sensitive question concerning all utopias: should the image of the ideal society be merely contemplated or should it be interpreted as a program for action? The implicit self-definition contained in the meaning of the word itself suggests that utopias are "no-places," infinitely distant from empirical reality, and this metaphorical distance stands also for the unbridgeable gap between ideal and reality, imagination and practice. The rhetorical drift of a utopian text, however — even when it does not profess explicitly political intentions — tends to imply an invitation to readers to consider the practicability of the utopian institutions. The ambiguity of the *political motives* of the utopian narrative has proven a watershed in the connotation of the term. The positive or negative evaluation of a utopia hinges on the perception of its politics: the more explicit this political intent, the more sharply divided its reception is among readers. Politically less explicit utopias are better tolerated as thought experiments or intellectual games, but even that credit may be denied by a predominantly conservative audience. The derisive or at least ironic connotation expressed by 2b,[7] which is perhaps the most widespread association in the mind of the public, apparently signifies such a conservative stance: in journalese, "utopia" is a satirical label attached to the ideas of daydreamers who harbor hopes of redeeming the world. This negative attitude is well summarized by Lord Macaulay's famous remark: "An acre in Middlesex is better than a principality in Utopia" (*OED* 370).

The preliminary examination of the various layers of encrusted meaning of utopia has outlined some of the sources of possible disagreement over the application and interpretation of the term. Utopia is a complex cultural phenomenon that unites aspects of different disciplines of cultural inquiry. In my opinion, the aspects outlined above — the literary, the social, the moral and the political — define the general field of reference within which other elements, such as the inherent psychological or anthropological, theological and other presuppositions of utopias, can be interpreted. Much of the disagreement over the exact meaning of utopia stems from either a certain hierarchy of value attributed to these aspects, or a differing interpretation of how relevant these aspects are for naming something "utopia" or "utopian."

This general analysis of the meanings of "utopia" is corroborated by Lucian Hölscher's meticulous study on the historical evolution of the concept. Unlike other authors presenting a historical survey of utopia and utopianism, including the Manuels or Martin Plattel, who seem to present their reconstruction of what they consider manifestations of utopianism rather than the actual evolution of the meaning of the term itself,[8] Hölscher makes a crucial distinction between the meaning(s) that the word denoted in the writings of contemporaries in various historical periods on the one hand, and modern attempts to apply a particular understanding of the term to a diverse group of earlier phenomena on the other. In the former, strict sense, the word "utopia" after its inception in More's book began to be loosely applied to other literary works similar in form, content, or intention, so it became the name of a certain kind of (as yet vaguely defined) literary genre (404). This was paralleled by the use of the word as a geographical metaphor for a happy and well-ordered land that is beyond ordinary human experience. The earliest appearance of "utopie" in a French dictionary is dated 1752, when the meaning was given with reference to Rabelais as "Région qui n'a point de lieu, un pays imaginaire" (Hölscher, 415, n.7). In German, the word "Utopien" was a French loan-word, which apparently became widespread only in the 1820s, denoting essentially the same idea: "Schlaraffenland," "Märchenland," etc. (415, n.8). Out of this geographical metaphor developed the more generalized meaning, both in English and in French, of "utopia/utopie" as a plan for a perfect society, a better constitution or even a small-scale social reform idea, as early as the late 17th and the 18th centuries. Such a transference is documented by a 1762 French dictionary entry ("On le dit quelquefois figurément de plan d'un Gouvernement imaginaire"; 416, n.9), while the *OED* cites an example for this meaning from as early as 1642 ("That new Vtopia of Religion and Government into which they endeavour to transform this Kingdom"; *OED* 371). Hölscher emphasizes that both the geographical metaphor and the reform idea meanings of the word contained a clear reference to their etymological origin, that is, More's book, and although both meanings carried an overtone of impossibility or impracticability, the word itself did not yet gain such a general negative connotation as, for example, "chimera."

The pivotal step toward a higher degree of abstraction was apparently made sometime during the late 18th and early 19th centuries, in all probability not independent of the turbulent political developments during and after the French Revolution that subsequently made an impact on the whole of Europe. Hölscher cites as evidence for this abstraction process the appearance and spreading use of various derived forms of the original noun: "utopist" in French in 1792, "Utopismus" in German also in 1792, while "Utopist" in German is first defined as a separate dictionary entry in 1836 (Hölscher, 416, n.11). The English language is a slight exception, since the adjective "utopian" in the sense of "an impossible idea" surfaces already in the political pamphlets of the English revolution (e.g., a 1659 quote: "Thats but a Vtopian consideration, a possibility which never comes into Act." *OED* 371), but the majority of such references date back to the late 18th and 19th centuries as well. As a result of this abstraction, "utopia" became a "politischer Kampfbegriff" (Hölscher 405) by the 1820s, used as a smear word to attack and debunk opposing political groups regardless of their actual political orientation.

The crucial shift of meaning resulted in an invariably negative overtone gained by the word in 19th-century political and theoretical debates. In the 18th century, "utopia" had already denoted an impossible fancy in written form, but the implied devaluation had been offset by the educational value attributed to utopias as moral examples. From the 1820s on, however, "utopia" and its derived forms simply implied that the theory or idea described as such is unrealistic, impracticable, and as a result, its value is zero. So as the word became abstracted from its etymological origin — More's book — and gained an autonomous meaning, it lost most of its earlier positive connotation as an entertaining albeit fanciful idea worthy of contemplation. In the frenzied political atmosphere following the French revolution, all political ideas could be described as "utopian": "Der Begriff war hinreichend allgemein geworden, und in allen politischen Programmen die Differenz zwischen Ideal und Wirklichkeit kritisch zu markieren." (Hölscher 405). From the 1840s, the charge of utopianism was primarily advanced against Socialistic and Communistic ideas, so that "utopianism" and "communism" almost became synonyms, and histories of utopia written in the late 19th century were primarily anti–Socialist tracts, while the various Socialist movements and sects often attacked one another with the term (406–7).[9]

Familiarity with this historical evolution of meaning is crucial for any intelligent discourse on literary utopias in the 20th century, since it helps to understand why the study of utopias as literary texts has emerged so painfully slowly and half-heartedly compared to the explosive growth of literary criticism in general. The literary criticism of utopias has been overshadowed by the predominant political understanding of utopias and utopian studies in general: the great majority of critics active in the field have been more interested in utopias as tools in the service of some sort of political agenda or documents of intellectual history than pieces of fiction to be appreciated in their complexity. Accordingly, the analysis of these works focused on the description of their imaginary communities, the most striking differences between their social arrangements and existing contemporary conditions, or the philosophical-ideological background of the author's social ideas.

I believe that this historical mingling of the two meanings of utopia — the literary genre and the "political battle concept" — has exercised an unfortunate influence on the criticism of utopian fiction. "Utopia" has become a politically charged term, and consequently, the act of reading utopias has all too often been understood as a political statement. While utopias undeniably tend to invite ideologically motivated interpretations more often than other types of fiction due to the elements of moral idealism and social satire that are, as I have argued before, their essential ingredients, they are nonetheless pieces of fiction and representatives of a generic tradition. My survey of the critical literature on utopias has uncovered surprisingly few studies that focus on the literary properties and the distinctive qualities that characterize utopian fiction, although only such an examination can fully evaluate the specific problems involved in narration, plot and character development of literary utopias. While I do not wish to question the legitimacy of alternative approaches to utopias, I am convinced that they are first and foremost literary texts, and they should be properly placed among literary genres and modes.

## The Criticism of Utopia: Genre, Method or Impulse?

The discovery — or creation — of a distinct tradition of utopias as texts concerned with a better or the best way of social life dates from the second half of the 1800s.[10] The earliest study providing some sort of theoretical approach to utopian literature, or the "novel of the future," is Felix Bodin's *Le Roman de l'avenir*, published in 1834,[11] and the first that uses the concept of "utopia" as the identifying label of a distinct tradition is Moritz Kaufman's *Utopias; or Schemes of Social Improvement, from Sir Thomas More to Karl Marx,* published in 1879 (Sargent, *Bibliography* 170, 181). The subtitle clearly reveals that the author's understanding of "utopia" is anything that passes for a comprehensive plan of social reform, rather than a specific type of literary text, representing an approach typical of the late 19th century. Utopian texts generated more interest among historians, philosophers and political activists than literary scholars: criticism of utopias remained a rather peripheral activity within the domain of literary criticism, and even when it was performed (mostly in magazine reviews), it was typically restricted to analysis of content — a selective discussion of some utopian institutions or inventions, with a varying mixture of sympathy and criticism.[12] Utopias have more often been used than read: used primarily as a quarry for social ideas, which then could be utilized in a number of ways, sometimes presented as reform proposals of some merit, sometimes paraded as the bizarre phantasmagoria of perverted thinkers. This approach, based on an implicit utilitarian concept of literature in general or at least of utopias in particular, made a more or less self-explanatory distinction between form and content: the fiction and its devices were typically taken for granted as a transparent and convenient cover for what was seen as a moral and/or political venture with a clearly discernible axe to grind.

A classic example of such "utilitarian" readings of utopias is Lewis Mumford's *The Story of Utopias* (1922), a pioneering effort to write a general history of utopias from Plato to the author's contemporary present. Mumford, an urban historian by profession, was one of the first to confront the difficulty of constructing a canon of utopian texts. Although he claims to have excluded what he calls "essays in politics" such as Thomas Hobbes's *Leviathan* or James Harrington's *Oceana*, as well as "any treatment of abstract idealisms" as untypical of the utopian method (*Story* 309), his "canon" is nonetheless a mixture of standard fiction (such as More, Campanella, Bacon, Mercier, Cabet, Bellamy, Hertzka, Morris, and Wells) and thinly disguised political tract, including works by Thomas Spence, Charles Fourier, and Theodor Herzl. The reason lies in his primary concern, clearly voiced in the Preface, to increase "awareness of the problems and pressures of the contemporary world," and "to uncover potentialities that the existing institutions either ignored or buried beneath an ancient crust of custom and habit" (2). And even though he is repelled by the static conception of life presented by most utopias as well as their rigid authoritarian regiments of social organization, his disappointment is offset by the inspiration derived from what he called "the utopian method of thought" (5), an approach viewing society as an organic whole whose harmony, balance and development requires creative and synthetic thinking. Although Mumford declares himself an anti-utopian in the sense that he does not believe in the redemptive qualities of any single utopian scheme, he nonetheless emphasizes the positive influence of utopias on the development of human society and culture. While utopias of escape provide a kind of psychological palliative, a welcome release from the immediate pressures of and conflicts with everyday existence, utopias of reconstruction offer a "vision of a reconstituted environment which is better adapted to the nature and aims of the human beings who dwell within it than the actual one" (21). For Mumford, most human art and literature belong to the former category, or has at least been inspired by such idyllic desires, while utopias of reconstruction are more than pure literature: they are documents of cultural and intellectual history, and Mumford turns to them with a historian's curiosity and a moralist's desire for an edifying lesson.[13]

Such an approach characterized much of utopian criticism in the late 19th and early 20th centuries. Critics either took literary utopias as exemplars of quaint and curious institutions out of which each reader can select what they like and jettison the rest, or they directed their attention to one single utopia, and passionately attacked or defended the alternative image of social relations it has presented, as, for example, in the extensive debate following Edward Bellamy's *Looking Backward* (1888) in the 1890s.[14] I do not wish to question the legitimacy of either, but neither approach does justice to literary utopias as pieces of fiction and representatives of a genre. Such "utilitarian applications" of literary utopias are, from a critical point of view, leading to a *cul-de-sac*, since they do not offer a perspective that enables us to place them within the literary tradition and appreciate them in their complexity. The ultimate futility of comparing utopias on the basis of the details of their social visions has been insightfully captured by Paul Ricoeur; he observes that it is extremely difficult

> to try to isolate a kernel of utopia.... A content analysis of utopias finally scatters completely; it dismantles the field to the point where it seems that we have before us dreams or social fictions that are unconnected.... If we look more generally at each utopian theme [such as family, property, social and political organization, religion etc.] ..., each one explodes in contradictory directions [270].

As a result, a thorough critical approach to utopias cannot be founded on a comparative examination of the institutions and social habits of individual utopias or a construction of a kind of composite utopia, since the actual ideas of individual utopias do not exhibit any kind of coherence. The genre's distinctive identity does not consist in any particular utopian social organization or a specifically utopian way of life but in the very act of "the presentation of *otherness*" (Williams, "Utopia and SF" 54), as well as the specific methods and techniques of presentation and narration, in short, the literary properties of utopian fiction.

Such an analysis of utopias as a literary genre rather than a series of reform schemes or documents of the history of ideas was initiated in the 1960s, notably by Northrop Frye and Robert C. Elliott. Frye in his classic essay, "Varieties of Literary Utopias," interpreted utopia with the help of myth and ritual: he described utopia as "a *speculative* myth," presenting "an imaginative vision of the *telos* or end at which social life aims" (109). This myth and the social practices described in it are — contrary to popular notions about utopias as ideal societies organized on a rational basis — no more rational than the well-known and existing traditions of the author's own society:

> Rituals are apparently irrational acts which become *rational* when their significance is explained. In such utopias the guide explains the structure of society and thereby the significance of the behaviour being observed. Hence, the behaviour of society is presented as rationally motivated.... The

utopian romance does not present society as governed by reason; it presents it as governed by ritual habit, or prescribed social behaviour, which is explained rationally [110–111].

Thus, the implied contrast between utopia and existing contemporary societies is not an opposition between rational and irrational organization, but rather a contrast between conscious and unconscious social rituals, where "the basis of the satire is the unconsciousness or inconsistency in the social behaviour he observes around him ... the typical utopia contains, if only by implication, a satire on the *anarchy* inherent in the writer's own society" (111).

Utopia as a social myth stands in a complementary relationship with another myth, the social contract, which purports to explain the origins of society. There is an implication in most utopias that the current state of affairs is a corrupted version of an earlier, superior way of life and the utopia seeks to restore this uncorrupted form of existence. As Frye puts it,

> The vision of something better has to appeal to some contract behind the contract, something which existing society has lost, forfeited, rejected, or violated, and which the utopia itself is to restore. The ideal or desirable quality in the utopia has to be *recognized*, that is, seen as manifesting something that the reader can understand as a latent or potential element in his own society and his own thinking [123].

This means that there is a kind of core ideal behind each utopia which can to some extent be reconstructed. In most Western utopias this is related to the myths of paradise or the Golden Age, inherited from Christianity and classical mythology, respectively. The two myths share a simplified social ideal, a primitive and peaceful form of existence in harmony with nature, with a minimum of social structure and organization. This ideal, called "Arcadian" by Frye, informs the pastoral convention in literature, which has been far more influential and significant in literary history than utopia proper.

Elliott — even though he does not explicitly acknowledge it — obviously utilizes Frye's concepts of myth and ritual in his own approach. He links the origins of utopia not only to ancient myths of the Golden Age, but also to such ancient rituals as the Saturnalia, during which social order was temporarily suspended and a kind of exuberant anarchy took its place: "The theme of the Saturnalia is reversal — reversal of values, of social roles, of social norms" (11). Such rites, including the various medieval Feasts of Fools or Lords of Misrule, involved a good deal of ridicule, mockery and other forms of satire directed against all sorts of worldly authority, since

a ritual reenactment of the Golden Age implied that social rules and limitations did not exist. Elliott concludes that

> utopia is the secularization of the myth of the Golden Age, a myth incar-
> nated in the festival of the Saturnalia. Satire is the secular form of ritual
> mockery, ridicule, invective — ritual gestures which are integrally part of
> the same festival. Thus utopia and satire are ancestrally linked in the cel-
> ebration of Saturn.... Satire and utopia are not really separable, the one a
> critique of the real world in the name of something better, the other a
> hopeful construct of a world that might be. The hope feeds the criticism,
> the criticism the hope [24].

In my opinion, these two critical essays have established the foundation on which most subsequent literary criticism of utopias should have
been built. The vital link between utopia and satire, especially, was rich
in potential that could have been utilized by subsequent critics. In addition, Frye makes an important distinction between the "straight utopia,"
which visualizes an ideal, or at least a more perfect social order, and the
"utopian satire," which mocks utopian ambitions by presenting them as
leading to tyranny or anarchy. His categories are somewhat misleading,
since he fails to point out that implicit satire is a constitutive element of
all utopias, and not only "utopian satires," while the latter by their nature
require a certain amount of—albeit vague and unexplicated — moral idealism. He probably intends to foreground that the satirical intent is explicit
and predominant in the works he calls "utopian satires," while the ideal
that forms the basis of satire remains implicit and inconspicuous, but it
would have been more felicitous to point out the complementary nature
of the two sub-genres. In the third essay of *Anatomy of Criticism,* an earlier work, where he incisively analyzes satire and its various types, he
observes: "Satire demands at least *a token fantasy,* a content which the
reader recognizes as grotesque, and at least *an implicit moral standard,* the
latter being essential in a militant attitude to experience" (224, emphases
added). The projection and explication of this implicit moral standard
into an image of a more perfect fictional human community constitutes
utopia, or, to quote Frye's brilliant definition, "a vision of the world in
terms of a single intellectual pattern" (310). Though Frye fails to explicate
the complementary generic link of utopia and its moral counterpart, dystopia or anti-utopia[15] in the "Varieties," he nonetheless establishes that
"straight utopia" and "utopian satire" are relative categories, since serious
utopias may seem morally inferior to existing reality for many — especially
later — readers.

Curiously, few subsequent critics followed up the critical insights offered by Frye and Elliott. The emerging utopian studies and its leading authors in the 1970s and the 1980s — Fredric Jameson, Darko Suvin, Tom Moylan and Carl Freedman — were all inspired primarily by Western Marxist thought, above all Ernst Bloch's unorthodox Marxist reinterpretation of the notion of utopia as a central motivation force behind human life and culture. Bloch had most probably built upon the work of a contemporary sociologist, Karl Mannheim, who, in his book *Ideologie und Utopie* (1929), employed the twin terms "ideology" and "utopia" to describe certain group consciousnesses that are incongruous with contemporary reality. Ideologies are usually proposed by socially dominant groups that want to justify the existing order of things, while utopias are proposed by rising social groups that seek to transcend it by changing the prevalent order of things. In other words, ideologies are oriented toward the past and are resistant to change, while utopias are oriented toward the future and try to encourage change. Mannheim's interpretation of "utopia" almost completely ignored individual utopias as well as "the historically evolved connotation of the term" (182) because his declared purpose was to uncover structural forces in history, while he considered literary utopias as such merely unique historical phenomena.[16]

Although there is no clear evidence to support it, it is a credible hypothesis that Mannheim's reinterpretation of utopia as a progressive social phenomenon that helps shatter the existing order of things[17] became a point of departure for Bloch in his three-volume magnum opus, *Das Prinzip Hoffnung* (written 1938–1947, published 1953–1959), in which he examines various manifestations of what he calls "Das antizipierende Bewußtsein" (47), motivated by hope for a better way of existence. The attraction of hope, or "das Noch-Nicht-Bewußten" (10), orients people not toward the past but toward future potentialities. The products of this orientation are called "utopian" by Bloch, and by this identification he expands the reference of the term to an unprecedented degree. He extends his investigation to all sorts of "images of desire" ("Wunschbilder"), from advertisements and color magazines, through thrillers, antiquities, foreign travels and dances to the theater and the film, then goes on to focus on more concrete or more explicit images of a better form of existence that he calls "Plan- oder Grundriß-Utopien" (12). He distinguishes medical, social, technical, architectural and geographical utopias as well as manifestations of similar fantasies in painting, poetry, music and philosophy. Images of life without illness, a society providing for the satisfaction of all needs, a technology offering total control over nature, buildings that express a striving for perfection, or faraway communities described by discoverers as living in perfect happiness — all these are considered by Bloch manifestations of the same desire to anticipate a better form of existence.

For Bloch, practically all manifestations of human imagination are to be interpreted through their "utopian function," and ultimately he subsumes all these manifestations under one single overarching desire, the desire for the "perfect moment" in the Faustian sense. In Bloch's vision, the "hope principle," or the utopian impulse, is magnified into a central and constitutive principle of human psyche and history, which incessantly drives us forward in search of a transcendent fulfillment of our radical longings. Hence the paradoxical nature of utopia: the search for it is doomed to be futile, because it "is always *elsewhere*, always escaping our actual horizons" (Freedman, *Critical Theory* 64), but in another sense this search is fruitful, because it inspires humanity to new insights and achievements, resulting in the element of *novum*, "the unexpectedly new, which pushes humanity out of its present towards the not yet realized" (Moylan, "Locus of Hope" 159).

In Bloch's hands, utopia has become a concept by which he intended to renew Marxism as a critical theory and enable it to approach all phenomena of culture with a radical deconstructive intent.

> For Bloch, utopia is not so much a matter of description or planning as it is a way of thinking and of reading: a utopian hermeneutic construes fragmentary prefigurations of an unalienated (communist) future in the cultural artifacts of the past and present, including many that on the surface may not seem particularly progressive [Freedman, *Critical Theory* 63].

Utopia is a lack that implies its own positivity, a kind of truth that can only be apprehended in a fragmentary way. It is a positive value that requires a ruthless negation of the actual *status quo*. "The essential function of utopia is a critique of what is present. If we had not already gone beyond the barriers, we could not even perceive them as barriers" (Bloch, qtd. in Freedman, *Critical Theory* 67).

Bloch's understanding of utopia, characterized by Carl Freedman as a "hermeneutic meaning" of the term, has little to do with what Freedman calls the "generic meaning," identifying a form of fiction originating from More's work ("SF and Utopia" 72–73). Bloch is fully aware that the term "utopia" had previously been applied mostly to "Staatsromane," that is, literary utopias, but he considers this a very narrow and, after the emergence of Socialism, hopelessly outdated use of the term.[18] As Bloch considers not only utopian fiction but practically all sorts of literature significant documents of the manifestation of the "utopian impulse," he offers a handy tool to deconstruct any literary text in order to reveal its explicit or implicit criticism of the *status quo*. Since the late 1960s, Marxist critical theory, inspired by the social and political movements of the time, recognized the potential of Bloch's theory to provide a critical view on capitalist culture (Csicsery-Ronay 116). The echo of Bloch is clearly audible, for instance, in the critical program of Fredric Jameson:

> Such is then the general theoretical framework in which I would wish to argue the methodological proposition outlined here: that a Marxist negative hermeneutic, a Marxist practice of ideological analysis proper, must in the practical work of reading and interpretation be exercised *simultaneously* with a Marxist positive hermeneutic, or a decipherment of the Utopian impulses of these same ideological cultural texts ["The Dialectic" 296].

Followers of Bloch's approach, named by Tom Moylan "critical utopia," have displayed a special attraction to science fiction as a genre particularly suitable for ideological deconstruction. As Freedman argues,

> science fiction as an aesthetic form is ... a privileged object of utopian hermeneutic. For the structural constitution of the genre on the Front, on the ontological level of Not-Yet-Being, renders science fiction a perhaps uniquely fertile field for the location of fragments of an unalienated futurity ["SF and Utopia" 81].

In other words, science fiction, with its future-oriented fictional imagination, presents a conscious or unconscious critique of the socio-cultural conditions of the present (or, to borrow the language of these critics, the contradictions of late capitalist society and bourgeois ideology), often by transposing its dominant cultural themes into elements of science fiction (e.g., Cold War appears as war against alien races, or the social emancipation of blacks is reflected in the relationship between men and robots, and so forth) or extrapolating some economic, social or technological trends and revealing their potential negative consequences (e.g., overpopulation, destruction of the environment, etc.). Such fictional themes can be interpreted as a subversive criticism of present conditions, and, sometimes by negation, as a fragmentary prefiguration of a better form of existence, "some authentic plenitude with which the deprivations of mundane reality are contrasted" ("SF and Utopia" 82).

## Suvin and Cognitive Estrangement

Thus, Marxist criticism, armed with the Blochian concept of the "utopian hermeneutic" or "critical utopia," began to focus on science fiction rather than literary utopias from the early 1970s on. The pioneer of Marxist science fiction criticism was Darko Suvin, who offered a new and sophisticated approach to the genre, utilizing — and, as some critics argue, also reinterpreting — Bloch's concept of the *novum* (*Prinzip* 227–235; *Metamorphoses* 64). His theoretical framework is based on a fundamental distinction between "naturalistic" and "estranged" fiction, the former term referring to prose genres that share a predominantly mimetic concern as opposed to other kinds of fiction creating an "alternative formal framework functioning by explicit or implicit reference to the author's empirical environment" (*Metamorphoses* 53), ranging from myth, folktale and romance to fantasy and science fiction. Suvin argues that science fiction is distinguished from and elevated above other related genres by what he calls "cognitive estrangement," a creative transformation of empirical reality based on "the narrative dominance or hegemony of a fictional 'novum' (novelty, innovation) validated by cognitive logic" (63).

Suvin's exploration of science fiction had important implications for the criticism of utopias: in a separate essay devoted to the genre, he places utopia within his theoretical system as one of the estranged genres, and defines it the following way:

> Utopia is the verbal construction of a particular quasi-human community where sociopolitical institutions, norms, and individual relationships are organized according to a more perfect principle than in the author's community, this construction being based on estrangement arising out of an alternative historical hypothesis [49].

Suvin's generic definition of utopia singles him out as the only major Marxist critic not to apply the term in the broad hermeneutic sense proposed by Bloch; in fact, he refers ironically to Bloch's overarching application of utopia as "a somewhat overweening imperialism" (61), and stresses the necessity of analyzing the "verbal construction" as an essential element of utopias.[19] After comparing utopia to several other estranged genres like myth, fantasy, folktale, and the pastoral, he concludes that utopia is differentiated by the presence of cognition, therefore he declares that "utopia is not a genre but the sociopolitical subgenre of science fiction" (61) because the *novum* in utopias is the "alternative historical hypothesis." This hypothesis is considered "cognitive" by Suvin because the imaginary human community depicted in utopias proper does not exist outside history or under improbably benevolent natural conditions, and its potential problems are addressed by human institutions instead of divine agents or other literary *deus ex machina*. Suvin does not fail to integrate Frye's and Elliott's insights either, when he stresses that

> utopia is a formal inversion of significant and salient aspects of the author's world which has as its purpose or *telos* the recognition that the author (and reader) truly live in an axiologically inverted world.... Utopia explicates what satire implicates, and vice versa [54].

Suvin's erudite and theoretically meticulous argument had the effect of a critical breakthrough and made his definitions of both science fiction and utopia widely accepted, serving as a starting point for subsequent inquiries for other — Marxist as well as non–Marxist — critics. His key term, "estrangement," is Suvin's translation of the German *Verfremdung* (6, n.2), which is Bertolt Brecht's neologism, adopted from 1936 on to replace the previously used — and more widely known —*Entfremdung,* translated as "alienation" by Suvin (Ritter 11, 655). While *Entfremdung* has a distinguished philosophical history, forming part of Hegel's philosophical system and popularized by Marx as a central concept of his early criticism of capitalist social conditions,[20] it was invested with an overwhelmingly negative meaning in the course of the 19th century, denoting a central social, cultural and psychological conflict in modern industrial societies (Ritter 2, 509–525). In Brecht's dramatic theory, on the other hand, estrangement functions as a positive idea, a ploy to create distance between the familiar reality and the observer and, as a result, make the familiar look strange, ironic, grotesque, unusual.[21] The shock produced by such de-familiarization is a creative one, because it generates reflection, criticism and a new kind of insight in the observer.

Suvin, however, extends the original meaning of "estrangement" when he lumps together non mimetic genres under the heading "estranged," employing the term essentially as a substitute for "fantastic." His avoidance of the more common expression probably serves the purpose of clarity, since "fantasy" in the late 20th century has become the identifying label for a distinct fantastic genre,[22] but describing whole literary genres as "estranged" departs radically from Brecht's original meaning, confusing a strategy of presentation with a fundamental literary mode.[23] No wonder that this generic label did not find a following among subsequent critics.

Estrangement defined as a literary strategy, on the other hand, offers a useful and productive way of approaching fantastic literature, demolishing historically evolved and often highly subjective distinctions between related fantastic genres. It emphasizes the same fundamental quality of fantastic literature that Kathryn Hume expressed in her simple and inclusive definition: "fantasy is any departure from consensus reality" (21), where the term "consensus reality" refers both to the world of the author ("world-1"), and the world of the audience ("world-2"). Unfortunately, Suvin's formalist devotion to generic precision coupled with his palpable Marxist rationalist-materialist bias moves him to set up the rather opaque qualification of "cognition" and then proceed on the unjustified assumption that "cognitive" (science fiction and its subcategory, utopia) is inherently superior to "non-cognitive" or "metaphysical" fantasy. Suvin employs the terms "cognition" and "cognitive" in a confusing way: understood in its dictionary sense, the noun simply means "acquiring knowledge," "gaining insight," and Suvin's contention that genres like the myth or the folktale are "indifferent to cognitive possibilities" because they do not "use imagination as a means of understanding the tendencies latent in reality, but as an end unto itself" (8) seems to deny them the right to carry any relevant meaning at all. To borrow Patrick Parrinder's witty observation, "A huge portion of the total literary output is ... thus labelled as 'Terra Non-cognita'" ("Suvin's Poetics" 37–38). Suvin's subsequent elaborations restrict his definition of "cognition": he argues that the word denotes a critical reflection on reality, and its methodology is analogous to modern scientific thought. As a result, his adjective "cognitive" becomes vaguely synonymous with "rational," although Suvin carefully avoids the latter term. He claims the noun "cognition" should be taken as an approximate synonym for "science" in its wider sense (German *Wissenschaft* or French *science*), that is, a systematic and rational understanding of the world based on hypothesis, testing and logical analysis. As a result, in science fiction "the cognitive — in most cases strictly scientific — element becomes the measure of aesthetic quality, of the specific pleasure to be found in SF. In other words, the cognitive nucleus of the plot codetermines the fictional estrangement itself" (15).

To use less elevated language, Suvin prefers science fiction to other fantastic genres because he claims that in good or "real" science fiction (he uses his definition normatively) the strategy of estrangement common to all fantastic genres is combined with a rationalist-critical approach to world-1, and the estranged world of fiction is constructed by the rules of scientific logic. His introduction of the *novum* as a literary category primarily serves the purpose of possessing a valid criterion to separate science fiction both from naturalistic fiction and metaphysical genres of fantasy. He defines the *novum* as a "cognitive innovation ... deviating from the author's and implied reader's norm of reality" (64). The *novum* should transform the whole fictitious universe or at least significant aspects of it, in order to fulfill the aesthetically significant purpose of the cognitive estrangement, that is, a critical investigation of the various potentials present in our empirical reality. Suvin argues that the *novum* should be "postulated on and validated by the post–Cartesian and post–Baconian scientific *method....* Science in this wider sense of methodically systematic cognition cannot be disjoined from the SF innovation" (64–65, emphasis retained). He declares all kinds of allegory, satire, and tall tales inimical to science fiction since they, by definition, do not possess a *novum;* he claims that allegorical and satirical inventions are used as "*immediately transitive* and *narratively nonautonomous* means for *direct* and *sustained* reference to the author's empirical world and some system of belief in it" (65, n.4, emphases retained). This is a highly controversial assertion, which, if understood strictly, should exclude most utopias from the realm of cognitive estrangement, as satire is an essential part of the utopian method. The presence of the *novum* and its "scientific" (that is, logical and consistent) application should also set science fiction apart from fantastic genres that "deny the autonomy of physics" (19), in other words, are not sufficiently materialist to Suvin's taste.[24] His dislike for all supernatural or irrational forms of fantasy manifests itself in a strongly emotional rhetoric by which, as one critic aptly remarked, Suvin attempts to "vomit the fantastic out of the body of SF" (Derek Littlewood, qtd. in Parrinder, "Suvin's Poetics" 38).

Suvin's insistence that the *novum* should be developed within the fiction "as a "mental experiment" following accepted scientific, that is, cognitive logic" (66), when tested on individual works of fiction, becomes little more than an excuse to justify his personal literary preferences. Isaac Asimov's *Foundation* series, for example, does not qualify as science fiction for Suvin because he considers psychohistory, the moving force behind most of the core trilogy, a transposed fairy tale device: "It pretends to explain away the supernatural by reassigning it to natural science.... However, the science is treated as a metaphysical and not physical, supernatural and not natural activity, as gobbledygook instead of rational procedure" (23). The observation is perspicacious, but it fails entirely as a criterion to separate pseudo–science fiction fairy tales from "genuine" science fiction. Suvin's favorite science fiction author, H.G. Wells, from whom he partly derives his concept of the *novum*,[25] never pretended to propose scientifically feasible or rationally verifiable inventions in his scientific romances:

> They are all fantasies; they do not aim to project a serious possibility; they aim indeed only at the same amount of conviction as one gets in a good gripping dream.... It occurred to me that instead of the usual interview with the devil or a magician, an ingenious use of scientific patter might with advantage be substituted.... I simply brought the fetish stuff up to date, and made it as near actual theory as possible [qtd. in Parrinder and Philmus 240–42].

The inconsistency of Suvin's specific value judgments is well illustrated by the fact that, in another essay, he himself observes that the "fantastic element" in Wells' scientific romances is "always cloaked in a pseudo-scientific explanation, the possibility of which turns out, upon closer inspection, to be no more than a conjuring trick by the deft writer" (209). If that is granted, however, it becomes extremely difficult to find any kind of reliable and objective yardstick to measure what passes for "cognitive estrangement" proper and what should be relegated to the periphery of the genre as "metaphysical gobbledygook" or "dark irrationality." Suvin's instinctive dislike for supernatural fantasy has prompted him in these early essays to try to erect a tall theoretical barrier between "metaphysical" genres and "cognitive" science fiction, but the more he tries to specify the generic difference between science fiction and other kinds of fantasy, the more he maneuvers himself into a complete cul-de-sac. The further Suvin progresses with his analysis of the central idea of the *novum*, the more biases — theoretical and ideological — he reveals in his approach, and eventually succeeds in elevating his own personal preferences and dislikes into an evaluative criterion. Parrinder notes the same tendency: "Suvin ... rapidly moves from quasi-neutral generic theorizing to the language of an ideological crusade" ("Suvin's Poetics" 38).

In his later writings, Suvin attempted to respond to his critics and correct some of the most controversial points of his system: for instance, he broadened the meaning of "cognition" by admitting the possibility of non-rational cognition and claiming that every metaphor has cognitive value ("Suvin's Poetics" 41, 45), but in the process, he went into the other extreme and stretched the reference of his pet concept to such universal proportions that it cannot but fail to function as a distinguishing criterion of science fiction. In my opinion, Suvin's failure to adequately defend his theory for cognitive estrangement is rooted in his ideological bias against non-rational and non-materialist forms of fantasy, which he consistently tried to keep out of the narrowly drawn boundaries of science fiction, and when his position became indefensible, he tacitly abandoned the whole project. With the benefit of hindsight, Edward James considers Suvin's entry into the field of science fiction criticism less revolutionary than commonly believed, since he essentially rephrased, in more erudite and subtle form, some of the previously dominant critical prejudices concerning science fiction ("Before the Novum" 19–28).[26] By stubbornly identifying the literary value of science fiction with its function of social commentary and critique, and insisting that science fiction criticism should focus on the original idea presented by the fiction rather than applying the general standards of literary criticism, he reiterated a conservative, content-based approach to science fiction that has a lot in common with the dominant trend in the criticism of utopias before the 1960s.

Despite my criticism of Suvin's specific formulations of his theory, I believe that his categories of cognitive estrangement and the *novum* can be applied fruitfully in critical investigation provided that they are relieved of their ideological ballast. Parrinder points in the same direction when he argues that estrangement and cognition are inseparable: "To the extent that countering habitualization renews our understanding and sharpens perception, genuine estrangement would seem to be an inherently cognitive process" ("Suvin's Poetics" 40). The validity of cognitive estrangement as a fictionalizing strategy could be maintained by eradicating Suvin's stubborn essentialist distinction between "rational science" and "metaphysical gobbledygook" in imaginative fiction: both are merely devices to create a novel and unusual setting for the story, a departing point for literary fantasy. The difference lies in the way the writers account for their own fantastic invention, in other words, the rhetorical strategy employed. Robert M. Philmus proposed a far more applicable definition when he argued that "science fiction differs from other kinds of fantasy by virtue of the more or less scientific basis, real or imaginary, theoretical or technological, on which the writer predicates a fantastic state of affairs" (*Into the Unknown*, 2). Philmus states unequivocally that the "scientific rationale" offered by the science fiction writer is merely an excuse "to account for the imaginary situation that the writer projects into some spatial or temporal region of the unknown" (2), as opposed to other kinds of fantastic fiction in which such a scientific excuse is simply missing or the mysterious and unusual events are explicitly presented as supernatural. This "scientific rationale" does not make a science fiction story any more original, coherent, logically consistent, in general more cognitive, than any other kind of fantasy. This is merely another literary convention that has emerged in parallel with the Enlightenment and the industrial revolution, relying on scientific explanation to make a fantastic idea credible to readers, and rooted in a positivistic faith in the potentially endless prospect of scientific progress and a philosophical optimism concerning the knowability of the world and its phenomena (I. F. Clarke 35–89).

Cognitive estrangement, then, is a fictionalizing strategy employed by all fantastic fiction, and, arguably, also by certain kinds of non-fantastic fiction, and its operation should be examined not only, perhaps not even primarily, through the *novum*, the original transformative idea, but through narrative method and rhetorical devices. As most critics agree that utopia is a form of literary fantasy,[27] the critical category of cognitive estrangement remains a valid tool to approach utopias, though not in the sense implied by Suvin's categorization of utopia as the sociopolitical subgenre of science fiction. From Suvin's argument that the quality and, in fact, the genuineness of science fiction is determined by the consistent and rigorous application of the *novum* in the story, one should logically conclude that criticism of utopias should primarily consist of the examination of the "scientific rigor" by which the imaginary community's institutions, habits, and cultural preferences are worked out from an underlying hypothesis or imaginary contract. But, as Frye reminds his readers in the "Varieties," human societies are not based on ultimately rational foundations, and social arrangements in utopias are not any more rational than in existing societies: only the rationalizations of the differing social rituals are different, and these rationalizations may or may not comply with Suvin's definition of the *novum*. In other words, a literary utopia's critical study should not consist of the examination and the embrace or rejection of the underlying social reform idea based on one's individual social and political preferences.

Although such a depoliticized critical approach is clearly alien from Suvin, his argument that a literary utopia presents an intellectual challenge to readers is fundamentally sound:

> Neither prophesy nor escapism, utopia is ... an "as if," an imaginative experiment.... Literary utopia — and every description of utopia is literary — is a heuristic device for perfectibility, and epistemological and not an ontological entity.... If utopia is, then, philosophically, a method rather than a

state, it cannot be realized or not realized — it can only be applied.... But apply a literary text means first of all (wherever it may later lead) to read as a dramatic dialogue with the reader. Besides requiring the willingness of the reader to enter into dialogue, the application of utopia depends on the closeness and precision of his reading [52–53].

As my intentions in this study could be described as the opposite of the Blochian "utopian hermeneutic" reading all literature as ideological texts hiding implicitly utopian fragments, I would like to construct a way of reading that would suit literary utopias more than other kinds of literature. I hope to devise a less ideologically oriented way of reading that could nonetheless explicate the process by which utopian texts, as Jameson put it, interrogate "the dilemmas involved in their own emergence as utopian texts" ("Progress Versus Utopia" 156).

## Utopia, Ambiguity, and Game

In my previous discussion of Suvin's theory of science fiction and utopia, I have pointed out that Suvin — alone among Marxist critics — integrated some of Frye's insights into his theory of utopia (e.g., the contract hidden in each utopia or the complementary relation between utopia and satire [*Metamorphoses* 51, 54]). He relied mostly on Frye's *Anatomy of Criticism,* which contains several important generic observations on utopia, although often made indirectly. In his fourth essay, Frye distinguishes between four fundamental forms of prose fiction: novel, romance, confession and Menippean satire. The last category, being the least obvious, is characterized as "extroverted and intellectual" (308), having a distinguished literary history from Lucian through Rabelais, Erasmus, Swift, and Sterne up to the 20th century.[28] Menippean satires contain rambling intellectual exchange between stylized characters acting as mouthpieces of ideas they represent as well as humorous, caricaturistic observations in a loose narrative form, which allows for the neglect of characterization and the violation of conventional rules of story-telling. That is why Frye proposes the term "anatomy," since this form is concerned primarily with a "dissection or analysis" (311) in the intellectual sense. Frye explicitly places utopias into this category: "The purely moral type [of anatomy] is a serious vision of society as a single intellectual pattern, in other words a Utopia" (310).

The crucial significance of Frye's distinction among forms of prose fiction consists in clearing utopian fiction from the charge of being bad novels. Frye argues that the discerning critic should stop looking for those qualities of the classic novel form — individualized characters, original plot, naturalistic social setting, and so forth — that utopia by its generic nature is not meant to offer. In addition, Frye touches upon the satirical generic traits of utopias in his third essay, where he groups several utopias and dystopias under the heading of "quixotic satire," based on an ironic contrast between the reality of everyday existence and another, imaginary world. The other world functions not as a practical alternative but as a provocative vision to challenge readers and shock them out of their complacency:

> Whenever the "other world" appears in satire, it appears as an ironic counterpart to our own, a reversal of accepted social standards.... [Quixotic] satire shows literature assuming a special function of analysis, of breaking up the lumber of stereotypes, fossilized beliefs, superstitious terrors, crank theories, pedantic dogmatisms, oppressive fashions, and all other things that impede the free movement ... of society. Such satire is the completion of the logical process known as the *reductio ad absurdum*, which is not designed to hold one in perpetual captivity, but to bring one to the point at which one can escape from an incorrect procedure [233].

Frye's generic insights are, by and large, compatible with Suvin's theory in several crucial points: both authors concur that the literary ancestry of utopias is significantly different from the "Great Tradition" of English novels celebrated by F.R. Leavis, and should be treated accordingly; that social satire, in a more or less explicit form, is a constitutive element of all utopias; that the satirical method requires the use of fantasy in utopias. There is an incompatible disagreement between them, however, with regard to the role of mimesis and fantasy in literature. The very idea of estrangement presupposes a cardinal distinction between mimesis and fantasy as two fundamentally different forms of literary imagination. Frye as an archetypal critic sees no such inherent gap between realistic and fantastic modes, having a far more sophisticated view on literary mimesis than Suvin. Starting from the premise that all literary works are verbal structures with a "hypothetical or assumed relation to the external world" (*Anatomy* 74), and this relation is governed by literary convention, or the accepted contract between author and reader about the hypothetical postulates of a given work, Frye goes on to argue that the concept "mimesis" as introduced by Aristotle and developed in Neoclassical tradition does not mean faithful verbal representation of phenomena in nature or human society and action (it cannot mean that since literature by definition does not have a truth value), but the creation of an ordered system of verbal symbols that "exists between the example and the precept" (84). The correspondence between such a verbal structure and the external world is strongest in case of explicit allegories and becomes less and less unambiguous as the structure of imagery becomes more complicated, ironic and paradoxical.

Applying Frye's concept of mimesis to utopias, one can observe a characteristically strong tendency toward allegory due to the generic need to refer back to the social environment (world-1) that is subjected to implicit criticism through the image of the other world. But as a result of the satirical method, the allegory is never quite direct and explicit. Satirical inversion turns familiar and unquestioningly accepted habits, methods, institutions upside down (e.g., the use of gold for chamber pots and slave chains in More's *Utopia*), with the result that they appear to the audience as weird, irrational, absurd, or simply as products of random chance rather than historical necessity or divine design. Such reversal, the primary vehicle of cognitive estrangement, sets up an ironic relationship between world-1 and the other world, investing the text with an ambiguous potential. This ambiguity is a generic, structural trait of literary utopias, since the author has no guarantee that the hypothetical postulate of the genre — that the other world presented is morally superior to world-1— will be accepted by readers. Most authors attempt to suppress this ambiguity by explicit rhetorical means, namely by staging a dialogue between two characters, one representing the *status quo*, the other the utopia, and rigging the argument in such a way as the spokesman of the utopia should emerge as the winner. Such slanted rhetoric invites the common charge of didacticism against utopias: as Hume puts it, "such literature demands full affirmation of its vision of reality and by implication asks for revisions in the reader's life" (103), and, as opposed to other kinds of fiction, utopias are difficult to enjoy if one does not accept the underlying premises. I disagree with this opinion. I believe that in case of utopias in which the allegory is not transparent or flawed, the fantastic invention, the other world gains an autonomous existence on its own and as such, becomes a counterbalance to world-1. The balance between world-1 and the utopia, as well as the complex interaction between them in the course of the narrative, generates the literary merits of utopias. This dynamic and by necessity ambiguous balance is negotiated by the narration of the fiction, often undermining the rhetorical intentions of the author.

Narration is a crucial problem for most utopias: the affective intent

requires that the "nowhere" of the story be presented in a sufficiently credible way to persuade readers to temporarily suspend their disbelief in the
feasibility of such an imaginary community. A serious utopia (as opposed
to a utopian parody) completely ruins its own ambition if the narrator is
explicitly presented as a frivolous or shady character, or if the way information is gained about the utopian community is beyond even fictional
credibility. For instance, a drunken sailor would hardly be an ideal narrator of a utopia, nor would it serve the rhetorical objective of the narrative if he started his story by relating how he traveled to Utopia riding on
the back of an albatross. Such frivolous devices are typically employed by
parodists like Lucian in his *Fantastic Voyage* or Cyrano de Bergerac in his
*Voyage to the Moon.* The requirement of fictional credibility establishes relatively strict limits to the fantastic imagination of the author, constrain-
ing him to alloy his fantasy with mimetic elements. On the other hand,
if mimesis in narration is overly successful, readers may fail to notice the
presence of fantasy in the narrative and simply take the story for a trave-
logue or a straight account of adventures that have really taken place. Such
an impression would also work against the rhetorical strategy of utopias,
since they want to challenge readers and provoke them into a reconsider-
ation of the values and institutions of world-2. The customs and practices
of a faraway country in themselves may fail to impress readers in such a
way; many would merely wonder at such exotic traditions or would ascribe
such practices to the "primitive habits of natives." The satirical method
can only be successful if readers are awakened to the imaginary character
of the country introduced to them but are nonetheless encouraged to
compare this fictional community to their own. Hence the attraction of
authors of utopia to the discussion form, a clash of ideas and principles
that highlights differences and invites readers to take sides in the debate,
while also orienting and occasionally prodding them in one direction or
another.

The roles assigned in the discussion depend on the author's choice
of the spokesman for the utopia and his (very rarely her) integration into
the narrative structure. If the narrator is identical with the person who
visited the utopia, he has to take up the debate with his listener(s). This
appears as a less fortunate rhetorical approach since the confrontation
between narrator/author and the listener/audience is too sharp: a devotee
of the other world argues passionately with his skeptical counterpart, leaving little room for mediation between points of view and subtle persuasion. A more promising situation is offered by a meeting between the

narrator and a visitor who returned from the utopia. In this case, the narrator must represent the values of world-1 against the "stranger," and his gradual surrender and persuasion by the utopian spokesman may induce a similar turnover in readers (cf. More's *Utopia*). A rhetorically similar scenario is set up when the narrator and the visitor are conflated into one character and he is confronted with a wise native of the utopia. In that case, the visitor has to argue for the world he has come from, but his and his readers' persuasion may be hastened by the fact that he directly experiences the utopia rather than merely hearing about it (cf. Bellamy's *Looking Backward* or Morris's *News from Nowhere*).

None of these techniques, however, can entirely eliminate the structural ambiguity of a literary utopia. Due to the contradictory demands of the need for the fictional credibility of the utopia on the one hand and the need for the recognition of the utopia as fiction on the other, the argumentative rhetoric cannot preclude the narrative's subversion of its own persuasive goal. If the utopian spokesman is a stranger, his credibility is always susceptible to distrust; if the narrator visited the utopia in person, the circumstances of the journey to the other world and back raise similar suspicions. These doubts cannot be erased from the text without ruining the rhetorical strategy of utopias: readers need to be both temporarily estranged from the values and practices of world-1 and driven to the recognition that the utopia represents not an existing historical alternative but a hypothetical possibility. Therefore, the author must allow a degree of ambiguity to enter the narrative; in fact, an authorial awareness of such an inherent ambiguity plays a creative role in good utopias. If the author embraces this ambiguity as a source of creative energy, and allows it to extend its influence over the narrative, he/she can keep readers in a sort of limbo while reading the narrative. They are invited to reconsider world-1 and compare it to the utopia; they are persuaded to temporarily suspend their disbelief in the possible existence of a fictitious country while being reminded of the imaginary nature of this community; they are hovering between the arguments presented by the protagonist of world-1 and the protagonist of the utopia; they may be second-guessing the motives of the author. Doubts are raised concerning the quality and rationality of world-1, but also concerning the viability of the utopia.

All these potential effects on readers are produced by cognitive estrangement: the *novum*, which is in this case the invention of a fictitious human community living by inverted or radically different social and moral rules, is a gauntlet thrown down to readers. On the other hand, the mimetic representation of world-1— either directly in the narrative frame or indirectly by the words and deeds of the protagonist of this world — exercises a constant restraint on this fictional challenge, literally and symbolically. After all, one person's account, experiences and arguments confront the consensus reality of the author and the readers (as long as they are near-contemporaries). However eloquently and convincingly the protagonist of the utopia argues in favor of the superiority of his "nowhere," the fictional conventions leave little doubt in the end that this excellent place is just fancy, an ideal beyond the reach of ordinary humans, the representation of desire, or whatever the reader takes it to be. A literary utopia is distinguished from a fictionalized political tract by the inevitable doubt it leaves behind: doubt concerning world-1 and world-2, doubt concerning utopia, doubt concerning the text and its motives.

Estrangement both induces and is produced by the inevitable ambiguity of utopias, and I have found it to work in more complex and more subtle ways than cognitive estrangement as described by Suvin. I completely agree with his idea that the *novum* and the cognitive estrangement it produces is a constitutive part of the rhetorical strategy of utopias. The particularly close conflict between the mimetic and the fantastic in utopias, however, manifests itself on another level, the level of narration, where it appears as the tension between the continuous endeavor of the text to establish credibility for the *novum* on the one hand, and its parallel and ongoing effort to undermine this credibility in indirect and subtle ways on the other. I propose to call the manifestation of estrangement on the level of the narration "narrative estrangement."

Narrative estrangement is produced by two forces pulling in opposite directions, and as a result, it is dynamic and controversial. One aspect of it — the well-known rhetorical strategy called "suspension of disbelief" — is a generic requirement of all fiction, mimetic and fantastic alike. The other, contrary aspect, aiming at subverting and occasionally annulling this suspension of disbelief, is much rarer, confined to certain kinds of fantastic fiction, where unqualified identification with the invented world is somehow not entirely desirable. As I have argued, it is mostly absent or far less significant in other sorts of science fiction since they do not require the explicit mimetic representation of world-1. In case of utopias, it both facilitates and is necessitated by the ongoing dialogue between world-1 and the utopia: both mutually question and relativize the other, just as narrative estrangement, on the level of narration, creates an illusion of hovering between the "what if" and the "what if not." In a sense, readers are asked to do two things at the same time: to believe and to doubt, to take fiction seriously while also smiling at it; in short, to play a game.

The theory of game as a fundamental element of human culture was first advanced by Johan Huizinga's classic study, *Homo Ludens* (1938), in which he extends his approach to literature as a whole, arguing that poetry displays all those features of human games that Huizinga deems essential. It is an activity freely undertaken by participants, without any physiological necessity or outer compulsion; it is pursued without any self-interest or further objective, its exclusive purpose is the pleasure it provides; it is carried out within clearly defined spatial, temporal and intellectual limits; it has a clear, visible order, governed by rules established by the players; and it involves the players deeply, inciting them to tension, effort, and enthusiasm, leading to an ultimate joy and release of tension (16–19, 142–145).

Although he focused his attention on poetry, his observations are valid for prose fiction as well, and utopias — by virtue of being hypothetical models of human communities possessing a relatively high degree of completeness and autonomy — are particularly suitable to be viewed as sophisticated games. Utopias are always clearly and obviously separated from world-1: they are located on distant continents, faraway islands, in valleys hidden by tall mountains, other planets, or in the future or the past. As I have discussed, the community is governed by a rational(ized) order, a social contract, which is duly exposed in the description or discussion, and which is of course created by the author, who acts as the maker of the rules of this particular game. Imagining and writing about a utopia is definitely not a necessary human activity in the strict sense; one may well consider it — and many hostile commentators have in fact called it — superfluous, idle daydreaming, satisfying Huizinga's first and foremost criterion about a freely undertaken activity. A well-written utopia most certainly engages its readers just like any other kind of good literature does: they get involved in it, imagine the community for themselves, begin to toy with the idea of living in it, formulate their own questions and objections to it; in short, they join the game initiated by the author.

Perhaps the only arguable criterion is selflessness: are utopias created and "played" without any axe to grind, like other games? I would argue that this particular criterion is exactly what distinguishes literary utopias proper from political tracts. The latter have an objective beyond the game itself, and view the fiction as a means to achieve some sort of political end (typically to propagate their own agenda), to the detriment of the literary qualities of the text (transparent allegories, heavy didacticism, etc.). But literary utopias, regardless of the political biases of their authors, are first and foremost intellectual and literary games, created by the author who invites readers to join in, to play with him/her and enjoy themselves.

Michael Holquist has explored some of the parallels between utopia and game, specifically, between utopia and chess. He points out that both utopia and chess are abstractions, simplified and stylized models of something far more complex and confusing: society and war, respectively.

> In each case what was rough is made smooth, what was chaotic is made orderly. The chess game has *rules*, the utopia *laws*. The chess game has its distinctive furniture, derived from battle. Utopia has its characteristic counters, derived from society.... Since utopia strives to reflect the more complex entity of the two, its furniture must be correspondingly more numerous and diffuse. It must find counters not only for rulers and warriors, but also for farmers, lawyers, philosophers, etc. Must utopias contain these elements, but they are all reduced to manageable essentials [135–36, emphases retained].

Both chess and utopia express a desire to control and manage something that is normally beyond human control; consequently, the simplification involves all aspects of the original. The space of both chess and utopia is strictly limited; the time of both is different from real time. While the time of chess is set by the clock, Holquist emphasizes that the time of utopia is different from the present, past or future in which the fiction is set; it is "hypothetical or heuristic time," existing only "as an enabling device for a certain kind of speculation" (138, 137). Utopias exist in an eternal, static present, unrelated to the present, past and future of world-1.

Utopia is also similar to chess in the inviolability of its laws or rules: a game functions only as long as its rules are followed; once any of these rules are broken, the game ceases to exist. In order to guarantee the stability and permanence of the rules, the figures in the game must be deprived of all autonomy and freedom: in the case of utopias it means that its human beings are literally mere pawns, they are custom-made robots obeying the rules of the game without qualms. That is also the reason why utopias are qualitatively different from novels: "People, like everything else in utopia, must be shriven of their idiosyncrasies, must be transformed into units that can be manipulated according to a restricted set of laws and presuppositions. In utopia, surprise is a heresy.... This society is by definition perfect, so that any changes in it can result only in a falling away, a decline.

Thus innovation is a crime in utopia, a sin against perfection" (Holquist 136, 139).

Holquist argues that utopia can be considered a strategic battle game just like chess: a battle between two sets of values, and the rules are established in such a way as to help utopian values to victory against the values of world-1. But one of the most universal characteristics of all games is that once the rules are set, the outcome of the game is impossible to determine, so any of the players may win. "The irreversibility of history is stemmed, and outcomes determined by the contingency of actual experience, can, in utopia, be reversed in the freedom of the utopist's imagination. Another set of laws obtains in the utopia, arbitrary but infinitely open to recombination. Utopia is play with ideas" (143). If one considers the utopia a game between the author and the readers, the analogy is obvious: although the author introduces the game and sets the rules, victory is ultimately declared by the reader, who may not come to the conclusion that the author has a winning side against world-1.

I am convinced that considering utopias as literary-intellectual games helps to establish an appropriate context for criticism. First of all, it is a healthy antidote against reading utopias as a manifestation of the author's political ideals. To offer a crude analogy, one can enjoy playing a game featuring kings and queens without being devoted to monarchy as a form of government. Just because a utopist proposes to play around with a hypothetical human community, he/she does not necessarily dream of living in it, or even if he/she does, the crucial difference between that game and real life is emphatically maintained in the narrative by means of cognitive and narrative estrangement. Second, the utopia-as-game approach reveals why it should not be the primary concern of literary criticism to praise or attack the politics of a particular utopia: if reading a utopia is engaging in a game, the reader's job is to try to play that game as well as they can, not to start arguing about the rules. The quality of a utopia is ultimately determined by how challenging and entertaining a game it proves to be, and that is, if not totally unrelated to, nonetheless not exclusively determined by the sociopolitical suppositions on which the game's rules are based.

Two of the most influential and also intriguing games among English literary utopias are Thomas More's *Utopia* and H.G. Wells' *A Modern Utopia*. In case of More's work, my interest lies in precisely how he constructs his narrative model, and how cognitive and narrative estrangement work in the text to couch his vision of Utopia in a delicate veil of ambiguity. Wells' book is not only an early–20th-century utopia, but a meta-utopia as well in the sense that it reflects on a four-century-long literary tradition. Wells made a significant attempt to rewrite the rules of the game in such a way as to overcome what he perceived to be the biggest drawback of the traditional form: the static, ahistorical character, which precludes the possibility of development and change. But Wells' attempt to establish a new game model was combined with significant innovations in the narration of utopia, which merits special attention from the critic. His oeuvre represents a definitive turn in the history of the entire utopian genre, and his long-ranging impact on 20th-century utopia, dystopia, and science fiction manifests itself in a variety of ways.

# Chapter 2

# Encounters with a Stranger

## *Pursuing Elusive Recollections*

Thomas More in *Utopia* describes the encounter that led to a long and passionate dialogue, followed by a lengthy description of "the best state of a commonwealth" (8), the following way:

> One day after I had heard Mass at Nôtre Dame ... I was about to return to my quarters when I happened to see him [Peter Giles] talking with a stranger, a man of quite advanced years. The stranger had a sunburned face, a long beard and a cloak hanging loosely from his shoulders; from his face and dress, I took him to be a ship's captain [More 1989, 9].[1]

This stranger, Raphael Hythloday, is explicitly identified in the subtitles of the two Books of the first, 1516 Louvain edition as the "author" of the discourse, while More is merely a "reporter" of his narration.[2] Despite the emphatic distinction between author and reporter, the narrative framework of *Utopia* received very little critical attention before the second half of the 20th century. The paramount question preoccupying critics and commentators has been the intention of Thomas More with his book; and most of them have come to the conclusion that reforming passion is so obviously permeating the whole work that Hythloday must be interpreted as the mouthpiece of the author, giving voice to More's critical views and reform ideas concerning contemporary Christian Europe.[3] Hythloday is also a necessary narrative device to describe an imagined faraway land that More — who left England only a few times during his lifetime and never traveled further than the Netherlands or Northern France[4] — could not have personally visited. This argument is doubtless supported by the overall rhetorical drift of the book, since

45

Hythloday's utterances dominate the dialogue in Book I, while Book II consists of his continuous, unbroken monologue describing his experiences in Utopia, with a very short, almost hasty, conclusion by More. At first sight it is difficult to believe that the author would give so much space for a character to expound his views if he did not agree or at least sympathize with them.

Nevertheless, this argument about the function of Hythloday as a transparent disguise of the author has at least two significant weaknesses, which have been duly exposed by several critics. One of them is that Hythloday is opposed in the debate of Book I not by another fictitious character but by More himself, who, while continually praising Hythloday's wisdom and intelligence, is far from agreeing with all his ideas: he accepts some, fails to comment on several others and vehemently disagrees with a few. If Hythloday is merely a disguise of More the author, what is the function of More the debater in the story? What does *he* represent, whose ideas does *he* express? The most influential answer to this question has come from J.H. Hexter, who submits *Utopia* to a textual analysis and, relying largely on extraneous sources, comes to the conclusion that Book II was written first, during More's sojourn as a royal ambassador in Flanders in 1515, together with a short introduction, which later became the opening part of Book I. Thus the original narrative design consisted of the encounter of More and Hythloday, immediately followed by Hythloday's account of Utopia. Therefore Book II represents More's "original intent" (*Biography of an Idea* 28), and the dialogue in which More himself is promoted from audience to a debating partner is an addition written later, in early 1516, in London. Hexter also offers a theory to explain why More changed his mind and inserted the dialogue; he argues that More was faced with a difficult choice after his return from the Netherlands: the decision whether or not to enter the service of Henry VIII as a royal councilor. This pressing personal problem was dramatized in Book I as an internal dialogue between two sides of himself (or possibly, between himself and his friend Erasmus), the debate between the realist and the idealist, the pragmatic humanist with noble ambitions and the independent-minded philosopher. But Hexter also struggles hard to maintain the notion that it is Hythloday who expresses More's own deep distaste for public service in the dialogue, and even tries to prove that More eventually entered royal service two years later as a result of a profound change in his inner conviction.

Such attempts to impute a clear authorial intent to *Utopia* by identifying Hythloday — or, for that matter, More the debater — as the representative of the author are inevitably wrecked by the inherent ambiguity of the narrative structure of the book itself: in a debate where a literary persona of the author is pitted against a fictitious character, it is very difficult if not impossible to make an incontestable case for either one or the other speaking the author's mind. Book II, despite its seeming straightforwardness, also raises serious questions at closer inspection. The most problematic aspects of Utopia have been its radical social egalitarianism, the absence of private property, and the high degree of religious toleration. The first two fly in the face of the social reality of More's own time, whereas the third seems to propose the heretical idea that there is more than one true religion, and they are all equally valid ways to achieve salvation. If these ideas were indeed professed by More, they suggest the image of a fearless critic and a bold reformer, who dares to imagine a society on an economic, social and spiritual basis that is completely different from his own. The only problem with that image is that it does not seem to correspond to the picture(s) of Thomas More presented by biographers and historians. It appears as if the author of *Utopia* and the historical Thomas More were almost complete strangers to each other.

For some reason, interpretations of *Utopia* have been all but inseparable from certain assumptions made about its author. One could almost say that the majority of interpreters were less interested in the book itself than what it reveals about More's character and political convictions. It is very interesting that this particular version of the "intentional fallacy" has been haunting the criticism of *Utopia*. The ambiguities of the book are almost invariably resolved with reference to the historical More, especially his subsequent public career and nonfictional writings. In my opinion, this irrepressible urge to try to harmonize the image of More with the interpretation of his most famous book emerges from the particular blend of mimesis and fantasy presented in *Utopia*. The text presents such a compelling picture of More encountering a wise traveler in Antwerp and engaging in an erudite discussion with him about the state of Christian Europe as opposed to a land of wise people in the New World that most readers could not resist the temptation to search for links between *Utopia* and its author. In practice, this has resulted in selecting one of the several public images of More in circulation and applying it to the text — sometimes rather forcefully. So in order to see how *Utopia* has been appropriated, we have to get acquainted with the public images of More, the elusive stranger whom everybody believes they know intimately.

## IMAGES OF MORE

The early biographers of More, from his own son-in-law, William Roper, who gave a partial eyewitness account of his life around 1557,[5] down to Cresacre More, his great-grandson, whose work, published in 1620, is mostly derived from previous biographies,[6] were primarily interested in More's life as an example of Christian virtue and his solid heroism in defense of Catholic doctrines. As John Guy puts it,

> They were lobbying to secure More's recognition by the Catholic church as a martyr and a saint. They were deliberately constructing an image.... Their "Lives" are hagiographical.... They blur the lines between "history" and "story," blending truth, fiction and "miracles" in ways that are unimaginable today ... they represent the "More" whom these authors have chosen to depict [11].

Although they failed in their efforts to ease the way toward More's canonization, because the defeat of the Armada in 1588 put an end to hopes of winning England back for Catholicism, and the interest of the Vatican in English martyrs of the Catholic faith was not reawakened until the 19th century, the long-term influence of these biographies proved decisive. After the re-discovery of More in the late 1800s, when he was beatified (in 1886), and the first modern scholarly works were written about him,[7] the saintly image presented by these early authors was revived with various modifications, and stamped on the mind of succeeding generations.

Apart from Roper, the only contemporary of More who left behind a detailed description of his character was his famous scholar friend, Desiderius Erasmus. The well-known letter to Ulrich von Hutten, written in 1519, contains much information that is not available from any other source: a description of More's physical appearance, his personal habits and tastes as well as interesting details of his family and household. Erasmus first met More in 1499, and afterward visited him several times during his spells in England, spending months in his house as a distinguished guest.[8] From Erasmus's portrait, we get the image of a very talented scholar and author, well-versed in both Latin and Greek, a friendly and amiable personality, an impeccably virtuous husband, father and public servant, and a pious Christian. Erasmus is the primary source for at least three crucial decisions in More's life: the first two in his mid 20s, when he was captivated by Greek literature and philosophy and wanted to devote himself to the full-time pursuit of scholarship, but under his father's pressure he decided to become a practicing lawyer.[9] At about the same time, he felt a strong attraction to the priesthood, but eventually renounced this ambition in order to have a wife and family.[10] Another turning point came around 1517 or 1518,[11] not long before Erasmus's portrait was written, when he was "dragged" into royal service despite his reluctance, since his outstanding talent and qualities proved so persuasive to King Henry that he refused to accept any polite excuses.[12] These assertions added a crucial feature to the public image of More: that of the virtuous and benevolent but misplaced intellectual, who was forced into a public career despite his desire to devote himself to his profession and his studies, and his honest and loyal service to the king eventually brought his own demise.

Erasmus's portrait has long been regarded as one of the most reliable accounts of More's character, since it was written by a close friend who maintained a regular and intimate correspondence with More during his whole career. The first scholar to question the reliability of the portrait was the eminent English historian, G. R. Elton: after examining available government records, he concluded that "by August 1517 More was a councilor," but he let Erasmus know about it only in April 1518, which could only mean that he did not want to admit to his friend that he joined royal service quickly and eagerly rather than unwillingly and hesitantly.[13] By questioning Erasmus's representation of More's true attitude, he also cast doubt on the generally accepted image of More as a reluctant courtier, and argued that More was motivated by a genuine desire to influence public policy for the better.[14]

John Guy in his recent assessment of More's reputation drew attention to another previously neglected aspect of Erasmus's letter on More: that it is not an objective description of a friend in a private letter, but a portrait intended to be published and make a public impression. According to Guy, "Erasmus sought to publicize throughout Europe what he considered to be the ideal of a Christian humanist life. He attributes to More the virtues immortalized by Cicero's *De officiis*, the 'golden text' of Italian and northern European humanism" (5). Concerning the choice between scholarship and holy orders on the one hand, and between legal career and marriage on the other, Erasmus "sought to create a model of *decorum* in which the clash between "action" and "contemplation" in their Christian and classical settings was resolved," while his description of More's reluctance to enter royal service is colored by a difference of opinion and mentality: Erasmus strongly disapproved of More's decision, since he himself made a point of maintaining a lifelong independence from all clerical and secular powers, therefore it suited his purposes more to emphasize the "unwillingness" of More to give up the same (32–33, 48). In brief, Guy argues that Erasmus's public portrait of More is the example of a different kind of idealization: he sketched up the image of an ideal humanist.

For English Protestants, the most significant aspect of More's life and career was not the circumstances of his death or the motives of his crucial decisions in early life, but his persecution of heretics during his chancellorship. The image of More as a fanatic and cruel inquisitor of Protestants was popularized by John Foxe's *Acts and Monuments* (1563), the "holy" book of Protestant martyrology (Guy 107–108). Although Foxe dropped some of the worst charges against More (including the accusation that he personally tortured a heretic with ropes) from the second edition of his book in 1570, his hugely influential work made an indelible impression on the English Protestant public. This strongly unfavorable picture stood in diagonal opposition to that of the author of *Utopia*. The spirit of religious tolerance displayed in the book could hardly be reconciled with the ferocious hunt for heretics described by Foxe. One influential resolution of this dilemma was put forward by the Anglican bishop and historian Gilbert Burnet in 1684, who argued that the young More was a Protestant reformer at heart, who saw the shortcomings of the Catholic church and dogmas very clearly as his criticism voiced in *Utopia* testifies; but when he became Lord Chancellor, he betrayed the ideals of his youth, and turned into a fanatic opponent of the Reformation. Burnet thus postulated a huge spiritual and intellectual rift in More's career, which his early Catholic biographers were careful to conceal (Guy 14–15, 109). His theory shifted the emphasis from More's personal "crimes" against Protestants to the cruel and intolerant attitude of Catholicism, then still a pillar of royal power, which forced More into conformity, and therefore the Church was to take most of the blame for the persecution of heretics. The "rediscovery" of More as a forerunner to Protestant reformers was completed in the 18th century, when his final stand against Henry VIII was interpreted as a defense of the right to the freedom of individual conscience against a dictatorial state (Guy 109–10). This interpretation of More's last days was popularized by a very successful play, Robert Bolt's *A Man for All Seasons* (1960).

More's early Catholic biographers, probably in order to protect the saintly image they were trying to produce, were evading the topic of heresy hunting. Biographers favorably disposed toward More began to counter the persecution charges only from the late 19th century. While disproving many of the false accusations, they tended, however, to try to clear him of all charges of religious persecution, and struggled to prove that More opposed heresy for political rather than doctrinal reasons (to prevent sedition and political unrest), and did not take an active role in the burning of heretics.[15] More's attitude to heresy and heretics is the most hotly debated issue in his career, in which biographers tend to take quite radical and emotionally colored stands. Guy, in an effort to re-examine the matter from an objective historian's point of view, comes to the conclusion that More, although he cannot be accused of illegal acts or personal cruelty toward heretics, was very active and energetic from as early as 1521 in the pamphlet warfare, and considered the defense of the Church and its doctrines a religious duty as well as a political obligation, in which the application of the full power and authority of the State was perfectly justified (Guy 113–22).

The 19th century gave rise to yet another public image of More: that of the forerunner of Socialist, or later Communist, doctrines. Karl Marx, in the first volume of his classic foundation of Socialist economic doctrine, *Das Kapital* (1867), referred to the famous "sheep-parable"[16] of Book I of More's *Utopia* to illustrate the original accumulation of capital in early–16th-century England and its impoverishing effects on landless peasantry.[17] Interestingly enough, Marx did not note Book II and the absence of private property outlined there, but his favorable references to *Utopia* paved the way toward a large-scale Socialist reinterpretation of More and his book. This was carried out by an eminent German Marxist, Karl Kautsky, who devoted a whole book to More and his *Utopia* in 1887. Here he opted for a literal reading of Book II, with special regard to the communal arrangement of life, work and property, and, largely on the basis of this single book, he proceeded to draw the picture of More as a Proto-Socialist, an early advocate of communist ideals. His book makes very strange reading: on the one hand, he surveys most of the literature on More available at the time, and subjects them to a penetrating analysis, showing their confessional bias and intentional or unconscious distortions.[18] This criticism, however, does not prevent him from performing a similar feat of distortive interpretation: he starts from the — never satisfactorily justified — axiom that More was a Socialist/Communist (the two terms he uses interchangeably), and reviews all other aspects of More's life and career from this angle.[19] In order to make good his claim, he carefully selects only those sources and references that support his points, uses lengthy quotations from *Utopia* as if they self-evidently reflected More's own opinion on various matters, and, with breathtaking audacity, he does not shrink from inventing false facts to prove his thesis.[20] But for all the grave defects of his book, Kautsky's lasting merit is that he refocused the discussion over More and *Utopia* by emphasizing, faithfully to the tenets of Marxism, the determining role of contemporary economic and social developments, while downplaying the importance of religion in More's career and outlook. In the meantime, however, he curiously reshaped the well-known saintly image of More by reinventing him as an early "saint" of Socialism, who progressed so far ahead of his time that he was not at all understood by his contemporaries. His version of More became a schoolroom commonplace in the Soviet Union and the satellite states of the Eastern Bloc during the 20th century.[21]

The multiplication of More's images in the public mind and scholarship alike was facilitated by the curious afterlife of *Utopia* itself. The original Latin text was published in five (probably limited) editions between 1516 and 1519, never to appear again in More's lifetime. In 1565–1566 it was included in More's *Opera*, printed in Louvain, and then it enjoyed a period of popularity among German and Dutch publishers in the 17th century,[22] but the first English edition was published only in 1663 in Oxford, not to be followed by any other for a century. For English readers, *Utopia* became familiar not in the original, but in Ralph Robinson's translation, first published in 1551, and kept in print fairly constantly, with nine editions throughout the next two centuries (Gibson 4).[23] Had it not been for Robinson, *Utopia* would have probably faded into obscurity in England until at least the late–19th-century rediscovery of More. As it happened, *Utopia* became somewhat dissociated from its author. During the 16th century, More was a well-known if controversial figure of recent English history, but *Utopia* was not counted among his outstanding achievements; Roper, his first biographer, does not even mention the existence of the book, and we do not find anything more than passing references to it elsewhere. For the generations living under the Tudors, who remembered the reign of Henry VIII vividly, More was apparently important for what he had done (or had not done), not for what he had written. But as the sharp lines in the profile of the historical personality (no matter whether this profile was faithful to the original) began to fade during the 17th century and afterward, More began to be associated in the public imagination primarily with a popular book. Outside England, where *Utopia* was also widely read but More's historical role was almost completely unknown, this association was even more dominant. As a result, when his beatification rekindled public interest in More in the late 19th century, scholars were faced with not one but several different "Mores," all handed down by different traditions and maintained by distinct groups, and they were forced to cope with these sharply different and contesting images: More the Catholic martyr, More the persecutor of Protestants, More the forerunner of Protestantism, More the enlightened Humanist, More the heroic opponent and victim of tyranny, More the Socialist pioneer.

## IMAGES OF UTOPIA

The disagreements and occasional bitter fights over the veracity or falsity of these portraits can be clearly traced in the various interpretations of *Utopia*. People who approached the work already tended to have some kind of a pre-existent image of its author, and bent their interpretation accordingly. The clamor of dissonant voices has been amplified by the fact that there had been little critical discussion of the book until modern times, and consequently, no widespread consensus in interpretation had been established that could have served as a touchstone for later scholars.

The first comments on *Utopia* naturally came from its obvious target audience, More's Humanist friends and contemporaries throughout Christian Europe. Most of these were not spontaneous but rather solicited opinions, duly attached to subsequent editions of the book, not unlike the quotes from positive reviews that appear on the back of modern paperback volumes. Most of the commending letters were secured by Erasmus, who was explicitly asked by More to solicit "the highest of recommendations, if possible, from several people, both intellectuals and distinguished statesmen" (qtd. More 1989, 114, n.4). The two most respectable "reviewers" were Jerome Busleyden — Flemish Humanist and Prince Charles's councilor who was visited by More during his 1515 embassy, and whose letter prefaced the 1516 edition — and Guillaume Budé — the foremost French humanist of the time, whose unusually long comment first appeared in the 1518 edition. For Busleyden and Budé, as well as for all the other commentators whose letters were collectively published in the 1518 edition, the task was essentially a diplomatic exercise: to offer unequivocal praise for the book without making any potentially embarrassing or sensitive remarks about its content. Significantly, none of them had anything to say about the dialogue in Book I, which contained the sharpest and politically most sensitive remarks about contemporary evils, explicitly criticizing Henry VII's England and representing the King of France in a

strongly negative light. Skirting the danger of being associated with any
of the topical references or controversial ideas, the commentators opted
for a general praise of Utopia as a fictitious example of the virtuous commonwealth.

Busleyden unequivocally interpreted the book as an allegory intended
to set a moral example to contemporaries: he repeatedly talks about "this
pattern of a commonwealth, this model and perfect image of proper conduct," which embodies the Four Cardinal Virtues of antiquity: "prudence
in the rulers, courage in the military, temperance in the private citizenry,
and justice among all men." He also praises the invention of removing all
private property, since it prevents all motives for "intrigue, luxury, envy
and wrong." In summary, he declares that More has done a great favor for
all future commonwealths by showing a pattern to follow in order to
remain strong and healthy states (More 1989, 127–28).

Budé's approach is similar, but he takes a longer view: he focuses on
human avarice as the root of all evil, and continues with a long diatribe
against the debasement of human law, both canon and civil, designed to
protect and assist human selfishness. He contrasts this to God's law, prom-
ulgated by Christ, who "left his followers a Pythagorean rule of mutual
charity and community property." Then he observes that Utopia seems
to be a place where "the truly Christian customs and the authentic wisdom" have been marvelously preserved by maintaining three crucial institutions: absolute equality of "all good and evil things among the citizens"
(presumably implying common property, social equality, the universal
obligation to work, etc.), dedication to peace and tranquility, and the con-
tempt for precious metals (118–19). But he immediately expresses his doubts
about whether such a place can truly exist, and goes on to question, gen-
tly and ironically, the authenticity of the account:

> I have decided, after investigating the matter, that Utopia lies outside the
> bounds of the known world. Perhaps it is one of the Fortunate Isles.... As
> More himself says, Hythloday has not yet told exactly where it is to be
> found.... If Hythloday is the architect of the Utopian nation, the founder
> of its customs and institutions from which he has brought home and fash-
> ioned for us the very pattern of a happy life, More is its adorner, who has
> bestowed on the island and its holy institutions the grace of his style, the
> polish of his diction. He it is who has shaped the city of the Hagnopoli-
> tans to the standard of a model and a general rule.... And yet he claims
> as his part of the task only the role of a humble artisan.... *He feared, of*
> *course, that Hythloday, who was living of his own free will on the island of*
> *Udepotia, might some day return, and be angry that More had left him only*

*the husks of credit for his discovery, having taken the best part for himself* [119–120].[24]

By calling Hythloday the "architect" of Utopia, Budé subtly hints that he considers Utopia a fiction, invented by Hythloday and cast into a literary form by More, although he does not seem to doubt the existence of Hythloday himself, only the reliability of his account. He implicitly confirms this reading at the end, when he commends the book, similarly to Busleyden, as "a seedbed ... of elegant and useful concepts" for the future use of mankind (121).

The crucial points of both letters concur: they praise Utopia as a great Christian allegory, a compendium of good social institutions, and single out the absence of private property as a particularly positive example, but otherwise refrain from analyzing the social arrangements of Utopia in detail. Since lavish encomia were common practice among Renaissance Humanists, it is impossible to tell how much of their praise was perfunctory and how much of it was motivated by honest enthusiasm for the book. Judging by the letters themselves, Busleyden is more brief and reserved in his appreciation than Budé, who did not know More personally and did not even address the letter to him, but nevertheless unfolded his views in greater detail.[25] The other letters and commendations included in the first four editions are either effusive praises for More's great talent without any specific critical observations, or — as in the case of the letters of Peter Giles and More himself— they join the "authenticity game" initiated by More, and mention various trivial details about the meeting with Hythloday and his subsequent career in order to playfully reinforce the illusion of factuality. (The ancillary materials are discussed in detail on pages 63–70.)

The most authoritative opinion on *Utopia* would have certainly come from Erasmus, who took care of the preparation of the first edition in Louvain in 1516 as well as the third and fourth editions in Basel in 1518 (Barker 218–21). He, however, curiously refrained from any comment on the book until August 1517, when, in a very brief letter written to his Basel publisher, Johann Froben, he praised More's exceptional talent but did not say a word on the merits or virtues of *Utopia* itself (More 1989, 114–15). In his portrait of More included in a letter to Hutten in 1519, he briefly referred to *Utopia*, whose purpose was "to show whence spring the evils of states: but he modeled it on the British [i.e., English] constitution, with which he is thoroughly familiar" (Allen 8). The silence of Erasmus is all the more peculiar since he as editor probably spent considerable time and effort on the text, and, according to the title page of the 1517 edition, he contributed at least some of the marginal glosses of the printed version (More 1989, 125). It is hard to believe that he had no distinct opinion on the work as a whole, but why he kept it secret remains a mystery. The reason he himself offered at the opening of his letter to Froben, namely, that he mistrusted his own judgment because of his close friendship to More, sounds rather disingenuous: Humanists were rarely prevented from praising a friend by scruples about their potential bias. Possibly, he may have refused to comment because he had a low opinion of the book, which he, out of respect for his friend, wanted to keep to himself. His eulogy of More in the letter to Froben contains some implied reservations: in effect he says that More could have unfolded his genius more completely if he had had the opportunity to study in Italy, and if he had devoted all his time to writing and scholarship. This wording might obliquely hint at Erasmus' dissatisfaction with More's actual achievement so far, including *Utopia*. In his letter to Hutten, he also made a remark on the "unevenness in the style" (Allen 8) of *Utopia*, and justified it on the grounds that the first book was written later and hastily. On the whole, however, it appears rather improbable that Erasmus would have taken all the trouble to edit, correct, and see through the press three editions of a book he otherwise disliked,[26] and obtained several written tributes to it from distinguished friends exclusively out of loyalty to his friend. After all, he would have risked his reputation by promoting an inferior piece of writing. If that is granted, one may conjecture that the most probable reason for his silence was caution: Erasmus, who was known to be a rather timid and diplomatic personality, very sensitive to political implications of his deeds,[27] may have perceived some potential risk in More's outspoken criticism of contemporary Europe, and thought it best not to reveal his opinion on any specific aspect of *Utopia*. If this conjecture is correct, then one may add that Erasmus had a prophetic instinct: he foresaw that More's book would continue to raise problems that were political as well as literary in nature.

As mentioned above, *Utopia* was revived after More's death in the mid–16th century by Ralph Robinson's English translation, and achieved surprising popularity in Protestant England given the fact that it was written by a staunch Catholic. That Robinson himself was aware of the danger he incurred by the translation is clear from his dedicatory epistle addressed to William Cecil, in 1551 secretary to King Edward VI, and Robinson's former schoolmate (More 1890, 68). In the epistle he explains his motives for translating More's work and remarks about him:

Sir Thomas More the author ... [is] for the excellent qualities, wherewith the great goodness of God had plentifully endowed him, and for the high place, and room, whereunto his prince most graciously called him, notably well known...: therefore I have not much to speak of him. This only I say: that it is much to be lamented of all, and not only of us Englishmen, that a man of so incomparable wit, of so profound knowledge, of so absolute learning, and of so fine eloquence was yet nevertheless so much blinded, rather with obstinacy, than with ignorance that he could not or rather would not see the shining light of God's holy truth in certain principal points of Christian religion: but did rather choose to persevere, and continue in his wilful and stubborn obstinacy even to the very death. This I say is a thing much to be lamented. But letting this matter pass, I return again to Utopia. Which ... is a work not only for the matter that it containeth fruitful and profitable, but also for the writer's eloquent Latin style pleasant and delectable [More 1890, 66–67].

Robinson is thus careful to dissociate himself from More the obstinate heretic; he chose *Utopia* for translation not because of his author but because of the qualities of the book. His caution is all the more reasonable if we take into account that he was dedicating his work to a high-ranking official of the son of Henry VIII, who — or rather his government led by the Duke of Northumberland — was sympathizing with the doctrines of Continental Protestantism. The irony of Robinson's careful disclaimer is that he could not foresee the future: Edward died two years later and was succeeded by Mary, determined to restore Catholicism in England. Accordingly in 1556, when Robinson's translation was issued again, the epistle containing the condemnation of More's religious views was replaced by a short foreword to "the Gentle Reader," in which neither More's nor William Cecil's name is mentioned, but Robinson muses on a quote from Terence that compares human life to a game of dice and says that "if that chance rise not, which is most for the player's advantage, that then the chance, which fortune hath sent, ought so cunningly to be played, as may be to the player least damage" (More 1890, 71). It is difficult not to see a degree of self deprecating irony in this remark as Robinson no doubt felt somewhat uncomfortable about his anti–Catholic comment made in print just five years earlier, and may have also wondered about the swift turn of fortune in the great "gamble" of national politics.

Two years later, at the accession of Elizabeth, the tables turned once more, and perhaps as a consequence of the popular anti–Catholic sentiment following the reign of "Bloody Mary," Robinson's text was not published again until 1597 (Gibson 4). But the fact that it became well-known and popular through the first two editions is illustrated by a remark made by Sir Philip Sidney in his *Apologie for Poetrie* (published posthumously in 1595), where he praised *Utopia* with the following words:

> But euen in the most excellent determination of goodnes, what Philosophers counsell can so redily direct a Prince, as the fayned Cyros in Xenophon, or a vertuous man in all fortunes, as Aeneas in Virgil, or a whole Common-wealth, as the way of Sir Thomas Moores Eutopia? I say the way, because *where Sir Thomas Moore erred, it was the fault of the man and not of the Poet*, for that way of patterning a Common-wealth was most absolute, though hee perchaunce hath not so absolutely perfourmed it [Sidney 18–19, emphasis added].

Sidney's enthusiasm is justified by the underlying idea of his tract, that is, to argue in favor of the importance and utility of "poetry" (at that time still designating literature in general) in the spirit of the Horatian idea "to teach and delight." For him, *Utopia* was an outstanding example of the best qualities of "poetry:" it entertains the reader and at the same time persuades them about the best moral values not by abstract argumentation but by describing a convincing example, being therefore superior to both philosophy and history. This understanding was essentially in line with the Humanist reading of More as the author of a great Christian allegory. What is novel about Sidney's comment is that he allows for certain unspecified defects in this image of the virtuous commonwealth, unlike the earlier commentators (after all, the author had a shady reputation in Sidney's time), but he justifies his own high regard by making a distinction between artistic intention and its realization: even with the noblest intentions, a fallible man is prone to commit errors, and thus More's perfect commonwealth inevitably has its disagreeable aspects; yet it does not disparage his merit of attempting to sketch such an ideal social organization. Thus Sidney asserts the pragmatic value — teaching ethics through entertainment — of *Utopia* while carefully avoiding any consideration of the actual ideas of the book or specifying where exactly More "erred."

The cautious "rehabilitation" of More on the basis of *Utopia*, initiated by Sidney, was completed by Gilbert Burnet. Burnet was the first to delve into the specific arrangements of More's ideal commonwealth by focusing on the religious tolerance of Utopians, and recast the author of *Utopia* as a Protestant reformer at heart. His bold thesis opened a long debate over More's religious views in which *Utopia* was not examined as an autonomous literary work but used as a quarry for the religious ideas of More before the Reformation started. The ultimate issue at stake was the moral integrity of More: did he have consistent views on the problems

and doctrines of the Church, or did he give up or betray his pre–Reformation ideals owing to religious zeal, conformity or expediency? Chambers,
in his influential biography published in 1935, still considers it so important to clear More of all charges that, in the chapter entitled "The Meaning of *Utopia*," he deals predominantly with the interpretation of religious
freedom and tolerance in Utopia (118–24). He concludes that More was
fully consistent with the premise of his work, since he wanted to produce
an ideal commonwealth based exclusively on reason and the Four Cardinal Virtues of pagan antiquity. As a direct result of that starting point,
there is no official religion in Utopia, but tolerance is strictly limited to
people who accept divine providence and the immortality of the soul as
inviolable doctrines.[28] Atheists are despised and cast out of society, forbidden to argue their views in public. Otherwise, Utopians allow religious
argument and attempts at persuasion, but only by peaceful and rational
means. Chambers argues that these ideas were not heretical since More
emphatically described an ideally wise and prudent state of pagans who
are unfamiliar with Christ's teaching; therefore they have made the most
reasonable arrangements for the peaceful coexistence of various religions.
This system, however, has nothing to do with More's own religious convictions; therefore it has no relevance upon his subsequent attitude toward
Protestants. Chambers returns to this problem once more in a later chapter, where he compares Utopian religion with More's treatises against heretics, and takes pains to demonstrate the difference of opinion between More
and English Protestants on a number of doctrinal and practical reform
measures (Chambers 245–56). He sums up this difference with a famous
quote from one of More's anti–Protestant treatises: "Reason is servant to
Faith, not enemy."[29] Utopia is based on Reason alone, whereas the Catholic
church is built on Faith in God's revelations transmitted by Christ. More
was a staunch defender of the unity of the Church, and he placed the
authority of time-hallowed institutions ahead of individual ideas or criticism. When he was critical of practices within the Church, he was attack
ing the debasement of worthy ideals by corrupt individuals, but the ideals
themselves were, for More, above criticism. His distaste for the ideas of
the Reformation was aggravated by what was seen by More as the aggressive propagation of these ideas, and the violent abuse of their opponents.
Therefore Protestants are not only a danger for the Church: they are threatening the stability of the realm, inciting dissent and civil unrest.

Chambers's demonstration of the consistency of More's religious views
effectively annihilated the arguments underpinning the image of "More

the Protestant forerunner," and recovered *Utopia* for the Catholics who had apparently been clueless to square it with More's subsequent martyrdom. But perhaps his most important innovation was the dichotomy he set up between the ideal society presented in the book and More's own views. Earlier, no interpreter had explored the possibility that Hythloday's description in Book II is not identical with More's own ideals and preferences — except for those who dismissed the whole book as a kind of joke. Chambers's subtle interpretation emphasizes More's intention to criticize the moral conditions of contemporary Europe explicitly in Book I and implicitly in Book II, where he satirized many of its follies by sketching a morally superior pagan society. Chambers's approach paved the way for the "humanistic interpretation" of *Utopia,* unfolding after the war, which locates the core of the work in the serious political-ethical content it offers and considers it largely as a theoretical treatise expressed in a metaphorical form (Logan 8–9). Perhaps the most influential study of this school was J.H. Hexter's investigation of the composition of More's *Utopia,* already alluded to in the opening part of this chapter. Taking his cue from Erasmus's letter to Hutten, which claims that More "began with the second book, written at leisure, and then ... added the first rapidly" (Allen 8), he detects a broken seam in the text of Book I where More the narrator, instead of reproducing Hythloday's description of Utopia, begins a lengthy dialogue about some other, apparently not too closely related topics. Hexter concludes that what More must have written afterward is the bulk of Book I, which he then inserted here: "He pried open a seam at the place where Hythloday's discourse originally had begun and inserted the addition there" (Hexter 21). Hexter goes on to draw important conclusions from this hypothesis: that in its present form Utopia does not represent a "unified literary design, ... the consistent working out of a preconceived plan" (28), but it includes an internally consistent description of an imagined ideal state (that is, the opening part of Book I and most of Book II), written "at leisure" in Antwerp, during the royal embassy's prolonged stay in the Netherlands in 1515, and a more or less coherent dialogue about certain issues (that is, the second, longer part of Book I) that More was concerned with after his return to London in early 1516 (15–30). Hexter dubs this larger and later part of Book I "The Dialogue of Counsel," and argues that it dramatized More's own internal struggle about whether to enter royal service or not.

Hexter's textual analysis and his meticulous justification of it has become generally accepted, and served as a starting point for subsequent textual investigations. On the other hand, many critics felt compelled to reject the conclusions he drew from that analysis. Several subsequent commentators emphasized that, regardless of the circumstances of the composition, More had decided to publish *Utopia* in the form it became known to us, and therefore the interpreter has to approach the text with the assumption that it is a coherent and consistent whole. The most recent development of this school focuses on the appreciation of the original nature of the ideas advanced by More and suggests that *Utopia* is above all a remarkable piece of Renaissance political theory.[30]

Another rival critical current, following the lead of Seebohm and Kautsky,[31] carried on the literalist interpretation by focusing on the social criticism and political reform ideas of the book, and linked this to the contemporary economic, social and political situation in England and Europe as well as More's personal background as a Northern Humanist and a citizen of London.[32] Such interpretations tend to see More as the spokesman of a distinct group — the London merchants, or the Erasmian Humanist reformers — and argue that he had specific political intentions with his book beyond mere moral satire and criticism: he actually put forward a blueprint for reform and wanted to actively influence the England of his day. This argument is greatly weakened by the fact that *Utopia* was written in Latin and never appeared in England during More's lifetime, a rather ineffective way to propagate one's political reform ideas in one's own country. Besides that, no persuasive evidence is known to support the claim that More ever seriously attempted to promote or suggest reform proposals similar in spirit to the social arrangements in Utopia when, as Lord Chancellor, he was one of the more powerful officials of the country.[33]

An interesting version of this "political blueprint" reading of Utopia was worked out by German critics in the 1920s who argued that More's agenda was to propagate English colonization of North America, and in the description of Utopian practices of planting surplus population overseas, as well as the description of Utopian methods of waging war, he provided moral justification of subsequent English efforts to build a colonial empire.[34] Their argument was reinforced by the fact that More's brother-in-law, John Rastell, made a failed attempt to establish a colony on Newfoundland a few months after the publication of *Utopia*. From this evidence, even Chambers draws the conclusion that "colonization and transatlantic adventure meant much to the writer of *Utopia*," as if Rastell's journey in itself were incontrovertible proof that he took the idea from More's book or his personal encouragement (Chambers 132, 134–35). This argument has very recently been rehashed in a convoluted form by Jeffrey Knapp to justify his thesis, namely that More's *Utopia*, together with Spenser's *Faerie Queene* and Shakespeare's *Tempest*, revolves "around three interlocking issues: the problem of an island empire; colonialism as a special solution to the problem; and poetry as a special model of both problem and solution.... The purpose of Nowhere for More, Spenser, and Shakespeare ... is rather to turn the English into imperialists by differentiating their other-worldly potentiality from their other-worldly island" (7). In his effort to prove that Utopia "could ... be taken, and intended, as colonialist propaganda" (21), Knapp decided to disregard all other aspects of the book that would refute his thesis, and magnified the description of Utopian colonies and war strategies into "the fully articulated national policy of colonization" (22). His justification is thin: he considers Book I primarily as a critique of expansionism by Hythloday, which is controverted by his praise of Utopian colonialism in Book II. He resolves this contradiction by distinguishing between European struggles for conquest and the colonization of the New World: the latter can be morally justified by arguing that these lands lie waste and unoccupied, as the Utopians justify their own colonial expansion. Then he goes on to argue that the parallels between Utopia and England reveal More's ambivalent intention to direct his audience's attention westward, not eastward. The whole argument deliberately overlooks crucial counter-evidence (e.g., the circumstances of publication, the narrative framework and the predominant rhetorical drift of the text), and casually muddles textual evidence, biographical information, and psychoanalytic meditation over More's ambivalent motives.

After World War II, the explosive development of literary criticism opened a new critical approach to *Utopia*, which began to examine the book as a literary artifact. Critics increasingly drew attention to the neglected literary aspects of the work, such as the significance of the narrative framework, the implicit characterization in the dialogue of Book I, and the role of pervasive and ambiguous satire in Utopia. They investigated in detail the influence of classical satirical works,[35] and raised questions about More's attitude toward his own creation, the admirer of the island, Raphael Hythloday. C. S. Lewis went as far as suggesting that *Utopia* is a mere *jeu d'esprit*, "a holiday work, a spontaneous overflow of intellectual high spirits, a revel of debate, paradox, comedy and (above all) of invention, which starts many hares and kills none" ("Thomas More" 391). Their approach aroused the dissatisfaction of the representatives of the other schools, since the literary analysis of *Utopia* often arrived at conclusions radically different from the earlier ones. Those who focused on *Utopia* as a satire discerned in it an ironic distance created between More and Hythloday, and refused to accept the description of Utopia or Hythloday's position in Book I as ideas self-evidently attributable or attractive to More.[36] This was described by a representative of the Humanist school as "suspicious and diminishing" reading.[37]

As this short survey of the critical tradition may have illustrated, there are few issues around *Utopia* on which modern critics would share a consensus, apart from considering it a great book, albeit for different reasons. It is conspicuous, however, that most of the disagreements about the book — regardless of how much evidence is available to support the respective argumentative positions — ultimately boil down to a clash of differing images about the author. The rival arguments are supported by biographical evidence and references to More's polemical writings, and the opposing position is rejected because it contradicts or subverts the image of More one party has in mind. The observer is often under the impression that Kautsky used a particularly apt metaphor when he compared More to the body of Patroclus being fought over by various parties. Although the fight and the ensuing scholarly efforts have brought to light a lot of important information and several interesting ideas, Thomas More continues to remain a stranger to us.

With all due respect to those scholars who have participated in the fight over More, I would like to avoid the pitfalls of entering into a critical argument about the intentions of the author as discernible in *Utopia*. Since my objective is not to uncover what *Utopia* reveals about Thomas More but rather to examine the crucial features of the book that have become the model of a genre it helped establish, I would like to focus my attention on the book as a literary artifact as much as possible. I am primarily interested in the particular blend of mimesis and fantasy created in the book as well as the sources of ambiguity in *Utopia*, which    as I argued on pages in a previous section ("Suvin and Cognitive Estrangement")— I consider not an accidental feature but an inseparable quality of a fully realized literary utopia.

## The External Frame

*Utopia* is a book of frames, and this poses a dilemma for any interpreter from the start. Where does the book exactly begin? The obvious

answer is that the book begins at the beginning, where More commences
to tell his story starting with his embassy to Flanders. None of the early
Latin editions[38] of the book, however, begin there: each of them has several letters and other introductory material prefacing the main text. The
amount and arrangement of this material varies from edition to edition.
The best-known modern critical edition, Volume 4 of the Yale edition of
*The Complete Works of Thomas More*, considers the 1518 Basel editions the
most reliable (clxxxiii–cxciii), and follows their order of arrangement: the
letter of Erasmus to Johann Froben (the printer of the Basel editions),
Guillaume Budé to Thomas Lupset (the printer of the 1517 Paris edition),
a map of the island, the Utopian alphabet and a specimen of Utopian
poetry (referred to in critical literature as *Tetrastichon*) together with its
approximate Latin "translation," a six-line poem on Utopia (usually called
*Hexastichon*) written by a certain Anemolius, whose real identity is
unknown, a letter of Peter Giles to Jerome Busleyden, the letter of Jean
Desmarez to Giles, followed by his poem on the island, two verses on the
book by Gerhard Geldenhouwer and Cornelis de Schrijver, the letter of
Busleyden to More, and finally the first letter of More to Giles (More
CW44 2–45).

When surveying this dizzying amount of ancillary material, one can
more or less clearly separate them into three categories. The majority of
the letters and the poems are laudations on the book and its author, and
two of them, Budé and Busleyden, offer some critical observations as well
(discussed on pages 53–55). The letters written by More and Giles seem
more relevant, since they can be regarded as extensions of the book itself:
the narrator of the story and the participant of the debate offer some additional (or, from the reader's point of view, introductory) comment on
Hythloday and the circumstances of the dialogue. The 1516 Louvain edition employed More's first letter to Giles (identified by its opening words
as *Pudet me*), which accompanied the finished manuscript of *Utopia*, as a
"Prefatio," and most modern editions (even those which excluded the other
letters and comments) followed this example. More wrote a second letter
to Giles (identified as *Impendio*) after *Utopia* had been published, which
was in turn incorporated into the second, 1517 Paris edition, placed after
the main text, and that is where it appears in the Yale edition as well.
Finally, we have some additions, such as the map, the alphabet and the
example of Utopian poetry, which are clearly intended to playfully reinforce the authenticity of the account.

The most obvious and direct impression is of course the shower of praise and admiration lavished on the book and its author by a number of distinguished contemporaries. It must have become clear even to the uninitiated that More is a person greatly appreciated by several of the great Northern Humanists, such as Erasmus, Busleyden and Budé. This way, the personal credibility and respectable social standing of More is well established even before the reader has come across a single word of his own. Such an impressive introduction is obviously an effective way of boosting the reputation of an unknown author.[39]

If the commendatory letters are disregarded and those written by Giles and More are singled out, they show that Giles, in his letter addressed to Busleyden, is primarily concerned with reinforcing the impression of authenticity, begun with the Utopian paraphernalia added to the introductory material. He praises both More's skills as a writer[40] and Hythloday's wisdom and experience, whom he places ahead of Ulysses and Vespucci — two names he is going to repeat in connection with Hythloday at the beginning of Book I. He emphatically affirms the truthfulness of Hythloday's account, as if he were responding to Budé's doubts (referred to on pages 54–55): "It was perfectly plain that he wasn't just repeating what he had heard from other people, but was describing exactly what he had seen close at hand with his own eyes and experienced in his own person, over a long period of time" (124). He also reveals that he added the Utopian alphabet and the Tetrastichon, "which Hythloday showed to me after More had gone away" (125). He provides an explanation why More did not happen to know the geographical location of the island: More was disturbed by one of his servants, while Giles could not hear the crucial words of Hythloday because of the loud cough of somebody else. He vows to find it out as soon as possible, but there is contradictory news about Hythloday: some say he died; others claim he returned to Utopia. The fact that the name of the island is not known to cartographers was also explained by Hythloday: "For, he said, either the name that the ancients gave it has changed over the ages, or else they never discovered the island at all. Nowadays we find all sorts of lands turning up that the old geographers never mentioned" (126).

Giles's letter reveals an intimacy with the "author" of Utopia. He talks about him as an acquaintance he has met more than once, since he has given Giles evidence about Utopia and also answered several of his questions. But he also contributes to the air of uncertainty surrounding Hythloday since he does not know where he currently is or whether he is alive at all. The letter also confirms More's reliability by emphasizing his faithful reproduction of Hythloday's words. Although the letter precedes More's *Pudet me* letter, it is actually a response, since More complains in it about forgetting to ask where exactly Utopia is.

More's prefatory letter to Giles opens on the note of apology. More is apologizing for sending the book so late, almost a year after their meeting in Antwerp, when all he had to do was "repeat what you and I together heard Raphael describe" (3). He tried to reproduce, as faithfully as possible, not only the content of their discussion but also Raphael's casual and simple Latin style, which was indeed an easy task. The only reason for his delay was his "many other obligations" (4) — and here, as if by accident, the reader is offered a brief introduction to the narrator by himself. The reporter of the discussion with Raphael spends most of his time as a busy lawyer and judge, and when his working day is over, he acts as a dutiful husband, father and head of the household: "I have to talk with my wife, chatter with my children, and consult with the servants. All these matters I consider part of my business, since they have to be done unless a man wants to be a stranger in his own house" (4). So, the only time he can devote to writing and scholarship is stolen from sleeping and eating: "Almost the whole day is devoted to other people's business and what's left over to my own; and then for myself— that is, my studies — there's nothing left" (4). He goes on to urge Giles to correct any mistake that may have been made unwittingly, and even asks a rather trivial question about the length of the bridge in the capital of the island to show that "I've taken particular pains to avoid untruths in the book" (5). He also wants to find out the exact location of the island since there is a man who is eager to go to Utopia to convert them to Christianity, and "he has decided to arrange to be sent there by the Pope, and even to be named Bishop to Utopians" (5). Then, with a sudden turn of mind, More begins to complain about his doubts whether he actually wants to publish his book at all, since there are so many different people with varying tastes and expectations (he sketches a whole gallery of comic types), who are quick to judge one's book bad or unsatisfactory.

This letter is unquestionably crucial in setting the frame of the book for the reader. According to it, the book is nothing more than a scrupulously honest and faithful recollection of a debate that took place among the author, the addressee of the letter and a third person called Raphael Hythloday. In a few words, the unknown author of *Utopia* is revealed as a busy man with many conflicting duties. Finally, there is some anticipation concerning future reactions and negative criticism about the book.

The whole letter is written in an ironic mode (it is most obvious in case of the comment about the anonymous person wanting to become Bishop of Utopia, as More reassures Giles that he is not motivated by personal ambition or greed, but purely by religious zeal), and thus sets the tone of the whole work. Both More and Giles are anxious to emphasize and re-emphasize that the fiction is actually fact, that the conversation has indeed taken place, that the island and its inhabitants exist, that there is nothing untruthful in the book except for unintended errors. As More puts it, "If anything is in doubt, I'd rather make an honest mistake than say what I don't believe. In short, I'd rather be truthful than correct" (5).[41]

The ambiguity of the above line is very subtle. If the narrator believes in the truthfulness of his own account, it is morally superior to a recollection that may happen to be correct, that is, faithful to actual reality, but does not correspond to the narrator's conviction. But the relevance of authorial intent (and its honesty) is immediately shown as marginal by the concomitant assertion that the author is nothing more than a scribe, a recorder of the words of somebody else, and therefore he cannot be held responsible for anything more than the errors of recollection. This way, More pulls off three different feats in one stroke: he makes an elegant claim for the *captatio benevolentiae* of the reader, sends a double-barreled message about his own truthfulness for those who perceive the irony, while, to those who read the letter straightforwardly, he excuses himself in advance for any accusation that there are lies in the book, and shifts responsibility for content to Hythloday.

More's subtle game with the notion of "honesty" is an excellent example of what I have proposed to call "narrative estrangement." While he heavily emphasizes the faithfulness of the reportage — he makes every effort to convince his readers that his book is an exercise in literary mimesis — he carefully reserves the right to say "falsehoods" as long as the decency of his intentions are not questioned. But even this statement is open to at least two interpretations. The naïve reading is that More does not want to deceive anybody with his story, while he himself may have been deceived by his informant, as it often happens with good men. But in a literary sense, saying falsehoods with an honest intention means writing fantasy. Thus More's statement may also be understood as an assertion that the "truth" of the book should not be measured by comparing it to empirical reality but by appreciating the author's honest intention of setting a moral example.

The ironic renunciation of authorship may be motivated by some apprehension about the reaction of the audience; such worries are evidenced by More's self-portrait, which emphasizes the lack of time he can devote to his art (a handy excuse for stylistic or structural weaknesses), as well as by his lengthy complaint about callous and unappreciative critics at the end of his letter. His description is worth a closer look. He dismisses most readers as uneducated and unable to appreciate learning; out of the remaining minority, the pedantic critics expect something highbrow and overcomplicated in style; admirers of the classics automatically denigrate anything written by a contemporary; solemn and dull readers cannot tolerate satire and wit; some others simply cannot formulate a firm opinion on anything; the alcoholic critics dissect and condemn everybody's work without exception; and finally, even those who liked a book often refuse to give proper credit to the author for it.

By exclusion, the "ideal reader" posited by More can be reconstructed from this list of complaints: it is somebody who is well-educated but not biased in favor of classical literature, somebody appreciating informality, wit and irony, and somebody disposed favorably toward the author. Interpreted as an indirect plea, it asks the reader to give the author the "benefit of the doubt," to read attentively but not to take everything in the book necessarily literally. But here again, ironic ambiguity about the sincerity of More enters the picture: after all, he did publish the book, exposing himself to critics who

> condemn every author by his writings, just as they think best, plucking each one, as it were, by the beard. But they themselves remain safe — out of range, so to speak. No use trying to lay hold of them; they're shaved so close, there's not so much as the hair of an honest man to catch them by [6–7].

More's subtle use of irony, already evident in the opening letter, seems to signal his determination not to offer up much of his hair to his opponents. This is even clearer in his second, *Impendio* letter to Giles, added to the second edition of the book, which returns to the question of whether the book is fact or fiction. More reacts to the remark of an anonymous critic of the book, purportedly reported by Giles, who said, "If the story is offered as fact (says he) then I see a number of absurdities in it; but if it is fiction, then I think More's usual good sense is wanting in some matters" (112).

More's response is two-pronged. On the one hand, he questions the relevance of declaring something an absurdity; on the other, he questions the critic's judgment:

I don't see why he should think himself so acute (or, as the Greeks say, so sharp-sighted) just because he has noted some absurdities in the customs of the Utopians, or caught me putting forth some half-baked ideas about the constitution of their republic. Aren't there any absurdities elsewhere in the world? And don't other philosophers, when they describe a society, a ruler, or a pattern of private life, sometimes say things that won't hold up? [113].

In other words, More indirectly claims that there is no clear line of distinction between feasible institutions and absurdities: the empirical world is as full of them as the history of philosophy. Reason and nonsense do not dwell in two separate worlds; they exist side by side in reality as well as in fiction. As a result, he chastises his critic for violating the unwritten rules of both mimetic and fantastic interpretation: once the story is accepted as fact, every aspect of it should be unconditionally considered faithful to actual reality; once it is identified as fiction, the question is no longer the feasibility of institutions but the wisdom and significance they carry.

Then follows a brilliant paragraph, in which More describes what he probably would have done if he had had any intention of creating a fictitious republic — in other words, if he had wanted to "lie," rather than being "scrupulously honest":

There's no denying that if I had decided to write of a commonwealth, and a tale of this sort had come to my mind, I might not have shrunk from a fiction through which the truth, like medicine smeared with honey, might enter the mind a little more pleasantly. But I would certainly have softened the fiction a little, so that, while imposing on vulgar ignorance, I gave hints to the more learned which would enable them to see through the pretence. And so if I had merely given such names to the ruler, the river, the city and the island as would indicate to the knowing reader that the island was nowhere, the city a phantom, the river waterless and the prince without a people, that would have made the point. It wouldn't have been hard to do, and would have been far more clever than what I actually did....

But I see, my dear Giles, some men are so suspicious that in their circumspect sagacity they can hardly be brought to believe what we simple-minded and credulous fellows wrote down of Hythloday's story.... If the doubters are not satisfied even with these witnesses [i.e. other people whom Hythloday also told his story], let them consult Hythloday himself, for he is still alive.... Let them get the truth out of him, let them put him to the question and drag it forth. I only want them to understand that I answer only for my own work, not for anyone else's credit [113–114].

This passage is the most eloquent example of More's use of narrative estrangement: understood straightforwardly, it is a flat denial of the fiction-

ality of the book and the "cleverness" of the author, and a repeated assertion of Hythloday's responsibility for content. For those perceiving the
irony, it summarizes the essence of the book as More sees it and offers some
clear clues to lay to rest any potential doubts about authorship, since More
in fact explains the etymology of the speaking names he invented for
Utopia. Placed after the main text of the book as it was, it gives all readers a reassurance about the correctness of their interpretation, just like the
way the opening letter simultaneously foregrounds the author and denies
his ultimate responsibility for the text. The tone of both letters is apparently utterly serious, but the underlying irony subverts it and shrouds the
letters in a veil of uncertainty. The reader is faced with an option already
at the start: to read the book with a belief in Hythloday's existence and
the credibility of his account, or doubting the same. On the surface, the
introductory material makes every effort to convince readers of the first
option, but the choice is left to them.

Thus, the outer frame of the book proves to be not only lavishly dec-
orated but delusive as well: does it frame a mirror or a painting? The ironic
ambiguity of More's statements essentially capture a problem that is central both to *Utopia* and all subsequent utopias: their uneasy position strad-
dling the mimetic and the fantastic modes of literary representation. As a
result of its peculiar narrative situation, there are two kinds of possible
doubt involved in the interpretation of *Utopia*: the authenticity of Hythloday and the authenticity of More. More as the author of the book can only
warrant the faithfulness of his own reportage — the problem of whether
Hythloday told the truth still remains open to question. The casual
remarks about Hythloday communicate contradictory messages; everybody claims he exists, but nobody seems to know where exactly he is. He
is out of reach, just like the island he has talked about. It is therefore crucial to reconstruct how the main text itself introduces More's informant
and what that introduction reveals about the authenticity of the narrative
on Utopia.

## The Stranger

The first internal frame of *Utopia* is the journey of the author, Thomas
More, who is identified in the title[42] as "citizen and sheriff of the famous
city of ... London" (8), to Flanders with an embassy sent by King Henry
VIII to discuss and settle "some differences of no slight import with

Charles" (8), Prince of Castile. Continuing a theme from his prefatory letter, More deftly elaborates on his self-portrait while the narrative situation of the main text is sketched up. To the roles of lawyer, family man
and scholar, the highly respectable position of royal diplomat is added
here, which should lend even more credibility to his account. The authenticity of the frame is reinforced by some casual name-dropping: talk about
Cuthbert Tunstall, the leader of the English embassy, or the Fleming
Georges de Themsecke[43] does not seem to serve any rhetorical purpose
other than dispelling any lingering doubt of the reader about the reality
of the journey. His friend Giles, whose letter preceded the main text, is
introduced in very appreciative words as well. The frame also foregrounds
another, hitherto neglected aspect of More's encounter with Hythloday:
that it took place outside his native England, in a country where More
himself was a stranger, separated from his family and country for "more
than four months" (9). Although he refers to his "ardent desire for my
native country, my wife and my children" (9), the reader might infer from
the prefatory letter that being away from home had its own advantages,
for instance being relieved from the burdensome duties of legal work and
family that he complained of. In a sense, he could suspend his other roles,
including that of the diplomat, in order to play the scholar for a while,
enjoying the intelligent and inspiring conversation of his Humanist friend.

After setting the stage for the story, the second internal frame opens
with the entry of the main hero. During his stay in Antwerp, More is
introduced to a stranger by Giles, who looks like a ship's captain, but Giles
identifies him as a traveler called Raphael Hythloday, and "there is no man
alive today [who] can tell you so much about strange peoples and unexplored lands" (9). So the unfolding plot seems to resemble a standard traveler's tale: the narrator, while being abroad, meets a foreigner who has
visited faraway lands, and tells the tale of his experiences. Hythloday, however, is distinguished by some peculiar features: he has a strange-sound-
ing name that    depending on how people choose to interpret it    provides
an ambiguous comment on his character.[44] And he is described as not
merely a traveler but also a philosopher, whose sailing, according to Giles,
"has not been like that of Palinurus, but more that of Ulysses, or rather
of Plato" (10). The comparison is very significant, because it identifies two
key features of Hythloday: that he traveled widely and gathered a lot of
experiences (like both Ulysses and Plato), and that he is able to interpret
his experiences on a philosophical plane (like Plato). But the parallel alludes
to other characteristics of Hythloday: both figures he is compared to are

Greek, not Roman (he is not like Palinurus, who was the pilot of the ship
of Aeneas, and thus related to the founders of Rome), and Giles goes on
to reveal that he has more expertise in Greek than in Latin "because his
main interest is philosophy, and in that field he found that the Romans
have left us nothing very valuable except certain works of Seneca and Cicero" (10). Instead of a mere skipper, which More at first sight believes him
to be, readers are faced with a reincarnation of an ancient Greek traveler-
philosopher. Only one of the two persons he is compared to, however, was
a living person: Ulysses is a epic hero, whereas the historical authenticity
of Plato, despite some dubious stories extant about his life and travels, has
never been questioned. The text seems to suggest already at the beginning
that Hythloday the philosopher is unquestionably real, while Hythloday
the traveler may be fictitious.

The half-fictitious character of the stranger is subtly reinforced in the
course of the introduction. Giles tells More that Hythloday is from Portugal and he "accompanied Amerigo Vespucci on the last three of his four
voyages, accounts of which are now common reading everywhere" (10).[45]
The most obvious explanation to his nationality is that Portugal took a
leading role in exploration from the mid–15th century on, and, despite
Columbus' journey and the Spanish discoveries, in the first decades of the
16th century Portugal was ahead of Spain both in overseas experience and
commercial success. Vespucci also made his later journeys in Portuguese
service, therefore the Portuguese Hythloday could be attached to him quite
naturally. I believe, however, that choosing Portuguese as the nationality
of Hythloday was a convenient device for another reason: as a powerful
critic of existing European countries, he would have commanded less credibility if introduced as a Spaniard, Frenchman, Italian, or German, somebody from the well-known countries of Europe. He had to be introduced
as an *outsider*, but nevertheless somebody familiar with European conditions, and a Portuguese person may well have been the closest thing to a
"marginal European" in the early 16th century.

Hythloday in a sense continued Vespucci's narrative where the other
left it off: he did not return with him from the fourth journey, but "he got
Amerigo's permission to be one of the twenty-four men who were left in
a garrison at the farthest point of the last voyage" (10).[46] From that base,
he befriended the local inhabitants, and with the help of their prince he
and his five companions crossed the land by "rafts when they went by water,
wagons when they went by land" (11), visiting several towns and countries,
until they eventually reached the Indian seaport Calicut via Ceylon.

Giles's brief account of Hythloday's adventures is conspicuous because in essence it means that he encircled the globe, traveling west across the Atlantic and the "New World" and reaching the Portuguese bases in India from the east. If that is true, he is unduly modest about his achievement, since he is the first person ever to carry out such a journey: the expedition of his compatriot, the Portuguese Magellan, set out for the same trip only in 1519, three years after the publication of *Utopia*, incidentally in the service of the King of Spain. Hythloday's somewhat hazy account of his trip suggests that they were traveling southward as well as westward, crossing the "desolate and squalid, grim and uncultivated" (11) equatorial region and finally reaching sea-faring people, where they could continue their journey by ship, eventually reaching India.[47]

The discussion between the three of them begins in the garden of More's house (which he earlier called "hospitium" or "visitor's quarters," while referring to Hythloday as "hospitus" or "stranger," thus reinforcing the similarity between the two of them [More CW4 48])[48]; Hythloday himself reveals some details about his travels. For those who have read classical works of geography, the account of his journey resembles the concepts of antiquity about the world more than it does the experiences of early discoverers. Hythloday seems almost eager to assure his audience that his experience did not contradict ancient beliefs about the unknown regions of the world:

> To be sure, under the equator lie vast empty deserts, scorched with the perpetual heat. The whole region is desolate and squalid, grim and uncultivated, inhabited by wild beasts, serpents and men no less wild and dangerous than the beasts themselves. But as they went on, conditions gradually grew milder.... At last they reached people, cities and towns which not only traded among themselves and with their neighbours, but even carried on commerce by sea and land with remote countries.... The first vessels they saw were flat-bottomed, ... with sails made of papyrus-reeds and wicker, occasionally of leather. Farther on they found ships with pointed keels and canvas sails, *in every respect like our own* [11–12, emphasis added].

This is not what the Spanish and Portuguese travelers found in the equatorial region and the Southern hemisphere, but rather the image of the world ancient geographers worked out, based mostly on conjecture.[49] Hythloday's account implicitly confirms that under the equator lies the mirror image of the northern hemisphere, in terms of not only geography and climate but social and cultural development as well, but no contact is possible between its inhabitants and Europe because of the impenetrable hot desert in the equatorial zone.[50] The uncivilized savages of the equatorial zone give way to inferior civilizations whose nautical techniques resemble the Egyptians and the North Africans, until finally they reach countries equal in culture and sophistication to Europe. Perhaps the only reason why they still have not discovered Europe earlier is the one inferiority revealed by Hythloday, namely, that they had not known the compass. Hythloday even remarks that he is worried about their sailors, who, equipped with the compass, might become rash and "this discovery ... may become the cause of much mischief" (12). There is a good deal of, apparently unconscious, irony in the fact that such a seemingly bold explorer as Hythloday cautions about the "Southerners" made reckless by the compass, an invention that was essential for European sailors to discover the New World. From More's introductory summary, he appears a passionate observer of social and political institutions, assembling a virtual collection of case studies in his head, which he willingly uses to evaluate familiar practices in Europe. The overall result of these comparisons is a kind of equilibrium: "While he told us of many ill-considered usages in these new-found nations, he also described quite a few other customs from which our own cities, nations, races and kingdoms might take lessons in order to correct their errors" (12). The societies living "underneath" are indeed like us in every respect: they have commendable institutions worthy of imitation as well as customs that appear inferior in comparison.

Thus, the essence of his story makes it obvious that his journey is leading to what Joseph Hall a century later would call "mundus alter et idem"[51]: a place that is in many ways similar to the well-known world of 16th-century Europe, but not identical with it. Hythloday's "mirror" is emphatically different from both those of Vespucci and of Ulysses. On the one hand, there is no trace of colorful and primitive natives who receive European travelers with a mixture of curiosity, awe and fear: Hythloday has seen well-developed cultures that are close or equal in sophistication to Europe. On the other hand, his account is focused on the customs and institutions of the people he supposedly visited, not on spectacular and improbable adventures, the usual stuff of ordinary sailors' stories. As More puts it,

> We made no inquiries, however, about monsters, which are the routine of travelers' tales. Scyllas, ravenous Celaenos, man-eating Lestrygonians and that sort of monstrosity you can hardly avoid, but to find governments wisely established and sensibly ruled is not so easy [12].

The "routine of travellers' tales" is illustrated by two famous references to Homer's *Odyssey*[52] and one to Virgil's *Aeneid*.[53] The message is obvious: Hythloday is not a mythical adventurer like Ulysses and Aeneas, and his story carries wisdom instead of cheap thrill or horror. His experience is derived neither from travels in the existing New World, nor from voyages into classical epics, but from visits to ancient books of philosophy and learning.

The second frame of Book I thus specifies the subject of the book: Hythloday, not entirely unlike a modern anthropologist returning from a field trip, is going to evaluate the communities he has examined by comparing them to European culture. But the undercurrent of the narrative suggests that the counterpart of this comparison is unreal: just as Hythloday is an imaginary traveler, the world he discovered had been imagined or at least predicted by the ancients. At this point, the reader of the narrative is again faced with a choice: to believe or disbelieve the authenticity of Hythloday's account.[54] One possibility is to accept that he is telling the truth and he verified the image of the world pictured by classical tradition. This is exactly what Columbus was trying to achieve when he set out to find the east coast of Asia by sailing westward — but his error and his consequent failure became obvious by the second decade of the 16th century, not the least because of Vespucci's trips. Alternatively, it requires just one step of the mind to follow the lead of Giles's comparison and identify Hythloday with Ulysses, an imaginary traveler whose adventures and experiences are also merely fictitious — but the narrator's dismissive remark about the famous monster stories of *Odyssey* draws a clear line of distinction between them. Thus the most plausible reading of Giles's parallel describes Hythloday as a traveler in the realm of philosophy, whose strange lands are lying just beyond the intellectual horizon, on the "other side of the equator" waiting to be "discovered" by Europe. The ancient and the modern are alloyed in this wondrous journey: Hythloday's travels take him back to the world of the ancients, but his discoveries still have the effect of strange novelty. It is as if the ultimate end of his journey was to rediscover something that is familiar but somehow still unknown; to hold up a mirror that projects an image that is intimate but at the same time strangely unusual.

This way, as if peeling off the layers of an onion, the reader is led toward the center of the narrative. We are given a sense of the place, the situation, and the background of the people present before a single word of Hythloday is quoted by More the narrator. In all appearance, the text is a summary of an encounter with a stranger whose circumstances are utterly credible. But there are also subtle hints and markers placed here and there to estrange readers from a mimetic interpretation and allude to an alternative way of reading, which views the text as fictitious and ironic. This tension between rhetoric and meaning, solemnity and subversion, surface and depth is gradually building up in the course of the narration, and becomes a dominant influence over the subsequent text.

## The Dialogue

After introducing the stranger and the main line of their conversation, More, or rather, the persona "More,"[55] makes an abrupt declaration about the present purpose of his narration: he would not like to repeat all he heard from Hythloday, but "now I intend to relate only what he told us about the manners and institutions of the Utopians, first explaining the occasion that led him to speak of that commonwealth" (12). Readers' expectations are disappointed, however, when the "explanation of the occasion" turns out to be a lengthy dialogue between him and Hythloday, during which the name of Utopia is hardly mentioned at all. This dialogue gives the bulk of Book I, and at first sight its relevance to the purported topic of the narration, that is, the description of Utopia, is rather tenuous.

From the reader's point of view, Book I appears as one huge digression, and that fact long puzzled interpreters, who as a rule chose to neglect it altogether, focusing on the seemingly more important part of the text, the description of the island in Book II.[56] While Chambers devoted two chapters to the analysis of More's presentation of Utopian society, he briskly declared, in a passing reference to the first part, that "when in any dialogue More speaks in his own person, he means what he says. Although he gives the other side a fair innings, he leaves us in no doubt as to his own mind" (147). Book I received its first thorough critical treatment by J. H. Hexter during his influential reconstruction of the composition of *Utopia*, when he explained it primarily on autobiographical grounds, claiming that the central problem of the dialogue — whether or not enter the service of a prince in order to turn one's wisdom and experience to good use — occupied More's mind at the time, and therefore the dialogue documents his intellectual conversion, in which Hythloday represents the earlier, idealist mentality, and "More" the later, practical frame of mind (*Biography* 113–55). Subsequent critics soon questioned his theory, however, arguing that More's personal dilemma would have hardly been adequate reason to expand the original version of *Utopia* so significantly, and proposing that "the Dialogue of Counsel," as Hexter dubbed it, provides a vital context to the description of the island. As a result, in the last forty years interpretations of the Dialogue have been multiplying rapidly.

Edward Surtz claims that Book I is superior to Book II due to its structural unity and the effectiveness of the dramatic dialogue. He compares *Utopia* to "a modern problem play, where the resolution or denouement is not conclusive and decisive" ("Literary Art" cxxxviii), in which Hythloday is portrayed as a radical humanist, while More assigns himself the role of the moderate humanist. Nonetheless, he alleges the existence of an unmistakable authorial opinion in Utopia pointing toward the unreality and unrealizability of Utopia: "The irony is pervasive, especially in Book II" (clii). Robert C. Elliott questions Surtz's confidence to discern More's own opinion: he foregrounds the satirical character of the dialogue, with Hythloday as the satirist and "More" as the adversary, speaking for the common opinion held by most readers, but treated ironically by the author, and clearly losing out to Hythloday in the end (31–47). Robin S. Johnson, on the other hand, declares "More" the winner of the debate, since he argues that Hythloday is shown to be a radical philosopher "blinded by his own Utopian vision" (66), unable to see the unbridgeable gap between ideal and possibility.

My interest in Book I is different from that of most commentators: I do not wish to decide who wins the debate, especially as it seems lopsided from the start: Hythloday's arguments get a lot more space than "More's" replies; the stranger's voice dominates the bulk of Book I. Under such circumstances, rhetorical victory can hardly be awarded to "More," who behaves as a polite and tactful listener until the second half of the book, and even then argues his point more briefly and less passionately than Hythloday. Accepting Surtz's description of Book I as a dramatic dialogue, I would like to find out what this dialogue reveals about the speakers, but especially the main speaker, the stranger who has allegedly visited Utopia: Raphael Hythloday.

The discussion is triggered by a question of Giles: why does Raphael, a man of so great wisdom and practical experience, not join the council of some prince? This way he could apply his knowledge for public benefit and also for his own interest and the advancement of his friends and relatives. Raphael's quick and categorical rejection reveals two traits of his character: his insistence on personal independence, and his indifference to personal advancement or financial gain. "More," who takes over the debate from Giles, also acknowledges this, but presses on with the first half of his friend's argument: the learning and experience of Raphael is so extraordinary that if he decided to enter public service, he could greatly benefit the populace by giving wise and noble advice to a king.

Raphael continues to disagree and, in support of his position, he offers some scathing criticism of contemporary government, where kings are more fond of war and conquest than proper peaceful government, and royal councilors are too arrogant, hypocritical, and jealous to accept anybody else's advice or opinion. As an example and illustration, he brings up England, which he also visited a few years earlier and where, at the dining table of the Archbishop of Canterbury, John Cardinal Morton,[57] Lord Chancellor of England, he entered into an argument with an English lawyer.

Here the dialogue takes an unexpected turn: Hythloday begins to dwell on his experiences gathered in England under the reign of Henry VII, since Morton was his Lord Chancellor from 1487 till his death in 1500, and any of More's English contemporaries could remember the period of his government with reasonable accuracy.[58] From this point on, the narration becomes quite complicated: "More" quotes the words of Raphael who in turn quotes a debate between himself and some others. The proper referential identity of the pronoun "I" has thus become considerably unclear, which confused many interpreters as well, when they understood Hythloday's words to be uttered by "More." In order not to falsify the rhetoric of the dialogue, however, one has to bear in mind throughout this part that "More" listens silently to Hythloday's account of a past episode.

The argument is provoked by the English lawyer's praise of the hanging of thieves, and Hythloday in his reply embarks on a radical criticism of the political and social circumstances of England. He is anything but restrained in his criticism: he condemns the practice of hanging thieves as both exceedingly cruel and ineffective since the cause of crime — extreme poverty — remains. As to the cause of this poverty, he provides a penetrating economic analysis, blaming the wasteful lifestyle and idle retainers of noblemen plus a specifically English problem, the enclosure of cultivated lands for raising sheep and selling the valuable wool, which turns people into beggars and thieves while also driving food prices up. He also proposes solutions to cure these evils: restore land to the tenants, restrict the right of the rich to buy up and enclose territories, reduce the number of idle servants, banish wanton luxury and gambling, and create job opportunities for the poor; otherwise the severity of punishments for theft is in vain. The lawyer's patronizing and fussy reply is cut short by Morton, who challenges Raphael to offer a better alternative to the punishment of theft. In his answer, he cites moral as well as practical arguments against the death penalty, and cites an ideal solution he supposedly saw among the Poly-lerites[59] in Persia, where thieves are not executed but sentenced to hard labor, treated humanely and thus benefit the whole community.

All these are radical words, which might easily be dangerous for an Englishman, especially when argued in public. But they are uttered by a foreigner, an outsider, who has nothing to gain or to lose by criticizing English social ills or the system of justice, and all this takes place at the informal dinner table of the head of government. At the table, everybody disagrees with him except the wise Cardinal, whose tentative endorsement of the idea (it would be worth a trial) suddenly provokes enthusiastic support from all others. Thus, the political treatise becomes a parable of ser-vility — the original motive of why Raphael has come up with the whole story.

Then another digression is added to the already long detour: Raphael goes on to relate a funny exchange between a "parasite ... who liked to play the fool" (26) and a friar at the table. The fool chimes in with the topic of settling the problem of thieves and vagabonds: he suggests that poor beggars should be distributed among Benedictine monasteries as lay broth-ers and nuns. When the friar present at the table wants to join in the fun and asks him what to do with poor friars, the fool replies that friars have already been taken care of: they are "the greatest vagabonds of all" (26), and therefore they should be arrested and put to work. The friar, stung by this reply, works himself into a rage and hurls all kinds of abuse and threats at the fool. Even the Cardinal warns him, "I think you would act in a more holy, and certainly in a wiser way, if you didn't set your wit against a fool's wit and try to spar with a professional jester" (27). The scene ends without any conclusion or resolution: the gentle and tactful Cardinal sends the fool out and turns the conversation to another subject.

At first sight, this last anecdote looks a perfectly superfluous and dis-pensable addition to Raphael's story, since it is connected neither to the criticism of English conditions nor to the servility of courtiers. It seems as if Raphael added it hesitantly as a humorous afterthought,[60] and the justification he offers for it is also quite tenuous:

> Though I might have shortened my account somewhat, I have recited it
> in full, so you might see how those who rejected what I said at first approved

of it immediately afterwards, when they saw the Cardinal did not disap-
prove. In fact they went so far in their flattery that they indulged and *almost
took seriously ideas that he tolerated only as the jesting of a fool.* From this
episode you can see how little courtiers value me or my advice [28, emphasis added].

This brief précis of a long digression leaves the reader slightly bewil-
dered. Did Raphael need such a tortuous story to drive home a rather simple point? His summary suggests that the real point of this lengthy anecdote
was not to criticize English social ills and their treatment, but simply to
illustrate the hypocrisy and obsequiousness of courtiers, and the actual
argument about English matters was merely the most convenient example
Raphael had at hand. The reaction of "More" seems to confirm the same:
he makes no reference to Raphael's diatribe against English conditions,
replying simply that "everything you've said has been both wise and witty"
(28), and praising Raphael's affectionate portrayal of the Cardinal, who
was also close to his heart. It is distinctly odd that "More," an Englishman and a royal ambassador abroad, offers no comment, no remark, no
counterargument of any sort in reply to such a massive attack on English
government and justice. Apparently both of them treat the actual subject
of Raphael's long lecture as a simple exercise in rhetoric in the service of
a seemingly more important goal: to surprise and confound the Cardinal's
courtiers, to demonstrate their lack of judgment and independent opinion by throwing some provocative reform ideas into the arena of the
debate.[61]
    But even if one accepts this, the scene between the fool and the friar
remains marginal in several senses, as John M. Perlette suggests in his brilliant deconstructive reading of the anecdote: just like the "parasite" in the
anecdote impersonates a fool and makes fun of the friar, the parasite-
anecdote imitates the previous dialogue and turns it into travesty, establishing multifarious interpretative connections between the two (233–39).
Although Hythloday seems unaware of this, the exchange between him
and the lawyer is implicitly paralleled by the verbal quarrel between the
fool and the friar; the lawyer and the friar are both portrayed as self-impor-
tant, arrogant and empty-headed, which calls for a parallel between
Hythloday and the fool. The fool is characterized the following way: "[He]
liked to play the fool, and was so good at it that you could hardly tell him
from the real thing" (26). So both characters dissemble, they hide their
real self for the sake of some purpose. The parasite wants to ingratiate
himself with the powerful Cardinal and his company by entertaining them

in return for the free dinner. He thinks he is clever by playing the fool, but in fact his awkward attempts to poke fun are merely tolerated by the Cardinal, who sees him for what he is: a simpleton, a man of no importance.

Hythloday's position is similar to the fool in two vital aspects: he is a stranger, an outsider to this group, who may be present at the table of the Cardinal only due to the tolerance of the host. His game, however, is much cheekier since his diatribe against English law, although expounded in a rhetorical battle with a lawyer, criticizes Morton by implication, who as Lord Chancellor was responsible for the dispensation of justice in England. Hythloday may believe himself to be clever, offering a shower of intelligent reform proposals in one breath, perhaps hoping to elicit some praise or approval from the Cardinal, while apparently unaware of the potential offense his harangue may cause. He does not realize that neither his praise nor his criticism matters much (after all, even his name in Greek carries the meaning "idle talk, nonsense"). The Cardinal probably sees through him just like the parasite, letting his words pass by as harmless, and even engages in some half-serious argument about reform, concluding with a rather condescending remark that "the experiment would involve no risk" (25). The essence of the episode is summed up by the Cardinal's advice to the angry friar: a wise man does not try to argue against somebody whose ideas are not serious.[62] Fools and jesters are not to be taken seriously, as Raphael summarizes the parasite-anecdote, unconsciously passing a judgment on himself.

The narrative thus frames the incisive criticism of English social problems and the system of justice as a mock-serious intellectual chat over the dinner table, a rhetorical battle of words to entertain the wise and tolerant man of power in his leisure hours. Furthermore, it continues to shade the character of Hythloday: the experienced traveler, the wise and serious philosopher is suddenly shown in a different light, as a rootless stranger who likes to entertain himself and his audiences with provocative debates, considering himself much wiser than he really is.

"More's" restrained and enigmatic reaction allows different interpretations. After all, he is confronted with a complete stranger who — soon after they were introduced to each other — launches a long-winded rhetorical attack on "More's" own country. Since it seems improbable that "More" really agreed with every single word he said, his silence may be a sign of mere courtesy, perhaps appreciating Hythloday's respectful portrayal of the Cardinal. Or it may suggest that he understood more from Hythloday's story than what the other wanted to tell, and accepted the Cardinal's advice not to take Raphael's provocation as a personal affront. Regardless of his wisdom or politeness, the portrait of Hythloday the philosopher is significantly modified by his double anecdote, aligning him with Plato or, rather, the hero of Plato's dialogues, Socrates: he employs radical proposals as rhetorical devices to throw his debating partners off balance, while these proposals do not necessarily represent more than a bold experiment in thought.[63] The parasite-anecdote reveals the subtle work of narrative estrangement: while the text presents an impassioned attack on the social problems of England (and by extension, all of Europe), it blunts the sharp edge of the criticism by ironically subverting both the seriousness of the criticism and the moral integrity of the critic. Hythloday the stranger is becoming ironically estranged by narrative means: he is placed in a complex web of textual connections which contextualize and thus relativize his character, his utterances and his subsequent presentation of Utopia.[64]

After Hythloday's long and complex lecture, "More" takes up the debate again: he presses on with his previous point that Raphael would still be an invaluable counselor to a prince, and he evokes the duty of wise men to serve the common good of mankind. As a support, he refers to Plato in the *Republic*:

> Your friend Plato thinks that commonwealths will be happy only when philosophers become kings or kings become philosophers. No wonder we are so far from happiness when philosophers do not condescend even to assist kings with their counsels [28].

"More's" rhetoric reinforces the link between Hythloday and Plato by setting up a contrast: if Hythloday is a real follower of Plato, he should take Plato's lead and help kings rule more wisely. Raphael retorts by saying that philosophers are glad to give advice and they have done so already in their works but people in power have never listened to them, as Plato's unlucky adventures in Syracuse show.[65] In essence, he claims to do exactly what "More" advises: he has learned from the example of Plato's failure and concluded that philosophers should keep their distance from men of power.

This time, he supports his position with a hypothetical example, imagining the reaction of the king of France and his council if he tried to advise them against conquest and in favor of improving the government of their country. Within this example, he makes another digression by citing the example of the Achorians,[66] "who live off to the southeast of the island of Utopia" (30). Then he embarks on another hypothesis picturing an unspecified king and his council, whom Raphael would try to dissuade of extracting more money out of their subjects, counseling him to rule for his subjects' benefit. In this imaginary exchange between himself and the council, Raphael again cites the example of an unknown country, the Macarians,[67] "who also live not far from the Utopians" (35). This lengthy double thought experiment (during which the name of Utopia, almost forgotten since the beginning of the dialogue, is mentioned twice, seemingly casually and accidentally) is one large, extended exercise in irony on Hythloday's part, ending in a poetic question: "Don't you suppose if I set these ideas and others like them before men strongly inclined to the contrary, they would "turn deaf ears" to me?" (35). But this time "More" does not hide his disagreement:

> To tell you the truth, I don't think you should offer advice or thrust forward ideas of this sort that you know will not be listened to.... This academic philosophy is pleasant enough in the private conversation of close friends, but in the council of kings, where grave matters are being authoritatively decided, there is no room for it [35].

"More's" counterattack is slightly unexpected, since so far he has been acting as an attentive and appreciative audience, apparently admiring Hythloday's wisdom and wit. But at this turn he strongly criticizes Raphael's in-your-face attitude of opposing a king and his whole council with a kind of stubborn idealism. What he prefers instead is a more practical, or perhaps political, philosophy that takes the given situation and its constraints into account and adapts its message accordingly. He uses the theatre as a metaphor to underline his point: "There is another philosophy, better suited for the political arena, that takes its cue, adapts itself to the drama in hand, and acts its part neatly and appropriately" (36).

Critics have identified the arguments forwarded by Hythloday and "More" in this exchange as the clash of two fundamental philosophical positions, with Hythloday representing the rigid moral absolutism of Plato, and "More" speaking for the Renaissance concept of *decorum*, a rhetorical idea emphasizing the right context for every message,[68] but their assessments of the outcome of this battle are diverse. Starnes argues that Hythloday cogently proves "More" wrong by demonstrating that Plato's idea of philosophers educating kings is impracticable (56–71). Johnson, on the other hand, sees in Hythloday's words a definite proof for his practical blindness, his isolation from human community "consumed ... by his utopian ideal" (41), while "More" represents the epitome of practical wisdom and tact. Hexter and Elliott judge the debate to be ultimately inconclusive: "Both arguments are coherent, eloquent, persuasive ... it is impossible to say who "wins" in the Dialogue of Counsel" (Elliott 38).

I agree with the proposition that simply by matching argument against argument, neither side can be claimed to have overpowered the other. Sylvester, however, offers a more literary interpretation when he suggests that Hythloday gradually undermines his position by moving from a historical situation — Morton's England — to "a hypothetical revision of contemporary history, and, finally, to a totally aloof fabrication" (298), while his examples from alien countries also take him further and further away, until he gets very close to Utopia — and very far from the known world. His observation is another instance of narrative estrangement at work, the text working against the speaker's rhetoric, subverting his argument and his moral integrity.

The same subversion, however, is also active in the case of "More." His sudden criticism of Hythloday's attitude is made curious in the light of his earlier silence: the same argument could have been advanced against Raphael after he finished his first anecdote, since the bold radicalism of his ideas in the lecture delivered at the Cardinal's table equaled that of his fictitious advice offered to the royal council. "More's" response seems to suggest that the difference between the two situations consists in the discrepancy between text and context. In the first case, the scene was a dinner table, a suitable place for an exchange of wit and ideas, satirical comments and mock-serious banter. Such a situation is perfectly suited to discuss unusual and radical notions without any risk or responsibility, and so Hythloday was free to argue, oppose, provoke, and enjoy the whole situation. To extend the theatrical metaphor: he had license to play the wise fool.[69] The emphatically hypothetical example of the French royal council has an inverse relationship to the Cardinal's supposedly real dinner table: it is a place where responsible thinking, moral earnestness and judicious statesmanship should rule, but in Hythloday's version it is a travesty of these ideals, and "More" seems to confirm that when he implicitly compares the whole scene to a comedy by Plautus (36). The dinner scene presents a contrast between comic context and serious content, whereas in the council the two positions are reversed: in an utterly serious context, the characters discuss greedy and depraved political ideas and, presented satirically, they thus shame and ridicule themselves. The dinner scene therefore becomes an example of high comedy, whereas the council, which should be a "serious play," turns into a low comedy. Thus, when "More" advises Hythloday,

> You pervert a play and ruin it when you add irrelevant speeches, even if
> they are better than the play itself. So go through with the drama in hand
> as best you can, and don't spoil it all just because you happen to think of
> another one that would be better [36],

his advice is anything but morally straightforward. It may be taken to
mean that among selfish and evil councilors, there is no place for honesty
and good counsel, so Raphael should strive not to "spoil" the pitiful comedy by pretending to agree with the others and chime in with similarly
cynical ideas on his own. Or "More" can be understood to suggest that
the kind of moral irony demonstrated by Raphael's headlong opposition
to the whole council is out of place in a political travesty; that where everybody is behaving foolishly, he has a responsibility not to act as a wise fool
and a teaser but as a practical-minded politician. The way he continues
his argument definitely points in that direction: "You must strive to influence policy indirectly, urge your case vigorously but tactfully, and thus what
you cannot turn to good, you may at least make as little bad as possible"
(36).

In my perception, there remains a degree of contradiction between
the metaphor and its literal "translation," since "More's" idea of "striving
to influence policy indirectly" for the better or the less bad does not appear
to be identical with "not spoiling the drama in hand" if the drama is not
about responsible and selfless policy-making at all. Regardless of whether
he argued radically or tactfully, Raphael would still be the odd one out in
a council where everybody opposes his noble ideas, and thus he would
inevitably end up as the spoiler of the play. Whichever is the ultimate
point of "More's" argument, however, both interpretations involve the
idea to dissemble, to hide your true self, to play a role — exactly what the
fool did in the parasite-anecdote, and what Hythloday, by implication of
the parallel, may have done at the Cardinal's table. So "More's" response
carries one more overtone: that real wisdom consists in knowing when to
play the role of the moralist, and when the role of the politician.

Raphael vehemently rejects the proposition, asserting his right to tell
the truth. Then he asks a double-edged rhetorical question: "What if I
told them the kind of thing that Plato sketches in his *Republic*, or that the
Utopians actually practise in their?" (36). The question purportedly suggests that he could bring far more radical examples than the ideas he cited
in his previous imaginative scenarios. But in the context of truth-telling,
the question offers another meaning: if truth is such an outrageous proposition, what if he told an elaborate story, a piece of fiction? Plato's hypo-

thetical Republic emphatically never existed outside the realm of ideas, and the parallel with Utopia, even though Raphael claims that they "actually practise" their ideas, again alludes to a similar unreality. Rhetorically, the undercurrent of the text carefully prepares the introduction of an elaborate fiction. The rest of his argument continues to carry an ironic duality: while he cites the example of Christ to show how little Christians have followed his commandments, although "he forbade us to dissemble them" (37), and therefore his teachings also would appear as absurd today, his illustration displays yet another gap between ideal fiction and practical realities. The upright moral message of his words is impeccable, but he displays a good deal of arrogance by dismissing all kings and councilors, almost the rest of humanity, as stupid, evil or merely hypocritical, while linking himself with Plato and Christ. Nonetheless, he also reveals the ambiguity in "More's" argument by saying that there is no middle road to take in a royal council; you either agree or disagree: "In a council, there is no way to dissemble or play the innocent. You must openly approve the worst proposals and warmly urge the most vicious policies. A man who went along only half-heartedly would immediately be suspected as a spy, perhaps a traitor" (37). For all these reasons, he sees for himself no other option but to keep away from politics because at least he can preserve himself from corruption.

This gradually intensifying argument is exciting because it presents a complex and ambiguous comment on both debaters. Hythloday is revealed as a stubborn and arrogant idealist, a determined outsider who refuses any compromise between what he considers ideal institutions on the one hand and social and political realities on the other. This intellectual position constrains him to act as the perennial critic who knows all too well that his advice is impractical and impracticable, and therefore he does not take seriously the act of giving advice itself, and ridicules all people who commit themselves to a position of adviser or councilor as dishonest, envious, hypocritical, and servile. His moral integrity, his uncompromising attachment to truth and truthfulness, however, hinges on his personal credibility: he repeatedly cites examples for superior institutions from obscure countries which he supposedly visited, but the "truth" of his argument would be ruined the moment it was revealed or believed that these examples are simply made up.

His debating partner, "More," also appears in a dubious light: he praises Hythloday as a man of great wisdom, urges him to enter public service and seems to agree with him on the ideals he advocates, yet he rebukes him for advocating these ideas, even in theory, at a royal council, while implicitly admitting that Hythloday's low opinion of royal politics is justified. The image of moral earnestness he projects at the beginning of the debate is thus undercut by his argument of political expediency and the virtues of playing the "proper role in the play." The reader inevitably begins to wonder: what is his motive for pressing Hythloday for public service, if he does not want him to speak his mind? What is the good of wisdom and experience if "More" proposes to place all that in the service of the great political comedy? Of course, both positions can be argued on a positive note as well: Raphael champions true Christian virtues and principles with unwavering loyalty, or, obversely, "More" is the epitome of practical wisdom and sober realism.

The reader, caught in the magnetic field of this amplifying tension, is under the full influence of narrative estrangement: it is difficult not to perceive the force of both arguments, yet the internal contradictions within both positions generate doubt and second thoughts about both speakers. The ironic ambiguity that was introduced into the text by the outer and inner frames as well as the introduction of the stranger is here combined with the moral ambiguity of the rhetorical positions. Hythloday has been considerably compromised by the effects of narrative estrangement, and the text has revealed his attraction to abstract moral fictionalization.

For Hythloday, then, the logical conclusion is that in a world where private property and material inequality rule, he can undertake no public office: only in a country with an entirely different set of social institutions could the fundamental antagonisms of Christian Europe be resolved. So he cites Utopia — here no longer in a fleeting remark but in an emphatic statement — as a country immensely superior to all European kingdoms by virtue of its institutions. There, with the elimination of private property, hardship and poverty have also disappeared. "More" continues to disagree, and his counterarguments are familiar. If there is no personal motivation of becoming wealthier, what makes people work harder? If there is no private property, how can it be guaranteed that people would not quarrel and fight for goods? If there is complete equality, how can people be governed? His ultimate opinion is, "It seems to me that men cannot possibly live well where all things are in common" (40).

Raphael's retort is predictable:

> I'm not surprised that you think of it this way ... since you have no idea or only a false idea of such a commonwealth. *But you should have been with me in Utopia and seen with your own eyes their manners and customs, as I*

*did....* If you had seen them, you would frankly confess that you had never seen a well-governed people anywhere but there [40, emphasis added].

Such a statement naturally begs the request to introduce the famous island in detail — and "More" indeed does so. An abstract but inconclusive argument about the best way to alleviate the social ills of Christian Europe thus gives way to a supposedly practical example. But even before Utopia is introduced in detail, the reality of the island is called into question by a seemingly innocent remark of Hythloday: the Utopians had never heard of "men-from-beyond-the-equator (that's their name for us)" (40) except when, about 1,200 years earlier, a ship was wrecked on the Utopian shore with some Romans and Egyptians. Because of their willingness to learn, they have acquired many useful aspects of Roman civilization through this accident, which means that they are not lagging behind Europe in their material culture either. The improbability of this historical incident amplifies the fictional quality of Utopia.[70] But the little story of Raphael is another link between classical antiquity and Utopia. It is an almost amusing sign of the Eurocentricism of Hythloday, the admirer of Utopia, that he cannot imagine the Utopians reaching the level of European civilization totally independently, without the benefit of Roman technology and culture. If the reader connects this story with the opening account of Hythloday's journeys and the explicit parallel he drew between Plato's *Republic* and Utopia earlier, the philosophical nature of the journey becomes ever more clear. There is a subtle but continuous layer in the text that works against the fictional suspense of the narrative, which sends signals and warnings that Utopia is not a real country but a philosophical fiction propounded by Hythloday.

After penetrating four successive frames — the prefatory letters, the setting of the scene, the introduction of the stranger, and the dialogue between him and the narrator — the reader finally reaches the core of the text: the description of the "new island of Utopia," as the title promised. In Book II, there is no duality in the text: what we have is the unmediated monologue of Hythloday; the whole island and all the institutions are seen through his eyes, and More's voice is not heard again until the brief conclusion. Book II is the rhetorical fulfillment of the promise made at the end of Book I: Hythloday is endeavoring to demonstrate that the institutions of Utopia should persuade anybody in doubt about the superiority of a commonwealth based on the community of property and social equality. Book I wraps this narration in several layers of ambiguity and estranges readers from Hythloday to a significant degree: the authenticity of Hythloday's experiences as a traveler is called into question, his sweeping condemnation of all European countries and men in power raises doubts about his discernment, the moral earnestness of his criticism is subverted by his refusal to participate actively in public life, and his tendency to tell philosophical tales is alluded to. The seemingly straightforward game of constructing a perfectly just, rational and stable human community thus appears rigged from the start, similarly to the game Utopians play — one of only two kinds of games they know since "gambling with dice or other such foolish and ruinous games" (52) are unknown among them (or perhaps forbidden). The game, according to Hythloday, is

> ingeniously set up to show how the vices oppose one another, yet readily combine against the virtues; then, what vices oppose what virtues, how they try to assault them openly or undermine them indirectly; how the virtues can break the strength of the vices or elude their plots; and finally, by what means one side or the other gains the victory [52].

While it is difficult to imagine how such a game could be played in practice, the real puzzle consists in the assignment of roles: who among Utopians may undertake to play with vices? Not to mention how an impeccably virtuous Utopian citizen will be able to manipulate vices well enough to have a chance of victory. Utopia cannot tolerate a morality game with an open-ended outcome: fate and chance have been carefully eliminated from the island. The end of the game is fully predictable: virtues always win.[71]

## The Conclusion

In the course of Book II, Utopia is presented by Hythloday as an economically self-sufficient, socially and politically stable country in which balance and order are made possible by the community of property and lifestyle, and maintained by the strict enforcement of a severe moral code. All in all, Utopian society is governed by two overarching principles: the subordination of individual interests to social interests, and the preference for stability over diversity and freedom. If we rephrase that in terms of the "social contract" theory, Utopian citizens trade in many of their individual rights for the guarantee of a moderate level of material comfort, and they submit to a rigorously disciplined way of life in return for the security of a well-ordered society. Hythloday's rhetoric is striving to convince his audience that the overall balance of this contract is positive for the individual citizens, while its benefits for society — order and stability — are obvious.

By the time Hythloday's narrative in Book II reaches its final topic, the reader may realize that the country he describes is the embodiment of one single overarching principle: rationality understood as social utilitarianism. Rational considerations in various disguises govern all aspects of Utopian life: the abolition of private property is a rational solution to poverty, material inequalities and economic rivalries; social and political institutions are organized in such a way as to guarantee that individuals uniformly fulfill their obligations to the community and in return get an equal access to all available commodities, benefits, and powers; their utilitarian moral philosophy is a subtle instrument to maintain strict social and moral conformity and thus stability; while their foreign policy and methods of war ensure that the Utopian way of life is not threatened from the outside but rather exported and occasionally foisted on neighboring countries. The uniformity of architecture, dress, lifestyle, customs, political and social institutions prevails in almost all aspects of Utopian life, and even their diversity of religious practice,[72] an oddly "liberal" aspect in an otherwise strictly regimented society, can be explained as a kind of psychological safety valve: as long as religious ideas do not break the spell of social conformity, they are considered harmless and their eccentricities tolerated. In fact, the whole complex of Utopian institutions appears as a closed logical system, in which inconsistencies are rarely detectable — as long as one accepts the underlying axioms, namely, that the greatest possible virtue of individual life is to be a good citizen of your community and the greatest social virtues are order, stability and permanence.

Raphael's lengthy and tortuous description of Utopia ends with a general peroration on why Utopia is superior to the nations of Europe. In his closing argument, he puts the strongest stress on the lack of private property and its positive effects: no greed, no hunger, no poverty, no financial constraints, no worries about the future. All these positive features shed a negative light on Christian Europe: "In other places men talk very liberally of the commonwealth, but what they mean is simply their own wealth; in Utopia, where there is no private business, every man zealously pursues the public business" (107). Carried away by the force of his passion, Hythloday even talks about "a conspiracy of the rich" (108) in European countries, who legislate exclusively with their own interests in mind, and use the powers of the state for their individual benefit. At the end of his passionate indictment of Europe, he concludes his rather conventional "money is the root of all evil" speech with the claim that Utopian institutions would have been adopted, "were it not for one single monster, the prime plague and begetter of all others — I mean Pride" (109).

Raphael's conclusion, however, is not the conclusion of the whole book. The narrative is rounded off with a very brief comment by "More," who says that he has found much of Utopian laws and customs "really absurd," above all "the basis of their whole system, that is, their communal living and their moneyless economy" (110). The only counterargument he offers is that such institutions would "utterly subvert all the nobility, magnificence, splendour and majesty which (in the popular view) are the true ornaments and glory of any commonwealth" (110). But he decided not to start arguing about the merits of Utopia since Raphael was tired, but also because "I was not sure he could take contradiction in these matters, particularly when I recalled what he had said about certain counsellors who were afraid they might not appear knowing enough unless they found something to criticise in other men's ideas" (110). So instead of open criticism, he offered some general praise for the Utopian way of life, and they left for supper with a vague agreement that they should find some other occasion to discuss these matters.

"More" the narrator's concluding words offer the only explicit connection between Book II and Book I, as they clearly refer back to the opening part of their discussion when Hythloday rejected the idea of joining a royal council by criticizing arrogant and conceited councilors. By choosing to hide his critical opinion and avoid conflict over a topic Hythloday has spoken so passionately about, "More" essentially reinforces the reader's impression about the same apparent difference of character that had been delineated by the end of their debate. He remains the same "practical-minded philosopher" who is careful to take context (in this case, Hythloday's exhaustion as well as his manifest emotional attachment to Utopia) into account when entering into an argument, while Hythloday's peroration expresses the same uncompromising moral idealism that he showed during their debate as well. The reader might suspect, however, that "More's" evasion is motivated not merely by expediency but also by the lack of appropriate counterarguments: for what he offers by way of criticism of Utopia — the lack of "nobility, magnificence, splendour and majesty" — is so feeble that it might even be considered ridiculous. The short interjection — "in the popular view" — however, is alluding to the presence of irony in the sentence, as if this counterargument were not

"More's" own opinion but the most common thing people would criticize in Utopia. His concluding sentence might be taken as a hint that he disagrees with Hythloday less than his words may convey and his careful distancing act is motivated more by political considerations, since he combines mild disapproval with cautious praise:

> Meantime, while I can hardly agree with everything he said (though he is a man of unquestionable learning and enormous experience of human affairs), yet I freely confess that in the Utopian commonwealth there are many features that in our own societies I would like rather than expect to see [110–11].

This conclusion can be interpreted in two ways: it is either an exercise in politics (praise for the man, a vague homage to his Utopia while maintaining its distance by suggesting disagreement with some of what he said), or it reflects a total incomprehension of the gist of Hythloday's narrative. As Raphael has emphasized throughout Book II and reiterated in his peroration, Utopia is founded on a completely different economic, social, and moral rationale from the one that governs Christian Europe, and this rationale has received a most consistent elaboration in all aspects of social life. Therefore, Utopia cannot be used as a source for individual reform ideas; it is a full-fledged alternative way to social existence. One either has to embrace it in full or reject it as such. Hythloday has obviously opted for the former, while his listener, "More," according to his last sentence, has either decided to sit on the fence or failed to grasp the radicalism embedded in Hythloday's account.

As far as the choice of the reader is concerned, I have labored hard throughout my analysis to bracket the temporal distance between world-1 of More and Hythloday and world-2 of myself. I consider it an irrelevant question whether a reader in the early 21st century finds Utopia a personally attractive social system or not. Our way of life has been changed beyond recognition by modern science, industrial technology and mass production, and our contemporary notions of individual rights and freedom as well as the desirable role of the state are so enormously different from those of the early 16th century that any judgment passed on Hythloday's Utopia from a contemporary point of view would reveal little more than varying degrees of incomprehension.

A legitimate critical project consists in playing the game with the author, and in the end make up one's mind about it. "More" (at least in the main text of *Utopia*) never seems to question the claim that Hythloday's account is about a faraway land he has personally visited. Nevertheless, even without the multiple instances of estranging effects in Book I, the reader is justified to doubt the existence of Utopia, and not only because of the "speaking names" of people and places. During the description it is made clear that Utopia has been created and shaped by the superior wisdom of one single ancient sage: King Utopus. The identity of King Utopus is worth some closer examination. While Hythloday tells quite a lot about his achievements and his outstanding role in the creation of Utopia, he reveals absolutely nothing about his personal origins or background. He is apparently a person out of nowhere, a mythical and mysterious stranger, who suddenly turned up, conquered the peninsula 1,760 years earlier[73] (nothing is said about where his soldiers came from or what ethnic group they belonged to), and turned the peninsula into an island by ordering his subjects to dig a 15-mile-wide channel across the isthmus connecting it to the mainland. He laid down the design of the capital Amaurot, which is carefully imitated by all the other cities. He was also the law-giver of the island who established by decree most of those social customs on which the uniqueness of Utopia lies. Utopia is therefore shown as an emphatically *artificial creation*: the island itself was brought into being, both physically and spiritually, by a victorious ruler. His colonization of the place was more profound and far-reaching than any known from the history of the Old World: he did not merely impose his rule over the natives, but cut them off entirely from the rest of the continent, built new cities out of nothing (and presumably destroyed earlier settlements), and imposed a complete set of novel economic, social and political institutions on the inhabitants. For all appearances, he created a perfect *tabula rasa*, since Hythloday does not mention any remains, material or cultural, from the pre–Utopian period. There is no other language spoken on the island; there are no pre–Utopian place-names (the reader is only told that the former peninsula had been called Abraxa[74] before Utopus came); the institutions of society show no signs of spontaneous development out of earlier cultures. The only aspect of community life where ancient traditions seem to have survived is religion: as a result of Utopus's decree of tolerance, a considerable degree of religious diversity still exists on the island, and one may conjecture that some of the local religious traditions have their roots in ancient, perhaps even pre–Utopian beliefs.

Utopus, the creator of Utopia in all the senses of the word, becomes the perfect incarnation of the philosopher-king of Plato. His power over his creation is unmatched by any in history, since he could mould both people and institutions completely to his liking. He had no opposition;

there were no rebellions against his iron will; nobody ever complained of being deprived of earlier wealth and privileges. Such a situation is extremely difficult to imagine in actual history, just like a perfectly static socio-polit-ical balance is impossible to maintain over more than 1,700 years. Such total dominance is imaginable only in fiction: King Utopus, the "king of no-place" is clearly a metaphor for the author of Utopia, who creates an island out of nothing, and peoples it with uniform citizens who all live the same way, dress the same way and think the same way — such unifor-mity could never be established in reality.

If King Utopus is a metaphor for the author, what is the role of Hythloday, the fictitious traveler? As I have argued, Hythloday was intro-duced in Book I as a visitor to ancient wisdom, who is striving to redis-cover something that has been known but somehow become obscured or forgotten. There is an extended ironic passage in Book II that reinforces the suggested affinity between Utopians and ancient Greek culture: Raphael tells that Utopians were eager to get to know the literature and learning of Greeks, and almost "miraculously" mastered the language in less than three years.

> I have the feeling they picked up Greek more easily because it was some-what related to their own tongue. Though their language resembles Per-sian in most respects, I suspect them of deriving from Greece because, in the names of cities and in official titles, they retain quite a few vestiges of the Greek tongue [78].

So Hythloday makes it explicit that he considers Utopians the descen-dants of ancient Greeks. His role in reintroducing them to the classics of ancient Greek literature and learning — most of Plato, much of Aristotle, as well as several works by Theophrastus, Plutarch, Lucian, Aristophanes, Homer, Euripides, Sophocles, Thucydides, Herodotus, Hippocrates and Galen (78–79) — amounts to a small "renaissance" in Utopia, coupled with the fact that the Europeans have also introduced them to the art of print-ing and the manufacture of paper, so it has become possible for Utopians to read the texts of these authors in "thousands of copies" (79). Thanks to Hythloday and his companions, Utopia has reached the level of 16th-century Europe both in learning and in technology.

The powerful irony in this passage — besides offering an explanation to why all the names in Utopia are Greek derivatives — lies in the implied contrast between the renaissance of Western Europe and that of Utopia. The rediscovery of ancient Greek learning triggered an enormous scien-tific, cultural, and subsequently social and political development in Europe.

But unlike Europe, Utopia has absolutely no need for this learning: what can they learn from Plato or Aristotle that they have not employed in their everyday social practice? They have an economico-socio-political organization that constitutes the fulfillment of the major principles of these ancient philosophers, so all they can gain by reading their works is a reinforcement of the essential rightness of their world view. Hythloday seems to believe that he has two valuable cultural gifts to present to Utopians: ancient learning and Christianity. The first is absolutely superfluous for them, while the second — although they are open to and in some ways ready for it — does not appear indispensable for their spiritual welfare. Hythloday is neither a professor nor a prophet to the Utopians — only a curious visitor who has some exotic tales to tell, and who soon becomes an overwhelmed admirer of the Utopian commonwealth. He himself reveals that Utopians like to have such touristic visits:

> Any sightseer coming to their land who has some special intellectual gift, or who has traveled widely and seen many countries, is sure of a warm welcome, for they love to hear what is happening throughout the world [79].

Utopia needs no other visitors but storytellers and admirers. Hythloday is both at the same time, but while he has passionately identified himself with Utopia, and estranged himself from his own birthplace, for Utopians he remained an exotic stranger, who might be entertaining but has no real pragmatic value. But for Europeans like More, he has likewise become an exotic stranger, who has deliberately uprooted himself, detached himself from his family, his native country and his native culture, and became a convert of a completely different social system. His fate is to be excluded from both worlds. Utopia does not need him, Europe cannot tolerate him, since he does not merely advocate reforms: what he demands is a *tabula rasa* and a rebuilding of European society from scratch. R. S. Sylvester raises the rhetorical question in his excellent essay on Hythloday, "Given Hythlodacus' isolation from the rest of humanity, can we really trust him to lead us into the promised land?" (297). After all, he could not fit into European society, and he could hardly fit into Utopia even if they accepted him. How could the restless traveler and stubborn-minded philosopher who has always "lived as it pleased him" tolerate the severe discipline and strictly ordered lifestyle (and the compulsory physical labor) of Utopia? Hythloday is a born misfit, whose curse is to envision a land in which his cherished principle — reason — could finally receive full reign. He wishes to be a King Utopus, the creator of the perfect commonwealth, but he remains only an "expert in nonsense." No wonder he disappears from the sight of Giles and "More" soon after their alleged meeting in Antwerp.

But Hythloday's failure is More the author's triumph: by creating a multi-layered, ironic text interwoven with fine threads of ambiguity, he has managed to deliver exactly that curious amalgam of amusement, suspense, criticism, bewilderment and challenging vision that is the distinctive feature of all great utopias written after him. That is why, despite century-long efforts of criticism, More and his *Utopia* continue to remain strangers, waiting to be revisited and rediscovered by every reader.

# Chapter 3
# Glimpses of a Moving Picture

## Anatomy of an Outdated Futurist

In a preface to a 1908 edition of the English version of *Utopia*, H.G. Wells offered the following comment:

> There are some writers who are chiefly interesting in themselves, and some whom chance and the agreement of men have picked out as symbols and convenient indications of some particular group or temperament of opinions. To the latter it is that Sir Thomas More belongs. *An age and a type of mind have found in him and his Utopia a figurehead and a token* [Parrinder and Philmus 234–35, emphasis added].

This somewhat condescending assessment of More would be readily adopted by several unfriendly critics to apply to Wells himself, who is seen by some as a mediocre artist with an unduly inflated reputation. His international fame rests largely on his "scientific romances," pioneering works of 20th-century science fiction, while in England he is also remembered for his Edwardian social novels written in a Dickensian vein. In the first half of the 20th century, however, he was most widely known as a prolific author of essays and pamphlets in which he tirelessly attempted to foretell various aspects of the future development of human civilization, and these social prophecies — although they have been largely forgotten by now among the general audience — exercised an enormous influence on a whole generation of intellectuals in the first two decades of the 20th century. George Orwell, who severely criticized Wells in a 1941 essay, nonetheless admitted,

> Thinking people who were born about the beginning of this century are in some sense Wells's own creation.... I doubt whether anyone who was

writing books between 1900 and 1920, at any rate in the English language, influenced the young so much. The minds of all of us, and therefore the physical world, would be perceptibly different if Wells had never existed ["Wells, Hitler" 198].

Although some of his popular appeal has survived into the late 20th century, his literary reputation is overshadowed by the fact that the majority of critics perceive a marked decline in the quality of his fiction produced after 1910, as his primary interest gradually turned from fiction to social activism in an effort to influence the course of world history, especially after the horrors of the Great War. Patrick Parrinder, perhaps the foremost critical authority on Wells, observes that after the publication of *The New Machiavelli* in 1911, "His English [critical] reputation reached, and passed, its peak. The more discerning critics had begun to perceive his artistic limitations as a contemporary realist" ("Introduction" 22). After 1920, the publication of *The Outline of History*, which sold over two million copies, Wells' fame reached unprecedented heights among the general public, and it continued to grow largely as a result of his educational, propagandistic, and general nonfictional output. This development, however, was paralleled by the emergence of the great generation of English modernists, who defined themselves partly in opposition to popular "Edwardian novelists" such as Wells, Bennett, and Galsworthy. As modernism gradually established itself as the dominant progressive force in English literature, Wells' occasional excursions into fiction looked increasingly inferior in comparison. Virginia Woolf, in her famous 1919 essay "Modern Fiction," ironically remarked that

> it can scarcely be said of Mr. Wells that he is a materialist in the sense that he takes too much delight in the solidity of his fabric. His mind is too generous in its sympathies to allow him to spend much time in making things shipshape and substantial. He is a materialist from sheer goodness of heart, taking upon his shoulders the work that ought to have been discharged by Government officials, and in the plethora of his ideas and facts scarcely having leisure to realize, or forgetting to think important, the crudity and coarseness of his human beings [1922–23].

While this judgment was contentious at the time, it became something of a critical commonplace by the second half of the 20th century, bolstered by the fact that Wells was unable to generate any substantial critical response or public success with his fiction after *The World of William Clissold*, published in 1926. His later attempts were simply passed over by readers and critics alike as feeble repetitions of earlier themes and characters, with a tedious overdose of Wellsian political and social opinions. As early as 1918, H. L. Mencken had accused Wells of a "messianic delusion" detrimental to the quality of his fiction, and later most critics came to share his opinion (Wagar, *Wells and the World State* 33; Parrinder, "Introduction" 25–27). By the late 1930s, not only his fiction but his ideas to reform and save the world have become outdated, a point made most eloquently by Orwell:

> If one looks through nearly any book that he has written in the last forty years one finds the same idea constantly recurring: the supposed antithesis between the man of science who is working towards a planned World State and the reactionary who is trying to restore a disorderly past.... On the one side science, order, progress, internationalism, aeroplanes, steel, concrete, hygiene: on the other side war, nationalism, religion, monarchy, peasants, Greek professors, poets, horses. History as he sees it is a series of victories won by the scientific man over the romantic man ["Wells, Hitler" 197].

Bernard Bergonzi, who initiated the critical reassessment of Wells in 1961, dismissed most of his *oeuvre* with one single gesture, "assuming as axiomatic that the bulk of Wells' published output has lost whatever *literary* interest it might have had" (165), and argued that his earliest work, the scientific romances published in the last years of the 19th century, represented the best and most enduring of his works due to their symbolic and myth-making power. He put the end of this early creative period to 1901, when the first major nonfictional work, *Anticipations*, was published, "where we see him ceasing to be an artist and beginning his long career as publicist and pamphleteer.... Wells' later attempts at the form all had a didactic aim, and suffered an according loss of imaginative power. They are no longer myths, merely illustrations of an argument" (21).

Bergonzi's dictum has been by and large accepted by literary critics,[1] except for his summary dismissal of the works of the 1900s. Biographer Lovat Dickson declares that Wells' decision to join the Fabian Society in 1903 had the consequence that "a novelist of great powers was lost to English literature" (137). Ingvald Raknem, who has investigated contemporary criticism about Wells' fiction, finds that "in the judgment of most critics, Wells had, by 1920, delivered his message. After that date, they argued, he deteriorated to such an extent that he was no longer able to produce great fiction" (5). Michael Draper discusses in detail the major novels from the first decade of the 20th century, and recognizes some merit in the novels written in the 1910s, but dismisses the rest as repetitions of earlier themes and motives with less and less artistic power. He sees the main cause in the fact that "by about 1910 Wells had used up as source material all the formative experiences he really cared about. Without these particulars to be true to, ... the way was open for him to restate his achieved world view with less rendering of experience and more discussion of it" (97–98).

The first decade of the 20th century is certainly a crucial period in Wells' career: he entered the new century with a second and lasting marriage to "Jane" alias Amy Catherine Robbins, who was to bear him two sons and remain unfailingly loyal and tolerant despite his numerous extramarital affairs; an improved health that became sturdier with time after his last breakdown in 1898; an escape from dogged poverty thanks to the income from his successful romances; and a freshly acquired fame as a talented young writer. He made friends with such respectable literary figures as Henry James and George Gissing, as well as with such upcoming writers as the late starter Joseph Conrad, Stephen Crane, Ford Madox Hueffer (Ford), and his most lasting friend, fellow young journalist and novelist Arnold Bennett (Dickson 93–107; Smith 151–68).

But he felt increasingly dissatisfied with the success of his romances; he longed for recognition as a serious novelist. He made his most ambitious efforts during the next ten years: *Love and Mr. Lewisham* was published in 1900, *Kipps*, after years of intermittent work, in 1905, *Tono-Bungay* and *Ann Veronica* in 1909, *The History of Mr. Polly* in 1910, and *The New Machiavelli* (after some search for a publisher) in 1911. All these novels are strongly autobiographical, their main hero emerging from lower–middle-class poverty to a decent middle-class existence through a combination of hard work and luck, and encountering a personal crisis usually due to a controversial love affair. As a rule, the social comedy version of this theme proved more successful, especially the adventures of the bumbling hero of *Kipps*: it was Wells' first book to sell more than 10,000 copies (Dickson 175). Of the serious novels, *Lewisham* did not attract much attention, but *Tono-Bungay*, which he intended from the start as his masterpiece, was enthusiastically received by several reviewers, including the young D.H. Lawrence (Parrinder, "Introduction" 19–20).

But his public reputation was becoming ambiguous with his entry into radical politics. After the resounding success of his first exercise in social prophecy, *Anticipations* (1901), Wells became an overnight celebrity: he was invited to lecture at the Royal Institution in early 1902, joined several distinguished and exclusive clubs, and his ideas of the future began

3. Glimpses of a Moving Picture

to circulate in middle- and upper-class drawing rooms. He also attracted the attention of the leaders of the Fabian Society, Sidney and Beatrice Webb, who persuaded him to join the Society in 1903 (Smith 92–98, 105–7). Wells was clearly flattered by the attention suddenly lavished on him and his ideas, and jumped headlong into political activism. His adventures with the Fabians lasted for five years, and ended in bitter disappointment, since Wells, flushed with his quick success and rising popularity, mounted an attack against the old leaders of the Society in order to transform the organization from a passive, elitist, middle-class social reform club into a propaganda machine for Socialism, and, incidentally, to take over leadership. The spiritual leader of the society, G.B. Shaw, challenged Wells' reform ideas and defeated him in a rhetorical battle at the meeting of the Executive Committee in December 1907. Wells continued to struggle on for a few months, but eventually resigned from the society in 1908 (Dickson 143–55).

During these years of feverish public activity and infighting, his literary output clearly received a propagandistic bent that was notably absent from his early romances. He followed up the success of *Anticipations* with *Mankind in the Making* in 1903, the first of his books in which he argued for the systematic education to improve the humanity of the future, and *A Modern Utopia* in 1905, in which he, in his own admission, tried to cast his ruminations on social and political issues into a literary form, aiming at a "shot-silk texture between philosophical discussion ... and imaginative narrative" (Wells 1994, xlvii). The same didactic tendency mars his subsequent scientific fantasies in the opinion of some critics: Bergonzi considers *The Food of the Gods* (1904) the first flawed romance because an imaginative opening idea degenerates into a didactic allegory as "his homiletic purpose becomes fatally obtrusive in the later chapters" (21). *In the Days of the Comet* (1906) was a weakly plotted novel in which a Socialist utopia is brought about by the absurd *deus ex machina* of a comet releasing a gas into Earth's atmosphere that completely erases all negative human traits and passions overnight, presenting a "true apocalypse ... a daydream" (McConnell 179). The scandal generated by a minor aspect of the latter book (the unrestricted "free love" between members of the regenerated post-comet world) brought Wells into an unfortunate press debate, in which Conservative reviewers attacked the book as a Socialist reform program in disguise (Parrinder, "Introduction" 15–16).

These enthusiastic years have fundamentally changed his intellectual attitude: although he kept professing that his true vocation is literature, the response he generated with his ideas persuaded him that he had a call-ing to influence receptive minds in a direction he saw as beneficial for the future of mankind. Some of his artist friends were becoming increasingly critical of what they saw as his mistaken interpretation of the role of the writer and writing. G.K. Chesterton accused Wells of being under the influence of "the great scientific fallacy; I mean the habit of beginning not with the human soul ... he does not sufficiently allow for the stuff or mate-rial of men" (104). What Chesterton saw as a flawed view of humanity, Ford Madox Hueffer ascribed simply to artistic carelessness (Parrinder, "Introduction" 17), and the same disagreement culminated in the famous James-Wells debate in 1914–1915, in which most later critics have judged the substance of James's criticism justified, and declared him the "winner" of the debate (Edel and Ray 65). Wells also provided his unfavorable crit-ics with an argument when in his *Experiment in Autobiography* (1934) he described himself as a "journalist," voluntarily giving up any claim to the title of "novelist" he professed himself so ambitiously in a 1911 essay. Many critics were ready to accept this statement as an admission of defeat, while others claimed that Wells simply drew a clear line of distinction between himself and the class of high-minded modernist literary artists in the tra-dition of Henry James who enjoyed their first vogue at that time.

Supporters and defenders of Wells' artistic achievement usually counter the summary judgment of the modernists in two ways. They may argue, following the example of Bergonzi, that Wells' overall literary achievement loses none of its significance by admitting that even the best of his realist novels fare poorly when judged by the exacting standards of modernist criticism, since his lasting merit lies in setting the standards for 20th-century science fiction, one of the most successful genres of popu-lar literature. The essence of this argument is that Wells is the acknowl-edged master of a different kind of literary tradition, which puts less emphasis on form, language and artistic self-reflection, and accords the highest value to the free play of creative imagination, and as such, it requires a different critical approach. As Frank McConnell put it, "His gift was for *imagining,* for realizing firmly, almost visually, the implications of his age's philosophy and science and for communicating those implica-tions to his readers with the urgency of myth" (11–12, emphasis retained). In Frye-ian terms, we could summarize their case in such a way as Wells was a master of the modern romance instead of the modern novel.[2]

Others focus their attention on Wells' cultural-intellectual influence rather than his literary merits. Warren Wagar, for example, sees the primary importance of Wells in "the abundance of his writing, in the variety of his interests, in his role as a popularizer of ideas and an encyclopedist of general knowledge, and in the satirical virulence of his social criticism" (*Wells and the World State* 4), and he compares him to the *philosophes* of the French enlightenment, Voltaire and d'Alembert, who were not so much academic thinkers as propagandists of new ideas, educators of the general public, devotees of social reform and faithful believers in the power of reason. Following Frye's model again, this assessment can be restated as a support for classifying Wells among the authors of "anatomies," books of fiction more interested in intellectual and social problems than plotlines and individualized characters.

The two propositions are not contradictory to each other: in fact, Wells' literary career can be interpreted as a development from the romance to the anatomy genre. In the early "scientific romances" the fantastic idea serves primarily as a starting point for an adventure that by and large follows the conventions of the romance. The story is centered on a lonely hero who is further alienated from his society by an unexpected twist — in Wells' case, a pseudo-scientific discovery (*The Time Machine* or *The Invisible Man*) or a fantastic event (*The War of the Worlds*) — and whose adventures and ultimate fate have a distinctly allegorical flavor: each story can be conveniently read as a fable cautioning about the potential dangers of certain moral and intellectual choices faced by man. But Wells had clearly become tired of this genre by the first years of the 1900s, and he abandoned this early formula. Following his ambition to deal with large-scale social problems in fiction, he began to experiment with a combination of the intellectual essay and social prophecy on the one hand and the conventions of fiction on the other. He conceptualized his own groping for a new form as the novelist's moral duty to expose contemporary issues in his essay "The Contemporary Novel," originally given as a speech in 1911:

> So far as I can see, it [the novel] is the only medium through which we can discuss the great majority of the problems which are being raised in such bristling multitude by our contemporary social development....
>
> You see now the scope of the claim I am making for the novel; it is to be the social mediator, the vehicle of understanding, the instrument of self-examination, the parade of morals and the exchange of manners, the factory of customs, the criticism of laws and institutions and of social dogmas and ideas.... The novelist is going to be the most potent of artists, because he is going to present conduct, devise beautiful conduct, discuss conduct, analyse conduct, suggest conduct, illuminate it through and

through. He will not teach, but discuss, point out, plead, and display....
We are going to write, subject only to our limitations, about the whole of
human life [Edel and Ray 148, 154–55].

Bergonzi called this Wellsian artistic manifesto a "misconceived attitude to the craft of fiction" because such discursive "contemporary" novels "lose their validity and interest as soon as the ideas and problems
discussed in them cease to be contemporary issues" (165). Henry James's
indirect response, in his extended critical essay entitled "The Younger Generation" in 1914, pointed out the same problem when he compared the contemporary literary scene to a "reservoir bubblingly and noisily full, at any
rate by the superficial measure of life" (Edel and Ray 179). He censured
the Edwardian generation, and Wells and Bennett in particular, for "saturation," a dense and detailed description and portrayal of certain aspects
of life without any apparent higher artistic intention. He commented ironically on Wells' overwhelming confidence as well as his tendency to write
verbosely and unreflectively about nothing else but himself and his own
interests:

> It is literally Mr. Wells's own mind, and the experience of his own mind,
> incessant and extraordinarily various, extraordinarily reflective ... of what-
> ever he may expose it to, that forms the reservoir tapped by him, that
> suffices for his exhibition of grounds of interest. The more he knows and
> knows, or at any rate learns and learns — the more, in other words, he
> establishes his saturation — the greater is our impression of his holding it
> good enough for us, such as we are, that he shall but turn out his mind
> and its contents upon us by any free familiar gesture and as from a high
> window forever open (Mr. Wells having as many windows as an agent who
> has bought up the lot of the most eligible to retail for a great procession)
> [Edel and Ray 189–90].

He concludes that Wells is an "adventurer" who wastes his fine material since he does not care much about the proper development of his story
or his characters: "The composition ... is simply at any and every moment
'about' Mr. Wells's own most general adventure" (192).

It would be difficult to disprove the validity of the Jamesian criticism
from the standpoint of the modern psychological novel: except perhaps
for one or two of his best social novels, Wells had little patience for careful composition and intricate characterization. But what James condemns
as a defect, the quality of "saturation" at Wells, Frye identifies in his *Anatomy* as a feature of a different genre tradition at work, that of the anatomy
or Menippean satire, which "deals less with people as such than with men-

tal attitudes," employs only stylized characterization, and "presents people as mouthpieces of the ideas they represent" (309). Menippean satirists, such as Rabelais, Swift, Voltaire, or Peacock, due to their intellectual preoccupations, "show [their] exuberance in intellectual ways, by piling up an enormous mass of erudition about [their] theme or in overwhelming [their] pedantic targets with an avalanche of their own jargon" (311). The encyclopedic interest and ambition, so explicitly declared by Wells in his claim for the novel cited above, turns his artistic program into a fine manifesto for the anatomy genre, with the mistaken use of the term "novel." Wells was predestined to be a writer of anatomies not only because of his intellectual preoccupations but also due to predilection for digressions, his fondness for staging learned discussions, and also his great talent for individual and social satire, all of which he often relished at the expense of the neatness of plot. Nonetheless, he is rarely recognized as a great satirist[3]; in my opinion, the explanation of this strange failure lies in his longstanding ambition to produce novels in the restricted sense rather than recognizing where his best creative talent works best and where he could utilize his full satirical potential.

This confusion about his own artistic goals is revealed by his own comments at different points of his career. In the prefaces of his early predictive nonfiction he repeatedly emphasized that these books are temporary excursions into a genre that is not central to his interest, and each of the sequels to *Anticipations* was accompanied by apologetic remarks about digressing from his main trade, which is fiction writing. In "A Note to the Reader" attached to *A Modern Utopia*, for example, he writes that "this may be the last book of the kind I shall ever publish" (Wells 1994, xlvi). Dickson compares this fitful search for excuses to "a man tempted to drink who swears that this will be positively the last" (103). The sweeping manifesto for "contemporary novelists" written in 1911 seems to bear witness to his lack of success in going dry: he adapted the definition of the novel to include explicit social criticism and the discussion of ideas he considered increasingly important. He happened to propose his novel definition at an apparent turning point in his career (though he himself could hardly be aware of that at the time): he was making unprecedented claims for treating every conceivable subject matter and demanded supreme sociocultural authority for creative fiction at a time when he had already published all his most significant and most successful literary works. Seen in this light, his comments in his autobiography in the early 1930s can be interpreted as a realization that his insistence on education and exhortation in his fiction resulted in more journalism than art, or in other words, the experiment in which he tried to marry essay and fiction had failed. But the real failure has been elsewhere: in his lack of boldness to experiment with the form and conventions of fiction as boldly as with intellectual ideas and social prediction. As far as his literary tastes were concerned, Wells remained a conservative at heart: a romancer who did not realize that his favorite genre was unfit for his favorite subject matter.

## The Wellsian Utopia

The ongoing debate on the quality of Wells' achievement is closely related to his assessment as a writer of utopias. A successful literary utopia requires all those skills Wells is credited with by his admirers: originality and boldness of creative imagination, a keen eye for contemporary sociocultural problems, and intellectual courage to advance new and unwhetted ideas. Wagar's parallel between Wells and Voltaire holds true in more than one way: as a writer of social fantasies, he entered the same tradition, the Menippean satire, that several of Voltaire's works (e.g., *Candide* or *L'Ingenu*) belong to. Nevertheless, the utopian inheritance of Wells is controversial: while he is unquestionably a towering figure of the utopian tradition, preoccupied through most of his life with the search for ideas to improve the future lot of humankind, it would be difficult to name any single book that embodies the ultimate Wellsian utopia. As Parrinder put it, "In retrospect his relationship to the utopian mode seems uneasy and paradoxical" (*Shadows* 96). This is partly because he was his own most powerful opponent, writing a number of dark prophecies of the potential dangers lurking in the future. Bright and somber visions, utopian and dystopian images of the future are alternating in Wells' *oeuvre*, sparking heated but ultimately fruitless debates about whether he was an optimist or a pessimist at heart.

Krishan Kumar argues that the recently fashionable view of picturing Wells as a fundamental pessimist who desperately wanted to compensate this personal trait with a willed belief in the ability of mankind to create a better world — an idea first put forward by Wells' son Geoffrey West — does not take into account a large segment of his published writings, which are ripe with utopian hopes and expectations (*Utopia and Anti-Utopia* 177–78). It is clear that pessimism was the dominant mood of the earliest and the last phase of his career, the period of the early scientific romances between 1895 and 1901, and the last gloomy writings written during World War II. But during most of his career, "The alternating moods of hope and despair continue throughout Wells' life, varying both with the state of the world and with the state of his personal life, physical and emotional" (*Utopia and Anti-Utopia* 178). Kumar is inclined to explain the pessimistic phases with personal reasons: the scientific romances were written during a period when he was poor and seriously ill, convinced that he would only have a few years left to live; and his last years, which were also overshadowed by a protracted illness, coincided with the darkest period of 20th-century history.

Other authors see less of a pattern of oscillation between opposing moods but rather one of consistent realism. Biographer David C. Smith does not consider Wells' last published writing, *Mind at the End of Its Tether* (1945), utterly pessimistic; it simply delivers a more austere form of the same message Wells had been sending out from the beginning of his career: that unless mankind makes a fully conscious, concerted and global effort to alter the course of its social and cultural evolution, the history of the race will end in disaster and extinction. His hopeful and gloomy visions of the future were projections of the two possible outcomes of this fundamental choice. "He did not think that negative ends had to come, but there was little evidence that they would not. It was up to our species, the only one since the beginning of time with the capacity to change the future.... Wells had believed it possible, but thought it very unlikely" (477).

The search for a definitive Wellsian utopia (or dystopia) is made all the more difficult not only because of the exceptional richness of utopian as well as dystopian themes and stories in Wells' output, but also because his own way of thinking, which relied to a large extent on intellectual experiment and improvisation. Wells' ideas never formed a consistent philosophical system; as Wagar observes,

> His emphases, moods, and alliances shifted from year to year, and his social thought is distributed through the pages of seven or eight dozen books written over a period of fifty years. Most of these books were not, to say the very least, written for posterity; they are often loosely reasoned, carelessly constructed, and intellectually slippery and shallow, so that any study of his thought is likely to display more of *l'esprit systématique* than Wells ever did [*Wells and the World State* 10].

Besides the lack of a discernible system, there is also the problem of the primacy of fiction over nonfiction: Wells was anything but restrained in pouring out his reform ideas in a number of pamphlets and tracts. The best-known is perhaps *The Open Conspiracy* published in 1928, which provided a detailed program of how Wells imagined utopia to be brought about by an alliance of enlightened and unselfish professionals in managerial and administrative positions who, prepared by a common theory of a post-democratic future world order, supersede the old elite and establish the first meritocracy in human history (Wagar, *Wells and the World State* 174–93). And even if nonfiction is deliberately excluded in line with a restrictive definition of utopia, there still remains at least a dozen books of fiction, from *The Time Machine* published in 1895 to *The Shape of Things to Come* in 1933, which could qualify as utopian or dystopian to a certain extent.[4] Despite their various similarities, it would be practically impossible to reconstruct a kind of composite Wellsian utopia and a complementary dystopia from them.

*A Modern Utopia*, published in 1905, is nonetheless a distinguished representative of his utopian imagination, "the nearest thing in his corpus to that book [the major utopian work]" (Parrinder, *Shadows* 96). Although several of his early scientific romances offer brief or long glimpses of various dystopian futures, *A Modern Utopia* is the first and also the most detailed presentation of his vision of a better future society (or alternative present); its fundamental ideas were to be often repeated with little variation in his subsequent writings.

It is also a central text to interpret Wells' development as a writer: it was written in that crucial period of his career when his ambition to win recognition as a great novelist was not yet divorced from his equally great desire to influence the future of the world, and when his ideas of contemporary social trends and the possible ways to influence these trends took lasting shape. Bergonzi remarks that his involvement with the Fabian Society deeply influenced his intellectual outlook:

> [His] shift from a dominantly individualistic view of human life to a collectivist one was made with great rapidity once Wells had started to absorb these [Fabian] influences, which provided him with a set of intellectual convictions on which all his later speculative activity was to be based.... He could undergo in a few months the kind of change in intellectual stance that would take another man as many years [169].

*A Modern Utopia* was written in the middle of this transition and bears a clear mark of his evolution: in 1905, he is no longer merely a writer of scientific fantasies, but he is still a dynamic young author willing to experiment with literary form and content. He has distinct social and political views, but he is not yet the well-known and tedious prophet of the world state. He still does not have international fame, but his writings are not yet received with politically conditioned enthusiasm or derision. It seems apt that he chose to write an "evolutionary utopia," not only reflecting the lasting influence of Darwinism on his thinking, but also documenting the ongoing and as yet still open-ended shift in his intellectual attitudes. *A Modern Utopia* represents his only sustained effort to consciously experiment with the formal elements of the genre, which furthermore offers a running commentary on the very process of the experiment. It is not only a utopia, but a "meta-utopia," a text about the possibility of composing a fictional utopia (Parrinder, *Shadows* 97–98). As such, it provides a comprehensive critique of the genre and also unwittingly represents the end of an era in its history.

## *The Modernity of Modern Utopia: Evolution and Narrative Estrangement*

The late 19th century was fascinated by everything that was, or could be claimed to be, new and modern. Wells was a representative spokesman for modernity in England, since he personally symbolized the new, upwardly mobile social groups that demanded a new social and political order. As Krishan Kumar argues,

> "New" was indeed the keyword of the age in which Wells grew to early manhood, the late Victorian and Edwardian age. In that sense his utopianism was a representative response.... There was Art Nouveau, the New Novel of Zola, the New Drama of Ibsen and Shaw, the New Music of Wagner, the New Journalism of Newnes's *Tit-bits* and Northcliffe's *Daily Mail*, the new Unionism of the unskilled trades, and the New Woman of the feminist movement. In the 1880s and the 1890s, any article in search of a buyer found it expedient to call itself "new".... The cult of modernity, with a new emphasis on the word "modern" as the desired progressive quality of novelty in art, politics or morals, dates from this time [*Utopia and Anti-Utopia* 169].

Modernity had a close association with "scientific" in the public mind. Wells, who came from a typical suburban lower-middle-class background, was less typically one of the first people of his generation to receive a predominantly scientific education in South Kensington, where he gained not only a solid grounding in contemporary natural sciences, but, as Philmus and Hughes put it, "assimilated the critical spirit of scientific inquiry" (2).

They argue that science, especially the Darwinian theory of evolution, prompted Wells to reject the anthropocentric view, which claimed that nature is teleologically oriented toward man, and nature's purpose and intent is in conformity with human ideals — an idea grounded in the traditional religious worldview (7). Instead, science provided Wells with a cosmic perspective on human destiny, since it suggested that both the biological development of all species and the whole progress of the universe are governed by strict and inexorable laws. Therefore, humanity was seen in a far more precarious position on earth than anybody had previously realized: we are small creatures in a vast universe, the emergence of the human race is most probably an evolutionary accident rather than the fulfillment of some divine purpose, and humanity is threatened by extinction and competition from other (perhaps extraterrestrial) species. On the other hand, this bleak view on the iron laws of nature and the universe is balanced in Wells' mind by the human perspective, which relates to the present and the future on a much smaller scale, and on such a scale human effort and initiative — the "plasticity," or evolutionary adaptability of the race — can significantly influence the future of the species.

Wells' choice of title equals a whole manifesto. Writing in the vein of an old and venerable tradition, his book will become distinguished from earlier works by a crucial feature: its modernity. He uses the term "modern" in both of its acquired senses: he intends his utopia to be new, recent, contemporary, as well as an improved, perfected version compared to earlier utopias.[5] Modernity, above all else, stands for dynamic development at the turn of the 20th century: the dynamism of the locomotive and the automobile, the dynamism of technological innovation, the dynamism of the bustling city life, the dynamism of the expanding suburbs, the dynamism of expanding empires. The established order of things had fallen apart over the previous hundred years; change and development had not spared anything. Under such circumstances, it must have looked outright ludicrous to present one's vision of the ideal society as a picture, frozen in time. In chapter I, the narrator makes clear that what distinguishes a "modern" utopia from all earlier ones is the advent of Darwin's theory that "quickened the thought of the world" (Wells, 1994 5).[6] After Darwin it had become impossible to imagine a static and unchanging state of happiness and perfection: "The Modern Utopia must be not static but kinetic, must shape not as a permanent state but as a hopeful stage, leading to a long ascent of stages" (5). The narrator's ambition, therefore, is to imagine an evolutionary utopia, where the ideal is not a timeless balance of perfection but a social and political structure open and flexible enough to allow development in a positive direction.

This opening axiom has crucial consequences. The image of an evolutionary or kinetic utopia must of necessity be incomplete and fragmentary — the narrator cannot aim at precise description or dwell on minute details, the standard feature of classic utopias, and should be constantly aware of the transitory nature of his vision. Furthermore, he should find a way to present rival or alternative ideas within the same framework. Such a requirement clearly puts a heavy strain on the traditional utopian narrative form. The dramatic strategy of classic utopias[7] — in line with the requirements of Suvin's cognitive estrangement — aims at giving a degree of credibility to the alternative human community, to acquire readers' consent to suspend their disbelief and give the fiction the benefit of the doubt, and to prepare them for a clash with their "normal" expectations. Nevertheless, a fundamental artistic problem that the narrator calls the "incurable effect of unreality" (7) of a utopian vision remains, which derives from the lack of recognizable physical settings, individualized characters and human conflicts, or in Frye's terms, the generic lack of novelistic qualities in utopias.

The narrator's response to all these problems is to dismiss the traditional narrative devices of utopias. The modern utopia can no longer be pictured as an island in the South Seas or a faraway country sheltered by tall mountains; it has to be imagined on a global scale. The journey motif is discarded with one single gesture: the two imaginary characters without any perceivable transition simply find themselves on another planet — the twin planet of Earth imagined to be lying beyond Sirius, while being physically identical with ours, "the same continents, the same islands, the same oceans and seas" (9).

Wells — who explicitly though ironically distinguishes himself from the fictional narrator, the "Owner of the Voice" (3–4)[8] — pulls off an unusual trick in the opening chapter: while starting on the note of a discursive essay treating the challenges faced by a writer of a "modern" utopia, and establishing his own fundamental criteria, he almost imperceptibly modulates the tone toward the beginning of a proper story. After a seemingly casual remark that on this hypothetical twin planet every natural feature should be so identical with Earth "that a terrestrial botanist might find his every species there, even to the meanest pondweed or the remotest Alpine blossom" (9), the narrator appears to be suddenly captured by the idea of a botanist in the Alps and immediately proposes a mental experiment to imagine him and a companion, who is the narrator himself, on an excursion in the Swiss Alps, having their lunch, and entertaining themselves with a discussion on Utopia.

> And behold! in the twinkling of an eye we are in that other world!
> We should scarcely note the change. Not a cloud would have gone from the sky.... Yet I have an idea that in some obscure manner we should come to feel at once a difference in things.... That would interrupt our Utopian speculations [10].

This sudden and tentative launch of the "story" harbors more than one layer of irony. By discussing and then dispensing with the traditional narrative devices of classic utopias, Wells is making gentle fun of these devices as such. If you are looking for the ultimate "noplace," forget about our small and familiar planet; go out into space where you can find vaster distances and more fundamental alienness than anywhere on Earth. If you want a replica of our familiar world in its physical conditions, do not bother making up facetious explanations, simply imagine that this planet is an exact copy of Earth in every conceivable way. And do not strain yourself by thinking up all sorts of wildly improbable ways of traveling there: simply suppose that your characters find themselves there in an instant. Wells' method is a satirical distillation of the way Gulliver is transported into various surreal places by Swift: improbability is carried to its logical extreme by stripping away all fictional plausibility.[9] It also exposes the central constitutive metaphor of all fictional utopias: the transposition of speculation into imaginative vision. When the utopian discussion of the two characters is interrupted by their finding themselves instantaneously in Utopia, imagination takes over from reasoning. This crucial moment of transformation, of the imaginative leap into a world where suddenly the familiar looks strange, and the *novum,* the transformative fictional invention, begins to rule, is half proposed, half described with all the experience of a prolific writer of scientific fantasies.

This opening provides a working demonstration of Wells' method of composition as described in his preface to his scientific romances in 1933:

> In all this type of story the living interest lies in their non-fantastic elements and not in the invention itself.... For the writer of fantastic stories to help the reader to play the game properly, he must help him in every possible unobtrusive way to *domesticate* the impossible hypothesis. He must trick him into an unwary concession to some plausible assumption and get on with his story while the illusion holds [Parrinder and Philmus 241–42, emphasis retained].

But in this case, Wells does not play the game properly, as he deliberately departs from his own rules at two points. His domestication of the impossible hypothesis *is* obtrusive, since he performs it with extra-fictional devices, registering his own speculations in a rambling essay rather than building up a proper story, a credible narrative situation. And he does *not* get on with his story while the illusion holds; quite the opposite, he constantly keeps the illusion at arm's length by sticking to an — occasionally rather awkward — conditional mood in his narration ("That *would* interrupt our Utopian speculations,... I *should* flick a few crumbs from my knee; *perhaps*,... I *imagine* his exclamation," etc. [10–11]),[10] which he also repeatedly breaks when he returns to the discursive essay tone of the chapter opening.

Robert C. Elliott considers the dominance of what he calls the subjunctive mood a weakness of the narration, "as though he were not willing to commit himself completely to the fictional reality of Utopia — as though Utopia were a hypothesis rather than a place" (115). This remark ignores the underlying assumptions of Wells' project that follow straight from his initial axioms. His Utopia is proposed as a tentative hypothesis, in which credible fictional illusion is not going to be created. Readers are not meant to be lulled by familiar fictional devices into a suspension of their disbelief; on the contrary, they are invited to ponder the theoretical and practical problems of creating a utopian hypothesis by watching the ongoing effort of the narrator to perform such a feat. It is not by accident that the narrator remarks *a propos* the lack of language problems in Utopia:

> We need suppose no linguistic impediments to intercourse. The whole world will surely have a common language, that is quite elementarily Utopian, and since *we are free of the trammels of convincing story-telling*, we may suppose that language to be sufficiently our own to understand [11, emphasis added].

The essay chapters, the casual extra-fictional remarks of the narrator inserted into the narrative parts as well as the extensive use of the conditional and the subjunctive are all part of this deliberate strategy, and they function as a second kind of estrangement. While the wildly fantastic setting of the story opens up the prospect of cognitive estrangement that is a generic requirement of fictional utopias, the narrative tools just described are in place to remind readers constantly of the contingency of the vision, in line with the starting proposition that a modern utopia has to be kinetic and thus elusive. The cognitive estrangement is thus itself estranged from the reader, suspending the suspension of disbelief, by means of what I propose to call "narrative estrangement," creating a weird feeling of hovering between two different modes, between fiction and essay, storytelling and self-examination.[11] This kind of estrangement is close to the Brechtian sense of *Verfremdung*, which inspired Suvin's own concept of estrangement (Suvin 6, n.2). In Brecht's dramatic theory, *Verfremdung* functions as a ploy to create distance between dramatic representations of reality and the observer, and, as a result, makes the familiar look strange, ironic, grotesque, unusual. In our case, the narrative estrangement exercised by Wells performs the same feat with the unfamiliar, the cognitively estranged fictional world of a utopia, presumably with the same objective as the one professed by Brecht: to generate reflection, criticism, and a new kind of insight in the reader/observer.

June Deery, in her insightful analysis of *A Modern Utopia*, points out several aspects of the operation of narrative estrangement, but without coming to a conclusion as to its ultimate significance. For example, she notes the deliberately "incomplete realism" of Wells' narrative, when "the author explicitly declines to fill in certain gaps in information and prevents the reader from doing so" (32), this way foregrounding both their absence from the fiction and the narrator's supreme authority to create or not to create them according to his will. She also stresses the ambivalent position of the "Voice," who sometimes speaks and acts as if he had complete control over his fictional vision, while on other occasions he is surprised by events and characters in his own vision, as if he was just a character in a story, occupying "several what we would ordinarily consider contradictory positions" (33). She describes the "traffic of ideas" from speculative essay into the Utopian story and occasionally backward, when a notion arising in the narrative is discussed in an essay chapter (34–35). She concludes,

> We are asked to quite consciously doublethink that Utopia exists as it is described but also that it is something the Voice is making up as he goes along according to gradually emerging principles. Discovery and invention are deliberately confused [35].

She is apparently unable to make any more sense of this strategy than ascribe it to an authorial intent to generate dramatic tension by means of form, but declares that "the manipulation often seems high-handed and careless" (39), primarily because the incompleteness of the fictional illusion hinders the smooth functioning of the particular mode of utopian realism she calls "imperative realism" (30). The term is meant to signify the ambition of a utopist to persuade readers that a particular utopia, although it does not exist in the sense of ordinary realism, ought to exist in a moral sense. This mode can only be functional if it succeeds in both making readers realize the fictionality of the utopian world — this is effected by means of the cognitive estrangement described by Suvin — and persuading them that it is a desirable fiction that should be real. Traditional utopias usually strove to achieve the latter objective by lengthy descriptions of the beauty, order, and prosperity of utopia as well as by rhetorical dialogues between spokesmen of the two worlds in which the pros and cons of contemporary reality v. utopia were all meticulously presented. Both methods were conventionally within the bounds of the fiction itself, in the latter case "the fictional subsuming the nonfictional" (Deery 30). Wells' chosen method, the narrative estrangement, on the other hand, not only foregrounds the fictionality of the fiction but also emphasizes its tentative and incomplete character, playing a seemingly capricious tug-of-war with readers, dragging them into a fictional world only to pull them out of it again, forcing them to contemplate the narrative as the narrator's mental experiment. Deery's final judgment is that such a strategy, quite apart from its careless and inconsistent execution, is detrimental to the ultimate persuasive ambition of a utopia.

Without intending to attribute more artistic consistency to Wells than actually presented in the text, I believe that his narrative estrangement as practiced here does have a larger function, which is on the one hand consistent with his self-professed experimental approach, as I have argued above, and on the other hand serves a narrative purpose that is quite distinct from the straightforward persuasive ambition of most traditional utopias. The key to this narrative purpose lies in the fictional relationship between the narrator and his companion, the botanist.

The narrator, as Deery also notes, is part of the rather complex narrative structure of the book consisting of "three successive frames," whose authors are H.G. Wells, author of "A Note to the Reader" and the appendix in the end; a nameless and faceless internal author called the "chairman," whose comments are italicized both at the beginning and at the end; and the main narrator, the "Voice," who "occupies different levels of fictionality in the main text" (Deery 29). He is introduced by the chairman, who describes the narrative situation as a crossover between a lecture delivered by the narrator sitting behind a desk with a manuscript in his hand, and a visual illustration of this lecture on "a sheet behind our friend on which moving pictures intermittently appear" (4). The visual illustrations are developed into a full "cinematographic entertainment" with the unexplained introduction of another character called the botanist, who will feature in the narration but will not have a voice of his own:

> There will be an effect of these two people going to and fro in front of the circle of a rather defective lantern, which sometimes jams and sometimes gets out of focus, but which does occasionally succeed in displaying on the screen a momentary moving picture of Utopian conditions [4].

This opening imaginative frame creates a double-barreled narrative: everything the reader is going to read is told by a person whose physical features fit Wells the author perfectly, yet he is emphatically distanced from him by the narrative frames. The narrator's lecture will occasionally fade into a moving picture or fiction in which the narrator is one of the main characters next to a certain botanist. So the narrator's position vis-à-vis the narrative is curious and contradictory: he is both a character in the story and the creator of the whole discourse, being both inside and outside his vision, a situation that creates a large potential for ironic self-estrangement. Fictional distance is created and destroyed with the same gesture; illusion is nurtured only to be crushed by the explicit discussion of the choices and decisions involved in creating it. While traditional utopias were "speaking pictures" (Manuel and Manuel 2) of an ideal state, the modern Utopia finds its corresponding metaphor in the new wonder of the 20th century: the movie, an essentially kinetic form of entertainment. It is noteworthy that this constitutive metaphor is described by Wells as a form of entertainment rather than art, which reveals an underlying attitude to his own utopia: it is a form of entertainment, a mental game with ideas, fantasy and narrative devices rather than a grimly serious artistic venture. Incidentally, the early technological imperfections of the new entertainment only increase the validity of the metaphor: the film projected on the screen is discontinuous and occasionally blurred, delivering only fragments of a whole, and the silent images (talking movies are still a wonder of the future) have to be accompanied by an explanatory voice. The result is what Wells termed "ratiocination": a combination of a series of visions and rational argumentation justifying them.

It would be logical to suppose that the narrator, the creator and "director" of the whole spectacle, has sovereign control over the whole fiction, including his own fictional double, and is free to give full play to his whims of fancy. The other main character, the botanist, at first does not seem to be more than one of such whims, inspired by a momentary impulse of the narrator to place such a character next to the narrator in the Alps of that other world. During chapter I, however, the botanist begins to undergo a sort of fictional emancipation as he suddenly interrupts the flow of the narrator's speculations when he wakes up to the possibility of meeting the utopian equivalent of his former love whom he had to relinquish back on Earth. The interruption, as well as the pathetic love story, angers the narrator:

> It is strange, but this figure of the botanist will not keep in place. It sprang up between us, dear reader, as a passing illustrative invention. I do not know what put him into my head.... But here he is, indisputably, with me in Utopia, and lapsing from our high speculative theme into halting but intimate confidences....
> Have I come to Utopia to hear this sort of thing? [16–17].

From this outburst it appears that the botanist, a construct of the narrator, seems to have acquired a certain degree of autonomy of his own. And rather than being interested in the lofty speculations of the narrator, he comes up with a cheap and corny unhappy love story, an unwelcome distraction. The intrusive presence of the botanist signals the possibility of an alternative attitude to the speculative experiment, or an alternative attitude to the narration. It seems as if the love story, the integral element of a true romance, surfaced here as an urge, nudging the discourse toward another, alien genre, but the narrator refuses to be drawn in that direction:

> What if instead of that Utopia of vacant ovals we meet relinquished loves here, and opportunities lost and faces as they might have looked to us?
> I turn to my botanist almost reprovingly.... "This is not the business we have come upon, but a mere incidental link in our larger plan" [18–19].

He also rejects another urge, arising in his own mind, which is to push the fiction toward parody by imagining encounters with the utopian doubles of various famous personages, for instance the British king, the German emperor, Theodore Roosevelt, the American president at the time, or Joseph Chamberlain, the influential British politician. Neither romance nor satirical parody, the story is launched at the end of chapter I as an estranged utopia, where the narrator is constantly aware of and constantly reminds readers of the speculative, experimental character of his narrative.

## *The Modern Utopia as Meta-Utopia: The Botanist as Reader*

In his authorial "Note to the Reader," Wells tells about his long struggle to find the form most suitable for his goals. Abandoning the standard argumentative essay he employed both in *Anticipations* and *Mankind in the Making,* he began to experiment with the discussion novel "after the fashion of Peacock's ... development of the ancient dialogue," then a combination of monologue and comments, employed by Boswell in his biography of Dr. Johnson, and finally with what he calls "hard narrative." Eventually, he rejected all of them in favor of "a sort of shot-silk texture between philosophical discussion on the one hand and imaginative narrative on the other" (xlvii). He emphasizes that his method is far less haphazard than it appears; he found it the most suitable to deliver "a sort of lucid vagueness" (xlvi).

One might say that by conscious experimentation, Wells rediscovered the anatomy genre, with its blend of intellectual dialogue, authorial comments and bizarre adventure. But *A Modern Utopia* is distinguished from earlier anatomies by the consistent use of narrative estrangement, which does not allow fiction and tract to blend smoothly, but maintains a somewhat forced distance by sharing with the readers every single consideration involved in the development of the fictitious story. This approach to writing about utopia allows Wells on the one hand to be vague as well as lucid, to justify his imaginative decisions at each turn, and to keep reminding his audience of the tentativeness of his vision. The ironic description of himself as the enthusiastic and excited "Owner of the Voice" suggests that Wells had an ambiguous attitude to his own prophetic self, which is also attested by his repeated assertions that his main vocation is literature, not futurology.[12] The device of narrative estrangement captures this partial alienation from himself, and allows him to ironically reflect on his own "ratiocinations" and thus cast a shadow of doubt over them. The "entertainment" offered by the book consists of several layers: the theoretical speculations on the "shape of things to come," as Wells would later call them, offer a sort of intellectual pleasure that is different from the halting and repeatedly interrupted story about the adventures of the narrator and the botanist in the narrator's own world of fiction, while the interaction between these two levels of the book gradually builds up to a complex and ambiguous commentary on both the narrator and his intellectual venture of imagining a modern utopia.

On one level, the book is a critique of the whole utopian tradition, begun by the implicit satire on the narrative devices of traditional utopias. In a sense, the very form of narration is part of this satire, since it parodies the classic utopian narrative situation of a stranger exploring Utopia with the help of a wise and omniscient guide. In this case, the narrator doubles himself and fulfils the roles of both guide and tourist, explaining to himself and his companion the botanist the rational considerations behind all phenomena they encounter. He structures his book by enumerating most of the fundamental problems tackled in one form or another by traditional utopias and discussing them from a "modern" point of view first, then incorporating his speculative conclusions into the next turn of the story. On occasion, this requires a rather strained split of consciousness, since the roles of author and actor, as Deery has also observed, are contradictory: during the speculations, the narrator is a know-all, occasionally making forward references to subsequent parts of the book as a decent essayist should,[13] but when he switches to the story, he feigns surprise at the new discoveries and ignorance about what to expect later. In both cases, he writes and behaves according to the conventions of the particular genre (systematic argumentation in case of the essay, suspense-building in case of fiction), but this split consciousness within the same fictional self functions as yet another aspect of the narrative estrangement. The tone of the discussion in the essay parts is apparently utterly serious, but irony creeps in when readers are reminded by the twists of the story that all these ideas and opinions are forwarded by a single individual, whose enthusiasm for his own mental construct is contrasted by the botanist, an often silly and uncomprehending but doggedly consistent critic of the unfolding utopian vision of the narrator. The botanist is a curious presence in the book, and critics have disagreed about his narrative function.

Mark Hillegas swiftly dispenses with the botanist as a "rather foolish" character (x) without stopping to consider his significance in the text. David Y. Hughes considers the botanist a "version of Wells," representing the rigid scientific, emotional and cultural conditioning he has brought with him, in which science stands for classification, and love is a stubborn attachment to a childhood ideal (73). This interpretation, however, is not consistent with the botanist's role in the course of the story: the "scientific professionalism" of the botanist receives a lot of emphasis at the outset of the book, only to disappear completely later on behind the image of a single-minded romantic obsession, while the botanist, despite his scientific training, is unable to develop any interest in the manifold wonders of Utopia. A few hints of similarity between the botanist and Wells the author notwithstanding, his role in the fiction resists such simplifying identifications.

John Huntington has offered perhaps the most sophisticated reading of the botanist by interpreting him as "an authentic voice of the Lover-Shadow" ("Amorous Utopian" 139), a submerged persona of Wells driven by his libido into a series of sexual escapades, as opposed to the dominant, rational persona committed to the scientific worldview and social reform schemes. In his view, the conflict between the narrator and the botanist is the fictional manifestation of a Freudian struggle between Wells' conscious and unconscious self. This interpretation may make sense in the context of Wells' private life (even though the botanist with his narrow fixation on and nostalgic longing for a single lost love is not exactly the fictional equivalent of the notoriously philandering Wells), but helps us little to interpret the botanist within the framework of this particular piece of utopian fiction.

Deery has somewhat vaguely claimed that "most critics agree that the botanist represents the personal life, the unpredictable, even rebellious, individual who is sometimes overlooked but who must somehow be accommodated in any utopia" (36). Since none of the critics she has cited in her endnote voiced this opinion in the form she has proposed, it can probably be taken as her personal interpretation of the botanist's role.[14]

From the clues offered by the narrator's asides, it appears that the growing fictional autonomy of the botanist is somehow inevitable, a necessary consequence of the way the utopian hypothesis has been set up. So despite his arbitrary emergence in the narrative, he seems to play an important and irreplaceable role in the whole imaginative experiment. In my view, the botanist is a crucial, perhaps the most crucial, agent in service of narrative estrangement. From his first interruption of the flow of the narrator's speculation, his intrusive presence signals the possibility of an alternative attitude to the speculative experiment, and/or an alternative attitude to the narration.

Their conflict emerges again in chapter II, when the exploration of Modern Utopia begins in the story by the descent of the two characters from the mountains and their entry into the utopian community. The metaphorical significance of this movement is clear: the visitors abandon their theoretical vantage point, the place of systematic contemplation and broad survey, and penetrate the "thick shrubbery" of an actual society in motion. The descent from the high peaks corresponds to a gradual surrender of a certain superiority over the narrator's own brainchild: by submerging themselves in the society below, the visitors inevitably get entangled in it, losing their freedom of action and the sovereignty of decision. It is hardly by accident that the botanist challenges the narrator's speculative vision again while they take a walk in a small Utopian town in the cool, moonlit evening, and observe a couple of lovers. The sight reminds the botanist again of his own unhappy love affair, and he begins to tell the whole story, generating more annoyance in the narrator.

> It is a *curiously human thing*, and, upon my honour, not one I had designed, that when at last I stand in the twilight in the midst of a Utopian township, when my whole being should be taken up with speculative wonder, this man should be standing by my side, and lugging my attention persistently towards himself, towards his limited futile self. This thing perpetually happens to me, this intrusion of *something small and irrelevant and alive*, upon my great impressions [33, emphases added].

This is a revealing comment: the narrator is annoyed by the botanist exactly because the latter is encroaching upon his liberty to dwell on his favorite utopian vision, but, as if by a slip of the tongue, the narrator admits that the "intruder" is something (somebody?) irrelevant but alive, while he is distracted from the "speculative wonder" of his newly fabricated utopian vision that is, in terms of the implied contrast, significant but dead. The "trite and feeble" (33) tragedy he is forced to listen to, with all its banality, appears more human and alive to him than his own grandiose utopian speculations.

The botanist, and his personal narrative, is clearly emerging as a rival to that of the narrator, an unimaginative and commonplace romance that is modulated by the middle-class setting, the lack of resolution and the cowardice of the male character toward a cheap mock-realist novel. This fiction, for all its sentimental and cliché-like features, seems more alive to the narrator than his own, and therefore the narrator has to fight and suppress it. The narrator's own distraction by the love story ("For a moment I forget we are in Utopia altogether" [36]), however, is emblematic of the way an average middle-class audience could be distracted by such a banal romance from the large-scale utopian speculations the narrator is engaged in. The lack of the botanist's enthusiasm for Modern Utopia may well be shared by many of the readers, and the narrator's struggle for dominance in the fiction is going on also for the readers' attention.

Thus, the botanist becomes the embodiment of a certain kind of implied reader, who approaches the narrator's imaginative experiment with expectations conditioned by Victorian fiction, supposing that a conventional love story, a romance, is an essential element of a fictional narrative, and revealing a lack of interest and comprehension for the narrator's exciting speculations, a feature typical of anatomies. The botanist is shown as a character so hopelessly bound to his own age and social customs that he is unable to make the full imaginative leap into Modern Utopia. He is becoming the spoiler of the narrator's fun, the slow, uncomprehending and pedestrian, but curiously alive critic of his personal utopia.

The narrator and the botanist clash again during the discussion of a rather banal aspect of Modern Utopia, the availability of alcohol. While the narrator cannot imagine the lack of good alcoholic drinks, the teetotal botanist disagrees. The narrator silences the botanist by declaring that this is *his* book, where he sets the rules, and in order to prove himself right, he orders beer from the landlord of the Utopian inn. This demonstration of the narrator's dominance over his own fiction is both comic — another instance of narrative estrangement since the argument about certain qualities of the imaginary world is settled within this world — and ironic, an unnecessary assertion of the narrator's fictional superiority over a banality. The narrator is insisting on his absolute liberty as creator when facing the threatening curtailment of this liberty both by the fictional world he has entered and the fictional companion he has created.

The next challenge comes in chapter IV, when the two characters meet a strange person, a kind of renegade of Modern Utopia, who treats them to a long tirade about the base and repellant artificiality of that world. The character is described by the narrator in strongly sarcastic terms: his face is ruddy, his hair is long and disordered, he wears strange leather and woolen clothes and sandals on his bare feet, and he rants on and on without listening to them. It turns out that he is a radical devotee of Nature, and criticizes modern society for its deviation from natural living, especially "the overmanagement of the world" (71). His rambling and elusive speech suggests more than it illuminates, and he disregards the questions of the two strangers. Nonetheless, the narrator realizes that the character represents a new kind of threat to his narrative: "Now had I come upon a hopeless incompatibility? Was this the *reductio ad absurdum* of my vision, and must it even as I sat there fade, dissolve, and vanish before my eyes?" (74).

The appearance, behavior and arguments of the "natural man" have the flavor of caricature; he looks like an exaggerated parody of those romantic back-to-nature enthusiasts who reject industrial civilization on principle and urge a return to some sort of primitive or pre-industrial lifestyle, faintly reminiscent of pastoral utopists like Jean-Jacques Rousseau or William Morris. He may also be seen as a parody of a standard narrative situation in classic utopias, the stranger(s) meeting an intelligent and enlightened local who patiently and systematically explains his whole world to them. Here the first talkative local they meet is not interested in them, disregards their questions, does not provide coherent information, and he is not a distinguished representative and spokesman of the utopian community, but a dissatisfied misfit. The narrator meets another rival in his own fiction who champions a different version of utopian vision, a vision emanating from the criticism of exactly those features of Modern Utopia — urban sprawl, dominance of science, technology and artificiality, bureaucratic invasion of individual life — that are presented by the narrator as positive achievements. The meta-utopian character of the text is in this way doubled: within a utopia criticizing contemporary social reality and reflecting on earlier utopian visions, we find hints of another utopia criticizing the fictional utopian reality — yet another instance of the narrative estrangement.

The confrontation with the misfit — even though his appearance and behavior discredits most of his opinions and arguments — challenges the narrator's vision of the World State as a smoothly functioning organic entity. The narrator is forced to tackle the problem of dissent in Utopia: in a genuinely human society, there must of necessity be a large number of people who disagree with and refuse to cooperate in the establishment and maintenance of the "perfect world." His Modern Utopia must be constructed in such a way as to contain and overcome this problem:

> If we are to have any Utopia at all, we must have a clear common purpose, and a great and steadfast movement of will to override all these incurably egotistical dissentients.... It is manifest this Utopia could not come about by chance and anarchy, but by co-ordinated effort and a community of design, and to tell of just land laws and wise government, a wisely balanced economic system, and wise social arrangements without telling how it was brought about, and how it is sustained ... is to build a palace without either door or staircase [75].

The narrator's attention is thus shifted from the "what" to the "how" problem: his conclusion is that he needs to imagine a group of people who are intellectually and morally capable of bringing about such a transformation, and who are organized enough to cooperate for that purpose. He seizes on a word dropped by the misfit about "voluntary noblemen" and begins to develop the idea in his mind: "I began to realise certain possibilities that were wrapped up in it.... Evidently what he is not, will be the class to contain what is needed here. Evidently" (76).

The idea of an evolutionary utopia is "evidently" extended at this point to the evolution of the narrative: the narrator's vision is being modified and corrected right before the readers' eyes, provoked by fictional interaction with other characters. While the natural man is already the second character in the story whose appearance is unexpected and unwelcome, and who threatens the narrator's sovereignty over his fiction, his challenge cannot be simply disregarded: "There was no denying our blond friend" (74). He is just as alive as the botanist and his love story, and the problem he raises — the problem of dissent in Utopia — is real. The narrator is constrained to admit: "I had not this in mind when I began" (75), and consequently he begins to ponder the problem of the establishment and management of Utopia, leading to his imaginative development of the order of the *samurai*.

By the beginning of chapter VI, the botanist, the implied reader is becoming distinctly hostile to the narrator's speculations. Their conflict again takes the form of rivalry between two genres, the anatomy vs. the romance. From the narrator's condescending description it turns out that

> my philosophical insistence that things shall be made reasonable and hang together, that what can be explained shall be explained, and that what can be done by calculation and certain methods shall not be left to chance, he loathes. He just wants adventurously to feel [103].

Their walk in Utopian Lucerne reminds the botanist of his latest encounter with his former love, and he recalls the incident in every sorrowful detail, which makes the narrator lose his temper again:

> I swear secretly.... Have not I, in my own composition, the whole diapason of emotional fool? Is not the suppression of these notes my perpetual effort, my undying despair?...
> "Don't you understand," I cry, "that we are in Utopia. She may be bound unhappily upon earth and you may be bound, but not here.... Here the laws that control all these things will be humane and just. So that all you said and did, over there, does not signify here — does not signify here!...
> I incline to fatalistic submission. I suppose I had no power to leave him behind.... The old Utopists never had to encumber themselves with this sort of man [104–105].

The resigned admission concerning the necessity of the botanist's presence offers another clue to unravel his significance in the story: he is assuming the distrustful skepticism of readers who are not taken in by ambitious theoretical constructions, who are not impressed by the grand vision of the organic World State, who are moved by individual suffering and emotional drama more than the indistinct promise of universal happiness. His dogged insistence on his own personal love story is more than mere obstinacy or narrow-mindedness; it foregrounds the problem of individual happiness and fulfillment in the Modern Utopia. The botanist's resistance to abstract philosophizing and his insistence on the vital importance of individual love exercises a restraint on the narrator, forcing him once again to change the course of his narrative, and subsequently consider the question of personal relations.

The reader is thus witnessing a strange development in the course of the first half of the text. The narrator is progressively working out and documenting the development of a speculative hypothesis — the framework of a modern utopia — and turning his own conclusions into a slowly and hesitantly evolving story, an emerging tangible fictional universe. In the meantime, the narrator's fictional double, the actor, has encountered a series of challenges in the narrative that questioned his direction and control over the fiction. By way of response, he has gradually detailed, refined and occasionally rectified his own vision, while getting increasingly entangled in his own narrative, losing control over it. His own creations, primarily the botanist, challenge his discourse, repeatedly veering it toward romance, and forcing him to give his experimental vision more substance than his starting hypothesis would allow. The more detailed and sharp the vision of Modern Utopia is, the more reminiscent it is of the static tableaux of classic utopias. The blurred moving pictures that were promised at the beginning tend to freeze into a fixed image. In chapter VII, he is suddenly awakened to have gotten himself into a fix:

> I had imagined myself as standing outside the general machinery of the State — in the distinguished visitors' gallery, as it were — and getting the new world in a series of comprehensive perspective views. But this Utopia, for all the sweeping generalisation I do my best to maintain, *is swallowing me up* [133, emphasis added].

The narrator's failure is in a sense the outcome of his success: his theoretical construct has become "curiously alive," a fiction gaining life and substance from its author's ability of "saturation" or density of description. The narrator, however, increasingly gets entangled in his own saturated world, overpowered by the sensuous details of Utopia, and hierarchy between author and actor is suddenly reversed: so far the narrator occasionally adopted the parallel persona of the actor, his own fictional double, to visualize and experience the world emerging out of his speculations, but he effortlessly slipped in and out of this role whenever he felt like it. Now the narrator appears to be suddenly captured by his own subordinate role, imprisoned in his own persona, unable to exercise control, reduced to a mere observer.

His attempted way out of this predicament is to twist the plot around in such a way as to stage a meeting with his Utopian self in London as a kind of denouement, eagerly expected by the narrator not only as an explanation to his open questions about Utopia but also as the symbolic end of his quest. As he remarks while still in Lucerne, "I find the interest of details dwindling to the vanishing point. That I have come to Utopia is the lesser thing now; the greater is that I have come to meet myself" (136–37).

## The Modern Utopia as the Expansion of the Self

The idea that in a Utopian world that is an exact replica of Earth one should find the doubles of well-known people, including his own *doppelgänger*, first surfaced in chapter I as a potential joke, to return later as an element of the plot (the Utopian authorities are confused about their fingerprints, which are identical with two Utopian citizens), until the chance to meet one's own Utopian self suddenly and retrospectively reinterprets the whole fictional journey of the narrator: what seemed earlier an experiment propelled by intellectual passion and curiosity has suddenly taken on a strongly personal and individual coloring. Meeting one's Utopian self promises a wealth of ironic opportunities, including a brilliant occasion for self-satire, since the narrator, an ironically distanced self of Wells who has already doubled himself into author and actor, is now about to meet a third persona of himself, an idealized but even further distanced self, distilling the conflict between the "real" contemporary world and the "imaginary" utopian world into an encounter between two versions of the same fictional individual. Part of the irony is that the narrator pretends to have lost his sovereign control over the narrative; the fictional construct has come into life and begun to operate by its own rules, and therefore the Utopian double is presented as an utterly autonomous character the narrator has not a trace of control over.

Wells, however, utilizes hardly any of these satirical opportunities[15]; instead, he suddenly abandons the method of narrative estrangement he has so far been employing reasonably consistently. The tone turns predominantly serious and straightforward, reminders of the fictionality of the whole situation disappear, and the opportunity to stage a lively exchange between the two selves is not explored. The first encounter, the only subject of the curiously short chapter VIII, is presented in rather emotional terms: "When I came to this Utopia I had no thought of any such intimate self-examination," the narrator confesses; "The whole fabric of that other universe sways for a moment as I come into his room.... I am trembling." The first confrontation leads to a resigned and nostalgia-colored meditation on opportunities and potentials left unexploited in the imperfect world of reality. The whole account is cut unexpectedly short with the enigmatic explanation that their first encounter was too "personal and emotional" to be recounted and it would "contribute nothing to a modern Utopia" (148). It is only suggested later that the narrator recalled his youth, with all its suffering, failures and lost hopes, and made a kind of confession to his double.

This egotistical turn of the narrator is paralleled by the characteristically self-absorbed botanist who is found in an agitated state in the hotel: he has seen the Utopian double of Mary, his love on Earth. His attitude to Utopia is completely transformed by the experience: he has suddenly become enthusiastic about the whole speculative venture since he thinks he has understood its purpose: "'You know I did not understand this,' he says. 'I did not really understand that when you said Utopia, you meant I was to meet her — in happiness.... It makes everything different'" (149). The narrator is trying in vain to explain that this Mary is a different person, with a different past, experiences and friends; the botanist refuses to listen to him and pins all his hopes on a future meeting with her.

The narrator's encounter with his double and the botanist's glimpse of the double of his love signifies an altogether different kind of ultimate objective for Utopia: the fulfillment of personal wishes and desires for both author and reader. The narrator wants to see himself in a world where he thinks he could have realized his full potential; the botanist wants to find the love he lost on Earth. Although the narrator seems to recognize that turning Utopia to the satisfaction of personal desires is yet another trap for his venture — as he puts it:

> Why should a modern Utopia insist upon slipping out of the hands of its creator and becoming the background of a personal drama — of such a silly little drama?... We agreed to purge this State and all the people in it of traditions, associations, bias, laws, and artificial entanglements, and begin anew; but we have no power to liberate ourselves [152].

— he nonetheless succumbs to the temptation when, in chapter IX, he describes his subsequent and more substantial encounters with his Utopian double. He starts out to summarize the exchanges between them in the same tract form employed in the first part of the book. But after explaining the basics of Utopian social theory and the rough history of the *samurai*, the essay is modulated into a conversation, with the Utopian double doing most of the talking: the narrator asks questions, expresses surprise or admiration, but on the whole acting as a polite and humble reporter, while the double takes over the narration. For the first time in the book, the dominant Voice is not that of the narrator, but his Utopian self. Although it is not much emphasized by the text, the change is significant: this time Utopia begins to explain itself through the mouth of the double. It seems that Modern Utopia has come to such a full life that it neither needs nor tolerates any further intrusion from its creator. On the other hand, Utopia is personified in another version of the narrator, who is not only autonomous but morally and intellectually superior to his "creator." The reader is implicitly offered a choice between two selves of the same character as a symbolic contrast between Utopia and reality.[16]

Actually, there have also been hints in the earlier chapters of the text that have pointed toward such a personalization of Modern Utopia. As David Y. Hughes has observed, envisioning the World State as an "undying organism" turns the evolutionary method into a "macro-biological metaphor of formidable sweep" (69). The method itself requires that the relationship between the state and the individual is to be seen in the analogy of an animal species and its individual specimens, but metaphorically, the World State assumes an organic existence on its own, reminiscent of the "body politic" allegory of medieval and early modern political philosophy. The personification of the World State into an organic entity and the provision of monopolistic dominance over all individual citizens may also be interpreted as a metaphor for the monopoly of the narrator over his fiction: a single will, a single sovereign intent determines all things in the Modern Utopia, despite the reassuring declaration of the narrator that "the State is for Individuals, the law is for freedoms, the world is for experiment, experience, and change: these are the fundamental beliefs upon which a modern Utopia must go" (53–54). Utopia is by nature a monopolistic venture, and a Modern Utopia seems to be no different. The disparity of individual human desires and intentions are subsumed in the World State, which is the exclusive property of its creator. As a result, the image of the World State inevitably assumes the features of the narrator, passing incontestable judgments on its own creatures with a firm sense of paternal superiority.

Such a personalization of Modern Utopia culminates in the detailed, occasionally even pettily pedantic, description of the strict discipline and ascetic austerity of the life of the *samurai* by the narrator's Utopian double, and especially during the portrayal of their mystical and synthetic religion centered around an infinitely complex and endlessly varied God, defying all explanations and definitions, and revealing itself only in complete solitude. This transcendental presence can only be contemplated in solitary meditation, and in order to facilitate such meditation, each member of the order is required once a year to leave civilization for at least a week, "go right out of all the life of man into some wild and solitary place, must speak to no man or woman, and have no sort of intercourse with mankind.... They must be alone with Nature, necessity, and their own thoughts" [178–179].

The account of the Utopian double's regular lonely journey suddenly waxes emotional and lyrical. The journey is both a test of physical endurance and the stoutness of heart as well as an occasion to stare nature in the face unaided by modern technology and civilization.

> I don't sleep much at nights on these journeys; I lie awake and stare at the stars.... Years ago, I went from the Nile across the Libyan Desert east, and then the stars — the stars in the later days of that journey — brought me near weeping.... All day long you go and the night comes, and it might be another planet. Then, in the quiet, waking hours, one thinks of one's self and the great external things, of space and eternity, and what one means by God....
>
> When I go among snows and desolations ... I think very much of the Night of this World — the time when our sun will be red and dull, and air and water will lie frozen together in a common snowfield where now the forests of the tropic are steaming.... I think very much of that, and whether it is indeed God's purpose that our kind should end, and the cities we have built, the books we have written, all that we have given substance and a form, should lie dead beneath the snows.... I remember that one night I sat up and told the rascal stars very earnestly how they should not escape us in the end [180–181].

This account is the emotional climax of the whole book and the key to the whole venture of imagining a Utopia. The iron discipline and the unwavering sense of duty of the *samurai* is rooted in a quasi-religious or metaphysical belief in their mission to maintain the human race, the "undying organism" metaphorically represented by the World State. The journeys in the wilderness serve as regular reminders of the precariousness of this organism constantly under threat from the chaotic forces of nature and cosmos. The religion of the *samurai* is nothing else but a dispassion-

ate sense of the calamities awaiting humanity and an unflinching determination to maintain their carefully constructed but fragile order against
all odds. This divine mission is at the heart of the Modern Utopia, and
the revelation of this divine mission has been prepared and deferred all
through the story.

The centrality of this episode is also signaled by the modified style
of narration: narrative estrangement has all but disappeared from the text
in the course of the discussion of the narrator and his Utopian double,
and there is no trace of irony in the lyrical account of the solitary journey. The text seems to verify the earlier assertion of the narrator: the essential point of imagining Modern Utopia has been to meet himself in a
perfected form, and allow his Utopian double to expound an "open-ended
cosmic mysticism" (Parrinder, *Shadows* 110). The whole journey through
Utopia, beginning with the descent from the mountains, continuing with
a series of encounters and challenges and ending with the arrival in London and the visit with his double, appears retrospectively merely as a transitory episode, a rite of passage between two solitary experiences. The first
one was in chapter I, right after the moment of the imaginary transition
into Utopia, when the narrator and the botanist looked up to the sky to
realize that they did not recognize the familiar constellations of the stars
above and "for the first time perhaps, we should realize from this unfamiliar heaven that not the world had changed, but ourselves — that we had
come into the uttermost deeps of space" (11). This "shock of dysrecognition" (Dick 99) of the stars is linked to the Utopian double's defiant confrontation with the stars, God and human destiny by taking place outside
society and civilization: both are essentially acts of the imagination. Imagining a Utopia is ultimately a solitary venture, which may start out of a
sheer impulse of making fun, and it may be continued as a pretence of
one person's tyranny over people, facts, habits and institutions, but ultimately, almost against the author's intention, it is constrained to account
for its own motives. And the ultimate motive of the narrator is revealed
by his double: a deep sense of anxiety that mankind is doomed to an eventual failure and extinction by the merciless laws of physics, echoing the
famous scene of the "dying world" from Wells' first scientific romance, *The
Time Machine*. The vision of Modern Utopia is evoked as a vague hope
that the concerted effort and determination of a global body of intelligent,
devoted and unselfish individuals, an improbably benevolent dictatorship
of the best of the best, might help defer or even avoid this threatening
fate.

## The Collapse of Utopia

But the book does not end here and on that note: after an awkwardly misplaced chapter X,[17] the thread of the story is picked up in chapter XI as the narrator arrives back in the hotel in a state of excitement. He feels that his venture has almost been completed: "This Utopia is nearly done. All the broad lines of its social organisation are completed now, the discussion of all its general difficulties and problems" (209).

In this almost Faustian moment, the whole edifice suddenly collapses. It is the botanist, the skeptical and uncomprehending but curiously "alive" critic of the narrator's imagination, the companion he had "no power to leave behind" (105), who becomes the destroyer of the Utopian vision out of personal frustration. As the narrator ironically comments on this turn with the benefit of hindsight:

> I forget that a Utopia is a thing of the imagination that becomes more fragile with every added circumstance, that, like a soap-bubble, it is most brilliantly and variously coloured at the very instant of its dissolution.... To find the people assuming the concrete and individual, is not, as I fondly imagine, the last triumph of realisation, but the swimming moment of opacity before the film gives way. To come to individual emotional cases, is to return to the earth [209].

But such an ending to the Utopian fantasy inevitably raises questions. The character of the botanist has been a nuisance all along the story, restraining and hindering the imaginative unfolding of the narrator's vision, but how can a fictional character possess the authority to actually put an end to the fiction itself? If there is any consistency in his narrative role, something must have empowered him to "burst the bubble."

A possible clue to this riddle lies in the botanist's function as an implied reader. While the narrator's quest has been fulfilled by encountering his Utopian self and receiving a vision about the *samurai* representing the future hope of humankind, the botanist's individual hope of regaining his lost love in Utopia has been crushed and even mocked by seeing his beloved woman happily united with the same hated rival who had won her hand back on earth. Deprived of the romantic reunion he sought and humiliated by the Utopia of the narrator, the botanist makes the "childish dreams" (212) collapse. Somebody who is adamantly reading a utopia as a romance cannot tolerate the loss of a happy ending.

More generally, the text seems to suggest that violent emotional reactions cannot be contained in the framework of Utopia. The fictional world has already been slightly shaken by strong and potentially destructive emotions before, for example, when the narrator was confronted with the misfit of Utopia, or when he first met his own double. But such moments of excitement, doubt and apprehension were nothing compared to the anger, exasperation and humiliation experienced by the botanist. But if Utopia cannot tolerate such emotions, is it possible for ordinary humans ever to occupy such a world? The botanist's passionate outburst — which also bursts the fantasy bubble — throws exactly this hard fact into the narrator's face: life cannot be conceived without pain and suffering, people are scarred by their past, and it is a childish daydream to imagine that humans can ever be delivered from unhappiness, failure, disillusionment and frustration.

It is yet another question how to interpret this end to Utopia. Has the botanist and all that he has come to represent in the book — selfishness, conventionality, unimaginativeness, sentimentality, but also pragmatism and distrust of rarefied speculations — triumphed over the unbridled optimism and reckless imagination of the narrator? Or rather, does this episode suggest that Utopia can only survive if it can exclude such people and such attitudes? The whole narrative drift of the text, however, has confirmed that people like the botanist are undeniable parts of reality, and as such, they have to be accommodated into any Utopian scheme, however small its claim to practicability. The narrator's own self-irony, referring retrospectively to his nearly completed Utopian vision as a "soap bubble," reveals the effect of the reality check exercised by the botanist.

The Utopian fantasy thus ends inconclusively and inconsistently: what started out as an ambiguously estranged fictional thought experiment with all the speculative criteria carefully established, is rounded off rather conventionally as a conversation-turned-daydream, while Wells the author apparently negligently jettisons his own narrative frame with the lecturer and the moving pictures. The whole speculation is explained as a discussion between two friends, or rather acquaintances, who have recently returned from a holiday in Switzerland and have been discussing the botanist's passion for a Lucerne woman over lunch in London. The sudden return to the ordinary reality of contemporary London retrospectively questions and undermines the confidence displayed by the narrator during most of the fiction. Modern Utopia, whose framework has been first speculatively worked out, then fictionally imagined and experienced, has proven merely a flimsy daydream that collapsed due to one person's wounded ego. Even though returning to the London of 1905 is a convenient device to demonstrate the moral superiority of the dream over the squalid and depressing reality,[18] the narrator's failure and intense disappointment is inevitable. His reaction is almost hysterical — he flatly denies the reality of the real world:

> You may accept *this* as the world of reality, *you* may consent to be one scar in an ill-dressed compound world, but so — not I! This is a dream too — this world. *Your* dream, and you bring me back to it — out of Utopia —.... It's all a dream, and there are people — I'm just one of the first of a multitude — between sleeping and waking — who will presently be rubbing it out of their eyes [215–16, emphases retained].

After jumping on an omnibus to get rid of the botanist's presence, he contemplates the bustle of the city and begins to meditate on the possibility of dreaming about Utopia when the solid fabric of the real world is so oppressively felt. His irrepressible optimistic spirit swells up again, and, in a genuinely prophetic vision, he glimpses the London of the future, and envisions the awakening of the future *samurai* in apocalyptic terms, as if an angel, "a towering figure of flame and colour, standing between earth and sky, with a trumpet in his hands, over there above the Haymarket, against the October glow" (219), could suddenly rouse all the potential *samurai* to recognize their true vocation as well as one another. But then his sense of reality reasserts itself, and admitting the impossibility of the millenarian vision, he finally asserts that Utopia will come into being step by step, slowly and gradually, in truly evolutionary fashion.

Patrick Parrinder argues that this final vision of the narrator captures the true evangelical motives behind Wells' "ratiocinations" (*Shadows* 109). Without contesting his excellent insight, I think the concluding musings of the narrator can also be interpreted in the context of the meta-utopian character of the whole book. In my opinion, the spectacularly inconsistent end to Modern Utopia, the abandonment of the carefully constructed narrative frame and the return to threadbare fictional conventions is the narrative equivalent to admitting the ultimate impossibility of the whole venture. The speculative experiment has failed: the starting axioms — the evolutionary character, the possibility of progress, the avoidance of a static image of perfection, the incorporation of anti-utopians like the botanist, etc. — do not allow a consistent working out of the hypothesis. For all his tremendous intellectual efforts, the last vestige of hope left for the narrator is nothing more than a recourse to the age-old millenarian vision of the "resurrection of the living" (220), a utopian *deux ex machina*. When the narrator's voice is silenced, and the chairman of the lecture — who has not been heard of since chapter II — suddenly takes over, he proceeds to summarize the same conclusion neatly.

> This Utopia began upon a philosophy of fragmentation, and ends, confusedly, amidst a gross tumult of immediate realities, in dust and doubt, with, at the best, one individual's aspirations. Utopias were once in good faith, projects for a fresh creation of the world and of a most unworldly completeness; this so-called Modern Utopia is a mere story of personal adventures among Utopian philosophies.
>   Indeed, that came about without the writer's intention [221].

So the chairman, or Wells himself (I think the distinction is no longer relevant here as the narrative frame has been abandoned before), claims that it is impossible to visualize individuals and the "comprehensive scheme" together in one equally sharp image: if he focuses on one the other becomes vague, indistinct and unreal. The "great scheme," the ideal society is often comprehended not so much as a rationally organized system but rather

> as a passion, as a real and living motive; there are those who know it almost as if it was a thing of desire.... But this is an illumination that passes as it comes, a rare transitory lucidity, leaving the soul's desire suddenly turned to presumption and hypocrisy upon the lips. One grasps at the Universe and attains — Bathos [222].

This final judgment is especially perspicacious if we apply it to the experiment with narrative estrangement: the failure of the narrator — and Wells the author — consists in being unable to overcome the challenge of the romance, that is, he could not contain and subsume traditional plot devices and reader expectations within the original and ambitious experimental narrative design he sketched out. His brilliant invention, the creation of a parallel universe that later became a staple device of 20th-century science fiction, coupled with a narrative strategy to estrange this cognitively estranged universe from readers, thus inviting them to reflect upon the enormous challenges involved in writing a literary utopia, is ultimately abandoned in favor of an inconclusive and hollow awakened-from-a-daydream ending lifted ready-made out of the cupboard of literary clichés.

But even this artistic failure seems to have a symbolic significance on the meta-utopian plane, expressing that the very essence of utopia is its fragmentariness and incompleteness, the tantalizing suggestion of a way of human existence that is beyond reach and beyond vision in its totality. Critics of A Modern Utopia invariably agree that the book was not written with sustained care and consistency. But despite these obvious flaws, there are occasional flashes of brilliance in the book on the level of both speculation and fiction that more than compensate for its weaknesses. As a social thinker, Wells was ahead of his time: several of his ideas — from the principles of the welfare state through the secularization of marriage and public morals to the transformative power of science and technology — have since become essential constituents of contemporary thinking. As a utopist, he had the rare courage to envision and justify in detail a 20th-century utopia while commenting on his own utopian ideas ironically and satirically. The narrative estrangement employed by Wells is nothing else but a correlative of his own ambiguity about utopianism — an undertaking that accounts for its own apocalyptic motives with rational speculation. His prophetic urge has been subordinated to a double "reality check": his own scientific-rationalist education and his powerful sense of irony, displayed in the same passage when the vision of the awakened *samurai*, who "will know themselves and one another," is suddenly interrupted by an earthly episode: "Whup! says a motor brougham, and a policeman stays the traffic with his hand" (219). The prophetic urge is the inheritance of the 19th century; the overwhelmingly ironic perspective is the prefiguration of the 20th.

## Chapter 4

# After Utopia? Anti-Utopia and Science Fiction in the 20th Century

Scholars dealing with the history of utopian fiction or other manifestations of utopianism routinely observe that the 20th century saw a radical decline in the intensity of utopian imagination (paralleled by an even more radical surge in utopian studies — a sign of fatal crisis?). The Manuels, in the end of their monumental work on Western utopianism, talk about the "twilight of utopia" (759). Robert C. Elliott wrote an essay on the "mighty fall" of utopia in this century, arguing that "utopia is a bad word today ... because we fear it. Utopia itself ... has become the enemy" (89). Chad Walsh devoted a whole book to the subject of the decline of the traditional utopia and the rise of the anti-utopia or dystopia in the first half of the 20th century; and the list could be continued.

To contradict the summary judgments above, Krishan Kumar remarks that there was no decline of utopian fiction in terms of numbers:

> In purely quantitative terms, utopias continued to appear in reasonable number. One might even say, knowing that this says very little, that more utopias have been produced in this century than in any preceding century. Without further evidence or assessment, all that this might point to is the successful operation of the mass publishing industry of our times [*Utopia and Anti-Utopia* 385].

The claim of a crisis of utopia in the 20th century is nevertheless true, he goes on to argue, at least to the first half of the century, since "no work of the utopian imagination appeared which caught the public fancy as had the utopias of Bellamy, Morris and Wells at the turn of the century" (386).

The successful books of the interwar and the early Cold War period (that is, the 1920s, 1930s and 1940s) are almost invariably dystopias, reflecting faithfully the mood and the intellectual climate of the times: two world wars, a great depression, the onslaught of totalitarian ideologies, the loss of faith in progress, the fear of technological civilization, and the threat of the total (physical, moral, or intellectual) annihilation of mankind.

To a superficial observer, it might seem as if the genre of dystopia or anti-utopia (the distinction will be discussed below) were the invention of the 20th century, but that is certainly not the case. Satirical attacks on utopian visions are as old as the utopian imagination itself: Plato's *Republic* was probably among the targets of Aristophanes' comedy *Ecclesiazusae*, and he utilized utopian themes for farcical purposes in other plays as well, for example, in *The Birds* and *The Clouds* (Elliott 21). These works could be called anti-utopian in the sense that they directed themselves against specific utopian ideas or the utopian impulse in general. But anti-utopia or dystopia as a more or less distinct literary genre only came into existence after the creation of the utopian archetype by More. Its formal requirement is the same as that of utopias: the creation of an imaginary place, a *topos,* with the intention to present an alternative socio-political arrangement. The difference lies in the *telos* of the anti-utopian narrative: instead of demonstrating the ideal or vastly superior qualities of this fictional community, they present a community where the quality of human life is significantly worse or inferior to the author's empirical reality. The most widely applied English term, dystopia, is derived from the understanding of utopia as "eutopia," or good place, whereas dystopias present a fictional description about a "bad place." Dystopias usually aim at two different targets: they criticize contemporary social reality and its hampering of the human potential, but at the same time reject the miraculous solution advocated by certain political reformers or utopian writers by demonstrating that the purportedly better social institutions produce a miserable way of life. The goal of these "negative utopias" is not merely to mock and ridicule utopias in order to entertain their audience but also to warn against the dire consequences of certain utopian ideas if they were ever applied in practice. The moral objective distinguishes dystopias from mere utopian parodies that revel in parody, farce, and absurd jokes; they utilize the same methods of irony and satire as utopias do, but their tone is often dark, their irony is biting, and their humor is bitter and dry, or altogether absent.

There is some critical disagreement surrounding the terms of anti-utopia and dystopia. Some critics use the two terms and related synonyms (negative utopia, utopian satire, inverted utopia, etc.) interchangeably, without much regard to semantic nuances; others prefer one term and studiously avoid using any other.[1] A group of utopian scholars insist on a more discerning usage. The eminent utopian bibliographer Lyman Tower Sargent remarks that "anti-utopia ... should be reserved for that large class of works, both fictional and expository, which are directed against utopia and utopian thought" (x). John Huntington provides a more detailed argument that anti-utopia and dystopia are not synonyms. He applies anti-utopia to an attitude that attacks the idea of constructing utopias, a "mode of relentless inquisition, of restless skeptical exploration of the very articles of faith on which utopias themselves are built," whereas dystopias share an interest with utopias in constructing a coherent imaginary world, but with an opposite moral value: "Both are expression of a synthetic imagination, a comprehension and expression of the deep principles of happiness or unhappiness" ("Anti-Utopian Logic" 123–24). His example is Wells' *The Time Machine*, representing "anti-utopianism at its purest" (124) by virtue of its complex vision of an antithetical future world. The distinction certainly makes sense with regard to theory (e.g., Karl Popper's criticism of closed societies is definitely anti-utopian, without an explicit dystopian alternative vision [157–68]), but its application to specific literary texts throws up several problems. Practically all dystopian stories display elements of anti-utopian skepticism; on that level, I see no way of separating anti-utopia from dystopia. On the other hand, there are a few anti-utopian works that deliver their skepticism and condemnation of utopian spirit without presenting explicit dystopias. The most notable example is Jonathan Swift's *Gulliver's Travels* (1726), in which the author's anti-utopian disposition is expressed through the most complex reflection on utopianism in world literature. Swift's attitude to utopia is fraught with ambiguity; he revels in presenting alternative utopian frameworks and then demonstrating their flaws and limitations. The Academy of Lagado in Book III is the outcome of "the utopian imagination run mad" (Elliott 59), while the land of the Houyhnhnms, apparently a pastoral utopia populated by rational speaking horses, is placed in a thoroughly ambiguous context with introduction of the human-looking but animalistic Yahoos and Gulliver's own controversial position between the two races. Swift is a towering figure in both the utopian and anti-utopian tradition, yet he never wrote an explicit dystopia.

As the above example shows, the historical relationship between utopia and anti-utopia is complex and ambiguous, and the dividing line between the two forms is far form clear-cut. Few modern readers of More's *Utopia* would find it an attractive place to live in, no matter how positively disposed they are toward utopian ideas in general, simply because our common notions about the ideal balance between social stability and individual fulfillment have shifted radically in favor of the latter since the early 16th century. In contrast, Joseph Hall's *Mundus Alter et Idem* (1609) is perhaps the earliest full anti-utopia in the English language, presenting a satirical description of a South Indian country where the various states embody all the traditional human vices and follies; yet some readers managed to see in it a positive celebration of bodily pleasures, an alternative Land of Cockaygne (Kumar, *Utopia and Anti-Utopia* 105). The readers' perception of that most elusive thing, the "authorial intent," as I have argued in chapter 1, is often crucial in determining the moral tone of a utopian text, and this is no less relevant in case of dystopias. Most modern dystopias strive to avoid this problem by sending clear and unmistakable signals about the quality of their fictional *topos*: writers of dystopias, especially in the late 20th century, almost competed to present the most gruesome, brutal, oppressive human society possible, avoiding even the slightest possibility of doubt that their nightmare world possesses any commendable qualities. Such single-minded concentration on the "badness of the bad place" makes many of these works somewhat dull and tedious; moral ambiguity is a necessary condition of both successful utopias and dystopias.

Kumar argues that up to the 19th century, "Anti-utopia was often concealed in utopia" (*Utopia and Anti-Utopia* 105), because utopian satirists presented their contemporary empirical reality in strongly negative light in order to make their utopian construct stand out against this dark background. In More's *Utopia,* for instance, the negative counterpart of the island of Utopia is contemporary Christian Europe, with its corruption, vices and self-seeking political leadership. Although the superior values of the fictitious utopian community are called into question and relativized by means of narrative estrangement, no attempt is made within the narrative to explicitly argue against the efficacy and wholesomeness of Utopia itself. One reason for the absence of the "dystopian impulse" may be that utopias before the 19th century are mostly considered harmless flights of fancy rather than actual realizable blueprints for an alternative socio-political framework.

Dystopia as a distinct genre emerges when the target of the negative satire is no longer merely the *status quo,* but also a utopian scheme advocating changes to it. The appearance of dystopias signals a changing attitude toward utopias: they are to be taken seriously and to be feared rather than hoped for. This is the age when utopia became a "political battle concept," to borrow Lucian Hölscher's phrase (see chapter 1, pp. 17–19); after the 18th century, when the Enlightenment and the French Revolution subverted previously generally accepted social notions about the necessity of certain institutions (e.g., the monarchy, the social hierarchy, the aristocratic elite's monopoly on power, the influence of the Christian churches, etc.), alternative socio-political ideas began to multiply with spectacular — and for some observers, alarming — rapidity. The prerequisite for such a shift of perspective is a novel view on human history, also popularized by the Enlightenment, which believes in the ability of human reason to transform existing social conditions and bring about a qualitatively better form of existence. As a result, utopian thinkers began to pin their hopes on the future rather than some distant island at the Antipodes, and, especially from the late 19th century, displaced their alternative visions into the near or distant future. Martin G. Plattel observes that the future perspective was a crucial shift in the history of utopias:

> The rationalistic faith in progress had less feeling for this playfulness [of Renaissance writers] and believed in an impending state of happiness. The utopian world was no longer far beyond reach. Its realization could be looked forward to because of the existing confidence that the world was continuously making progress toward its final completion [34].

Utopian fictions of the future inevitably became a political genre, because they in effect required authors to sketch up a history of the future that led to the fortunate state of affairs pictured in the story. Such a historical projection attempted to account for the otherness of the future by envisioning revolutions or other kinds of sudden and dramatic changes that swept away the *status quo.* By means of a fictional history, they sharpened the contrast between the inferior present and the glorious future and also implicitly suggested, even though within the bounds of fiction, a certain political alternative. The most influential archetype of this narrative venture was Edward Bellamy's *Looking Backward: 2000–1887* (1888), which spawned both enthusiastic admirers and imitators as well as angry criticism, among them William Morris's famous rejoinder in the form of an alternative utopia, *News from Nowhere* (1890).[2]

Dystopias are motivated by the same belief in the potentialities of human history but without the optimistic outlook of utopians. The influential Russian anti-utopian thinker of the early 20th century, Nikolai Berdyaev, voiced this new-found fear of future utopia with particular aptitude (no wonder that Aldous Huxley chose the French original of this quote as the motto of *Brave New World*): "Utopias seem very much more realizable than we had formerly supposed. And now we find ourselves facing a question which is painful in a new kind of way: How to avoid their actual realization?" (quoted in Elliott 89). The typical answer of dystopian authors in the 20th century is the insistence on individual liberty as a fundamental yardstick against which utopian promises of universal happiness are to be measured. Hence the characteristic dystopian narrative model: the story of the misfit, who somehow differs from the rest of the community and grows dissatisfied with the supposedly perfect conditions under which he or she is supposed to exist. As the hero begins to look for a way out of "utopia," the narrative centers on his or her struggle for unlimited personal freedom against what is revealed as an oppressive socio-political regime. The most influential early example of this model is Yevgeniy Zamyatin's *We* (1921), which was inspired by Wells.

The emergence of dystopia as an increasingly popular and relevant genre in the early 20th century coincided and overlapped with another literary trend: the rise of science fiction, one of the most spectacularly successful genres of 20th-century popular literature.[3] The generic relationship between utopia, dystopia, and science fiction is a contentious subject among critics, complicated by the fact that science fiction itself is a literary phenomenon notoriously difficult to define. As I discussed in chapter 1 (p. 28), Darko Suvin defined utopia as a subcategory of science fiction, arguing that the fantastic core idea, the *novum,* is present in the form of an imaginary, alternative social organization. But this definition is based on formal criteria, disregarding the two genres' historical development. The term "science fiction" was invented by American pulp magazine editor Hugo Gernsback in 1929 (adapted from his own, earlier and clumsier phrase, "scientifiction")[4] to market the stories appearing in his own magazine; as a result, it developed a strong association with sensationalist adventures, repetitive plot clichés, cardboard cutout characters, and poor writing style, all characteristic of the cheap popular magazines in the United States of the interwar era. Gernsback himself, however, repeatedly emphasized that his science fiction has notable forerunners among eminent 19th-century writers such as Edgar Allan Poe, Jules Verne, and H.G. Wells, whose stories he also reprinted in his magazine. The most widely held critical view essentially accepts Gernsback's "family tree" and considers science fiction as a distinct form of fantastic literature that is the product of the 19th century, shadowing the rapid and sweeping transformations in the economies and societies of Western Europe and the United States brought about by the industrial revolution and the succeeding development of modern science and technology. Brian Aldiss succinctly states that science fiction is "the fiction of a technological age" (Aldiss and Wingrove 14), borrowing its archetypal form from the gothic novels of the Romantic period, and his view is essentially shared by Patrick Parrinder (*SF Criticism* 1–28). Others seek the roots of the genre in the fantastic voyages of ancient literature, listing Homer's *Odyssey* or Lucian's *True History* as "early SF" or "proto–SF" stories (Roberts 21–30), and then continue the historical survey of the genre in the 17th and 18th centuries, the age when modern natural science as a distinct field of scholarship emerged, inspiring stories about voyages to the Moon and similar fantasies. Although I personally remain skeptical about the existence of "seventeenth-century science fiction" (Roberts 36–63) and prefer to consider these texts allegorical tales with a rather explicit satirical, moral, or theological axe to grind, such an approach to the history of science fiction has the distinct advantage of establishing an early common link between science fiction and utopia, since utopias from More to the late 19th century also followed the plot clichés of the fantastic voyage formula.

Such critical contentions aside, a general consensus exists concerning the identity of two most influential science fiction authors in the 19th century who decisively shaped the future of the genre: they were the Frenchman Jules Verne and H.G. Wells. Verne excelled in what he termed *voyages extraordinaires,* adventurous journeys to distant and exotic places of the globe, some of which remained within the boundaries of contemporary reality and credibility, while others clearly ventured into fantastic territories, like *Voyage au centre de la terre* (*Journey to the Center of the Earth,* 1863), *De la Terre à la Lune* (*From the Earth to the Moon,* 1865), or *Vingt mille lieues sous les mers* (*Twenty Thousand Leagues Under the Sea,* 1870). His characteristic attraction to giant machines and somewhat implausible plots makes him the father of the technological adventure story subgenre of science fiction, but his fiction hardly ever trespasses the territory of utopian imagination.[5] It is H.G. Wells' *oeuvre* where the emerging genre of science fiction and the still popular but slowly declining form of utopia converge (see chapter 3 for details). With his early scientific romances, written between 1895 and 1905, he established a mode of writing as well as a set of ideas, archetypal images, and plots for countless 20th-century science fiction writers to follow.[6] Wells' fertile imagination and restless spirit combined speculation about the potential changes of human life brought about by scientific-technological innovations with a rare sensitivity to the larger social and political trends of his age. Sam Lundwall called this quality of Wells his "political conscience" (48). As a result, his science fiction is always tinged with more or less explicit satirical criticism of his own age, while most of his utopian and dystopian visions are presented in a science fiction mode, typically by removing the fictitious society in space or in time and then delivering the narrator/protagonist there by some science fiction device (space or time travel). Wells was also unprecedented in projecting his alternating optimistic and pessimistic moods into distinct utopian or dystopian visions of the future of humanity, in a sense acting as his own fiercest critic. He welded science fiction, utopia, and dystopia together in several stories, and exercised an enormous influence on all science fiction writers as well as all utopists in the first half of the century.

One direct result of the Wellsian influence is the confluence of dystopia and science fiction. Mark Hillegas describes this phenomenon pertinently, although with a certain finicky dismissal of genre science fiction as a whole, emphasizing that the anti-utopias (his consistently preferred term) are merely "similar to pulp science fiction in their conventions and themes but greatly superior in their literary quality and significance of comment on human life" (*Future as Nightmare* 8). He also makes a reasonable distinction between anti-utopian science fiction and utopian satire in the vein of, for example, Swift or Samuel Butler's *Erewhon* (1872), pointing out that utopian satire of the latter kind is not concerned with achieving verisimilitude in his fiction: "The writer of science fiction presents what he intends to be taken as actual possibilities whereas the satiric utopist ... usually offers in this other world ... inversions, parodies, or grotesque variations of things in our world" (9). He adds, however, that combinations of the two approaches are also possible, and mentions Frederik Pohl as an eminent example of a science fiction writer occasionally producing satiric utopian fiction (one may add such distinguished practitioners of this subgenre as the American Robert Sheckley, especially his brilliant novelette "A Ticket to Tranai," or the more absurdist British Douglas Adams and his *Hitchhiker's Guide* series).

Hillegas' essential thesis is that Wells was more of a forerunner than an opponent to the ideas of 20th-century dystopians, since in his early scientific romances he displays the same "cosmic pessimism" as E.M.

Forster, Zamyatin, Huxley, or Orwell (18–20). Hillegas singles out *When the Sleeper Wakes* (1899), "A Story of the Days to Come" (1897) and *The First Men in the Moon* (1901) as Wells' most influential anti-utopias, with many of their images, social arrangements and story twists resurfacing in subsequent dystopias. In the early 1900s, he turned from scientific romances to social and political problems, producing fiction and nonfiction alike in which he propagated his ideas as a means to forestall such gloomy developments that he himself had envisioned in earlier dystopias (see chapter 3 for details). As Hillegas sums it up,

> The hero of the first two decades of the century became the symbol of everything most intellectuals hated, and his vision of utopia the object of scorn.... The anti-utopians attacked his vision, and ironically, they used as a vehicle Wellsian science fiction.... But in attacking the Wellsian utopia, the major anti-utopias are greatly indebted to it since much of their attack consists of parody and caricature [*Future as Nightmare* 57].

Thus Wells both directly and indirectly helped establish dystopia as a characteristic treatment of social themes in science fiction. In fact, post-war American and British genre science fiction authors produced dystopian pieces of fiction in huge numbers, as they extrapolated one or more of the various scientific, technological, economic, political or ecological threats emerging during the 20th century to their logical conclusions, almost invariably presenting nightmare visions of future humanity. Frederik Pohl and Cyril M. Kornbluth in *The Space Merchants* (1953) tackle overpopulation and the oppressive domination of global business companies; Ray Bradbury's *Fahrenheit 451* (1953) envisions an extreme philistine United States in which possessing and reading books is a crime; Kurt Vonnegut's *Player Piano* (1952) takes up the Forsterian theme of mechanization as a dehumanizing effect on people's lives; Walter M. Miller's *A Canticle for Leibowitz* (1960) charts the future history of a post-apocalyptic North America pushed back into a quasi-medieval way of life by nuclear holocaust; Philip K. Dick pictures a United States divided between victorious Nazi Germany and Japan in *The Man in the High Castle* (1962), or a decaying United States suffering from the impact of nuclear fallout in *Do Androids Dream of Electric Sheep?* (1968); J.G. Ballard's *The Drowned World* (1962) presents an unrecognizable future London after the melting of the polar ice caps raised ocean levels and destroyed most seaside cities of the world; and the list could be continued. While none of these books achieved the worldwide success and fame of the two classics, Huxley's *Brave New World* and Orwell's *Nineteen Eighty-Four*—due partly to the authors" low social status as "SF writers" rather than mainstream authors, which excluded them from large segments of the book market — their combined impact was a curious domestication of dystopia by the end of the 20th century: such fictional nightmares have become a kind of commonplace in popular culture, even to the point of provoking parodistic treatments.

The great dystopian wave of the half century between the end of World War I and the peak of the Cold War in the 1960s was followed, perhaps inevitably, by something of a return to utopia, albeit in a significantly different form. While the powerful social and political trends of the 1960s — the human rights movement, the youth revolution, sexual liberation, early feminism, the decolonization of the Third World, and the anti–Vietnam War protest, which by the late 1960s coalesced into an improbable brew of revolutionary world view, a mixture of Marx and Freud, Gandhi and Che Guevara, Bakunin and Mao — did not produce any comprehensive fictional account of their imagined ideal human communities despite their optimistic outlook and utopian expectations, they did prepare the way for a new kind of utopian literature, which received the name "critical utopia" from Tom Moylan. He argues that several science fiction novels of the 1970s — his examples are Joanna Russ's *The Female Man* (1974), Ursula K. Le Guin's *The Dispossessed* (1974), Marge Piercy's *Woman on the Edge of Time* (1976), and Samuel Delany's *Triton* (1976) — returned to explicitly utopian themes, but they present "the utopian society in a more critical light" (*Demand the Impossible* 44), juxtaposing alternative societies, examining their respective advantages and disadvantages, and exposing the ambiguity at the heart of any utopian venture also on the narrative level with fragmented story-telling, uncertain narrators, and other means. Although this flare-up of utopian science fiction was not followed by a larger wave of science fiction novels written in a similar vein, they did have a crucial significance: they rehabilitated utopia as a valid theme of science fiction after a deluge of dystopian narratives, and they helped break down the isolation between the "SF ghetto" and the "mainstream literature" deemed worthy of critical attention, as these novels became the favorite subject matter of several representatives of the new academic criticism of science fiction.

To conclude this sketchy genre history, while the distinct genre of literary utopia in its classic form has followed the fate of the verse epic and several other literary forms that lost the interest of readers by the 20th century, utopia as a literary theme is far from dead. Although science fiction is a much broader genre with a wide variety of subjects and narrative possibilities, it has preserved some of the central concerns of utopias, especially when it pictures imaginary human and quasi-human communities removed from the readers' present in space (on other planets), in time (in the future), or both. As Edward James argues in his essay on the relationship of utopia and science fiction, "Utopia has not disappeared; it merely mutated, within the field of sf, into something very different from the classic utopia" ("Utopias and Anti-utopias" 219).

In the following, I would like to examine two novels that demonstrate both the survival of the utopian impulse in dystopia and science fiction and the far-ranging impact of H.G. Wells in 20th-century English fantastic literature. Aldous Huxley's *Brave New World* is unique among early–20th-century dystopias in presenting a comprehensive fictional vision about a future World State that does not rest on the brutal oppression of its citizens by a powerful collectivist state; instead, he envisages a society in which "happiness" is the overriding concern of all individuals. The powerful ambiguity of Huxley's interpretation of this key utopian concept confers a special quality to the novel, amplified by the complex satirical references and allusions to the Wellsian utopia, the contemporary United States, and, perhaps less conspicuously, Shakespeare's *The Tempest*. It is this final literary paragon that my examination will focus on: although Huxley does not employ the method of narrative estrangement that is so central to both More's *Utopia* and Wells' *A Modern Utopia,* his employment of an English literary classic as an ironic model of plot and characters broadens the frame of reference in which his dystopian statement is to be interpreted and invests it with an additional layer of significance.

Arthur C. Clarke's *The City and the Stars* (1956) might look like an odd choice to represent the science fiction treatment of utopia, as his most widely discussed novel, *Childhood's End* (1953), is also concerned with utopian issues. My explicit intention in this case is to set the balance straight and argue in favor of the relevance of *The City and the Stars* as a representative example of Clarke's utopian imagination, which envisions ideal states of humanity only to look for ways to transcend this stagnant way of existence. Furthermore, I believe that Clarke's approach to utopia — deeply influenced by Wells and Olaf Stapledon — is also characteristic of science fiction as a genre, with its dynamic emphasis on progress and change, as well as a restless questioning of several aspects of human existence that are all too often accepted as given and unchangeable by most people.

## Caliban Stranded in Civilization: Huxley's Brave New World

The first half of the 20th century, especially the interwar period, saw the dynamic rise and success of the dystopia. Although this dystopian turn of mind produced works of fiction in practically all Western literatures,[7] the critical consensus invariably singles out two English books as the representative and also the most influential examples of the "20th-century dystopia"; Aldous Huxley's *Brave New World* (1932) and George Orwell's *Nineteen Eighty-Four* (1949). Krishan Kumar underlines the pivotal role of these two books when he writes,

> Anti-utopias such as *Brave New World* and *Nineteen Eighty-Four* have not only dominated their own times, the first half of the twentieth century, but have continued to attract a considerable following in our time.... No anti-utopia since *Nineteen Eighty-Four* has truly captured the popular imagination or become the centre of public debate. There has been no new anti-utopia to stamp its compelling image on the contemporary world, as a rival to those of Huxley's and Orwell's [*Utopia* 422].

Both books have achieved worldwide fame and shaped the imagination, the anxieties and even the language of generations to come. And they both have been the focus of many critical works that attempted to explain their vast impact.

Part of the explanation certainly lies in the fact that both novels succeeded in capturing the *Zeitgeist* of the early 1930s and the post-war 1940s, respectively. Huxley drew his inspiration primarily from "the horror of the Wellsian Utopia and a revolt against it," as he phrased it in a private letter (*Letters* 348), but he also directed his social satire against the early consumer society as it emerged in the United States during the "Roaring Twenties." Orwell's fictional world was evidently based on the two horrendous totalitarian regimes, Nazism and Stalinism, that emerged during the 1930s and waged a desperate and utterly destructive war against each other during the early 1940s. His bleak vision of the extreme totalitarian dictatorship that excludes even the possibility of resistance, escape, or rebellion has elevated his novel into an "ultimate dystopia," a fictional world unsurpassable in its inhumanity and hopelessness.

The two books had a fascinating afterlife. Orwell's last novel evolved into a major popular success by the 1950s all over the Western world (Rodden 44–50), and became a staple of American and Western European college reading lists as "an ideological superweapon in the cold war," to use the famous phrase of Isaac Deutscher (29), catapulting its previously rather obscure author into a posthumous cult figure status. East of the Iron Curtain, on the other hand, *Nineteen Eighty-Four* was considered a subversive and ideologically dangerous book by Communist governments, and it was banned until 1989–1990 in all Eastern European countries; only illegal translations or surreptitious English texts circulated among intellectuals and students. This forbidden fruit quality as well as numerous similarities between Orwell's oppressive fictional world and the drab reality of existing Socialism elevated *Nineteen Eighty-Four* into a underground cult status in Eastern Europe, and it preserved its popularity even two decades after the collapse of Communist regimes.[8]

In contrast, Huxley was already a well-established and internationally successful author when *Brave New World* came out,[9] and although the novel was mostly favorably reviewed (Watt 197–222) and enjoyed a period of international popularity in the 1930s, it never became a runaway success, soon to be eclipsed by the more explicit horrors of World War II as well as the subsequent fears and tensions of the Cold War. It remained steadily in print and was widely read in the West,[10] but never achieved a popular fame comparable to Orwell's book. But as Huxley's popular and critical standing took a nose-dive after his death,[11] and his numerous novels and essays[12] were relegated to the back shelves, *Brave New World* proved a uniquely resilient book in Huxley's *oeuvre* that preserved the interest of a wide range of readers, and became almost the only work that manages to maintain his reputation beyond a narrow circle of specialist critics. In Eastern Europe, *Brave New World* was largely forgotten outside of academia after the war; when a new edition was published in Hungarian in 1982 to commemorate the 50th anniversary of the novel's appearance, it had a quaint and curious impact on readers living under Socialism, who never experienced many of the social aspects satirized by the novel, such as material affluence, omnipresent advertisements, or an endless supply of available entertainments. However, the novel went into a new Hungarian edition in 2008, which seems to suggest a new lease of life in this part of the world two decades after the transition into Western-style free-market economy and consumerism.

From the vantage point of the early 2000s, one might indeed question the assumption common during the second half of the 20th century that Orwell's dystopia appeared more relevant or up-to-date than Huxley's.[13] Although the appearance of the first legal edition of *Nineteen Eighty-Four* in Hungary in 1989 was a symbolic breakthrough, signaling the loosening of state-controlled censorship and the concomitant decline of the Party's power, the history of Eastern Europe since 1990, characterized by free-market capitalism sweeping through these countries after almost half a century of nationalized and state-controlled economy, suddenly made the problems presented in *Nineteen Eighty-Four* look outdated and several aspects of *Brave New World* very relevant. People in this part of the world no longer felt a gripping fear from the all-too-powerful State; but they soon had to learn to respect and even fear the power of globalized business and big money interests. Instead of one or two strictly censored television channels, they could watch several dozen different ones; but art films, dramas, science and music programs quickly gave way to endless soap operas, cheap thrillers, talk and reality shows, all peppered with an ceaseless shower of commercials. Huxley's prophesy, made in his letter to Orwell, that "I feel the nightmare of *Nineteen Eighty-Four* is destined to modulate into the nightmare of a world having more resemblance to that which I imagined in *Brave New World*" (Letters 605) has not manifested itself in its frightful literal sense in Eastern Europe. Yet many contemporary readers, in Eastern Europe or elsewhere, would probably agree that our contemporary world, with mass media brainwashing to educate and manipulate the perfect consumers as well as the widely publicized scientific experiments with the cloning of animals (and, possibly, humans), provides chilling recognitions of similarity with Huxley's dystopia.

Most probably it is the unceasing currency of Huxley's social and cultural satire of unlimited commercialism and the ruthless scientific standardization of humans that keeps it popular among new generations of readers. This ever-present timeliness of the novel, however, tends to obscure the fact that *Brave New World* was as much a reflection on the English utopian tradition as a biting satire of the socio-cultural realities of the early 1930s. When Huxley set out to convey his disgust with the Wellsian utopia, consciously or unconsciously he utilized ideas from early Wellsian anti-utopias — especially the Selenite civilization of *The First Men in the Moon*, with its workers shaped from infancy to have the optimal shape and physical traits for their job, shows some striking similarities with Huxley's castes. This phenomenon was described by Krishan Kumar as "a case of Wells *contra* Wells" (*Utopia* 225). Despite Huxley's explicit dislike of Wells and his social ideas, Kumar sees a distinct pattern of underlying similarity between Huxley and Wells. Just like Wells, Huxley also shifted from an anti-utopian into a utopian mentality, as his last novel, *Island* (1962), testifies. And Kumar observes a comparable decline of literary artistry in the later novels of both authors (*Utopia* 226). Some recent research went so far as to question the prevailing notion of a headlong opposition between Wells' and Huxley's views. David Bradshaw, after a detailed examination of Huxley's newspaper articles and essays in the 1920s and early 1930s, came to the conclusion that Huxley, rather than being an avid anti–Wellsian, approved of crucial aspects of Wells' views aired in *The Open Conspiracy* and elsewhere, and he himself felt at least equivocal about some of his own social ideas, including the caste system (38–41).

Huxley's extant letters throw scant light on the exact development of *Brave New World*. Late in his life, he wrote that Wells' *Men Like Gods* "annoyed me to the point of planning a parody, but when I started writing I found the idea of a negative Utopia so interesting that I forgot about Wells and launched into *Brave New World*" (quoted in Baker 25). Jerome Meckier, after a meticulous examination of the extant typescript, came to the conclusion that the original idea of a Wellsian parody was subsequently modified into a more comprehensive satire of contemporary American economic and social developments. During a revision of the typescript between May and August 1931, Huxley added multiple references to "Our Ford," sniping at Henry Ford, the world-famous American pioneer of industrial mass production, who publicized his controversial ideas about paternalist "welfare capitalism" as well as efficient business and social organization in *My Life and Work* (1922).[14] Ford's name, conveniently similar to "Lord," as well as his breakthrough product, the Model T, were turned into brilliant multi-faceted symbols of the Brave New World by Huxley, travestying the shallowness and the idol-worshipping of an essentially faithless, utterly materialistic world.

> Wells's ideal of a rationalized society run by scientifically trained bureaucrats and Ford's confidence in the organizational skills that produce a well-run factory went together as ends and means. To universalize his antiutopia, Huxley realized, was to Americanize it, to become blatantly anti–Fordian [Meckier, "Americanization"].

Meckier also observed that the oldest part of the manuscript is not the opening chapters, but the ones taking place in Malpais, the Indian reservation in New Mexico. It seems that Huxley's original plan was to introduce the early life of John (the present chapter 8 of the novel), and then have Bernard return to the reservation to encounter his own abandoned lover (initially called Nina rather than Linda), and ally with his natural son, John, in an attempt to overthrow the World State, a typical plot

cliché of several dystopian novels, for example, Zamyatin's *We*.[15] The figure
of John was probably inspired by Huxley's late friend, D.H. Lawrence, who
was fascinated by the Native American cultures of New Mexico, and
employed a noble savage character in his novel *The Plumed Serpent*. But
in the process of writing Huxley apparently realized that the favorite gesture of anti-utopists, pitting "untouched" nature and the "natural man"
against the artificial, technicized puritanism of utopian visions, would not
suffice in this case. His strong critical sense and grotesque view of his contemporary world did not allow him to idolize the marginal, pre-industrial
culture and the abject poverty of New Mexico Indians as a credible alternative to the mechanized and uniformized Wellsian-American utopia.
Accordingly, he turned his Savage from a romantic hero into its parody.
Thesis and antithesis did not provide any synthesis — only a bitterly ironic,
satirical parable, which ends in the suicide of the hero rather than the liberation of the prisoners of Utopia.

Meckier provided a third fascinating insight from the examination
of the typescript: the text shows no trace of the intention that this work
in progress should receive *Brave New World* as its final title. In the final
version, at the end of chapter 8, almost at half-point in the novel, John
quotes Miranda from Shakespeare's *The Tempest*. Prospero's young daughter, who grew up in isolation on the island, utters the following words in
Act V when she first sees the company of shipwrecked noblemen, including his father's traitorous brother, Antonio, and his former accomplice,
Alonso, King of Naples:

> O, wonder!
> How many goodly creatures are there here!
> How beauteous mankind is! O brave new world,
> That has such people in 't!
> [V.1.181–84].[16]

John exuberantly cites Miranda's words in reply to Bernard's invitation to
come with him and Lenina to London. In Shakespeare's play, Prospero
reacts briefly and wryly to Miranda's innocent and misinformed outburst:
"'Tis new to thee" (V.1.184). Likewise, in Huxley's novel, Bernard supplies
the skeptical counterpoint: "Hadn't you better wait till you actually see
the new world?" (144). This unanswered question forecasts the entire second part of the novel's plot.

This famous scene is completely missing from the typescript. Huxley first refers to the novel by its final title only in February 1932, more
than half a year after the revision of the typescript had been completed

(*Letters* 358). "It seems incredible that these important pages were added between typescript and proof sheets," remarks Meckier.

After making this remarkable discovery, Meckier fails to raise the pertinent question: What made Huxley carry out yet another revision on the manuscript and choose as title a well-known Shakespearean quote from *The Tempest*? Strangely enough, the substantial critical literature on *Brave New World* never investigated the Shakespearean influence in any significant detail. Contemporary reviewers were primarily concerned with the characteristics of the book's dystopian world, especially the use of biological advances, conditioning, and hypnopaedia, as well as the caste-like social organization and its relation to contemporary phenomena, in other words, the topicality of the book's satirical references. Few of them commented on the novel's literary influences or its forerunners. Only Rebecca West (who used to be the extra-marital lover of H.G. Wells), perhaps the most insightful reviewer, pointed out that the confrontation between the Savage and the World Controller essentially paraphrases the famous encounter between Jesus and the Grand Inquisitor in Dostoyevsky's *The Brothers Karamazov* (Watt 201). Firchow, in his study 40 years later, expanded on this parallel, adding lengthy quotes from Dostoyevsky's novel, but without acknowledging the primacy of West's insight (126–28). Another reviewer, Charlotte Haldane, spotted the parallel between the Savage and Voltaire's famous "philosophical tale," *L'Ingenu* (1767), in which a Huron Indian makes innocently sarcastic discoveries about the absurdities of 18th-century France (Watt 208). But nobody considered the intricate influence of Shakespeare's works on John worthy of any extended comment.[17]

Subsequent critics also rarely went beyond dutifully explaining the significance of the title itself.[18] Miranda's unwitting misjudgment of the shipwrecked company sounds merely innocent and romantic at first sight. In the context of the drama, however, it receives a thoroughly ironic overtone, and casts a dark shadow on Miranda's future outside the enchanted island; with such naiveté, she can easily fall prey to the predatory instincts of ordinary humans. By choosing Miranda's words as the title of his novel, Huxley did more than exploit one of the numerous Shakespearean proverbs: he made an opening statement about his own novel, which immediately placed it in an ironic context. Just as Miranda is gravely mistaken to regard her father's former lethal enemies and traitors as goodly and beauteous people, Miranda's words are quoted by a character who has no knowledge at all about the reality of the World State. Readers familiar with the original Shakespearean context are given a fair warning to approach the author's conspicuous praise of his own fictitious world with a healthy dose of suspicion; Huxley's Brave New World is new to the readers, but they had better not share John's unequivocal enthusiasm about it.

In my conviction, Huxley's emphatic reference to *The Tempest* is by no means occasional nor accidental, despite the fact that it was added to the text at a very late stage of the creative process. By closer inspection, Huxley's novel displays such a number of similarities and parallels with Shakespeare's play in terms of characters and motifs that it cannot be regarded as a mere coincidence. In fact, I believe that *Brave New World* can be read as a comment and reflection on certain central themes of *The Tempest*, which adds a whole new interpretive dimension to the novel.[19] With a final decision that may have objectified a certain unconscious process of his creative mind, Huxley clearly reached beyond the Wellsian utopia and the Fordian United States to find a corresponding model in Shakespearean theater, more precisely one of the most complex plays of Shakespeare, which contains several utopian as well as dystopian themes and allusions. This way, he anchored the book more firmly in the general utopian tradition, thereby giving his novel a symbolic significance beyond the topical social satire. In order to unfold this symbolism, I am going to examine certain motifs of *The Tempest* in an attempt to shed new light on *Brave New World*.

## "Here in This Island We Arriv'd"[20]

Prospero's island, the scene of practically the entire plot of *The Tempest*, has been the subject of much critical speculation over the centuries. It has been identified with various islands in the Mediterranean,[21] but it has also been placed in the Bermudas of the Caribbean, where an English ship almost miraculously survived a great storm and was wrecked on a beautiful uninhabited island in 1609; the adventures of the ship's passengers were widely publicized at the time *The Tempest* was written (Kermode xxvi–xxviii; Greenblatt, "Introduction" 3052). So the island may be part of the Old World, or part of the New; several interpreters, however, felt tempted to locate it in the realm of the imagination instead of the map. Allegorical interpretations have seen in it an allegory of the theater, where the magician-poet (Prospero-Shakespeare) commands the spirits of the imagination and holds his audience under his spell.[22] Alternatively, the island may stand for the larger isle of Britain, united for the first time under

King James I, who inherited the English throne next to his native Scottish kingdom in 1603. James had a reputation for being a scholar-king with a thorough theological education but was also deeply interested in witchcraft and the spirit world (Croft 25–27), and his reign was threatened by a Catholic plot against him and Parliament in 1605 with a vague similarity to the plots against Prospero back in Milan, or on the island during the play. Yet another contemporary reference is provided by the fact that the play was performed at the royal court in late 1612 or early 1613 as part of the entertainment in honor of the betrothal and the marriage of James's daughter, Elizabeth, to Frederick, the Elector Palatine (Kermode xx–xxii; Greenblatt, "Introduction" 3047), an event reminiscent of the unification of Miranda and Ferdinand. A more recent postcolonial reading of the play has interpreted the island as a symbolic miniature of the recently discovered New World, America. This approach considers Prospero the embodiment of the white European colonist, who, armed with magic-like superior technology and weaponry together with a firm belief in his own moral and intellectual superiority, has taken possession of the newfound land without the slightest hesitation, and enslaved Caliban, the native of the island, who had lived there in harmony with nature (Vaughan and Vaughan 49–50).

The island carries different meanings for individual characters of the play itself. For Prospero, it is a place of refuge, where he landed after he had been dethroned and exiled from his native Milan, and where he was able to create a small new world for himself and his daughter. For Miranda, it is a place of innocent beauty where she grew up and was educated by Prospero; it is her school and playground in one. For Ariel, it is a prison, where she is bound to serve Prospero. For Caliban, it is a lost realm, his natural inheritance that was taken from him by the invading sorcerer, Prospero. For some of the shipwrecked company, it is a trap from which they see no way of escape; for others, it offers an opportunity to carry out their vile plans. In the famous monologue of the old, wise counselor Gonzalo, the island inspires a dream of the Golden Age, where

> I would by contraries
> Execute all things; for no kind of traffic
> Would I admit; no name of magistrate;
> Letters should not be known; riches, poverty,
> And use of service, none; contract, succession,
> Bourn, bound of land, tilth, vineyard, none;
> No use of metal, corn, or wine, or oil;

No occupation; all men idle, all;
And women too, but innocent and pure:
No sovereignty; ...
All things in common Nature should produce
Without sweat or endeavour: treason, felony,
Sword, pike, knife, gun, or need of any engine,
Would I not have; but Nature should bring forth,
Of it own kind, all foison, all abundance,
To feed my innocent people....
I would with such perfection govern, sir,
T' excel the Golden Age [II.1.143–64].[23]

At this point in the play, the island motif clearly overlaps with the contextual meaning it carries in utopian literature ever since Sir Thomas More created "the island as the perfect commonwealth" archetype for many subsequent utopias. More's island is even similar to Prospero's in the vagueness of its location (see chapter 2, pp. 72–74). The island is an ideal venue for an ideal society; it can be placed in a faraway part of the globe, at a safe distance from the familiar world, in those uncharted areas of the map where geographical facts tend to mingle with ancient myths and wild fantasies. Its remoteness and isolation may account for some of the more startling aspects of this utopian society, and may help suspend the disbelief of European readers — it functions as the literal *terra incognita* of fiction. The island as a literary device also offers a convenient plot that had been handed down ready-made from classical literature: the traditional topos of the adventurous sea voyage, where a traveler is driven off his course by a storm and ends up on an unknown island, gets into contact with its inhabitants, gathers information about their political organization, lifestyle and customs, and eventually manages to return to Europe to share his experiences and observations with the readers.

This conventional narrative tool remained in use for imaginative utopias until the 19th century. By that time, however, even the most distant nooks of the "South Seas" had been carefully mapped, and therefore the geographic discoveries made utopian islands anachronistic as places of symbolic displacement. On the other hand, the industrial revolution triggered a spectacular development of science and technology, and this modern magic offered a radically new perspective: a utopia removed from our world not in place but in time, located in the future. The future suddenly appeared reasonably predictable by projecting existing tendencies of present progress, and such a feat was performed to great international acclaim and controversy by the American Edward Bellamy in his *Looking Backward*

*2000–1887* (1888). Bellamy imagined a fully egalitarian United States in the year 2000 without private property, where all citizens live in plenty and happiness. H.G. Wells followed Bellamy's lead and enlarged his vision in *A Modern Utopia* when he pictured a utopian World State, reversing the relative role of the island versus the world. In Wells' book, islands are the places where deviant individuals — dissenters as well as common criminals and moral failures like alcoholics — are transported in order to be removed from the society of the normal utopians. It is no longer the ideal society that is spatially contained and separated, but the prison or purgatory to which criminals and misfits are constrained.

Huxley naturally adopted many of Wells' inventions, including the World State and the prison islands, for his Wellsian satire. During his discussion with the Savage, Helmholtz, and Bernard in chapter 16, Mustapha Mond refers to some special islands where the misfits of the World State are sent in order not to upset social stability. But these islands do not sound like extended concentration camps:

> He's being sent to an island. That's to say, he's being sent to a place where he'll meet the most interesting set of men and women to be found anywhere in the world. All the people who, for one reason or another, have got too self-consciously individual to fit into community-life. All the people who aren't satisfied with orthodoxy, who've got independent ideas of their own. Everyone, in a word, who's anyone [225].

Judged by this description, the population of those islands comprise the most intelligent and talented people of the planet. There they are apparently allowed to pursue their interests unhindered, which is probably the greatest gift an intellectually inclined person can get. The prison island is instantly transformed into a utopia for inquisitive minds. That is Prospero's story in a nutshell. He lost his dukedom because he was too much immersed in his scholarly pursuits, and transferred his government duties to his brother Antonio, who then abused his newfound power and drove his elder brother from the throne of Milan. But the exiled Prospero found a perfect refuge on the island. Armed with his books ("he [Gonzalo] furnish'd me/ From mine own library with volumes that/I prize above my dukedom" [I.2.166–68]), he set out to perfect his magical power, to educate Miranda, and to rule the island together with its spiritual and earthly inhabitants. In Gonzalo's words, he found "his dukedom in a poor isle" (V.1.211–12). In retrospect, his exile seems almost a blessing in disguise; relieved from the duties of a prince, he could concentrate on his primary interest, and became a most powerful scientist-magician.[24]

Prospero's happy exile on his island is a truly attractive opportunity for creatively inclined individuals. But the islands referred to by Mustapha Mond remain obscured by clouds of vagueness. What do exiles exactly do in these places? If their punishment involves the deprivation of the material comfort of the World State, then they are forced to take care of their own daily survival, thereby perhaps learning the hard way the value of human community they scorned before. That would be a more advanced version of those re-education camps invented by various left-wing dictatorships against members of the former privileged classes. Or they may be supplied with the most up-to-date equipment and technology to engage in creative work and research in the natural or social sciences. Here these talented artists and scholars can engage in investigations forbidden by the strict censorship of the World State, even attempting the ultimate social experiment: building a community of enlightened individuals, who are allowed the freedom of difference. In that case, the longing overtones of Mustapha Mond ("I almost envy you, Mr Watson" [225]) would be perfectly justified, since he was deprived of Prospero's opportunity. By choosing World Controllership over a life devoted to scientific research on an island, he missed the real, unconditioned and drugless utopia. Thus Mustapha Mond pictures himself as a Prospero marooned in the World State: a former scientist who chose to be a ruler instead of an exile.

That is, if we are to believe him. But there is reason to be cautious. He himself relates the story of the Cyprus experiment (221–22), where a community consisting of 22,000 Alphas was set up, supplied with all the necessary agricultural and industrial equipment. Since Alphas refused to do menial work and disobeyed orders, the outcome was total chaos, civil war and the violent death of the great majority of the inhabitants. "And that was the end of the only society of Alphas that the world has ever seen" (222).

This story begs the question: how would the exiles — by definition all Alphas and all rugged individualists verging on the eccentric — end up any better if they are left alone to manage themselves? There seem to be just two plausible answers. They are either carefully separated from one another and live alone or in very small groups, monitored and supervised by some kind of police, which is a far cry from the ideal of the free alternative community sketched up by Mond. But there is an even darker reading of Mond's subtext: that misfits are transported to these islands and isolated from the rest of the world exactly in order to kill one another off without disturbing the World State. In the latter case, the World Controller's apparent benevolence is all hypocrisy; he knows all too well that sending Helmholtz and Bernard to an island is the equivalent of signing their death warrant. A seemingly casual remark by Mond, made toward the end of his conversation with Helmholtz, reinforces this reading: "It's lucky ... that there are such a lot of islands in the world. I don't know what we would do without them. Put you all into the lethal chamber, I suppose" (227). The remark passes unnoticed by Helmholtz or the Savage, as it seems to suggest that the islands are a much more humane way of ridding the World State of its burdensome rebels. But placed in the context of the tell-tale unreliability of Mustapha Mond, it gains a more chilling meaning. There is eventually no difference between these islands and a gas chamber except that Brave New Worlders do not have to stain their hands with human blood, and they can maintain a hypocritical façade of mercifulness and humanity.

This interpretation further reinforces Mond's similarity to Prospero. His position in the World State parallels Prospero's situation on the island; the World Controller (as his title reveals) is vested with such a supreme authority that he seems to wield almost magical power. He can apparently do whatever he wants ("as I make the laws here, I can also break them" [217]), and although the existence of a Controllers' Council is mentioned, Mond seems to have no controlling authority above him. He is exactly the kind of enlightened absolute monarch as Prospero on the island: friendly and benevolent at first sight, but also condescending and imperious. They both exercise their power in full conviction of their moral superiority and they never doubt that their decisions are exclusively for the benefit of their subjects. They both appear as selfless and benign white magicians, but their characters reveal a streak of darkness at closer inspection.[25] Prospero is sometimes arrogant and easily works himself up into a rage over trifles, once abusing even his most obedient servant, Ariel; moreover, he is consistently very brutal and cruel to Caliban, which does not seem to be justified by Caliban's past attempt to rape Miranda, not to say that it is strongly short-sighted pedagogy. Mond forbids the publication of a book on the theory of biology that he considers highly original, and places the author under supervision. It is also Mond who, after a pleasant discussion with the Savage, does not allow him to join the others on the islands of exile, because "he [Mond] said he wanted to go on with the experiment" (239).

This propensity for experimenting on humans is perhaps the most striking parallel between the two characters. Mond, in his own account, overstepped the prescribed boundaries as a young physicist and was forced to choose between joining the intellectual exiles on an island or becoming one of the servants of the happiness of the World State, that is, becoming a member of the Controllers' Council. As he tells the arrested Savage, Helmholtz, and Bernard,

> "I chose this and let the science go." After a little silence, "Sometimes," he added, "I rather regret the science. Happiness is a hard master — particularly other people's happiness. A much harder master, if one isn't conditioned to accept it unquestionably, than truth." He sighed, fell silent again, then continued in a brisker tone. "Well, duty's duty" [225].

Again, there is something distinctly insincere, theatrical in this uninvited confession, which is repeated soon after, at the end of the same long monologue about the dangers of unrestrained science:

> One can't have something for nothing. Happiness has got to be paid for. You're paying for it, Mr Watson — paying because you happen to be too much interested in beauty. I was too much interested in truth; I paid too.
> "But *you* didn't go to an island," said the Savage, breaking a long silence.
> The Controller smiled. "That's how I paid. By choosing to serve happiness. Other people's — not mine" [226–27].

And immediately after this he drops his casual remark about islands and lethal chambers. An attentive reading of his performance reinforces the suspicion that he has been playing a role: the role of the selfless public servant, who has sacrificed his own happiness for the welfare of the World State, and discharges his duties as World Controller out of some sense of moral obligation. In the wider context of the novel, however, it becomes clear that he is lying. He has not given up science, only changed the field of study: instead of physics, he has taken up social engineering. He has been studying the behavior of Bernard and Helmholtz, and will probably continue to watch them after they have landed on their respective islands. But his number-one subject for experiment is John the Savage. Mond used Bernard as an unwitting tool to remove John from his "island," the Reservation, and dropped him into an alien environment to observe his "immune reactions."[26] He possesses the professional detachment of a natural scientist: he may feel some kind of sympathy for the subject of the experiment, but does not let it interfere with his decisions.

This attitude is the exact parallel of Prospero's, who has had years to develop his knowledge and power on the island. He broke the charms of the witch Sycorax and freed Ariel, but had only two humans to experiment on: his own daughter, Miranda, and Sycorax's son Caliban. The result was 50 percent success; he managed to shape Miranda in the way he wanted, but failed completely with Caliban, therefore enslaving him. Then his great opportunity comes: a whole group of human specimens turns up near the island, and Prospero can finally begin his great experiment. He subjects Ferdinand to a complicated series of tests and trials to find out whether he makes a suitable groom for Miranda; he makes King Alonso believe that he has lost his only son to break and chastise him; he gives various moral lessons to several others of the company.

The outcome is apparently a complete success. Ferdinand excels at the ordeal, winning Miranda's heart and hand; Alonso repents his crimes against Prospero; Stephano and Trinculo are punished by tormenting pains and public ridicule; and even the hopeless Caliban declares to "be wise hereafter,/And seek for grace" (V.1.294–95). But Antonio remains conspicuously silent throughout the final scene, showing no repentance and not thanking his brother for his forgiveness. The real test of Prospero's science will be to repeat his results outside the carefully controlled conditions of his laboratory: to prove that his subjects will be better people when they have returned to Milan and Naples. About that, however, the play supplies no information. Only Mond's experiment is followed up until the final outcome: the suicide of the subject.

## "A DEVIL, A BORN DEVIL, ON WHOSE NATURE NURTURE CAN NEVER STICK"[27]

The Savage is unquestionably the most interesting character — arguably the only fully realized character — of *Brave New World*. The figures of Huxley's early novels were almost all modeled on real-life personalities, including his own closest friends and acquaintances. In contrast, the Savage is the ironic echo of fictitious characters from literary tradition. His name is a clear reference to the famous noble savage of the French Enlightenment, and he can be considered a near-perfect realization of Rousseau's dream: a character both untainted by civilization and at the same time educated by one of the greatest poets of all time — William Shakespeare. He is a man of nature who grew up under primitive conditions like Caliban, but also a man of ideals with a wide-eyed romantic enthusiasm reminiscent of Miranda. And, similar to both Caliban and Miranda, he was born and raised on one of the few uncivilized islands allowed by the World State to exist: the New Mexican Savage Reservation, separated from the outside world by high-voltage electric fences instead of the ocean.

The Reservation surfaces in chapter 6 when Bernard invites Lenina to an unusual holiday. It is revealed as a curious mixture of a traditional Native American community that Huxley knew mostly from the writings of D.H. Lawrence (pueblo, Native American languages, fertility rites, pre-industrial living conditions) and some fragments of a past culture that actually derive from Huxley's present (fragments of Christianity, a volume of Shakespeare's *Complete Works*). The function of the Reservation from the point of view of the World State remains unclear. It could serve the purpose of scientific research like the study of "primitive societies," but there are few signs that the savages are actually studied by people from the World State.[28] The visit of Bernard and Lenina suggests the idea that the Reservation may have been preserved as a kind of curiosity, a human zoo or safari park, which "civilized" people can visit to be amazed and horrified by the Indians' primitive living conditions and bizarre rituals, and return to their own world with the comfortable assertion that they are infinitely superior to these creatures. But this idea is contradicted by the fact that entry to the Reservation is carefully controlled (Bernard needs the permit of Mustapha Mond himself), and there seems to be little interest in and few visitors to the place (Lenina, when confronted with Bernard's offer, finds the idea interesting but strange). When subsequently the Savage visits a lesson at Eton, students are taught a definition of the reservation: "A savage reservation is a place which, owing to unfavorable climate or geological conditions, or poverty of natural resources, has not been worth the expense of civilising" (164). It is difficult to imagine, however, that the World State, with its almost infinite financial and economic resources, would find it too expensive to improve the living conditions of a few thousand natives. The evidence available in the book best supports the hypothesis that the Reservation functions — or rather, functioned in the past — as a kind of "control group" to the great social experiment conducted in the World State. Perhaps the unknown creators of that carefully balanced, static, and artificially maintained society left nothing for chance and set aside a small group of "primitives" to make sure that if anything unforeseeable happens and the experiment goes awry, there is still a small pool of unconditioned, "natural" people left to draw upon for future purposes.[29]

In that case, the Reservation is an abandoned laboratory, just as Prospero's island will be deserted after twelve long years of study and experiments. One of the questions left unresolved at the end of *The Tempest* is exactly whether anybody stays behind after Prospero and Miranda depart with the royal ship. Will Caliban's desire be finally fulfilled so that he will become "mine own King" (I.2.344) again after "a tyrant, a sorcerer ... by his cunning hath cheated me of the island" (III.2.40–42)? Or is he going to leave with Prospero, who, in a cryptic utterance just before the end of the play, accepts some sort of responsibility or connection with him: "This thing of darkness I / Acknowledge mine" (V.1.275–276)? Even though Caliban is a living testimony to Prospero's failure as an educator, he has learned certain things from him, most importantly language, which set him apart from his once natural surroundings. He is no longer a mere human beast, and it is doubtful whether he would find his way back to his natural condition, whether he would enjoy his "kingdom" alone, without the company of any other human beings. By his education, he has been partly alienated from nature, without having been assimilated to the "civilization" of Prospero and his company, who would never accept him as their equal. In the eyes of Prospero's society, he would always remain a speaking animal, a circus spectacle, nothing more.

In the story of the young Savage, Huxley clearly paraphrased the fate of Caliban. His mother, Linda, was stranded in the reservation by accident like Caliban's mother, Sycorax, who was left on the island by sailors. Linda could not return to the World State because she turned out to be pregnant, an intolerable shame by Brave New World standards, so in a way she was banished from her civilization like Sycorax was from Algiers. Sycorax was, at least by Prospero's account, a wicked witch; Linda, by contrast, is just a miserable shipwrecked Beta, who was completely unable to understand the Indians' strict rules of acceptable social conduct. As a result, she remained an outcast among them: she was not killed, nor chased away, but allowed to live on the margin of the community, despised by all others.[30]

His mother's low social status as well as her different cultural background and sheer physical difference (blond hair, blue eyes, white skin) alienated her son, John, from his immediate community from the moment of his birth. So, rather than a "natural man" living in harmony with his environment, he is a double outcast, since he belongs neither to the native culture (his attempts to integrate into the Indian community are cruelly rebuffed due to his shameful family background) nor to the World State (despite his mother's clumsy attempts to transmit some of her own culture to him, including the ability to read). He becomes fully aware of his difference from his peers when he receives the Complete Shakespeare, which was "lying in one of the chests of the Antelope Kiva ... for hundreds of years" (137). For the illiterate Indians it was apparently a piece of worthless junk. But for John, it is the book of magic, like old Mitsima saying magic over his feathers and his carved sticks and his bits of bone and stone ... but better than Mitsima's magic, because it meant more, because it talked to *him*; talked wonderfully and only half-understandably, a terrible beautiful magic [137].

Shakespeare became his real educator, his Prospero. Shakespeare gave him a wonderful new language to express his rage, misery, or melancholy, and to console himself in his darkest moments. He also gave him ideas about a wonderful world outside the reservation. From Shakespeare's plays, mingled with Linda's fabulous stories about her birthplace, the Savage formulated his personal utopia of the Other Place, where everything is strange and wonderful and infinitely better than in the Reservation. From Shakespeare, he also received a book of magic, which he uses not as literature but as a source of powerful charms that he murmurs to invoke help in the most important moments of his life. When he attempts to kill Popé, the hated lover of his mother, he keeps repeating Hamlet's words ("a man can smile and smile and be a villain"[31]; "Remorseless, treacherous, lecherous, kindless villain"[32]; "When he is drunk asleep, or in his rage/ Or in the incestuous pleasure of his bed"[33]). When he is not allowed to join the other boys in the initiation ceremony and is chased away with stones, he sits down at the edge of a canyon, just a step away from death, and lets the blood from his wound drop down into the abyss: "Drop, drop, drop. Tomorrow and tomorrow and tomorrow..." (142).[34] These are Macbeth's famous words after the death of his wife and shortly before his own. When John is admiring the soma-drugged and sleeping Lenina, he speaks with Troilus's[35] and then with Romeo's[36] words. And of course, when invited to come with Bernard and Lenina to the "Other Place," John expresses his enthusiasm with Miranda's famous utterance.

The brief autobiographical portrait of chapter 8 sketches up a peculiar character. John the Savage grew up as an outcast on an island of natives, a lonely man who equates civilization with a series of magical roles from his sacred book, and, in order to give meaning to his isolation and otherness, he tries to adapt these roles to himself. While doing so, he reminds one simultaneously of the primeval rites of the Native Americans ("these words like drums and singing and magic" [137–38]) and the role-playing of a 19th-century romantic hero. In the character of the Savage, these two seemingly opposing qualities are merged. He is a Caliban devoid of all the characteristically negative features attached to Shakespeare's beast: his physical deformity, his sloth, his lechery and his treachery. Instead, he is filled with the romantically positive qualities of Miranda: beauty, enthusiasm, impeccable morality and straightforward honesty. The result is a true incarnation of a noble savage, a Caliban and a Miranda merged in one personality. He also displays the defects common to both Caliban and Miranda: he never experienced the world beyond his island, so his imagination is bound by his natural environment. Perhaps as a result, he has a distinctly naïve, infantile, immature character, which makes him highly vulnerable to the realities of the "Other Place."

The rest of story of the Savage in *Brave New World* can be read as Huxley's bitter and darkly cynical afterthought to the fate of both Caliban and Miranda in *The Tempest*. Their combined *alter ego*, John the Savage, leaves his island to face his utopia. As all decent utopists would do, he expects to find people there who share his own values and preferences, in short, who are like him. Predictably, he is utterly disappointed. His values are all turned upside down in the Other Place. Physical beauty is a common feature to all people, and therefore it has lost its distinguished place; passions are to be avoided since they are considered dangerous to social stability; the ruling morality is that everyone belongs to everyone else, and therefore love and exclusive partnership are signs of deviance. "Civilization" receives him with the same mixture of curiosity and repulsion as the members of the shipwrecked company wonder at and simultaneously recoil from Caliban. Out of his natural environment, John has no guidelines of behavior, and he resorts to a variety of poses taken from his magical book. He acts a longing but scrupulously chaste Romeo or Ferdinand toward Lenina, dreaming of a heroic deed to prove worthy of her hand, but when she wants to have sex with him without any ceremony, he turns into a mad, raging Lear, ranting about the lechery of women (189–96).[37] What he does not realize is the total inappropriateness of both poses: chivalrous love as well as moral outrage have no meaning in this "brave new world."

Miranda's words surface twice more in John's mind, every time with a more sarcastic overtone. First when he is shown around in a factory full of identical Bokanovsky-groups, the sight of whom makes him sick and retch; the second time when he has just left the hospital ward where his mother died, and in the vestibule of the hospital he is confronted with a large crowd of identical Delta menial workers, queuing for their soma ration. But this second time the words receive a new meaning in John's mind:

> Miranda was proclaiming the possibility of loveliness, the possibility of transforming even the nightmare into something fine and noble. "O brave new world!" It was a challenge, a command [209–10].

Inspired by this understanding, John makes a pathetic attempt to incite revolt among the semi-moron Deltas in the name of freedom, while borrowing poses from Shakespeare again and quoting short passages from *Julius Caesar* and *As You Like It*.

> Do you like being babies? Yes, babies. Mewling and puking ... Don't you want to be free and men? Don't you even understand what manhood and freedom are? ... Very well, then ... I'll *make* you free whether you like it or not [212].

And, confronted with the total incomprehension of the Deltas, he throws their soma tablets out of the window with an angry and desperate gesture. In the resulting riot, he is arrested and taken to the World Controller.

This failed rebellion, which could signal the dramatic climax of the story, is merely a sarcastic, ridiculous episode here. The conditioning of Brave New Worlders makes the concept of freedom meaningless for them, and they do not have any possible motive for revolt since they are perfectly happy with their lot. John has recourse to Shakespeare again and again when looking for models of behavior just like he did at the Reservation, where the knowledge of Shakespeare gave him a sense of superiority over the Indians, a superiority of art over rite. But outside the Reservation-island the charms no longer work, because he has stepped out of the magic circle where art has a moral and emotional validity. In Brave New World art has been overcome by the artificial, and therefore any role he picks from it is totally inappropriate and ridiculous. The most fatal deficiency of the Savage, however, is that he does not understand Shakespeare's art, only parrots his text, as a child recites poems by rote. This way, the language of his master fails miserably; and with it, the education of the Savage proves a failure. He could say with Caliban:

> You taught me language; and my profit on't
> Is, I know how to curse. The red plague rid you
> For learning me your language! [I.2.365–67].

In such a predicament, John has no other choice but to retire to the other part of his soul, the savage man. After the meeting with Mustapha Mond, he leaves civilization and tries to construct a small, private "reservation" for himself in the way he learned from the Indians: his last, desperate attempt to find his personal utopia. Here he attempts to purify himself from what he sees as the contamination of civilization. His earlier childish but amiable behavior has given way to ascetic self-mortification and the aggressiveness of a hunted animal. He no longer speaks Shakespeare, but rages in Zuñi at his recurring visitors from civilization. Eventually, a final encounter with Lenina unleashes his suppressed sexual desires in the form of a murderous rage, flogging her to death and then succumbing to an "orgy of atonement" (254). The next day, faced with what he perceives as a complete moral failure, he escapes into suicide.

The failure of the Savage to come to terms with the discrepancy between the Other Place of his dreams and the reality of Brave New World makes a sad and bitter story, but he can hardly be viewed as a tragic hero. It is a matter of subjective judgment whether that should be considered the novel's artistic merit or its deficiency. One possible interpretation of the Savage's fate is that tragedy has no meaning in Brave New World. There is no worthy cause to sacrifice oneself for, no overwhelming, fatal passions to follow to the end, no wrathful gods to satisfy, and no sympathy or catharsis to be expected from spectators. Besides, children rarely have the stature necessary for a tragic hero. The story of the Savage's lonely childhood probably generates sympathy in readers, but during his bumbling adventures in the World State the Savage remains a distant and comic figure throughout, full of good intentions but completely unable to understand the society around him. His occasional tantrums remind one of a petulant adolescent, evoking little compassion. He is a "salvage and deformed slave,"[38] but his deformity is not physical but mental: an incurable romantic utopianism. His portrait and fate is Huxley's judgment about that deformity, presented by an intrusive author with a cold and wry smile.[39]

## "SUCH STUFF AS DREAMS ARE MADE ON"[40]

Sleeping and dreams are recurring motifs throughout *The Tempest*. Sleep is a common metaphor for a special state of consciousness, when the iron laws of everyday reality lose their grasp on the human mind, something akin to the products of fantasy or the effects of magic. For the passengers of the royal ship as well as for the audience, the entire experience on the island has an enchanted, dream-like quality. This magical attribute of the place is voiced with charming beauty by the oddest character, Caliban, in his famous monologue:

> Be not afeard; the isle is full of noises,
> Sounds and sweet airs, that give delight, and hurt not.
> Sometimes a thousand twangling instruments
> Will hum about mine ears; and sometime voices,

That, if I then had wak'd after long sleep,
Will make me sleep again: and then, in dreaming,
The clouds methought would open, and show riches
Ready to drop upon me; that, when I wak'd,
I cried to dream again [III.2.133–41].[41]

For Caliban, the island is a source of wonderful, mesmerizing dreams, soothing the memories of his daily toil and suffering. On this wondrous island, sleep is routinely used as a tool of magic by Ariel and Prospero. Ariel rescues the ship from the storm while putting the entire crew to sleep, and the sailors remain asleep aboard while the noblemen and Ferdinand are landed on separate parts of the island. Prospero, after telling Miranda (and the audience) their history on the island, casts a sleeping spell on her in order to converse with Ariel. Being asleep in these cases represents a state of safety and blessed unconsciousness.

But sleeping on the island can also be a source of mortal danger. When the rest of the shipwrecked noblemen fall asleep, Antonio drops a hint to Sebastian that the situation presents a unique opportunity to make himself king of Naples. Sebastian pretends not to take the hint, as if Antonio was speaking in his dream:

surely
It is a sleepy language, and thou speak'st
Out of thy sleep. What is it thou didst say?
This is a strange repose, to be asleep
With eyes wide open; standing, speaking, moving,
And yet so fast asleep [II.1.205–10].

But Antonio presses on with his argument, persuading Sebastian that the others' sleep is his great opportunity ("what a sleep were this / For your advancement!" II.1.262–63). Eventually, they are thwarted in their murderous plot by Ariel, who awakens Gonzalo just in time to avert disaster. Caliban also suggests to Stephano and Trinculo that they should murder Prospero in his sleep to become lords of the island. Sleeping and dreaming in these episodes figure as metaphors of death, just like in Prospero's famous monologue when, after cutting short a beautiful spectacle of spirits, he meditates on the transience of the human experience:

We are such stuff
As dreams are made on; and our little life
Is rounded with a sleep [IV.1.156–58].

Despite the ominous plots and murderous intentions, however, nobody is killed or injured during the drama, as if the magical circle of the enchanted island would protect all lives within its boundaries; just like in a dream where many dangers may befall the dreamer, yet they escape without any harm. The characters repeatedly express their doubts whether they are in the real world or in some strange dream; the power of Prospero holds them in captivity but also protects them from danger.

The significance of sleeping and dreaming is no less central to *Brave New World*. Hypnopaedia is employed as an essential method of the postnatal conditioning of artificial humans in the hatcheries, in order to instill the fundamental moral laws in the members of the various castes.

> They stepped over the threshold into the twilight of a shuttered dormitory. Eighty cots stood in a row against the wall. There was a sound of light regular breathing and a continuous murmur, as of very faint voices remotely whispering.... Rosy and relaxed with sleep, eighty little boys and girls lay softly breathing. There was a whisper under every pillow. The DHC halted and, bending over one of the little beds, listened attentively.
> "Elementary Class Consciousness, did you say? Let's have it repeated a little louder by the trumpet." ...
> "Alpha children wear grey. They work much harder than we do, because they're so frightfully clever. I'm really awfully glad I'm a Beta, because I don't work so hard. And then we are much better than the Gammas and Deltas. Gammas are stupid. They all wear green, and Delta children wear khaki. Oh no, I don't want to play with Delta children. And Epsilons are still worse. They're too stupid to be able... [41–42]."

The Director of Hatcheries, who guides students around the Central London Hatchery, triumphantly declares that sleep-teaching is "the greatest moralizing and socializing force of all time" (42), because these incessantly whispered opinions and judgments form the basic guidelines of behavior for all the citizens of the World State.

> "The child's mind *is* these suggestions, and the sum of the suggestions *is* the child's mind. And not the child's mind only. The adult's mind too — all his life long. The mind that judges and desires and decides — made up of these suggestions. But all these suggestions are *our* suggestions!" The Director almost shouted in his triumph. "Suggestions from the State...."
> A noise made him turn round.
> "Oh, Ford!" he said in another tone, "I've gone and woken the children" [43].

The parallel with *The Tempest* is unmistakable: the disembodied voices whispering irresistible commands in the ears of babies to cast an unbreakable spell on their minds for their entire life are nothing more than a rationalized version of the sorcerer's magic. The entire book asks the crucial moral question whether the scientific "magic" performed by the World State is white or dark sorcery. The sleeping children in the hatcheries are apparently safe and protected from all danger — unless one considers the murmuring voices the greatest insidious threat on their independent mind. All through the novel, a number of Brave New Worlders repeat slogans and judgments they unconsciously learned in childhood, without ever realizing that these sentences are not their own thoughts or opinions but simply instructions planted into their minds by their conditioning. This gives readers a disquieting impression of World State citizens as mere automatons, pre-programmed organic androids. One such deeply ingrained command is to turn to the magic drug, soma, whenever they face difficulties, depression, or any kind of negative experience. Soma invariably relaxes people and cheers them up while, when taken in a larger dose, it reliably puts them to sleep. Lenina goes on an "soma holiday" for almost a whole day after the shocking experiences in the Reservation (145), and she tranquilizes herself with soma again after the disappointing date with John at the feelies (173). Bernard also knocks himself out with soma — even though he earlier often mocked Lenina and others for using the stuff— when he suffers public humiliation for failing to bring John to the VIP party he organized (178).

John recalls her mother, Linda, being asleep a lot from the *mescal* brought by his Indian lover, Popé, which was her way of escape, in the absence of soma, from the miserable reality of Malpais (131). The child John once made a feeble attempt on Popé's life while he was drunk and sleeping next to Linda — a clear reference to Caliban's plot to murder Prospero (138–39). Linda, once back in the World State, can only tolerate her own old, bloated, and ugly self among a society of healthy, beautiful, and young-looking people by staying permanently on soma, retiring to a dream world and slowly killing herself in the process. As her doctor explains to John,

> *Soma* may make you lose a few years in time.... But think of the enormous, immeasurable durations it can give you out of time. Every soma-holiday is a bit of what our ancestors used to call eternity [157].

Soma, then, is the universal magic potion of the World State — the stuff to comfort, tranquilize, and anaesthetize anybody at any time, without side effects. Soma is the ultimate escape from the tough side of utopian reality, the ultimate medicine to alleviate any complaints in this perfectly happy society. Soma is the ultimate guarantee that people remain stable, reliable, good citizens; "Christianity without tears — that's what *soma* is," says Mustapha Mond (235). Brave New Worlders are taken good care of; as Mond sums it up,

> The world's stable now. People are happy; they get what they want, and they never want what they can't get. They're well off; they're safe; they're never ill; they're not afraid of death; they're blissfully ignorant of passion and old age; they're plagued with no mothers or fathers; they've got no wives, or children, or lovers to feel strongly about; they're so conditioned that they practically can't help behaving as they ought to behave. And if anything should go wrong, there's *soma* ... that's the price we have to pay for stability [218–19].

The outcome of this social mechanism is a society of children.[42] If the citizens of the World State share any character trait with John the Savage, it is their infantility. They are supervised by Mustapha Mond and the other World Controllers, the benevolent magicians who guarantee their safety and welfare, while making sure that they all develop into standardized, identical, interchangeable individuals fitting well into a standardized society. From their carefully controlled environment, all the undesirable aspects of human existence are excluded. As a result, they slumber through their life in a state of blissful ignorance, a kind of wakeful dream, from which they are normally never shaken, nor do they want to be roused.

So, what began as a satire of the Wellsian Utopia and developed into a pungent criticism of contemporary United States, eventually became a symbolic assessment of utopianism utilizing key motifs of a Shakespearean classic. The most powerful blow of Huxley's anti-utopian pamphlet is amplified through the manifold references to *The Tempest*: that utopia is a dream that can finally be realized as long as human individuals are reduced to manageable, controllable items. The modern magic of science and technology finally enables humanity to enlarge the utopian island to a World State in which they remain safe and happy, everybody "inside ... an invisible bottle" (221), oblivious to what they have lost, or rather, never had: freedom, individuality, love, passion, art, science, religion. The argument staged between Mustapha Mond and John in chapters 16 and 17 is set up in such a lopsided way that the outcome can hardly be in doubt; the formidable intellect of the World Controller can easily brush aside the Savage's half-instinctive, emotional and poetically inspired objections. As several of my students have remarked at classroom discussions, if the measure of any utopia's success is the happiness of its inhabitants, Huxley's Brave New World *is* a well-planned and effectively executed utopia. It is a society of children in a state of peaceful sleep, listening to whispering voices that tell them what they should dream of.

## *The Return of the Great Ones: Arthur C. Clarke and His Cyclical Utopias*

If a science fiction fan in Europe or in the United States were asked to randomly list the greatest authors of their favorite genre, the name of Arthur C. Clarke would probably figure among the top five. Clarke is undoubtedly one of the most famous of all 20th-century science fiction writers, and probably the single best-known British author in a genre that came to be dominated by American writers and publishers.[43] Fellow science fiction author Gregory Benford described him as "the greatest living science fiction writer" (McAleer 385). His worldwide fame largely rests on his contributions to a classic science fiction movie, Stanley Kubrick's *2001: A Space Odyssey* (1968); Clarke developed the script from his own early short story in collaboration with Kubrick, and subsequently published a novelized version of it. The movie was a breakthrough hit: a visual tour-de-force, an art movie that raised philosophical questions about the origin and destiny of humankind while ending on an enigmatic note with the birth of the "Star Child," a new kind of superhuman entity. His participation in the project gave Clarke a name recognition both inside and outside the science fiction genre that was equaled by none except perhaps the incredibly prolific Isaac Asimov (McAleer 224–25). His other novels, stories, and nonfiction (mostly essays on the future of science and technology) confirmed his image as the elder statesman of science fiction until his death in 2008.

Despite his popularity and high reputation among readers and fellow writers alike, he failed to endear himself to the fledging academic science fiction criticism that emerged mostly from the 1970s onward. An extensive search uncovered only a short introduction to his work from 1980 (Rabkin, *Clarke*), two monographs (Hollow and Reid; the latter adorned with the grossly exaggerated title *A Critical Companion*), and one volume of essays devoted exclusively to his art, published in 1977 (Olander and Greenberg). *Science Fiction Studies,* arguably the foremost critical journal on the genre, published merely four essays that focused on Clarke's work (two of which were reprinted with revisions in the essay volume listed above) since its foundation in 1972, and none at all since 1985. Critics have tended to ignore him or make only passing references to his work, often dismissing him as a "typical" hard science fiction writer, strong on scientific extrapolation but weak on characterization and literary style.[44]

What can explain this glaring discrepancy between his popular and critical reputation? In a sense, he may have gone out of fashion by the 1980s. Clarke's most dynamic period was certainly the 1950s, when he published two of his arguably greatest novels, *Childhood's End* (1953) and *The City and the Stars* (1956), as well as several of his classic short stories, such as "The Sentinel" (originally written in 1948), the basis of the story of *Space Odyssey*, "The Nine Billion Names of God" (1953) and "The Star" (1955).[45] In parallel, he wrote several nonfiction volumes on the future of space exploration as well as the wonders of the oceans, as he fell in love with scuba diving (the main reason why he moved permanently to Sri Lanka in 1956). Perhaps his most enduring nonfictional work is a series of essays, originally written for *Playboy* magazine from 1961 on and collected as *Profiles of the Future* (1962), in which he summarized his views of the future prospects of humanity as well as his general philosophy of science. So Clarke was at the height of his powers well before the admission of science fiction into academia as a genre worthy of serious critical attention. After a period of literary hiatus in the 1960s, when he published very little imaginative literature, focusing mostly on popularizing science (even though his most resounding success, *2001: A Space Odyssey,* dates from this period), he returned with several more novels in the 1970s (*Rendezvous with Rama*, 1973; *The Fountains of Paradise* 1979). They collected all the greatest science fiction prizes based on readers' votes, but nonetheless were passed over by fastidious critics as repetitions of familiar themes written in an earlier science fiction idiom that looked increasingly pale when compared to the work of the "New Wave" of science fiction writers (Roberts 297–98).

Critics from inside the science fiction subculture have also found fault with Clarke's work. Sam Moskowitz, in his survey of the masters of the genre in 1966, makes some distinctly reserved comments on Clarke's popularity, attributing it primarily to the fortunate accident that one of his nonfiction works was selected by the Book-of-the-Month Club in 1952. "His 'failings' as a writer are many in the realm of science fiction. For the most part he was not an innovator. As a literary technician he was outclassed by a number of contemporaries. His style, by current standards, was not 'modern'" (390). Moskowitz's strongest charge against Clarke is his stories' lack of originality; he repeatedly points out with apparent relish the sources of his borrowed ideas for each major work. His judgment stands only if one accepts his underlying premise that the primary value of an science fiction story lies in the originality of ideas it exposes, an outdated critical position prevalent among the "first generation" of fans-turned-critics in whose ranks Moskowitz belongs.

In my opinion, such reductive prejudices applied to Clarke as "typical hard science fiction author" or "derivative, unoriginal science fiction writer" tend to misinform the views of most critics both inside and outside the academia. For one thing, I have strong doubts whether Clarke's inclusion in the "hard science fiction" camp is justified on the basis of his most original and powerful work. Although Gary Westfahl makes a distinction between what he calls "microscopic" and "macroscopic hard science fiction" of Clarke, I rather agree with Algys Budrys, who remarks that "Clarke, educated and intelligent, is supposed to be one of the big guns in 'hard' science fiction.... He is in fact the author of a clutch of mystical novels and only one or two 'hard' ones" (quoted in Westfahl). Rabkin also observes, "Hard sf seems to be a stylistic trope for Clarke, rather than the heart of the matter" (McAleer 386). The seemingly incompatible styles of Clarke's writing have been most incisively analyzed by Peter Brigg, who distinguishes between Clarke "the Projector," "the Wit," and "the Mystic." His extrapolative and carefully researched hard science fiction works go under the first heading, while he described the style of the third type of writings as "enigmatic sentimentalism," "communicat[ing] an urgent wish for man to explore the wonders of the universe and reveal its basic being" (35). Brigg emphasizes Clarke's ambition in this mode to go beyond the scientifically grounded extrapolation and reach into the unknown beyond the limits of human knowledge. Such passages are strongly evoking in readers that sense of wonder that is often used to describe the most fundamental experience of reading science fiction. Clarke is able to open up vast vistas of both space and time and successfully drives home the tininess of the scale of human existence and ambitions from the cosmic perspective. Brigg also points out that Clarke's metaphysical speculations produce open-ended and ambiguous plot conclusions, suggesting both hope for an infinite evolutionary potential for humankind as well as a diffuse melancholy over the fact that these future stages of development are beyond the reach or the comprehension of ordinary humans. This speculative interest in the ultimate destiny of mankind reveals the influence of Olaf Stapledon, whose work *Last and First Men* (1930) was one of Clarke's formative experiences in his early teenage years (McAleer 21).

The tenuous critical consensus regards *Childhood's End* as Clarke's most original and artistically satisfying novel. It was singled out by Robert Scholes and Eric Rabkin in their pioneering critical introduction to science fiction as a representative work of the genre on account that "of all utopian science fiction, the most widely respected and enthusiastically read is *Childhood's End*" (217). Edward James illustrated the novel's ongoing popularity by remarking that it typically features on poll charts as "one of the top three of the 'Ten Greatest SF Novels of All Time'" (quoted in Roberts 213). In the essay collection of Olander and Greenberg, no less than three essays center on this novel. The other most often cited and analyzed work, partly on occasion of its popular success and cultural influence, is *2001: A Space Odyssey*. But the rest of Clarke's fictional *oeuvre*, including his voluminous short stories as well as the rest of his twenty-odd novels, receives scant attention.[46]

Clarke's earliest novel, *The City and the Stars,* belongs to these rarely discussed novels, even though it might be called the most representative of all his pieces of fiction, because Clarke reworked it several times during the first two decades of his writing career. "The opening scene flashed mysteriously into my mind, and was pinned down on paper, around 1935" (quoted in McAleer 42), when Clarke was still in grammar school. He recalls the chronology of composing *Against the Fall of Night* in 1978 the following way: "My notebook says that Opus 21 was 'Begun *c* 1937. First draft finished at Colwyn Bay late 1940. Completely rewritten August 1945–January 1946. Typing completed 23 February 1946'" (Clarke, "On Moylan"). Clarke ultimately published this version under the title *Against the Fall of Night* in 1948, having worked on the text intermittently for more than a decade, but he apparently remained dissatisfied with it. After the breakthrough success of *Childhood's End* in 1953, he revised the novel again during a long sea voyage to Australia in 1954–1955 and published it as *The City and the Stars* in 1956 (McAleer 113, 122). He would return to the story one more time late in his career, when Gregory Benford persuaded him to co-author a sequel to the novel, *Beyond the Fall of Night* (1990; McAleer 360).

Opinions are divided over the merits of the novel. The eminent science fiction writer Frederick Pohl considers it Clarke's finest novel (McAleer 43); critic Eric Rabkin also referred to it as "one of his greatest works" (*Clarke* 30). Gary K. Wolfe, while remarking in a slightly apologetic tone that it is "admittedly in many ways a flawed novel" ("Structure and Image in SF" 104), proceeds to a perceptive and insightful analysis of the book.

Edward James believes that in *The City and the Stars* as well as in *Childhood's End*, Clarke expresses "the classic sf objections to utopia.... He describes a classic utopia, and then shows it as fatally flawed" ("Utopias and Anti-Utopias" 221). Moskowitz, faithful to his creed that Clarke is mostly a derivative writer, presents a laundry list of forerunners and influences. He suggests that Clarke took the fundamental idea of an eternal city with sophisticated machinery serving a decadent human population from John W. Campbell's 1934 short story "Twilight," while the elevated poetic style of certain passages "reflect[s] the method of Clark Ashton Smith in capturing a mood but with a shallower rhetorical depth. A bow should also be made here in the direction of Lord Dunsany" (384). The conclusion's vast cosmic vistas are clearly reminiscent of Olaf Stapledon. Moskowitz ultimately dismisses the novel with the final comment, "Clarke essentially changed nothing when he expanded the novel to *The City and the Stars* in 1956" (384). This statement is patently false; while the essence of the plot indeed changed little, the focal image of the whole story, the eternal city of Diaspar, has been fleshed out into one of the memorable utopian visions in the history of science fiction.

That the core idea was long occupying Clarke's imagination is testified by a remark in a short essay published in 1939 on the unexplored opportunities lying open to science fiction:

> few of the really fundamental ideas of fantasy have been properly exploited. Who has ever, in any story, dared to show the true meaning of immortality, with its cessation of progress and evolution, and above all, its inevitable destruction of Youth? ... And who has had the courage to point out that, with sufficient scientific powers, reincarnation is possible? What a story *that* would make! [Clarke, "Reverie" 23].

The passage is revealing in several ways. Clarke makes it clear that the inspiration for the story is derived from what he calls "fantasy"—others may prefer the term "mythology"—and his project consists in giving an science fiction treatment to two of humanity's ancient dreams, immortality and reincarnation. Clarke's definition of immortality is overwhelmingly negative: he is a passionate believer in Wells' evolutionary perspective, which equates the survival of the human species with its capacity to progress and change.[47] His faith in the necessity of "new frontiers" for the development of civilization is stated most succinctly in his essay "Rocket to the Renaissance," in which he writes, "It may well be that this beautiful Earth of ours is no more than a brief resting place between the sea of salt where we were born, and the sea of stars on which we must now venture forth" (*Profiles* 90). Significantly, Clarke does not share Wells' gloomy view of the eventual demise of humanity and all terrestrial life due to the "heat death of the universe," epitomized by the Time Traveler's visit to the Earth "more than thirty million years hence," when he sees a snowy, silent, red beach illuminated by a dying sun with no sign of life except from some greenish vegetation on the rocks (*Time Machine* 74–75). Partly due to the explosive development of astrophysics in the first half of the 20th century, partly under the influence of the more optimistic vistas of Stapledon and J. D. Bernal (whose influence he readily acknowledged on several occasions; cf. *Profiles* 204), Clarke considers the end of the universe such an incomprehensibly distant prospect that should not cause humanity to lose heart or faith in the future. As he put it with characteristic pathos and irony in the concluding essay of *Profiles of the Future,* "Eternity, like Infinity, is a concept which no human mind can really grasp," but scientific evidence does suggest that "our Galaxy is now in the brief springtime of its life ... in a few fleeting billions of years, will the *real* history of the Universe begin" (210).

Aware of the staggering abyss of time ahead, he ventures to stretch out his story's framework of time to an evolutionary scale, following in the footsteps of Stapledon (Hollow 39). In the prologue of *Against the Fall of Night* the narrator casually remarks that spaceships ceased to arrive at Diaspar "half a billion years ago" (4), and at the opening of the story proper, protagonist Alvin is shown the earliest records of Earth's past, when oceans still covered the now desert planet: "His ears were still ringing with the boom of breakers stilled these thousand million years" (5). This nearly unfathomable time gap between our civilization and the "eternal city" of Diaspar may serve several purposes. On the one hand, a thousand million years is enough time for such a drastic climatic change to take place as the one that provides the background to the novel. The vast oceans of Earth dried up completely, making the entire terrestrial flora and fauna extinct and leaving an endless salty and sandy desert behind. In the earlier version of the novel, Diaspar appears immediately in chapter 1 as the last refuge of humanity on an inhospitable planet, the ultimate utopian island in the lifeless wilderness: "the desert lapping round the island that was Diaspar" (5). On the other hand, the enormous gulf of time lends credibility to the miraculous perfection of the technology that keeps Diaspar going. After a billion years of scientific development, readers may be more inclined to accept that Diaspar's inhabitants are surrounded by invisible machines that can be controlled by thought and are able to create anything from furniture and food to reborn (or rather recreated) human individuals. Clarke here offers an illustration to his later dictum that came to be called Clarke's Third Law: "Any sufficiently advanced technology is indistinguishable from magic" (*Profiles* 2), which could be rephrased in such a way that science fiction and fantasy differ merely in the way they justify the miraculous in their plot. The city's inhabitants neither know nor care how exactly the machines that sustain their finite world function, a well-established symptom of cultural decadence in science fiction at least since Wells' *The Time Machine*.

More importantly, the billion-year time gap between empirical reality and fictional reality offers Clarke a chance to focus on the past of the future, a rather rare perspective in such a stubbornly future-oriented genre as science fiction. The entire story is concerned with the re-discovery of the "ancient past" of Diaspar and Earth — how the city ended up as the last human settlement on the planet (a universal but untrue belief, as it turns out) and how Earth became a bleak desert isolated from the universe, which, according to legends, once used to be humanity's backyard. This perspective, which looks back upon a glorious past and seeks to discover the secrets of the ancient great people whose deeds and achievements are shrouded in legend, relates the story to the genre of high fantasy rather than conventional science fiction. This generic relation is confirmed by the opening of *The City and the Stars* (which is completely missing from the *Against the Fall of Night*):

> Like a glowing jewel, the city lay upon the breast of the desert. Once it had known change and alteration, but now Time passed it by. Night and day fled across the desert's face, but in the streets of Diaspar it was always afternoon, and darkness never came.... It had no contact with the outer world; it was a universe itself.
>
> Men had built cities before, but never a city such as this.... Diaspar alone had challenged Eternity, defending itself and all it sheltered against the slow attrition of the ages, the ravages of decay and the corruption of rust.
>
> Since the city was built, the oceans of Earth had passed away and the desert had encompassed all the globe. The last mountains had been ground to dust by the winds.... The city did not care; Earth itself could crumble and Diaspar would still protect the children of its makers, bearing them and their treasures safely down the stream of time [9].

This is hardly the opening of a technological hard science fiction story, a story of scientific extrapolation and meticulous explanation — this is the start of a mythical fantasy tale, placed outside historical time. C.N. Manlove observes that a distinguishing feature of Clarke's art is "the way he can create images that go on resonating through the mind, like struck bells" (143). He also adds the significant remark that this particular talent relates Clarke's best work to "the genre of fantasy with its reliance on archetypal images" (143). His examples are the black monolith in *Space Odyssey,* the huge alien spaceship in *Childhood's End,* and the giant cylinder found in the solar system in *Rendezvous with Rama,* but the city of Diaspar clearly belongs to the list. These images are central to the entire story; the narrative offers a detailed description of them; this leisurely contemplation again reminds Manlove of fantasy stories. The origin and true purpose of these focal images is shrouded in mystery; readers receive only tantalizing glimpses of the entire truth; each uncovered secret reveals larger and more difficult puzzles.

The symbolic power of Diaspar is not merely registered but also examined insightfully by Gary K. Wolfe, who devotes close attention to the iconic significance of "the technological city" (*Iconography of SF* 109) in both a 1977 essay and the follow-up monograph. He argues that science fiction as a genre is rather anti-metropolitan, because the symbolic principles represented by the city — centralization, collectivism, xenophobia, stability, confinement, and artificiality, among others — typically stand in diametric opposition to the core values espoused and expounded by science fiction, such as dispersion, individualism, discovery of the unknown, expansion, and a new harmony with the environment. He comes to the conclusion that, although science fiction is an eminently urban literary genre, the dynamics of its plot conventions support the breaking down of barriers and penetration of the unknown beyond, hence the recurring conceit of the hero escaping from a confining, suffocating urban environment as well as the favorite image of a giant city in ruins (*Iconography of SF* 88–94). This would imply that science fiction is also an essentially anti-utopian genre, since, as Lewis Mumford observed, "The first utopia was the city itself" ("Utopia, the City" 3).

Wolfe interprets Clarke's city as a progeny of early–20th-century visions of automated cities of the future, especially E.M. Forster's dystopian story, "The Machine Stops" (1909), itself a reaction to Wells' dark visions of gigantic and oppressive future mega-cities in "A Story of the Days to Come" and *When the Sleeper Wakes.* Forster, however, eliminates the necessity of human labor in favor of a fully mechanized environment, which works as an alienating influence, and focuses on a misfit whose overwhelming desire is to escape from the subterranean city to the surface. In his wake, science fiction cities become "at once tombs of a dying technological culture and potential wombs that preserve the race for its eventual rebirth into the universe" (*Iconography of SF* 109), an apt description of the eventual function of Diaspar in *The City and the Stars*.

Clarke's narrative in its final form presents Diaspar in deliberately ambiguous terms. While the rather hasty opening chapter in *Against the Fall of Night* is simply labeled "The Prison of Diaspar" (5), *The City and the Stars* uses no less than six chapters to provide a more intricate and balanced view of the city. At first sight, it is a wonderful and glorious achievement of humankind, indeed the ultimate technological utopia. As I have mentioned above, the city's machinery has achieved such perfection in controlling matter that renders Diaspar a place of constant miracles. Individual apartments consist of no perceivable physical space, neither walls or ceiling nor furniture; anything the inhabitants need can be created and abolished at will via telepathic orders to invisible machines. Telecommunication between individuals is also instantaneous and requires no separate device; they can talk to or "visit" one another without leaving their home or lifting a finger. Vehicles are rendered superfluous by the moving walkways that crisscross the city, consisting of partly fluid, partly solid matter, and "peristaltic fields" carry people up and down along tunnels in the vertical direction (32–33). Human relationships are free from traditional constraints; individuals may have a wide range of sexual partners or form lasting bonds with only one person. Since families no longer exist and sex has no reproductive function any more, it has simply become of the countless pastimes by which the inhabitants may entertain themselves. Other such activities include various sports, creative and artistic pursuits ranging from mathematics and philosophy to painting and sculpture, or a joint participation in the Sagas, fictitious adventures in virtual reality that create a perfect sensory illusion, indistinguishable from reality.

> They were not bored, for they had access to everything that had happened in the realms of imagination or reality since the days when the city was built. *To men whose minds were thus constituted,* it was a completely satisfying experience [33, emphasis added].

Nature has been almost completely eliminated from Diaspar; its last vestige is the Park that occupies the very center of the city, surrounded by towering skyline (which makes it vaguely reminiscent of New York's Central Park) as well as a perfectly circular River that flows into itself (25). The patent absurdity of such a waterway only reinforces the dominant feeling of artificiality that the Park is supposed to alleviate by screening out the surrounding architecture with a narrow forest. The geometric cen-

ter of the Park is home to the oldest building in Diaspar, the Tomb of
Yarlan Zey, the legendary creator of the Park and, possibly, of Diaspar (the
classical architecture and the contemplative expression of the "great man"
calls the Lincoln Memorial of Washington D.C. to mind).

The entirely artificial environment of Diaspar supports a thoroughly
artificial kind of humanity. Instead of being born, they emerge fully grown
but with an undeveloped mind from the Hall of Creation, where mysterious machines reproduce them from intricate patterns preserved in the
memory banks of the city.[48] It takes about twenty years to reach mental
maturity and accommodate themselves to living in Diaspar — and after this
"childhood," they regain the memories of their innumerable earlier lives.
Their average life span is well over a thousand years, and they never die;
when they grow tired of material existence, they choose to terminate their
body by retiring into the memory banks again, but before doing that, they
carefully sift through their memories, selecting those worthy of preserva-
tion. Jeserac explains to Alvin that

> at any moment, Alvin, only a hundredth of the citizens of Diaspar live and
> walk in its streets. The vast majority slumber in the memory banks, wait-
> ing for the signal that will call them forth on to the stage of existence once
> again. So we have continuity, yet change — immortality, but not stagna-
> tion [22].

So, the city combines the two communities that were located on the opposite banks of the Nile in ancient Egypt: the town of the living and the
town of the dead. About ten million people have a bodily existence at any
time in Diaspar (14), while a billion other people are stored in the city's
"mind" as a vivid memory of a human person, recalled in a mysteriously
random way to physical being every few millennia. The hidden presence
of hundreds of millions of people who hover in a state of technological
limbo between life and death lends Diaspar a strangely haunted quality.
Sometimes it appears as if the marvelous technology animated the entire
structure of the city rather than its human inhabitants: "Its outward
appearance ... merely hinted at the hidden marvels of technology without
which all these great buildings would be *lifeless sepulchres*" (28, emphasis
added). The striking image of machinery breathing life into a dead city
implicitly suggests that the human inhabitants are not capable of the same
feat. The city gives birth to and devours its own countless children (it is
described as "an artificial womb" [16]), only to return them to existence
in the unspecified future — this fact strengthens the impression of Diaspar as an organic entity, a weird immortal mother figure, as Rabkin pointed

it out, also comparing it to a "pyramidal cocoon" ("Unconscious City" 31). The metaphor is particularly apt, since even the awakened children of the city are unable to exist either physically or mentally outside its boundaries. As part of the thorough-going "reconstruction" of the human body and mind carried out by the legendary ancestors,[49] all the citizens of Diaspar possess a strong in-built feeling of agoraphobia, which renders them unable even to contemplate the desert outside or imagine leaving the city's protective shelter. This psychological barrier makes them captives of the city, and essentially deprives them of any meaningful free will.[50]

At closer inspection, the human society of Diaspar displays striking similarities with the World State of Huxley's *Brave New World*. It is an artificially created and maintained community that relies on technology for its very survival and daily existence. The precarious balance between social stability and individual satisfaction is achieved by modifying the natural properties of the human mind, adapting people to the strictures of their physical and social circumstances. Given the apparently limitless powers of science and technology at their disposal, Diaspar's "founding fathers" did not need to bother with such crude methods as prenatal conditioning and sleep-teaching. They simply created perfected versions of humans, removing such problematic emotions as extreme anger and rage, violence, or any other strong passions, as well as curiosity and adventurousness.[51] Although the resultant society is not as revoltingly vulgar as the World State with its exclusive interest in consumption and mindless entertainment, Diaspar's citizens nonetheless resemble those gentle, placid, and bland characters that populate Arcadian visions of the Golden Age. They carry on an uncomplicated and contented life, never desiring what they cannot get. As a result, they appear slightly less than fully human, featureless nonentities, interchangeable parts in the "single mighty machine" (28) that is Diaspar.

Lacking any significant individuality, the human inhabitants fade in importance compared to Diaspar itself, which unfolds in the first few chapters as a multifarious symbol: an island in a sea of desert, a bulwark against the surrounding wilderness, an ark carrying the last representatives of humanity "safely down the stream of Time" (47), and, as a closed and perfectly self-contained world, it also bears resemblance to another science fiction icon, the spaceship. But besides these convenient parallels, organic metaphors are increasingly associated with Diaspar: "a living organism, and an immortal one" (43), "full of eyes and ears and other more subtle sense organs which kept the city aware of all that was happening within it" (43). The city's fully automatic and self-sustaining technology, which preserves Diaspar's physical appearance down to the last atom as well as its human cargo for eternity, is managed and controlled by the Central Computer, which is the "overmind" of the city with its "all-but-infinite intellect" (66), effectively exercising power in the city instead of its putative government, the Council.

> It was difficult not to think of the Central Computer as a living entity.... Even if it was not alive in the biological sense, it certainly possessed at least as much awareness and self-consciousness as a human being [66].

This superhuman intelligence, which is at the same time the "sum total of all the machines in Diaspar" (66), gives a quasi-human appearance to the city. Rabkin has a distinctly negative view of this entity, describing it as a monstrous parasite: "They [the citizens] have something like immortality at intervals, but she [Diaspar], feeding on them, goes on forever" ("Unconscious City" 32). I think this is a negatively biased interpretation, disregarding the fact that the inhabitants of Diaspar do not feel oppressed or exploited by the city's prodigious machinery rendered at their service. The relationship is described in the novel as a "perfect symbiosis" (46), and that seems to me much closer to the actual state of affairs. And when one of the citizens — Alvin, the main hero of the story — grows dissatisfied with this static symbiosis, the Central Computer first tacitly, then overtly, assists him in breaking down the isolation of Diaspar.

Alvin fulfills the conventional role of the misfit in this utopia. He is soon revealed to be a Unique, "the first child to be born on Earth for at least ten million years" (22), carrying no memories of his earlier lives. Probably as a result, he is different from his fellow citizens, feeling unhappy and discontented in Diaspar. His curiosity for the outer world is not hampered by the irrational fear felt by the others, so he develops a desire for leaving the city and discovering the desert around it. He is aided in his venture by Khedron the Jester, the other odd character in Diaspar, whose role, as he explains, is to add "calculated amounts of disorder" (45) into a far-too-well-ordered society. Khedron is the first figure in the story who permits himself critical remarks about utopia, calling it a "frozen culture, which cannot change outside of narrow limits" (44). He also raises the question whether individuals in Diaspar have any free will at all. Although he is from the same mould as the rest of the population, fearful of the outside world and any substantial change, he decides to help Alvin when he tells Khedron his plan to find an exit from the city. Khedron's motive, besides his curiosity to see where Alvin's stubbornness leads him, is a vague dissatisfaction with his fate in Diaspar:

> Sometimes he felt resentment that the intelligence which had contrived Diaspar with such infinite skill could even now, after all these ages, make him move like a puppet across their stage [58].

So, the description of Diaspar gradually modulates its tone from an almost enthusiastic admiration of the wonders of the city to an explicit criticism of the limitations of human existence within it. Ambiguity creeps into the story when Alvin's otherness is revealed, and his discussions with Khedron and his tutor, Jeserac, expose several mysterious aspects of Diaspar: the purpose of the Uniques (Khedron tells Jeserac that there were fourteen other Uniques in the history of the city, but they all disappeared without a trace), the source of the irrational fear of all others from the outside world, and ultimately, the reason why the remaining humanity retired and closed itself up in Diaspar a billion years ago, abandoning not only the universe but also the rest of Earth.

In other words, Alvin questions the very foundations of the social contract that is the *raison d'être* of Diaspar. The official explanation about the enigmatic Invaders who supposedly pursued humanity back to Earth and allowed them to survive only on condition that they would never return to space, sounds like a scary fairy tale.[52] Alvin, who behaves somewhat like a restless teenager (his age fits but he lacks the appropriate hormonal background due to the lack of physical growth of people in Diaspar), starts out as an instinctive rebel, looking for an exit from utopia simply because he is mentally different, capable of crossing the city's boundaries unlike all the others. He does not know if there is anything worthwhile to discover outside; he simply wants to explore for the sake of the experience. Rabkin sums it up simply: "Alvin needs to be born" ("The Unconscious City" 33). In an allegorical sense, his departure from Diaspar is the beginning of his adulthood, when he questions the received wisdom of the elders about the proper way of life.

Alvin's search eventually uncovers a secret underground transport system accessible from the Tomb of Yarlan Zey, and he embarks on a lonely journey to Lys, the only other human community in existence. Lys proves to be the complementary utopia to Diaspar; it is a rural country rather than a single giant city, consisting of small communities that grow their own food, keep animals, and live in proximity to tamed and charming nature. Although they are familiar with advanced technology, they prefer to avoid excessive reliance on machinery: "The tools and the knowledge were there, but they were used only when it was essential" (104). They still procreate in the traditional way, and therefore their life span is short and they age visibly. Their most peculiar feature is their telepathic ability, which Diaspar's citizens apparently lost except when giving orders to machines.

The emergence of Lys as an alternative utopian community dramatically broadens both the actual and the fictional horizon of the story. So far, readers have seen the society of Diaspar from the inside — alternatively from Alvin's, Jeserac's and Khedron's points of view, with some explanatory comments from the omniscient narrator — and received an ambiguous account of its positive and negative aspects. With Alvin's discovery of Lys, an explicit comparison is invited. Unlike in the case of Diaspar, however, readers do not get an insider's glimpse of how telepathic communication transforms all aspects of human life. Lys is consistently seen through Alvin's eyes, who marvels at its many alien and strange ways, some of which (e.g., the existence of children and animals or the proximity of nature) are obviously used as a ploy by Clarke to drive home the extreme artificiality and barrenness of life in Diaspar. Alvin is most captivated by the sight of children, who disappeared from Diaspar when the Memory Banks were installed ages ago: "Sometimes it seemed to him that they were not human at all, their motives, their logic and even their language were so alien.... And yet, even while they baffled him, they aroused within his heart a feeling he had never known before" (106). As Alvin learns to understand and appreciate Lys, the tremendous technological achievements of Diaspar grow ever so relative in his eyes. His instinctive discontent develops into a conscious critical mentality aided by his knowledge of an alternative way of life.

For readers, the adoption of such a critical mentality toward Diaspar comes much more easily, as the essence of the antithetical relationship between the two communities is obvious: Lys represents the pastoral ideal that historically predates the utopian archetype created by More and harks back on representations of Arcadia in ancient literature (Frye, "Varieties" 125–26; Davis, *Ideal Society* 22–26), in which people live their life in harmony with nature and one another. The inhabitants of Lys continue to have families and children; thanks to their telepathic ability, they are essentially unable to lie or conceal their thoughts and feelings, and therefore they develop very deep affection and loyalty to each other. Their shunning of machine aid in their everyday life (although they are not ignorant about technology[53]) strengthens the community bonds, and their lifestyle evokes deep-seated ancestral memories of the wholesomeness of country life.[54] In an imaginary contest between the two communities with contemporary readers to jury, Lys would probably win hands down, unless the prospect of immortality tilted the scales in favor of Diaspar.

At least one author, Gary K. Wolfe, speculated on the significance of names of the two utopian communities. In Wolfe's interpretation, the name of Lys refers to the Hellenic Elysium, while Diaspar has a Hebraic character, with its name suggesting "the Babylonian exile" (*Iconography of SF* 113). The latter half of his insight remains obscure, since he does not justify his opinion, but probably he refers to the similarity between the name of Diaspar and the word "diaspora,"[55] which was originally applied to the Babylonian exile and dispersion of ancient Jews in the 6th century B.C. (Boadt 384–86). This association offers several interesting insights into the origin and history of Diaspar, since the Babylonian exile is "a huge lacuna in the historical narrative of the Hebrew Bible" (Albertz 3), about which only fragmented glimpses are provided in the text, while the exile is characterized in the books of Kings as the end of history for Israel (Albertz 8–12). Diaspar does represent the end of human history with its eternal and essentially unchangeable world, and the history of Diaspar is similarly shrouded in mystery as the history of the Babylonian exile. The Central Computer, the powerful and omniscient guardian of humanity in Diaspar, was compared by Rabkin to "a clear image of God" (*Clarke* 34). On the flip side, however, contemporary understanding of "diaspora" implies the displacement and scattering of population from its original homeland (modeled on the second diaspora of Jews under the Roman Empire after 70 A.D.). In science fiction, "diaspora" is commonly used as a reference to the outward spread of humanity from Earth to various planets far and wide across the Galaxy. Examined from this angle, the parallel looks rather tenuous, since Diaspar's citizens remained on their home planet and huddled together in a single city rather than scattering. I am inclined to agree with Edward James, who points out the name's anagrammatic reference to "Paradis(e)" ("Utopias and Anti-Utopias" 221). The city of Paradise and the country of Elysium are presented as two radically different approximations to the ideal human community.

Yet Lys does not lack some shortcomings, either. Its inhabitants display an ingrained sense of superiority and a kind of xenophobia toward Diaspar.[56] Their leader, Seranis, offers the following justification to Alvin why he must not return to Diaspar with information on the existence of

Lys: "If the gates were opened, our land would be flooded with the idly curious and the sensation seekers. As it is now, only the best of your people have ever reached us" (98). This could just as well serve as a concise summary of contemporary European immigration policies. Lys shares Diaspar's aversion to the outside world even though they are not born with a psychological inhibition.[57] Alvin, who sought to escape the constrictions of Diaspar, finds himself in another kind of trap in Lys: he must stay or his memory will be telepathically erased before he returns to his home city.

From this point on, the plot follows an almost schematic pattern, described by Wolfe as "a series of ever-widening circles" (*Iconography of SF* 116). Alvin, confronted with a new threat on his sovereign freedom of will, sets out on a second quest with his new friend, Hilvar, to find an escape from that predicament, and incidentally, to uncover the fundamental secrets of humanity's past billion years. He visits the ruins of Shalmirane, the alleged scene of a legendary battle between Earth people and the Invaders who chased them back to their home planet. At Shalmirane, he is confronted with a new mystery: an ancient sentient being that looks like a giant polyp. This being is, in a sense, an organic equivalent of Diaspar: it is immortal because it has recurring life cycles during which its body disintegrates and its cells continue an independent existence in the depth of the dark lake, until they gather and reconstruct the polyp again.[58] The polyp turns out to be the last disciple of a bygone religious prophet called the Master, and it is patiently waiting for the fulfillment of his last prophesy, the return of the "Great Ones." Alvin persuades the polyp, which is undergoing the decomposing period of its life cycle, to lend him its assistant, the ancient robot of the Master. With the robot, Alvin gains a loyal servant and an invaluable link to the distant past. The robot helps him to escape from Lys and, after the Central Computer removes the block on its mental circuits imposed by the Master, the robot retrieves the Master's ancient spaceship from the sand-covered, abandoned port of Diaspar.

Aided with the ship and the robot, Alvin sets out on its farthest and boldest journey of discovery, crossing half of the galaxy to examine the Seven Suns, an apparently artificial constellation in the center of the Milky Way. The change of perspective in the novel is sudden and dramatic; the opposition between Diaspar and Lys, the exclusive concern of the plot so far, shrinks visibly in importance when the spaceship rises high above the Earth and Alvin is able to glimpse both communities from above. Lys looks like a "green island in an ochre sea," "an emerald stain against the rusty desert," while Diaspar "was glittering like a many-coloured jewel" (189). The beautiful image (far from commonplace when the book was written, as colored space photographs of Earth did not become available until the late 1960s) symbolically confirms Alvin's efforts to resolve the antagonism between the two remaining human communities of Earth and reestablish a new synthesis out of this age-old pair of opposites. The rest of the plot is concerned with the larger opposition between the Earth and the universe, the next great unknown penetrated by Alvin. His trip represents a giant leap not only spatially; he dives deeper into history as well, searching for knowledge about the aeons before the foundation of Diaspar and the decline of Earth. In this case, however, he cannot find clear answers, only tantalizing glimpses of ancient mysteries.[59] These enigmas — the other significant addition to the earlier version of the story in *Against the Fall of Night*— are never explained in the story, and they remain marginal to the plot. Their common feature is gigantism: the vast superhuman scale of the white marble column, the mindless sea predator, the alien spaceship and the rectangular corral not only dwarf the visitors but also put their own home civilization as well as their personal ambitions into a unflattering perspective. Like latter-day Gullivers in the abandoned land of giants, Alvin and Hilvar feel overpowered by a sense of awe but also futility.

> Alvin felt a strange weariness come over him. He had seen so much, yet learned so little.... He looked at the stars scattered like dust across the vision screen, and knew that what was left of Time was not enough to explore them all.
> A feeling of loneliness and oppression such as he had never before experienced seemed to overwhelm him. He could understand now the fear of Diaspar for the great spaces of the Universe, the terror that had made his people gather in the little microcosm of their city [216].

In the exact moment when Alvin loses hope, a kind of *deus ex machina* arrives in the form of Vanamonde, a peculiar creature existing as "a pure mentality" (224), who has infinite knowledge of the past but nonetheless possesses an immature, infantile intelligence. Relying on Vanamonde as a source, the telepathic scholars of Lys are able to reconstruct the "true history of the Galaxy." The summary provided by the Lysian Callitrax bears all the marks of a heroic legend. Although he reveals that the Invaders never existed and humanity never ruled the Galaxy, he sketches up an even more outlandish tale on an enormous canvas of time. Humanity's history essentially consisted of two phases. First there was a long period of physical and mental self-perfection after they made contact with superior alien races, leading to a presumably utopian stage of existence ("He [mankind] had banished disease; he could live for ever if he wished, and in mastering telepathy he had bent the most subtle of all powers to his will" [238]) and entry into an interstellar association of races that came down simply as the "Empire." The crowning achievement of the Empire was a huge experiment to create a pure mentality with no bodily existence: "They strove to create a brain whose components were not material, but patterns embossed upon space itself.... It could endure as long as there was an erg of free energy left in the Universe, and no limit could be seen for its powers" (239). This stupendous venture to develop an unprecedented kind of disembodied intelligence free from all the shackles of matter is difficult to understand otherwise than an effort to create a genuine transcendent God. As Callitrax remarks, "This was a conception common among many of Earth's ancient religious faiths, and it seems strange that an idea which had no rational origin should finally become one of the greatest goals of science" (239). The first experiment somehow went astray and produced the Mad Mind that was "either insane or ... implacably hostile to matter" (240); after a long and colossal struggle, it was imprisoned in an artificial Black Sun. The second effort created the good-natured but childish Vanamonde. Thus the Empire succeeded in reestablishing the age-old duality between good and evil, and the eventual perspective of an apocalyptic struggle is forecast when the artificial prison of the Black Sun dies and the Mad Mind is let loose again: "At the end of the Universe, as Time itself was faltering to a stop, Vanamonde and the Mad Mind must meet each other among the corpses of the stars" (254). After setting the stage for this titanic galactic battle, the races of the Empire mysteriously departed from the known world, embarking on an immense journey to find "something very strange and very great, far away around the curve of the Cosmos, at the other extremity of space itself" (241), and leaving behind the conservative remnants of humanity on Earth, who gradually sank into decadence and locked themselves up into the settlements of Diaspar and Lys.

As this brief summary shows, the novel that started out as a high fantasy tale seeking to reveal the secrets of the glorious and mysterious past of humanity's future ends with the discovery of a future history that reads like a mythical legend. The ultimate venture of the combined science of all the intelligent races in the Galaxy has a religious end; and after achieving their goal, they disappear from the world. The teachings of the Master are proven to be quite true in the end: humanity was indeed reduced to the fate of waiting for the return of the ancient, olympian "Great Ones," whose true history and identity fell into oblivion or was deliberately destroyed. Seen from this semi-transcendental historical context, the significance of both Diaspar and Lys dwindles to infinitesimal. What was first presented as a utopian state of existence proves to be a decadent, stagnant stage in the history of humankind, a desperate effort to stave off total extinction.

The cosmology of Clarke's tale combines the linear view of history that characterizes the Judeo-Christian-Islamic tradition with the cyclical view of history predominant in the philosophy of Hinduism and Taoism. While the ultimate end of the universe seems a distant but inevitable fate, brought about by an apocalyptic battle of good and evil forces that reads like a pared-down version of John's Revelations, the more modest history of humanity against this monumental eschatological setting consists of upward and downward cycles, outward into interstellar space and back to the tiny speck of dust that is Earth. On an even smaller scale, life in Diaspar also consists of lengthy and uneven cycles of annihilation and rebirth, reminiscent of the Hinduist concept of reincarnation except the body is always the same and the process is aided by magical machinery. In Diaspar, however, this endless repetitive cycle supports a long-term stasis, the arrest of historical change, forcing individual humans to languish in a sort of limbo, which is anathema to an evolutionary thinker like Clarke. Closing the memory banks and restoring the normal cycle of life and death equals a return to the evolutionary cycle, which makes adaptive change and development possible. The cosmic cycles of human history carry the hope of the eventual redemption of mankind, which is allegorized by Clarke either in the form of an ascent to a higher level of existence (the conclusion of *Childhood's End* or *2001: A Space Odyssey* both provide memorable examples) or a mysterious departure, as in this novel.

Although Clarke himself does not explicitly invite such an interpretation, the ultimate cause of humanity's decline on Earth may be understood as their loss of faith: after the first great cosmic experiment failed and the new God proved to be evil, they did not have the courage to join the second effort and fled headlong back to Earth, where they created Diaspar, a stable but unchanging city gripped by a deep fear of outer space and the obscure menace it harbors.[60] Having no God to rely on, and having lost the departed "Great Ones" too, they replaced a true deity with an artificial one: the all-powerful Central Computer that took care of all citizens from birth to death. From a theological point of view, Diaspar clearly amounts to a heresy, which, as Thomas Molnar argues, is an essential characteristic of all utopias. Putting an end to the reign of this false God and breaking the cycle of eternal reincarnation that chains people to the same form of existence is what the conclusion of Alvin's story holds out as promise.

The end of the book suggests a new beginning, a new upward cycle. Jeserac voluntarily submits himself to a psychological experiment conducted by scientists of Lys and, with the help of a specially constructed Saga, overcomes his mental terror from leaving Diaspar. After the Saga is over, in which Yarlan Zey himself instructs Jeserac, "You are no longer afraid" (247), Jeserac wakes up and finds himself in Lys, which he can admire for the first time. A symbolic first step toward the reunification of the people of Diaspar and Lys has been made. Alvin, chastised and humbled by his discoveries, returns to Diaspar and embraces the city as his real home. His personal journey has been a rite of passage to adulthood: "He had discharged his destiny; now, perhaps, he could begin to live" (249). Although he never found out his own role in the plan of Diaspar's makers with certainty,[61] he is content to look ahead to helping the reintegration of the two communities after aeons of separation as well as the great task of bringing back life to the rest of Earth. "He believed that Diaspar must escape from the prison of the memory banks, and restore again the cycle of life and death.... Sometimes he thought he would give all his achievements if he could hear the cry of a new-born child, and know that it was his own" (250–51). With a symbolic final decision, he renounces the opportunity for further journeys of exploration and sends the spaceship out of the Galaxy to seek contact with the representatives of the departed humans: "They will return, and I hope that by then we will be worthy of them, however great they have become" (253).

So the optimistic conclusion of the book rests on two hopes: the restoration of life on Earth and the second coming of the "Great Ones." The cyclical character of the human saga is reinforced by the closing image of the novel: a simultaneous sunset and sunrise on opposite sides of the Earth, observed by Alvin, Jeserac, and Hilvar from outer space. A limited utopia is destroyed to make way for a renewed search for a more complete, more satisfactory way of existence, a symbolic new journey for humankind, and this headway to the future has been opened up by a cyclical journey into the ancient past. Clarke's ending carries echoes of the *Tao Te Ching*:

> Hold fast to the Way of ancient days
> To guide us through our present world;

To know how things began of old
Is to be grounded in the Way [Laozi 59].

It is hardly by coincidence that Clarke finished the revision of his novel on a long sea voyage from London to Australia, which marked the start of his new life, culminating in a permanent residence in Sri Lanka. His consistent optimism about the ultimate fate of humankind may be based more on sheer hope and blind faith than on scientific extrapolation, for which he is so highly regarded by science fiction fans; but it reflects the fundamental utopian impulse that science fiction has preserved from a venerable literary tradition.

# Conclusion

Krishan Kumar has pronounced the following solemn sentence over utopia:

> Utopia, in the course of this century, has fragmented, both in its form and in its audience. The classic literary utopia, invented by More, has declined: in quality if not in quantity, in relevance and in appeal if not in ingenuity. Utopia can still flourish in social theory ... and utopian social movements — cults, communes, therapeutic missions — have thrived as never before. There has even been an interesting revival of the utopian novel among certain contemporary groups, as among the feminists. But this serves only to underline the weakness of the utopia as a central symbol, capable of evoking a response from society as a whole [*Utopia and Anti-Utopia* 420].

Do we indeed witness a general, lasting — and possibly fatal — decline of utopian genre in the course of the 20th century? In my opinion, the answer cannot be reduced to a simple "Yes" or "No." On the one hand, H.G. Wells' *oeuvre* definitely represents the end of a long era of utopian fiction. His meta-utopian reflections on utopian experiment have foregrounded and exposed an essential quality at the heart of genre: its irrevocable and unbridgeable moral ambiguity. While Kumar claims that a general feeling of ambiguity entered the perception of the genre relatively recently, in the early 20th century, in my analysis of two utopias — the archetypal text of the whole genre and what might be considered the last comprehensive literary reflection on the genre — I have attempted to demonstrate the continuous and structurally necessary presence of this ambiguity. While it is a valid claim that the somber history of the 20th century has contributed greatly to a general skepticism toward any utopian ideas, the public distrust has not changed this essential quality of literary utopias, only brought it to the surface of the public mind.

Perhaps the only major difference between the 20th century and earlier ages is that literary utopias have lost their innocence in the public eye. The emergence, reign and brutality of two totalitarian ideologies, Nazism and Stalinism, have made readers wary of even the most innocuous fantasies that seem to present overarching proposals about how people *should* live. It has become fashionable in the past 50 years to read literary utopias of the past as unconscious demonstrations of the totalitarian ambitions of their authors, each of them a little paper dictator ordering their hapless creatures around with a malicious and self-satisfied smirk. The fictitious social contracts offered by most utopias are also rejected wholesale: historical experiences warn against embracing an overpowering state; the breakup of traditional religious and moral value systems make recipes for universal justice and happiness suspect. Contemporary readers, as a rule, seem to ask more suspicious and skeptical questions than their predecessors. Is it possible to make *everybody* happy in a human community? Can happiness be guaranteed by means of social institutions at all? How could a uniform social rationale incorporate the variety of worldviews, attitudes, preferences, and lifestyles that characterize modern Western societies? These suspicions gave rise to the famous dystopias of the 20th century, which in turn have spawned a huge literary following. The modern dystopias have all sided with individual freedom and diversity as opposed to traditional utopian ideas of stability, order and social harmony, faithfully reflecting the preferences of post-war Western societies. The entertaining and challenging games of past centuries appear in the suspicious eyes of contemporary readers as inhuman social machines, suppressing individual ambitions and aspirations in the name of the "greater social good," as 20th-century totalitarian regimes have done. Perhaps the most famous theoretical representative of this general suspicion is the philosopher Karl Popper, who has traced the seeds of totalitarian ideologies in the oeuvre of the most famous historicist political philosophers, Plato, Hegel, and Marx, in his well-known study, *The Open Society and Its Enemies* (1945).

But the strong skepticism of modern readers does not mean that utopia is dead and least of all that it is superfluous. Popper may well have been right concerning political philosophy, but I am convinced that no literary utopia is guilty of the crime of totalitarianism. Authors of fiction all resemble King Utopus: they are absolute rulers, but their kingdom is a "no-place," and their demise is imbedded in their own fiction. The imaginary community can never be more than a vague suggestion, a miniature model of the huge, sprawling and swarming complexity of existing human societies, being always somewhere else, out of reach for ordinary humans. Its inaccessibility is inevitably symbolic: it is a land to be visited, contemplated, admired and reported about, not a land to dwell in. It is a land of desire, rationalized into a model community with a fictitious social contract, whose creator is the author of the text. As the author has unlimited control over his model, the outcome is by necessity more systematized, more ordered, more uniform than anything existing in either world-1 or world-2. Rough edges are carefully smoothed, antagonistic conflicts of interest and attitudes are miraculously removed, and vexed social problems disappear by one magical stroke. The outcome is a simplified social model whose underlying rationale can be made explicit, and therefore it resembles the rules of a game. Reading a utopia is therefore, as I have argued, playing an intellectual game, in which victory is always declared by the individual reader, and they have every right to declare the author the loser.

Therefore, utopias have not become illegitimate despite the history of the century; nor has the public demand for challenging cognitive estrangements disappeared. What has changed is the starting point of a (post)modern utopian project: what H.G. Wells had to realize as the outcome of his meta-utopian experiment — the ultimate impossibility to construct and fictionally present a global utopian vision — authors coming after him have to face and reckon with from the start. Such fundamental awareness of the precariousness, relativity and fragility of the utopian vision lies at the heart of such novels as Aldous Huxley's *Island* (1962) or Ursula K. Le Guin's *The Dispossessed* (1974). But utopian imagination has not subsided; Brian Attebery has observed of the 20th century, "From H.G. Wells to Samuel Delany, science fiction is full of utopias, dystopias, ambiguous utopias, and 'heterotopias'" (5). While science fiction has no all-encompassing utopia in the traditional mould to offer, it offers numerous utopian fragments in the form of various human communities, usually estranged in space and time. The science fiction transformation of utopia is, beyond the general skepticism of the century, due to two main reasons. On the one hand, the fundamental fictional conventions of science fiction (the acceptance of the contemporary scientific paradigms, including the necessity and value of evolution and development, the pseudo-scientific rationalization of the *novum* and the exclusion of explicitly metaphysical agents) are incompatible with any static society where perfection, however defined, rules. On the other hand, the narrative conventions of the genre demand more elements of romance: dynamic plot, individualized characters, human conflicts, elements that are missing from classic utopias.

One outcome is what Tom Moylan called "critical utopias": texts written in the science fiction convention, presenting an explicitly and simultaneously critical perspective on both world-1 and the utopian alternatives they visualize. But the utopian imagination, defined more broadly, underlies much of science fiction, especially when science fiction authors seek solutions elsewhere than classic authors: instead of putting their faith in superior social institutions and education, they propose fantastic and drastic transformations of human body and mind, resulting in a radically new form of humanity. Such specimens of cognitive estrangement may not be found utopian in perspective by many readers, but the motivation to imagine a better human community is still present, and the readers continue to be challenged by these visions. The multiplication and fragmentation of utopia as well as its dissolution in a wider generic context is an inevitable consequence of both the individualistic moral attitudes and the multiplicity of values and ideals of the contemporary West. But even if utopia as a distinct genre may have declined, science fiction — with its wider scope of themes and motifs, greater variety of narrative models and strategies, and larger potential for moral ambiguity — has in fact replaced utopia in the second half of the 20th century as the literary genre most suited for an imaginative inquiry into the human condition, which in turn means that there is no cause for mourning utopia — it is alive and well since, as Suvin remarks, "For all its adventure, romance, popularization, and wondrousness, SF can finally be written only between the utopian and the anti-utopian horizons" (*Metamorphoses* 61–62).

# Chapter Notes

## Introduction

1. For a detailed explanation of the etymology, see chapter 1.

## Chapter 1

1. *The Oxford English Dictionary,* 2nd edition, Vol. XIX (Oxford: Clarendon, 1989), 370–71.

2. The information of the *OED* is contradicted by the Manuels, who claim, "In the sixteenth and seventeenth centuries, descriptive works that imitated the *Utopia* were called utopias, with a minuscule" (Manuel and Manuel 1). But they do not cite a single source or evidence to justify their statement and do not specify which language they refer to: Latin, English, French or maybe all of them?

3. Or it may be removed in time, but that is a later development of the genre: visions of utopias located in the future first surface in the English tradition in the second half of the 18th century: *The Reign of George VI 1900–1925* (1763), *Anticipation, or The Voyage of an American to England in the Year 1899* (1781) (Sargent, *Bibliography* 12, 13), and temporal displacement became a common device only in the 19th century, shadowing the diffusion of the belief in historical progress and the predictability of the future (Plattel 33).

4. The derivation from the Greek compound is even clearer in the name of the legendary king who supposedly founded Utopia: King Utopus (see chapter 2).

5. At this point, it may be useful to distinguish one more shade of meaning: in italicized form, *Utopia* is the widely used short title of More's book itself, although it is not the title More himself gave to his own work; see chapter 2 for details.

6. The ambiguity of the term is revealed by a six-line poem on Utopia (usually called "Hexastichon"), inserted before the text of *Utopia* itself, ostensibly written by a certain Anemolius. The short, playful poem makes an ironic statement about the purpose of Utopia and makes explicit the two different possible interpretations of the name of the island. Several critics have jumped to the conclusion that the poem is written by More, but there is no conclusive evidence for that, since most of the introductory material is known to have been provided by More's friend Peter Giles. But authorship of the poem aside, the ambiguity is not an invention of subsequent criticism but contained in the original coinage itself.

> *Utopia* priscis dicta, ob infrequentiam,
> Nunc civitatis aemula Platonicae,
> Fortasse victrix, (nam quod illa literis
> Deliniavit, hoc ego una prestiti,)
> viris et opibus optimisque legibus
> *Eutopia* merito sum vocanda nomine
> [More CW4 20, emphasis added].

The best interpretative prose translation is the following: "The ancients called me Utopia or Nowhere because of my isolation. At present, however, I am a rival of Plato's republic, perhaps even a victor over it. The reason is that what he has delineated in words alone I have displayed in men and resources and laws of surpassing excellence. Deservedly ought I to be called by the name of Eutopia or Happy Land" (Ginzburg 3).

7. The combination "Utopia-monger" in definition 3 also carries the same negative overtone.

8. The Manuels claim that the meaning of the term "utopia" began to expand already in the 17th century to "denote general programs and platforms for ideal societies, codes, and institutions that dispensed with the fictional apparatus altogether" (2). But their specific references are only to an English royal physician writing about a "Christian utopia" in 1647 and a vague claim that Milton used the term similarly on one occasion. This seems rather meager evidence to support such an ambitious statement. They contradict themselves when they later state that the first critical consideration of "utopies sociales," as distinct from utopian novels, dates from 1840 (10). Therefore it is far from convincing that their distinction between fictional utopias, which they call "speaking pictures," and nonfictional utopias, which they term "discursive, argumentative utopia" (2), is a contemporary development or their own interpretative reconstruction. They argue that nonfictional utopias became more prominent in the 18th and 19th centuries, when utopian thinkers such as Morelly, Condorcet, Fourier and Owen addressed themselves directly to the reformation of the entire human species, while utopian fiction in the traditional sense continued to flourish. Since their interpretation of the term "utopia" is inclusive rather than exacting, it certainly fits their approach to devote more attention to what they term "nonfictional utopias" and their authors.

Plattel outlines a broadly similar tendency of historical development, supported by a similarly slim body of evidence. He perceives a shift in utopian literature from the 18th century onward: while utopias of the Renaissance are primarily concerned with imagining a Christian paradise on earth, authors of the Enlightenment anticipate the progress of mankind along reasonable lines. This 18th century belief in the ability of science and reason to discover and explain the laws of history spilled over into the 19th, notably in the oeuvre of Hegel, Spencer and Marx. But Plattel discerns one more historical turn in the late 19th century: the steady progress of science and technology enables society to "assume control over its own future.... The future lies open to man as a bundle of many possibilities" (34). He believes that the utopian thinking of this period is characterized by an unprecedented openness to the various potentialities of the future in contrast to the traditional utopian ambition to provide an absolute ideal and anticipate a kind of millennial end of history. His observations are interesting, but his application of "utopia" to the ideas of various philosophers and thinkers is at least lacking in adequate justification.

9. This cultural association between utopia and socialism was so firmly established in common use that Adam Ulam could declare: "Those two words were once thought to be closely associated, if indeed not synonymous. With all due respect to Sir Thomas More's copyright, creation of utopias is a nineteenth-century phenomenon and so is socialism" (116).

10. In Sargent's bibliography, the most comprehensive available, I have found 26 book-length secondary works published before 1900 and classified by the compiler as somehow related to "utopian literature," and out of these, 17 came out after 1880, apparently signifying a rising scholarly and public interest in utopian ideas as the 19th century was drawing to a close. But sheer numbers can be misleading: if one disregards works concerned with one single author (7 out of 26) — Morus, Campanella, Condorcet, Hertzka and, above all, Bellamy — as well as those dealing with the history or the contemporary ideas of Socialism or Communism (another 7 out of 26), which have apparently been taken by Sargent as a loose synonym for "utopianism," only 12 books are left, 5 of which came out before 1880 (Sargent, *Bibliography* 167–97).

11. Cf. I.F. Clarke's discussion of the book, which was a partly a survey of earlier fictional attempt to predict the future, partly an attempt to produce the author's own extrapolation (69–72).

12. Cf. the contemporary reviews of Wells's *A Modern Utopia*: they invariably focused on the institutions and other arrangements in Wells's version of the better world, comparing the book to William Morris's *News from Nowhere* and Plato's *Republic*, but only one reviewer, T. H. Warren, made passing references to the inventive way of presentation and the "most ingenious creation ... the sentimental 'botanist'" (Parrinder, *Critical Heritage* 110–21, 120).

13. Cf. his conclusion after summarizing the social institutions and lifestyle of More's *Utopia*: "To grasp the living reality and spurn the shadow — this is the substance of the Utopian

way of life.... In this Utopia of the New World every man has the opportunity to be a man because no one else has the opportunity to be a monster. Here, too, the chief end of man is that he should grow to the fullest stature of his species" (78).

14. Cf. Kumar's summary of the contemporary influence of the book (*Utopia and Anti-Utopia* 133–36).

15. The shades of difference between these terms is discussed in chapter 4.

16. His concentration on "historical forces" that work toward shattering the existing order has led him to single out Thomas Münzer as a representative early utopian rather than Thomas More, who invented the term and founded the literary genre. For Mannheim, Münzer was a religious revolutionary who gave expression to the ambitions of a large oppressed social group, the poor peasants and artisans. His active political role and his role as a prophet of a social class apparently elevates him above More in Mannheim's esteem, since More has not exhibited any reformist zeal outside his single utopian book (180–81, 190–97).

17. Mannheim's achievement lies in his meticulous theoretical treatment of the progressive nature of the utopian mentality, not in the recognition itself that utopias can have a positive moral value, since that insight had been aphoristically put forward by several earlier authors, most famously by Oscar Wilde in his 1891 essay "The Soul of Man under Socialism": "A map of the world that does not include Utopia is not worth even glancing at, for it leaves out the one country at which Humanity is always landing. And when Humanity lands there, it looks out, and, seeing a better country, sets sail. Progress is the realization of Utopias" (43).

18. Cf. Bloch's comment on meaning of the concept: "der Begriff Utopie sowohl ungemäß verengert, nämlich auf Staatsromane beschränkt wurde, wie vor allem auch, durch die überwiegende Abstraktheit dieser Staatsromane, eben jene abstrakte Spielform erhielt, die erst der Fortschritt des Sozialismus von diesen Utopien zur Wissenschaft weggehoben, aufgehoben hat. Immerhin kam, mit allen Bedenklichkeiten, das *Wort* Utopie, das von Thomas Morus gebildete, wenn auch nicht der philosophisch weit umfangreichere *Begriff* Utopie hier vor.... Ja, Utopisches fällt mit dem Staatsroman so wenig zusammen, daß die ganze Totalität *Philosophie* notwendig wird..., um dem mit Utopie Bezeichneten inhaltlich gerecht zu werden" (13, 14, emphases retained).

19. He makes his theoretical position crystal clear at the outset of his essay: "I propose to confine myself here to a consideration of utopia *as a literary genre*.... I propose that an acknowledgment that utopias are verbal artifacts before they are anything else, and that the source of this concept is a literary genre and its parameters, might be, if not the first and the last, nonetheless a *central* point in today's debate on utopias" (38–39, emphases retained). In his critical analysis of several earlier definitions, he finds a proper emphasis on the literary character of utopias lacking (40–48).

20. Cf. "Der Kommunismus bestimmt sich als Aufhebung der Entfremdung" (qtd. in Ritter, vol. 2, 512 from *Ökonomisch-philosophischen Manuscripten* [1844]).

21. In Brecht's own words: "Einen Vorgang oder Charakter verfremden heißt ... zunächst einfach, dem Vorgang oder dem Charakter das Selbstverständliche, Bekannte, Einleuchtende zu nehmen und über ihnen Staunen und Neugierde zu erzeugen" (qtd. in Ritter, vol. ll, 653). Suvin also remarks that the earliest form of the concept was first proposed by Russian Formalists in the form of Shklovsky's *ostranenie* (6).

22. Suvin's application of the term "fantasy" includes all tales of the supernatural, especially gothic and supernatural horror stories, which may explain his insistence on "horrible helplessness" and "black timelessness" as typical features of fantasy stories. This contradicts the widespread contemporary understanding of "fantasy" as a more restricted and more recent genre that juxtaposes certain elements of myths, legends, religions, folktales, and premodern history to create a static world with pre-industrial technology and the widespread presence of magic and the supernatural. Classic examples of this type of fantasy include Robert E. Howard's *Conan* series in the 1930s, and J.R.R. Tolkien's *Lord of the Rings* trilogy (1954–1955), which in turn gave rise to a whole tradition of "sword and sorcery" fiction. Sometimes this latter type of fantasy is called "high fantasy" or "heroic fantasy" by virtue of their fully developed secondary world, while gothic and horror stories, relying on supernatural intrusions into a realistic contemporary world, are referred to as "low fantasy" (Clute and Nicholls 409).

23. Brecht as a playwright was striving to create a new kind of critical mimesis, in which the audience is encouraged to control their identification with characters and action, to keep their distance from the representation of life on stage. His application of *Verfremdungseffekte* was restricted strictly to formal conventions of the theater, essential elements of the drama — such as

setting, characters, and plot—remained within the bounds of mimesis. Brecht wrote naturalistic plays that were to be estranged from the audience by means of theatrical devices.

24. His normative and, in the final assessment, rather arbitrary distinction between cognitive and non-cognitive fantasy with the transparent purpose to accord a higher value to the cognitive kind calls to mind Marx and Engels's well-known distinction between utopian and scientific socialism, where the adjective "scientific" was meant to impute the same positive value to Marxist socialism as "cognitive" to science fiction (Marx and Engels, section III, chapter 3).

25. Cf. Suvin's identification of the *novum* with what Wells called "fantastic element, the strange property or the strange world, [which] is used only to throw up and intensify our natural reactions of wonder, fear and perplexity" (*Metamorphoses* 208; Parrinder and Philmus 241).

26. Parrinder also notes that Suvin's ideas carry less novelty at closer inspection — the emphasis on cognition is reminiscent on Hugo Gernsback's original definition of science fiction as fiction with a scientific explanation, while the idea of the *novum* was essentially laid down by H. G. Wells as early as 1933 ("Suvin's Poetics" 37).

27. Although this point is not beyond dispute: Kathlyn Hume remarks that several theorists refuse to consider utopias as fantasy, "preferring instead to call them speculative fiction, since they do not violate any laws of physics" (22). Hume herself rejects this idea on the grounds that utopias strive to represent a desire for perfection that is unavailable in our world. But her remark on the controversial relationship between utopia and the fantastic sheds light on an important problem: traditional utopias (by which term I refer to utopias written before the late 19th century, when typical science fiction methods of estrangement—space or time travel—were, as a rule, not yet employed in utopias) tend to have more affinity with mimesis than other fantastic genres.

28. Frye's examples include Swift's *Gulliver's Travels*, Voltaire's *Candide*, Burton's *Anatomy of Melancholy* (from which Frye took the name for the whole genre), Walton's *The Compleat Angler*, Sterne's *Tristram Shandy*, Peacock's *Headlong Hall* and *Nightmare Abbey*, Samuel Butler's *The Way of All Flesh* and *Erewhon*, and Aldous Huxley's *Point Counter Point* and *Brave New World* (308–12).

## *Chapter 2*

1. All subsequent quotes from *Utopia* are taken from More 1989, unless otherwise indicated.

2. "A discourse by the extraordinary Raphael Hythloday, as recorded by the noted Thomas More" (More 1989, 8). Book II has a slightly different subtitle carrying essentially the same meaning (More 1989, 42).

3. Cf. a representative opinion by one of the most authoritative 20th-century critics of More: "Thomas More appears in his *Utopia* and his early non-polemical works as a zealous Catholic *reformer*.... The *Utopia* contains, in a more or less disguised form, his ardent views on public and private morals, war and peace, economic suffering, social inequality, national politics, international intrigue, contemporary education, current philosophy, and formalistic religion" (Surtz, *Praise of Pleasure* 2–3, emphasis retained). All the views listed above by Surtz are expressed in the book by Hythloday, either in the dialogue with More or in the description of Utopia, while More, his opponent in the debate, often argues with him or at least refuses to endorse his opinion.

4. "In 1515 when he wrote Martin van Dorp of the University of Louvain in defense of Erasmus, More mentioned that he had studied for a time in Paris and Louvain in 1508.... He tells Dorp that he was in neither Paris nor Louvain for a long time, but it is hard to say what a 'long time' means." (Marius 51–52). More's next journey abroad was the royal embassy of 1515, which inspired *Utopia*. During the next three years, he was sent on two diplomatic missions to Calais (at that time under English rule), and accompanied Henry VIII and Wolsey to the Netherlands on their negotiations in 1520 and 1521. His later diplomatic journeys took him to France in 1527 and 1529 (Elton 100–102).

5. I call Roper a "partial eye-witness" because he is the only one among More's biographers who knew him intimately, but only during his later years. Roper married More's eldest daughter, Margaret, in 1521 (Chambers 174; Marius xv), and he himself writes at the beginning of his *Life*, "I was continually resident in his house by the space of sixteen years and more," which means that he moved into More's house around 1518 or 1519 (Roper 3). Therefore he witnessed

More's public career and final years, but he had no direct knowledge on his early life; considering that, he may have relied on stories and hints from More, his elder contemporaries, and the oral tradition within the family, which might not always be reliable, especially as Roper was writing more than twenty years after More's death, probably around 1557 (Guy 7; Marius xv).

6. Besides the work of Roper, Cresacre More's other primary sources were Nicholas Harpsfield's *Life and Death of Sir Thomas More*, which was completed in 1558, but remained unpublished until 1932 (probably owing to the succession of Elizabeth and the return of official Protestantism to England), and Thomas Stapleton's Latin *D. Thomae Mori Vita*, published in Douai in 1588, intended for the English Catholic exiles and the international public opinion (Guy 8–11; Kautsky 112–14).

7. The Catholic biography of T.E. Bridgett, *Blessed Thomas More* (1891), and the Socialist interpretation of his life and *Utopia* by Karl Kautsky, *Thomas More und Seine Utopie* (1887).

8. Reynolds 21–22, 52–59, 66–72, 87–95, 105, 112–20, 128–31, 154, 180–81. Erasmus stayed in More's house for some time in July or August 1516 while More was probably working on *Utopia* (Reynolds 116; Hexter 101–2). Afterward, he returned only once more for a brief visit in April 1517 (Reynolds 128). Their last personal meetings occured in June 1520 and in August 1521 in Bruges, where Henry VIII and Cardinal Wolsey, respectively, conducted ceremonious negotiations with Emperor Charles V and Francis I of France: More was in Henry's diplomatic service, while Erasmus accompanied the Emperor as councilor (Reynolds 154, 180–81).

9. "As a young man he took up Greek literature and philosophy — to the distress of his father, an upright man and usually of sound sense; who being himself an authority on English Law, thought fit to check these studies by cutting off all supplies, and, indeed, More was almost disowned, because he seemed to be deserting his father's profession.... Yet, after making trial of the schools, he turned his strong and quick wits to the law with such success that no one's counsel was in greater demand, and no professional lawyer had a better practice" (Allen 5).

10. "To theology, too, he applied his mind with vigour. When still scarcely more than a youth, he gave lectures on Augustine's City of God which were well attended.... At the same time with all his strength he turned toward the religious life, by watching, fasting, prayer, and similar tests, preparing himself for the priesthood.... And he had almost embraced this ministry; but being unable to master the desire for a wife, he decided to be a chaste husband rather than a priest impure" (Allen 5–6).

11. The most famous criticism of Erasmus' statements about the chronology and conditions of More's entry into royal service was put forward by G.R. Elton (87–92). Guy devotes a whole chapter to the discussion of when exactly More was recruited to the King's Council and whether he was really unwilling to accept the position, and he eventually rejects Elton's claims (chapter 3, especially 50–58).

12. "He had resolved to be content with this position [i.e., that of a London City judge in civil cases], which gave him dignity without the more serious risks of public life. But more than once he was constrained to serve on embassies; and his sound conduct of these so delighted King Henry VIII that he could not rest till he had dragged More to Court. *Dragged* is the only word; for no aspirant was ever more eager to go to Court than More was to avoid it" (Allen 7).

13. "There really is no evidence at all that he lived twelve years against the grain [i.e., he served as a royal councilor 12 years despite his will], and he followed Henry's call at so early a date that he cannot have hesitated long. But he did not like to admit all this to Erasmus, so much so that he allowed him to suppose that no decision had been taken even while, as king's councillor, he was negotiating at Calais and expecting Erasmus to visit. More, it would seem, respected Erasmus' known opposition to a scholar's involvement in affairs sufficiently to prevaricate about his own contrary view.... At any rate, in trying to understand More's place in government, we should abandon the conventional talk about his reluctance to enter it. He went with his eyes open; he meant to make a career.... In short, his entry into the Council was a serious matter, not the act of a man pulling face privately at those with whom he worked publicly" (Elton 92).

14. "He had accepted office ... because he had become convinced that the scholar must, if pressed, take his learning and wisdom into the service of princes" (Elton 110).

15. Cf. Chambers' summary of his chapter on the issue: "More's hatred of heresy has its root, not in religious bigotry, but in the fear of sedition, tumult, and civil war characteristic of sixteenth-century statesmen" (270).

16. "Your sheep, ... that commonly are so meek and eat so little; now, as I hear, they have become so greedy and fierce that they devour men themselves. They devastate and depopulate fields, houses and towns" (More 1989, 18–19).

17. Cf. Marx 674, note 193: "'Utopiá'-jában Thomas Morus beszél arról a furcsa országról, ahol a 'juhok felfalják az embereket.'" Cf. also the lengthy quote from the original text on 688–89, note 221.

18. Kautsky 107–30. The only source he cites with approval is Erasmus, whose letter he reproduces fully in German translation.

19. Cf. the opening of section 2: "Es ist nicht unsere Aufgabe, eine eingehende Biographie Mores zu liefern.... Wir haben es hier nur mit dem Kommunisten More zu tun und seiner geistigen Entwicklung ... vor allem der Entwicklung seiner ökonomischen, politischen, religiösen Anschauungen" (131).

20. Cf. section 2, chapter 5, where he claims, without a single piece of evidence, that More's *Utopia* had a huge influence on contemporary English humanists and politicians, including Henry himself: "Daß die 'Utopia' Mores Einfluß in London selbst sehr steigerte, dürfen wir wohl annehmen, wenn wir auch keinen direkten Beweis dafür haben.... die große Wirkung der 'Utopia' auf ihre Zeitgenossen, eine Wirkung, der sich auch Heinrich VIII. nicht entziehen konnte. More hatte mit seiner 'Utopia' ein politisches Programm entworfen, das allgemeinen Beifall errang, er war damit in die erste Reihe der englischen Politiker getreten.... er war ein politischer Faktor geworden, den man gewinnen oder vernichten mußte" (Kautsky 190–91).

21. Cf. the afterword of Tibor Kardos in the Hungarian translation of *Utopia*: "The greatness of More begins when he divines some of the fundamental principles of the scientific socialism of the future, even though he cannot turn it into a closed reasoning, that is into science.... The joy of life in the new society is guaranteed by the fact that nobody possesses any kind of private property, so they are free from the most horrible power that alienates human emotions. The inhabitants of Utopia produce together, consume the common property, labor for them is joy and heroism, culture is a daily pleasure. When More declares that the practical and univeral foundation of the new society he boldly steps into the future" (More 1989, 152, 160–61; my translation from Hungarian).

22. There were 10 editions between 1591 and 1689 in Wittenberg, Frankfurt, Hanover, Cologne and Amsterdam (Gibson 3).

23. It may be interesting to note that this was not the first vernacular version of *Utopia*: the English translation was preceded by a German (1524), an Italian (1548), and a French (1550) version, and was soon followed by a Dutch translation (1553), which virtually guaranteed its dissemination in most major European languages.

24. The italicized passage is written in Greek in the original.

25. This impression is reinforced by Busleyden's comment on his own prefatory letter made in his accompanying letter to Erasmus, in which he described it as a tribute to Erasmus — and by implication not a tribute to More or the book (More CW4, clxxxiv).

26. Erasmus' extant letters prove that he suggested a new edition after the first Louvain edition because he was dissatisfied with its quality, and in March 1517 he repeatedly asked for a corrected copy to use it as a basis for the edition of the new version, although there is no evidence that he ever received one from More. In any case, he sent a corrected copy to Froben in May 1517, which served as the basis for the 1518 Basel editions (Barker 219–20).

27. Cf. his denial of the authorship of the pamphlet on Pope Julius II (Chambers 108).

28. "So he [King Utopus] left the whole matter open, allowing each person to choose what he would believe. The only exception was a positive and strict law against anyone who should sink so far below the dignity of human nature as to think that the soul perishes with the body, or that the universe is ruled by blind chance, not divine providence" (More 1989, 98).

29. Quoted by Chambers without specification of source on 121 and again on 245.

30. Cf. Davis 42–61, Logan, Starnes.

31. Seebohm's study on the Oxford reformers was a pioneering work on the beginnings of English Humanism, and he drew the first detailed picture of More as the junior member of a circle of distinguished Humanists. Kautsky implicitly acknowledged his influence in the description of More's Humanist background (Kautsky 115–16).

32. "More's *Utopia* expresses the various reforming purposes of the statesman, the lawyer, the merchant, the humanist, and the man of religion. These purposes were, of course, intertwined and overlapping as well as distinguishable. The middle class, in its inconsistent and only partly conscious campaign against feudalism, had the merchant as its chief economic power and the humanist as its ideological shock groups — with More active in both groups. The *Utopia*, incorporating many views acceptable to the London merchants, presented a program of social reform, and was, first of all, a humanist tract" (Ames 8).

33. "Was More a Utopian reformer as Lord Chancellor? Were his actions governed by a philosophical impetus towards social justice and the perfection of the commonwealth...? The evidence is inconclusive, but unpersuasive. More was adamant that Wolsey's system of access to 'equal' and 'impartial' justice irrespective of social status should be maintained.... But this was no more than the Lord Chancellor was bound to do by virtue of his oath of office. If equitable jurisdiction is itself to be equated with Utopian reform, then Wolsey was as much a Utopian reformer as More.... The notion that Utopian communism was the solution — 'the only possible solution' — to the catalogue of social evils in the reign of Henry VIII was entirely alien to More's practical outlook in the courts" (Guy 140–41).

34. "If the population throughout the entire island exceeds the quota, they enroll citizens out of every city and plant a colony under their own laws on the mainland near them, wherever the natives have plenty of unoccupied and uncultivated land. Those natives who want to live with the Utopians are taken in.... But those who refuse to live under their laws the Utopians drive out of the land they claim for themselves; and on those who resist them, they declare war. The Utopians say it's perfectly justifiable to make war on people who leave their land idle and waste yet forbid the use and possession of it to others who, by the law of nature, ought to be supported from it" (More 1989, 56). Chambers cites Hermann Oncken and Ernst Tröltsch as proponents of this view (132–34).

35. Cf. Branham, McCutcheon, "Denying the Contrary" and "Cicero's *Paradoxa*," "The Shape of Utopia" in Elliott 25–49.

36. "It is no good looking behind Hythloday's words to concealed or unacknowledged meanings: Hythloday *is* only the words that the words of Thomas More say he speaks.... *Utopia* has the shape and the feel — it has much of the form — of satire.... one must read the *Utopia* with an eye — and an ear — to complexities of the kind one finds in Horace and Alexander Pope, testing the voices of the speakers against the norms of the work, weighing each shift of tone for possible moral implication. The meaning of the work as a whole is a function of the way those voices work with and against each other: a function of the pattern they form" (Elliot 28–32).

37. R.M. Adams, quoted Logan 6.

38. The reference here is to the first four editions of the book in which More may have had a hand, although there is no proof in support of the conjecture that he indirectly contributed to any of the editions: 1516 Louvain, 1517 Paris, and two editions, both in 1518, Basel (More CW4 clxxxiii–cxc; Barker 219–21).

39. As I have mentioned earlier, there is textual evidence for that intention, since More explicitly asked Erasmus to secure such commendatory letters (More 1989, 114).

40. "As often as I read it, I seem to see even more than I heard from the actual words of Raphael Hythloday," although "Hythloday himself showed no mean gifts of expression in setting forth his topic" (124).

41. The translation of this crucial line in More CW4 is the following: "If there is doubt about anything, I shall rather tell an objective falsehood than an intentional lie — for I would rather be honest than wise" (41). The Latin original of this is the following: "nam ut maxime curabo, ne quid sit in libro falsi, ita si quid sit in ambiguo, potius mendacium dicam, quam mentiar, quod malim bonus esse quam prudens." The marginal note remarks: "Nota Theologicam differentiam inter mentiri et mendacium dicere" (More CW4, 40), which is translated as "Distinction between an Intentional Lie and an Objective Falsehood" in More CW4 (41) and "distinction between a deliberate lie and an untruth" in More 1989 (5). The editorial note of More CW4 makes it clear that the distinction is not theological but classical: it comes from *Noctes Atticae* by Aulus Gellius, a popular text among Humanists. According to Gellius, the distinction between "mentiri" (lying) and "mendacium dicere" (telling a falsehood) consists in the speaker's attitude: "One who lies is not himself deceived, but tries to deceive another; he who tells a falsehood is himself deceived.... A good man ... ought to take pains not to lie, a wise man, not to tell what is false" (qtd. in More CW4, 291–92). This distinction between an "honest" man and a "wise" man is reiterated by the last sentence of the passage — as long as it is interpreted as a straightforward statement.

42. As several critics and commentators are careful to emphasize, the original title was much longer and far more informative. The title page of the first edition published in Louvain in 1516 begins as follows: "Libellus vere aureus nec minus salutaris quam festivus de optimo reipublicae statu, deque nove Insula Utopia" (More 1971, 1). Surtz considered the modern brief title misleading since he claimed that the original title clearly identifies "the best state of a commonwealth" as the overarching theme ("Work of Literary Art" cxxv). Starnes drew attention to the fact that

already the title itself establishes a parallel and calls for a comparison with Plato's *Republic* by using the term (3). There is also a long, slightly modified subtitle at the beginning of both Books, which repeats the "best state of the commonwealth" theme but adds the important fact that it is "the discourse of ... Raphael Hythlodaeus, as reported by ... Thomas More" (More CW4, 47, 111).

43. As far as the historical authenticity of these people is concerned, Cuthbert Tunstall was a well-known and influential bishop and politician in Henry VIII's time, and he is named chief commissioner by the royal commission issued in May 1515 which appointed the members of the embassy. Georges de Themsecke is also a historical person, a councilor of Charles, and also provost or dean of several important churches in the Low Countries (including Cassel, which is mentioned by More). Charles often employed him on various diplomatic missions (Surtz, "Utopian Embassy" 278, 284).

44. Most English-language sources agree on the Greek etymology of the name: a compound made up of ὕθλος (*hythlos:* nonsense, stupid or idle talk) and δαίεσθαι (*daiesthai:* to distribute), which is variously translated into English as "nonsense peddler" (More 1989, 5, n.9) or "dispenser of nonsense" (More 1965, 8). The Yale edition quotes the late-17th-century editor of More's *Opera*, G.J. Vossius, who recognized the word δάϊος (*daios:* knowing, cunning) in the name, therefore interpreted the name as "expert in trifles" or "well-learned in nonsense" (More CW4, 301). Starnes interprets the whole name as "the healing (one) of God [i.e., Raphael], knowing nonsense" (24), which he in turn explains as a reference to Socrates. The Hungarian translator of *Utopia*, Tibor Kardos, following the early 20th-century German commentator, H. Brockhaus, uses another meaning of δαίεσθαι (to burn) to interpret the name as "burning babbler" and claims that it refers to the passionate but absurd ideas and argumentation of Hythloday (Morus 1989, 165, n.7). Another meaning of δάϊος is "destructive, hostile," which would lead to the meaning "destructive babbler," a very negative reference to Hythloday's character.

45. Two versions of Vespucci's travels are extant: an undated private letter written to the Medici, which was first published in Latin in 1503, usually referred to as "Epistola" (the original Italian version is lost); and a letter written in Italian dated September 4, 1504, which first appeared in print around 1505 (referred to as "Lettera"), and was translated into Latin and published in the *Cosmographiae Introductio* in 1507 (Vespucci iv–x). It was the latter version, published under various titles, such as *Quattuor Americi Navigationes* or *Mundus Novus,* that became extremely popular in the second decade of the 16th century: people read it pretty much as they had read earlier books of fancy on imaginary lands, since his adventures sounded at least as fantastic, extraordinary and unbelievable. In fact, the authenticity of Vespucci's accounts has been passionately debated by modern scholars, because there are a number of contradictions between the Medici letter and *Mundus Novus,* for example, the former mentions only two voyages, and therefore the authenticity of the first and the fourth voyage in *Mundus Novus* is not universally accepted ("Vespucci" 336–37).

46. "[W]e sailed 260 leagues further on [along the coast of Bahia, present Brazil], till we arrived in a harbour: where we decided to construct a fort, and we did so: and left therein 24 Christian men whom my partner had for us, whom she had collected from the flagship that had been lost: in which port we stayed quite 5 months making the fortress and loading our ships with verzino [dye-wood]: as we were unable to proceed further, because we had not men [enough] and I was deficient of many pieces of shiptackle. All this done, we determined to turn our course towards Portugal...: and we left the 24 men who remained in the fort with provision for six months, and 12 big guns and many other arms, and we pacified all the land's people.... We went, quite 30 men of us, 40 leagues inward: where I saw so many things that I omit to tell them, reserving them for my 4 Giornate. This land lies 18 degrees south of the equinoctial line, and 37 degrees to the west of the longitude of Lisbon, as is demonstrated by our instruments" (Vespucci 44).

47. George B. Parks, in his essay devoted to the geographical authenticity of Hythloday's journey, discusses the possibility of whether Hythloday crossed the equator from the south, since Vespucci's account of his fourth journey (quoted in the previous note) tells that the fort in which his 24 men were left behind (including Hythloday, according to *Utopia*) was 18 degrees south, and Hythloday at the end of his own journey eventually reached Calicut on the northern hemisphere. I think that the southern latitude provided by Vespucci is irrelevant, because More never mentions it in *Utopia*, while he makes it explicit that Utopia is in the southern hemisphere (Hythloday even says that Utopians called them "men-from-beyond-the-equator" [40]) and that during their journey, they were moving away from the equator, into a temperate zone similar but

not identical with our own (11), which — even though More does not refer to any points of the compass — can only mean a southern-southwestern direction. From this point of view it is irrelevant whether the starting point of his journey was a little south of the equator or north of it — the primary significance of the description is that he penetrated a region of the globe where no European traveler had ever visited before. Parks, although using extraneous evidence, such as contemporary maps of the world, which More may or may not have known, also comes to the conclusion that Hythloday was travelling south or southwest, turning north at an unspecified point to eventually reach India (226–31).

48. This insight has been provided by Benedek Péter Tóta, whose generous help I would like to gratefully acknowledge.

49. Classical geographers, who had no direct knowledge of the southern hemisphere, postulated that there should be a temperate zone in the south as well, but the two temperate zones are separated by a hot, infertile and uninhabitable tropical zone (which they probably imagined along the lines of the Sahara). Parks notes that More's description of the tropical zone is based on this classical theory of geographical symmetry rather than contemporary evidence of explorers, since Hythloday claims to have seen deserts, which Vespucci did not mention. But, according to Parks, More also extended the classical theory as he postulated a symmetry of civilization as well as climate (233–36).

50. Starnes (76–77) adds to this classical concept a medieval Christian tradition that held that the Earthly Paradise from which Adam and Eve were expelled was located in the southern hemisphere, and Dante also placed his Mount Purgatory opposite to Jerusalem in the southern hemisphere. From this evidence he goes on to set up an interesting, but in my view rather strained, thesis that Utopia was intended as the mirror image of London in the southern hemisphere just like Mount Purgatory was that of Jerusalem, and the relationship between Utopia and Mount Purgatory was also a parallel to that between London and Jerusalem. Since I am unaware of any reference to Dante in any part of *Utopia*, I think that without textual support Starnes's theory is little more than intelligent conjecture.

51. Joseph Hall: *Mundus alter et idem sive Terra Australis ante hac semper incognita longis itineribus peregrini academici nuperrime lustrata* (1605). His work, perhaps the earliest dystopia, purported to describe the "great southern land" at the antipodes, but it was actually a satirical attack on the Catholic church.

52. Scylla is a twelve-legged, six-headed monster with three rows of teeth in each head, living in a large cave on a huge rock and hunting animals and sailors from the sea, while Lestrygonians are gigantic cannibals who ate one of Ulysses' fellow travelers and destroyed all ships except his own. *Odyssey* XII, 80–99, and X, 100–132.

53. Celaeno is one of the harpies, the frightful and disgusting winged creatures with claws and female heads, who tells Aeneas an ominous prophesy. *Aeneid* III, 210–58.

54. The problem of Hythloday's credibility was first raised and incisively analyzed by Sylvester.

55. It seems reasonable to make a distinction between More as a participant in the debate and the reporter of the conversation on the one hand, and More the author of the text on the other. The underlying irony of the superficially serious text should warn any reader against making an automatic identification between the two *personae*, and during the analysis of Book I "More" will denote the character in the narrative.

56. Cf. the survey of the critical history of Utopia on pages 53–63.

57. Morton was More's benefactor, in whose court the young boy was raised and educated between about 1490 and 1492, and it was probably also Morton who sent him to Oxford (Marius 20–25). This may explain Hythloday's admiring and affectionate portrayal of him.

58. Hythloday even provides a clue to pinpoint the exact date of the episode: "It was not long after the revolt of the Cornishmen against the King had been put down with great slaughter of the poor folk involved" (15). The Cornish rebellion broke out in 1497, and therefore the episode at Morton's dining table must have taken place either in the same year or the year after (More CW4, 313).

59. Greek compound created by More: πολύς (*polys*: much, many, numerous) + λῆρος (*leros*: nonsense, idle talk), meaning roughly "people of much nonsense" (More CW4, 343).

60. His hesitation is expressed at the beginning of the anecdote as well: "I don't know whether it's worthwhile telling what followed, because it was silly, but I'll tell it anyhow, for there no harm in it, and *it bears on our subject*" (26, emphasis added).

61. Such rhetorical exercises constituted a common practice in the legal training of lawyers at the inns of court, where "professional lawyers used to argue hypothetical 'cases' in readings and

moots" (Guy 192). The testimony that led to More's conviction for treason cited More's words
that had been uttered as part of such a hypothetical argument.

62. Cf. Harry Berger's comment: "Morton humors Hythloday as he humors the lawyer,
friar and parasite — a Chaucerian gallery eminently qualified to bring on an attack. He amuses
himself with them, is amused by them, allows them to vent their vanities and theories at his table,
and dismisses them when it is time 'to heare his sueters'" (qtd. in Johnson 57).

63. Cf. Starnes' comment on the multitude of parallels between Hythloday and Socrates
(24–25), and his summary judgment: "More intended his learned readers to see Raphael's position as similar to that of Socrates in the Platonic *Republic*" (24).

64. Perlette in his essay suggests further possible parallels between Hythloday and "More,"
"More" and the friar, "More" and the fool, "More" and Cardinal Morton, and so forth, by which
he illustrates the dialectical nature of the text (240–43). While his explanations are invariably
ingenious, I find some of his arguments a bit preposterous.

65. Diogenes Laertios reports that Plato was invited by the tyrants of Syracuse, Dionysius
I and II, to reform their country and establish the ideal state he had in mind. The experiment
ended with total failure (Starnes 32, n.31).

66. Greek compound created by More: ά- (*a-*: without) + χῶρος / χωρίον (*choros / chorion*:
place, country, land), meaning roughly "people without a country" (More CW4, 358).

67. From the Greek word μάκαρ (*makar*: happy, blessed), meaning "the happy ones."

68. Cf. Surtz, "Literary Art" clxxi.

69. Cf. Greenblatt's brilliant investigation of the relevance of theatrical metaphors in More's
writings: he talks about More's "lifelong fascination with the games people play" (12) and emphasizes that "we keep in our minds the image of More sitting at the table of the great in a peculiar
mood of ambition, ironic amusement, curiosity, and revulsion. It is as if he were watching the
enactment of a fiction, and he is equally struck by the unreality of the whole performance and
by its immense power to impose itself upon the world" (13).

70. According to introductory part of Book I, Hythloday had to cross the uninhabitable
torrid zone of American continent overland in order to reach the "south seas" and those civilizations beyond the equator that are equal in development to Europe. If impenetrable heat as well
as a huge land mass separates Utopia from Europe, how could a European ship in ancient times
be blown so far away from its course and wrecked on Utopian shore? This is yet another remark
that reinforces the doubt that Hythloday has never carried out the journey he is talking about.

71. This ruthless rationality of Utopian games is both symbolized and inverted with a savage irony in the end of Orwell's *Nineteen Eighty-Four*, when the physically and mentally broken
and "corrected" Winston Smith muses over a chess problem and realizes: "'White to play and
mate in two moves.' Winston looked up at the portrait of Big Brother. White always mates, he
thought with a sort of cloudy mysticism. Always, without exception, it is so arranged. In no chess
problem since the beginning of the world has black ever won. Did it not symbolize the eternal,
unvarying triumph of Good over Evil?" (238).

72. Contrary to common misconceptions, freedom of religion does not exist in Utopia,
since two beliefs are expressly forbidden: "that the soul perishes with the body, or that the universe is ruled by blind chance, not divine providence" (98). In other words, they do not tolerate
atheist ideas that deny the existence of an immortal soul and divine intervention into human life.
This is also explained by utilitarian considerations: without a belief in some sort of God, people
might not tolerate the strict regimentation of Utopian life.

73. The 1,760 years mentioned in the text (when subtracted from 1516) give the fictitious
date of the foundation of Utopia as 244 B.C., when Agis IV, whose fate is described in Plutarch's
*Parallel Lives*, became king of Sparta (More CW4, 395–96).

74. The name, properly Αβραξας (*Abraxas*), is an allusion to the heresiarch Basilides, who
postulated 365 heavens, and called the highest heavenly sphere or supreme power Abraxas, since
the value of the Greek letters in the name add up to 365. According to the Yale edition, "More
uses the term, less to designate the island as a heaven on earth, than to indicate its mythical nature,
since it has no more being than the Abraxas of Basilides" (More CW4, 386).

# Chapter 3

1. With the notable exception of Richard Hauer Costa and Robert Bloom, who have made
out a case for some novels written in the 1910s and in the late 1930s, respectively; they have argued

that these novels, such as *Mr. Britling Sees It Through* (1916), *The Undying Fire* (1919), *Brynhild* (1937) and *Apropos of Dolores* (1938), are worthy of reappraisal as significant aesthetic achievements in their own right, even when measured by the strict standards of Henry James. They have failed to generate wider interest in these works (Costa 87–99; "H.G. Wells").

2. Cf. Frye's description of science fiction: "It is ... a mode of romance with a strong inherent tendency to myth" (*Anatomy* 49).

3. Frye does not list him among his gallery of authors producing anatomies; he only refers to him once in the *Anatomy* as the "low mimetic writer" of Tono-Bungay (155).

4. As a guideline, I used Lyman Tower Sargent's bibliography, which lists, besides *The Open Conspiracy*, 13 books of fiction by Wells, four of which are described as dystopian in character (Sargent 54–108). His list is the following: *The Time Machine* (1895), "A Story of the Days to Come" (1899, dystopia), *When the Sleeper Wakes* (1899, dystopia; slightly altered edition in 1910: *The Sleeper Wakes*), *The First Man in the Moon* (1901, dystopia), *The Food of the Gods* (1904), *A Modern Utopia* (1905), *In the Days of the Comet* (1906), *The World Set Free* (1914), *Men Like Gods* (1922), *The Dream* (1924), *The Autocracy of Mr. Parham* (1930, dystopia), *The Shape of Things to Come* (1933), *The Holy Terror* (1939). The list excludes those stories that present an apocalyptic destruction of large segments of contemporary society but do not provide any description of what comes after, such as *The War of the Worlds* (1898) or *The War in the Air* (1908).

5. The word "modern" is derived from Latin "modo," meaning "just now," "very recently" or, combined with future tense, "immediately." From this evolved the late Latin adjective "modernus," which entered French. It became current in the 16th century in contrast to "ancient," which referred to the age and cultural products of Greek and Roman antiquity. Raymond Williams claims that in this comparative sense, "modern" had a predominantly unfavorable connotation until the 19th century: in the eyes of the Renaissance and the Neoclassical period, modernity struggled in vain to achieve the same level of excellence as the ancients. During the 19th century, however, the hitherto ambiguous connotation of the word underwent an opposite development, until it became almost synonymous with "better, improved, more efficient." From this connotation the verb "modernize" is derived, which has been used since the 18th century to describe the improvement of buildings, and also changes made to the language or the adherence to current tendencies in fashion (*Keywords* 174).

6. Subsequently, all numbers in brackets in the text and the footnotes of this chapter refer to the 1994 Everyman edition of *A Modern Utopia*, unless indicated otherwise.

7. In chapter I, the narrator casually lists several of the most famous authors and books of the genre, from Plato's *Republic* and *Laws*, through More's *Utopia*, Campanella's *City of the Sun*, Cabet's *Icaria*, Howells's *Artruria*, Bellamy's *Looking Backward* and Morris's *News from Nowhere* down to Hertzka's *Freeland*, which may serve as an illustration that he is familiar with the generic tradition (7).

8. The narrative frames of the book will be discussed below. The distinction between Wells and the narrator is ironic, since the narrator's description is a satirical and rather unflattering self-portrait: "a whitish plump man, a little under the middle size and age, ... agile in his movements and with a slight tonsorial baldness — a penny might cover it — of the crown. His front is convex. He droops at times like most of us, but for the greater part he bears himself as valiantly as a sparrow.... And his Voice ... is an unattractive tenor that becomes at times aggressive" (3).

9. Cf. Wells's remark in an introduction to his scientific romances written in 1933: "My early, profound and lifelong admiration for Swift, appears again and again in this collection" (Parrinder and Philmus 242). V. S. Pritchett also observes that "in his best narratives Wells goes back to the literary traditions of the early eighteenth century" (34).

10. It was Robert C. Elliott who first called this narrative manner "the subjunctive mood" (114–15) and the term was taken up by David Y. Hughes as well (67); following their example, it has become a widespread term to characterize the narration of *A Modern Utopia*, but nowhere did they ever justify its use. As Géza Kállay pointed out, "subjunctive" as a grammatical category cannot be applied to Wells' narrative since it relies mostly on various forms of the conditional to express the tentativeness of fictionalization. I would like to thank him for this insightful comment.

11. Such a mixture of fiction and essayistic exposition is a generic feature of anatomies or Menippean satires, as emphasized by Frye: "The Menippean satirist, dealing with intellectual themes and attitudes, shows his exuberance in intellectual ways, by piling up an enormous mass or erudition about his themes or in overwhelming his pedantic targets with an avalanche of their own jargon" (*Anatomy* 311).

12. Parrinder cites a similar instance of self-satire from his student days when he drew a sketch of himself surrounded by incomplete manuscripts with grandiose titles such as "Wells design for a New Framework for Society" and "All about God" ("Experiments" 12).

13. For example, "The discussion of the Utopian state of affairs in regard to such property [i.e., property over wife and children] may be better reserved until marriage becomes our topic" (57).

14. In her endnote, she cites Hughes and Huntington, discussed above, as well as Parrinder, whose only brief reference to the botanist is the following: "[He] expresses humanity's recalcitrance in the face of the utopian spirit" (*Shadows* 103).

15. There are occasional jabs at contemporary people and phenomena (e.g., an ironic but nonetheless respectful tribute to William Ernest Henley, a poet and critic who died in 1903, and whose poetry and criticism of the Book of the Samurai is supposed to have been incorporated into the Book itself), including a satirical aside about a certain English writer who was thinking about an organization similar to the *samurai*, but his ideas were "pretty crude in several respects" and "a little vague" (156)—a reference to Wells's earlier predictive nonfiction, *Anticipations* (1901) and *Mankind in the Making* (1903), in which he called for a voluntary association of "New Republicans."

16. Of course, this "reality" is also a fiction but not self-consciously so: the narrator as "author"—as opposed to the narrator as "actor"—is presented as the lecturer introducing readers to an alternative vision to their own familiar world, so by implication he stands as the representative of contemporary reality within the whole fiction.

17. The chapter is essentially a separate essay, forcibly interpolated into the narrative for no apparent reason and following rather clumsily from the previous parts of the text, arguing for the essential equality of races and the stupidity of all racist theories and philosophies. The point driven home is that Modern Utopia should not be imagined as the dominance of white Europeans in the role of the *samurai* over "inferior" races, but as a truly synthetic World State in which people of different races have an equal chance to succeed. Despite its laudable message, it has the most tenuous connection to the rest of the book, not linked to fictional events before or after, except for a brief interlude, supposedly an earlier exchange between the narrator and the botanist, in which the botanist's conventional and unthinking racism is presented as an illustrative point (200–201).

18. Perhaps the best satirical aside is a newspaper placard with the latest headlines they glimpse: "MASSACRE IN ODESSA. DISCOVERY OF HUMAN REMAINS AT CHERTSEY. SHOCKING LYNCHING OUTRAGE IN NEW YORK STATE. GERMAN INTRIGUES GET A SET-BACK. THE BIRTHDAY HONOURS—FULL LIST" (214). Racial hatred, murder stories, imperialist political rivalry and royal awards for the pillars of the establishment—these are the news of the day.

# Chapter 4

1. Hillegas, for instance, consistently calls the anti–Wellsian fictional dystopias of the early 20th century "anti-utopias" (*Future as Nightmare*). Kumar also consistently avoids the use of "dystopia," while he uses "anti-utopia" in a very broad sense, applying it not only to pieces of fiction but also to various documents of political philosophy (*Utopia and Anti-Utopia* 99–104).

2. The impact of Bellamy's book is well demonstrated by Sargent's bibliography, which lists a large number of books, articles and pamphlets written in reaction to it (176, 189, 192, 202–3, 224, 228, 232, 252, 275, 278).

3. "Science fiction is one of the major literary success areas of the second half of the twentieth century" (Aldiss and Wingrove 13); "Science fiction has come to permeate our culture in ways both trivial and/or profound, obvious and/or insidious" (Disch 11). Although these are claims made by practicing science fiction writers, so they are liable to exaggerate the success and cultural impact of science fiction, the substance of their statements are corroborated not only by book sale figures but, for instance, by the spectacular success of Hollywood blockbusters and major network soap operas utilizing science fiction scripts and ideas (Roberts 264–94).

4. Cf. Parrinder, *SF Criticism* 2.

5. With the exception of an early novel, *Paris au XXe siecle* (*Paris in the 20th Century*), written in 1863, in which he made an attempt at picturing a future France, but it was rejected by his publisher and did not see print until 1994; and *Les Cinq millions de la Bégum* (*The Begum's*

*Fortune,* 1879), which is a rather thinly allegorical re-enactment of the Franco-Prussian War of 1870 between two imaginary communities, one French, one German, established on U.S. soil (Roberts 132, 139–40).

6. Wells is universally recognized as an outstanding practitioner of science fiction, whose influence has extended well beyond the English language: "With all his strengths and weaknesses Wells remains the central writer in the tradition of SF" (Suvin, *Metamorphoses* 219); "the greatest science-fiction writer of them all" (Disch 61); "If ... I were pressed to name the greatest novelist to have worked in the science fictional idiom, I would name Herbert George Wells" (Roberts 143); "Wells is the Prospero of all the brave new worlds of the mind, and the Shakespeare of science fiction," declares Brian Aldiss (Aldiss and Wingrove 133). Arthur C. Clarke summarized Wells's significance in an encyclopedia article as follows: "Wells is considered the father of modern SF ... because ... he made ideas the center of his work and originated or definitively adapted most of the ideas that became the subject matter of later writers down to the present, focused his work on the nature and fate of the human species, and established the tone of pessimistic irony that has become traditional with literary SF ever since" (Gunn 499).

7. A non-representative collection of examples includes the Russian Yevgeny Zamyatin's *Mi* (*We*, 1921), the Czech Karel Capek's *Válka s mloky* (*War with the Newts*, 1936), the Hungarian Sándor Szathmáry's *Kazohinia* (1941), the Swede Karin Boye's *Kallocain* (1940), the American Jack London's *The Iron Heel* (1908) and Sinclair Lewis's *It Can't Happen Here* (1935), and Russian-American Vladimir Nabokov's *Bend Sinister* (1947), among several others.

8. For example, *Nineteen Eighty-Four* finished among the top twelve at a nationwide poll in 2005 to find the most popular novel in Hungary, on a par with such popular children's classics as A.A. Milne's *Winnie-the-Pooh* and Antoine de Saint-Exupéry's *The Little Prince*, or such blockbusters as J.K. Rowling's *Harry Potter and the Sorcerer's Stone* (http://www.fn.hu/konyvek/20050611/nagy_konyv_top_12/).

9. Cf. Firchow 21–23. His younger contemporary, C. P. Snow, described him as "the most significant English novelist of his day" (Watt 226) in 1933. Huxley was considered a major contemporary English novelist by Hungarian writers, critics and intellectuals in the 1930s: several of his novels were translated, almost each of his new books was promptly reviewed in literary magazines, and he was placed on an equal level with, or occasionally even above, such famous contemporaries as D.H. Lawrence or Virginia Woolf (Pintér).

10. Cf. Murray 256. A slightly cynical comment made on occasion of the novel's 75th "birthday" suggested that at least part of this steady popularity is due to British and American secondary school literature teachers, whose favorite essay assignment is a comparison between *Brave New World* and *Nineteen Eighty-Four* (Derbyshire).

11. There is hardly any other English author who went so swiftly out of fashion in 20th-century critical appreciations as Huxley. While in the interwar period his fiction and nonfiction were both followed with great interest and often became the subject of heated debates, in 1969, a few years after Huxley's death, the preface of Jerome Meckier's study discusses the prevalent view that Huxley is an outdated representative of the 1920s (*Satire and Structure* 1–3). Late-20th-century surveys of modern English literature tend to simply omit him from their gallery of significant authors. In 1960, David Daiches deleted his chapter on Huxley from the revised version of his classic appreciation of the modern novel (*Satire and Structure* 1). Volume 7 of *The Pelican Guide to English Literature* devotes only a few passing references to him under the general heading of "The Comedy of Ideas," in the company of G. B. Shaw, H. G. Wells, G. K. Chesterton, and George Orwell (Churchill 243). But while Orwell received a separate essay in the following volume 8, Huxley only merited a few unfavorable comparisons with Iris Murdoch in another essay, where the author offers a devastating summary of Huxley's work as "fashionable fiction tempered by a flattering sense of intellectual weight," and, by way of final judgment, offers the following dictum: "In art, cleverness is not enough" (Dawson 214).

12. One biographer listed more than 40 volumes published in Huxley's lifetime, discounting various anthologies and collections; this number includes novels, essay collections, travel accounts, short pamphlets, a biography of his famous grandfather, the Darwinist biologist T. H. Huxley, as well as several volumes of poetry and one comedy (Watts 169–71).

13. Cf. the famous critical remarks made by Orwell and Huxley about the other's dystopia. Orwell argued that Huxley's imaginary society would not last long due to the lack of a distinct ideology of the ruling class, and also the lack of a clearly definable motive to rule: "There is no power hunger, no sadism, no hardness of any kind. Those at the top have no strong motive for staying at the top, and though everyone is happy in a vacuous way, life has become so pointless

that it is difficult to believe that such a society could endure" (Watt 333–34). Huxley, in a private letter to Orwell shortly before the latter's death, in turn questioned whether a dictatorship based on an extreme form of sadism would endure. "I believe that the world's rulers will discover that infant conditioning and narco-hypnosis are more efficient, as instruments of government, than clubs and prisons, and that the lust for power can be just as completely satisfied by suggesting people into loving their servitude as by flogging and kicking them into obedience" (*Letters* 605).

14. Even Ford's book appears briefly in the novel; when the Savage is taken to the World Controller, he finds it in Mustapha Mond's study, "bound in limp black leather-surrogate, and stamped with large golden T's ... MY LIFE AND WORK, BY OUR FORD" (216). In Huxley's parody of Christianity, Ford's book appears as the gospel of Brave New World.

15. Although Huxley consistently denied having read the Russian's novel before writing *Brave New World*, several critics argue for the opposite, based on textual and circumstantial evidence. Cf. Baker 36–45.

16. All subsequent quotes from *The Tempest* refer to the Arden Shakespeare edition, edited by Frank Kermode (6th edition, 22nd reprint, London: Routledge, 1994)

17. With the odd exception of a Hungarian reviewer, Andor Németh, but he considered this aspect a major failure of Huxley's novel, interpreting it as a weakness of his social satire and criticism, since he brings up nothing else to oppose the technocratic nightmare of Brave New World but a bunch of literate quotations of poetry. In my opinion, this is a superficial and mistaken reading of the novel.

18. Cf. Firchow 119; Watts 72; Meckier, *Satire and Structure* 181; Murray 256. Nance discusses the recurring use of the quote in the novel in some detail (77–78).

19. There is evidence that Shakespeare's play was on Huxley's mind around the writing of the novel. One year before the appearance of *Brave New World* (that is, about the same time as he was actually working on the text of the novel) he published an essay in which he predicted the survival of traditional culture and "culture-snobbery" over the gathering forces of stupidity and ignorance (Firchow 129–30). The title of the essay — "Foreheads Villainous Low" — was also taken from *The Tempest*: they are Caliban's words to Stephano and Trinculo, urging them to hurry up with Prospero's murder, or else he is going to turn them "to apes / With foreheads villainous low" (IV.1.248–49). So, despite the late invention of the novel's title, it is far from conjecture to suppose that elements of *The Tempest* were present and working in Huxley's imagination while writing *Brave New World*.

20. *The Tempest*, I.2.171.

21. A remark by a member of the shipwrecked company reveals that the ship was sailing back to Italy from the wedding of the king of Tunis and the daughter of the king of Naples (II.1.67–68.). On the basis of this, the island can be looked for among the many tiny islets located around Sicily. Cf. Vaughan 32.

22. Cf., for instance, the ingenious and powerful allegorical reading by G. Wilson Knight, who identifies Ariel with Shakespeare's art in action, and Caliban with the world of creation, physical reality (Knight, especially 204–12 and 220–23). Cf. also Kermode's commentary on Knight and allegorical approaches in general (lxxxi–lxxxv). Frye's comment is also worth noting: "In *The Tempest* the play and the play within the play have become the same thing: we're looking simultaneously at two plays, Shakespeare's and the dramatic structure being worked out by Prospero" ("The Tempest" 172).

23. Critics have traced this passage back to Montaigne's famous essay "Des Cannibales" ("Of Cannibals"), which happens to be the earliest influential treatment of the "noble savage" in European literature, inspiring both Shakespeare in *The Tempest* and authors of the French Enlightenment like Voltaire and Rousseau (Kermode xxxiv–xxvi).

24. One might even wonder why he wants to return to Milan at all. To find a suitable husband for Miranda? To deprive his villainous brother of his usurped throne and restore the moral order? To free his native Milan from Neapolitan dominance? To return to human society and enjoy the company and respect of fellow human beings again? All of these motives can be considered, but none seems really convincing. To take revenge on those who plotted against him looks like a more plausible ambition, and there are signs in the play that his original intentions were less magnanimous than the eventual outcome. But after some gentle prodding from Ariel, he declares, "With my nobler reason 'gainst my fury/ Do I take part: the rarer action is/ In virtue than in vengeance" (V.1.26–28). So he forgives Alonso, Antonio, and Sebastian, and at the end of the play he makes preparations to return to Naples — and then to Milan — with them. But his

brother's obstinate and ominous silence suggests that he is not prepared to accept Prospero's return and his fall from power without resistance. So, the apparent harmony of the play's conclusion hides a considerable degree of uncertainty about Prospero's return to human society.

25.  Cf. Géher about Prospero: "Something is not quite right about Prospero. (He is magnanimous, yes — and still he is not a great soul. He has outbursts of a sort of petty and nervous annoyance, and he seems to be disturbed by an inferiority complex, which he compulsively offsets with an air of unpleasant, chilly superiority.) ... Although he is performing white magic, Prospero's mantle is black. He is a dark figure, like Hamlet." (373–74, my translation from Hungarian). Frye is more categorical: "In this play too our feelings about Prospero may vary: sometimes we may think of him as a human providence or guardian angel, sometimes as a snoopy and overbearing bully" ("The Tempest" 172).

26.  Cf. the Savage's "allergic reaction," although artificially induced, after his meeting with Mond: "'Did you eat something that didn't agree with you?' asked Bernard. The Savage nodded. 'I ate civilisation.... It poisoned me; I was defiled'" (238).

27.  *The Tempest*, IV.1.188–89

28.  The only indication in this direction is the lesson visited by the Savage at Eton, where the students are shown a film about a religious ceremony of the Native Americans, which makes both students and teachers laugh violently. Even here, "savages" are not the object of study but a strange and funny curiosity.

29.  Similar large-scale social experiments did take place, as the Mustapha Mond reveals, on Cyprus and Ireland (221–22).

30.  At one point she is referred to as a "she-dog" (141), reminiscent of Prospero's animal epithet for Sycorax: "blue-ey'd hag" (I.2.269).

31.  137; *Hamlet* I.5.108, with minor errors.

32.  137; *Hamlet*, II.2.590.

33.  138; *Hamlet*, III.3.89–90, with minor errors. Actually, it is an interesting question why the Savage commits several errors while quoting Shakespeare: does Huxley mean to suggest that the Savage's memory is imperfect, or is it Huxley himself who quotes imprecisely from memory?

34.  *Macbeth*, V.6.19.

35.  "Her eyes, her hair, her cheek, her gait, her voice;
Handlest in thy discourse, O! that her hand,
In whose comparison all whites are ink
Writing their own reproach; to whose soft seizure
The cygnet's down is harsh" (148; *Troilus and Cressida*, I.1.56–60).

36.  "On the white wonder of dear Juliet's hand, may seize
And steal immortal blessing from her lips,
Who, even in pure and vestal modesty,
Still blush, as thinking their won kisses sin" (148; *Romeo and Juliet*, III.3.36–39, with an error in line 36).

37.  "The fitchew nor the soiled horse goes to't with a more riotous appetite. Down from the waist they are Centaurs, though women all above. But to the girdle do the gods inherit. Beneath is all the fiends.' There's hell, there's darkness, there is the sulphurous pit, burning, scalding, stench, consumption; fie, fie, fie, pah, pah!" (195; *King Lear*, IV.6.122–29, with a minor error).

38.  The Dramatis Personae of *The Tempest*.

39.  In fairness to Huxley, it should be pointed out that later he rather regretted the fictional fate of the Savage. In a 1946 introduction to the novel, he wrote, "If I were now to rewrite the book, I would offer the Savage a third alternative. Between the utopian and the primitive horns of his dilemma would lie the possibility of sanity" (*Brave New World* 9).

40.  *The Tempest*, IV.1.156–57.

41.  A portion of Caliban's famous words are quoted in *Brave New World* by Mustapha Mond when John praises the music in the air as one of the few advantages of civilization. John reacts with surprise: "'I thought nobody knew about that book here, in England.' 'Almost nobody. I'm one of the very few. It's prohibited, you see'" (217).

42.  This is exactly what John shouts at the Deltas when he wants to incite them to rebellion; see p. 165.

43.  Arthur is ... the most read science fiction writer in the world, and his British agent has the numbers to prove it," said Gregory Benford in 1989 (McAleer 385).

44. Cf. such comments like "More than any other SF author, Clarke has been faithful to a boyhood vision of science as saviour of mankind.... His literary abilities are traditional, and his prose is often workaday" (Aldiss and Wingrove 249); or "[His first two novels] suffer from the rather wooden prose which ACC later fashioned into a more flexible instrument, though he was never able to escape an occasional stiffness in his writing. They are, in effect, works of optimistic propaganda for science, with human problems rather mechanically worked out against a background of scientific discovery" (Nicholls 229).

45. Clarke himself listed these three stories among his top five, along with "Dog Star" (1962) and "Transit of Earth" (1971), his personal favorite (McAleer 107).

46. A rare exception is Robin Anne Reid, who — probably to redress the imbalance in the critical literature noted above — decides to neglect all of Clarke's work published before the 1970s and devote her attention exclusively to his late novels published after his decision to return to fiction writing. She claims that "his later work shows development of the themes that were important in his earlier work, and some interesting developments in style and characterization as well" (27). Apparently, she has been unable to convince the critical community of the wisdom of her choice; the review in *Science Fiction Studies* sums it up as "a high school crib" and deplores the title "Critical Companion" when it willfully leaves out the earlier and more influential half of Clarke's fiction (Ruddick, "Crib Notes").

47. John Hollow considers Wellsian influence on Clarke so fundamental that he launches his investigation of Clarke's *oeuvre* by declaring that "appreciation of Clarke's stories and novels might well begin by seeing them as having appeared, as do the stars at evening, against the dark background of the far future anticipated by Wells' best-known scientific romances" (2).

48. As Alvin's tutor, Jeserac, describes his own future: "Nothing will be left of Jeserac but a galaxy of electrons frozen in the heart of a crystal" (21). The boldness of Clarke's vision may be better appreciated if one is reminded that electronic data storage was in its infancy at the time the novel was written. This is also a significant revision compared to *Against the Fall of Night*, where the longevity of Diaspar's population is not explained.

49. Some of these changes to the "original primitive form" of the human body are described, such as the disappearance of the navel, nails, teeth, and all bodily hair except on the head, while the male sexual organ "was more neatly packaged when not required" via "internal stowage" (26). A skeptical reader may wonder how exactly the inhabitants of Diaspar cope with such everyday functions as chewing their food or urinating.

50. This feature of Diaspar links it to More's *Utopia*, where the citizens' rights to leave the island or even their own hometown are severely curtailed, albeit not by psychological means (More 1989, 60). Also reminiscent of More is the obscure, half-mythical origins of the city; the "legendary ancestors" arranged all aspects of life in Diaspar, casting it into an unbreakable mould, like King Utopus on the island of Utopia.

51. The novel carefully avoids any specifics about how these changes are brought about; Gregory Benford remarks that Clarke wrote the first version before the discovery of DNA, and "biology really had been left out of the entire story" (McAleer 360). Clarke admitted that he deliberately neglected biological aspects because "he'd never known anything about biology and was interested in the metaphor machines" (McAleer 360).

52. In fact, Rabkin identifies several traditional fairy tale motifs in the novel's plot (*Clarke* 30–34).

53. Rabkin, in his desire to formalize and sharpen the opposition between Diaspar and Lys, makes a blatantly false assertion about Lys: "Unlike the people of Diaspar, those of Lys still reproduce sexually; unlike the people of Lys, those of Diaspar still exercise their minds. Obviously a union is needed" ("Unconscious City" 33). Rabkin here confuses technology with science; the people of Lys, while they do not rely on advanced technology in their everyday life, are presented in the text as possessing a superior scientific knowledge to the citizens of Diaspar exactly because it is them who still exercise their minds, not only in telepathic communication, but also in various scientific projects, for instance in their long struggle to protect Lys from the encroaches of the desert and preserve its water resources (96).

54. Clarke reveals in his foreword to the 1968 edition of the novel that it was partly inspired by the contrasts he experienced when he moved from his rural Somerset homeland to London.

55. The Greek word (in noun and verb form) appears in the Septuagint in Deuteronomy 28:25 and 28:64 as well as in Jeremiah 15:7 as a prophetic threat to Jews who deviate from the Law. This link between the name of Diaspar and "diaspora" was suggested by Vera Benczik in a personal conversation. She also suggested another association, the word "despair," which may be

understood as the motivation behind creating an eternal city to defy the threat of total extinction. I would like to thank her for these two ideas.

56. When Alvin returns to Lys for the second time, he makes an attempt to persuade the Assembly of their leaders about the values and beauty of Diaspar (184). This eulogy of Diaspar, very similar in tone to the opening description of the city quoted above, carries a good deal of irony, coming from the mouth of the very person who was so discontented with his life in the city that he sought and found a way to escape from it.

57. Wolfe remarks, "Clarke's explanation of the stasis of Lys is less satisfactory than his account of Diaspar, since the Lysians know of Diaspar and do not have to contend with the problem of immortality" (*Iconography of SF* 113). I would add that Lys is supposed to be a spontaneously evolved society, unlike Diaspar, which makes it hard to understand how they lost human curiosity and adventurousness, which was almost certainly bred out of the citizens of Diaspar. Fear of the legendary Invaders seems somewhat meager an explanation for this extreme caution.

58. The parallel between the polyp and Diaspar is reinforced in the narrative when the polyp's disintegrated stage reminds Alvin of "the manner in which the inhabitants of Diaspar spent their quiescent millennia in the city's memory banks" (134). The polyp is seen as a victim of its biology: "Because of its immortality, it could not change, but was forced to repeat eternally the same invariant pattern" (134).

59. Examining the planets around the Central Sun, they encounter an enormous white column in the middle of a huge amphitheater on a completely deserted planet, erected in memory of the Master ages before; another planet covered in thick green vegetation where nature "has run amok" (204) and where a giant sea creature tries to swallow the spaceship (an episode that may have inspired a similar story twist in *The Empire Strikes Back*); a large number of artificial white domes on a third planet as well as the wreckage of a huge spaceship next to one of them; and a immense corral on a fourth one, built to contain a colossal creature that nonetheless escaped.

60. As Callitrax says, "Since it [Earth] had always been drained of its most adventurous spirits, our planet had inevitably become highly conservative, and in the end it opposed the scientists who created Vanamonde. Certainly it played no part at all in the final act" (241).

61. The story suggests two alternative solutions: either the Uniques were created in a deliberate effort of the "founding fathers" to periodically seek a way out of the eternal cycle of existence in Diaspar, or they functioned as a subversive tool in the hands of a minority group of dissenters who opposed the idea of a permanent arrest on the future development of the city. The saga that removes Jeserac's ingrained fear of the outer world supports the second version, but its creator, the psychologist Gerane, admits that the words he put into the mouth of Yarlan Zey are a convenient historical fiction even though they are "consistent with all the we know about Yarlan Zey and the origins of Diaspar" (248).

# Bibliography

## Primary Sources

Adams, Douglas. *The Hitchhiker's Guide to the Galaxy.* New York: Wings Books, 1989 [1979].

Ballard, J. G. *The Drowned World.* SF Masterworks Series. London: Gollancz, 1999 [1962].

Bellamy, Edward. *Looking Backward 2000–1887.* New York: Signet Classic, 2000 [1888].

Bradbury, Ray. *Fahrenheit 451.* New York: Ballantine, 1991 [1953].

Butler, Samuel. *Erewhon.* Ed. Peter Mudford. London: Penguin, 1985 [1872].

Clarke, Arthur C. *2001: A Space Odyssey.* London: Arrow Books, 1968.

_____. *Against the Fall of Night.* New York: ibooks, 2005 [1948].

_____. *Childhood's End.* New York: Del Rey, 2001 [1953].

_____. *The City and the Stars.* London: VGSF, 1993 [1956].

_____. *The Fountains of Paradise.* SF Masterworks Series. London: Gollancz, 2001 [1979].

_____. "On Moylan on *The City and the Stars.*" *Science Fiction Studies* 14, vol. 5, part 1 (March 1978). Available at http://www.depauw.edu/sfs/backissues/14/notes.html (accessed March 27, 2009).

_____. *Profiles of the Future: An Inquiry into the Limits of the Possible.* London: Indigo, 2000 [1962].

_____. *Rendezvous with Rama.* New York: Harcourt Brace Jovanovich, 1973.

_____. "Reverie." *The Collected Short Stories.* London: Gollancz, 2001 [1939], 22–23.

Delany, Samuel R. *Triton.* New York: Bantam, 1983 [1976].

Dick, Philip K. *Do Androids Dream of Electric Sheep?* London: HarperCollins, 1993 [1968].

_____. *The Man in the High Castle.* London: Penguin, 2001 [1962].

Forster, E.M. "The Machine Stops." 1909. In Douglas R. Barnes and R.F. Egford (eds.). Twentieth Century Short Stories. Cheltenham: Nelson Thornes, 2001.

Huxley, Aldous. *Brave New World.* London: Grafton, 1977 [1932].

_____. *Brave New World Revisited.* London: Grafton, 1983 [1959].

_____. *Island.* London: Grafton, 1976 [1962].

_____. *Letters of Aldous Huxley.* Edited by Grover Smith. London: Chatto & Windus, 1969.

Le Guin, Ursula K. *The Dispossessed.* SF Masterworks Series. London: Gollancz, 2001 [1974].

Miller, Walter M. *A Canticle for Leibowitz.* New York: Bantam, 1997 [1959].

More, Thomas. *The Complete Works of St. Thomas More: Volume 4, Utopia.* Edited by S.J. Edward Surtz and J. H. Hexter. New Haven: Yale University Press, 1965.

_____. *Utopia.* Translated by Ralph Robinson. Edited with an introduction by Maurice Adams. London and Felling-on-Tyne: Walter Scott Publishing 1890 [1556], 65–200.

_____. *Utopia.* Translated by Paul Turner. Harmondsworth: Penguin, 1965.

_____. *Utopia.* Facsimile of the 1516 Louvain edition. Menston, Yorkshire: Scolar Press, 1971.

_____. *Utopia.* Norton Critical Edition. Translated and edited Robert M. Adams. New York: Norton, 1975.

_____. *Utopia.* Translated by Robert M. Adams. Edited by George M. Logan and Robert M. Adams. Cambridge: Cambridge University Press, 1989.

Morris, William. *News from Nowhere*. Edited by Krishan Kumar. Cambridge: Cambridge University Press, 1995 [1890].
Morus, Tamás. *Utópia*. Translated with an afterword and notes by Tibor Kardos. Budapest: Európa, 1989.
Orwell, George. *Nineteen Eighty-four*. Signet Classics, The New American Library. New York: Harcourt, Brace, 1961 [1949].
_____. "Wells, Hitler and the World State." *The Penguin Essays of George Orwell*. London: Penguin, 1984 [1941], 194–99.
Piercy, Marge. *Woman on the Edge of Time*. New York: Fawcett Books, 1995 [1976].
Pohl, Frederik, and Cyril M. Kornbluth. *The Space Merchants*. New York: Ballantine, 1983 [1953].
Russ, Joanna. *The Female Man*. Boston: Beacon Press, 1986 [1974].
Sheckley, Robert. "A Ticket to Tranai." *Citizen in Space*. New York: Ballantine, 1955, 108–47.
Skinner, B. F. *Walden Two*. Indianapolis: Hackett, 2005 [1948].
Stapledon, Olaf. *Last and First Men*. London: Penguin, 1937 [1930].
Swift, Jonathan. *Gulliver's Travels*. Edited by Peter Dixon and John Chalker. London: Penguin, 1985 [1726].
Verne, Jules. *From the Earth to the Moon*. New York: Barnes & Noble Books, 2005.
_____. *A Journey to the Center of the Earth*. New York: Limited Editions Club, 1966.
_____. *Twenty Thousand Leagues Under the Seas*. New York: Oxford University Press, 1998.
Voltaire. *The Huron; Or, Pupil of Nature*. Translated by William F. Fleming. *The Works of Voltaire: A Contemporary Version*. Vol. 3. Paris: DuMont, 1901, 64–163.
Vonnegut, Kurt. *Player Piano*. New York: The Dial Press, 1999 [1952].
Wells, H. G. *Anticipations*. Leipzig: Tauchnitz, 1902 [1901].
_____. *Experiment in Autobiography*. Vol. I. London: Gollancz and Cresset Press, 1934.
_____. *The First Men in the Moon*. London: Penguin Classics, 2005 [1901].
_____. *The Food of the Gods*. Leipzig: Tauchnitz, 1904.
_____. *In the Days of the Comet*. Leipzig: Tauchnitz, 1906.
_____. *The Invisible Man*. Leipzig: Tauchnitz, 1908 [1897].
_____. *Mankind in the Making*. Leipzig: Tauchnitz, 1903.
_____. *Men Like Gods*. Whitefish, MT: Kessinger, 2005 [1923].
_____. *Mind at the End of Its Tether*. New York: Didier, 1946 [1945].
_____. *A Modern Utopia*. Edited by Krishan Kumar. London: Everyman, Dent, 1994 [1905].
_____. *New Worlds for Old*. Leipzig: Tauchnitz, 1908.
_____. *The Open Conspiracy*. San Diego: Book Tree, 2006 [1928].
_____. *The Shape of Things to Come*. Edited by John Hammond. London: Everyman, Dent, 1993 [1933].
_____. *The Time Machine*. Edited by John Lawton. London: Everyman, Dent, 1995 [1895].
_____. "Utopias." *Science Fiction Studies* 9 (1982 [1939]): 117–21.
_____. *The War of the Worlds*. London: Everyman, Dent, 1993 [1898].
_____. *When the Sleeper Wakes*. Edited by John Lawton. London: Everyman, Dent, 1994 [1899].
_____. *The World Set Free*. London: The Hogarth Press, 1988 [1914].
Zamyatin, Yevgeny. *We*. Translated by Clarence Brown. London: Penguin, 1993 [1921].

## Secondary Sources

Adams, Robert P. *The Better Part of Valor: More, Erasmus, Colet, and Vives, on Humanism, War, and Peace, 1496–1535*. Seattle: University of Washington Press, 1962.
Albertz, Rainer. *Israel in Exile: The History and Literature of the Sixth Century B.C.E.* Leiden: Brill, 2004.
Aldiss, Brian W. "Wells and the Leopard Lady." In *H. G. Wells Under Revision: Proceedings of the International H. G. Wells Symposium, London, July 1986*, edited by Patrick Parrinder and Christopher Rolfe, 27–39. Cranbury, NJ, and London: Associated University Presses, 1990.
_____, with David Wingrove. *Trillion Year Spree: The History of Science Fiction*. New York: Atheneum, 1986 [1973].
Alexander, Peter. "Grimm's Utopia: Motives and Justifications." In *Utopias*, edited by Peter Alexander and Roger Gill, 31–42. London: Duckworth, 1984.
Allen, P.S., and H.M. Allen, eds. "Letter by Erasmus to Ulrich von Hutten from Antwerp, 23

July 1519." In *Sir Thomas More: Selections from His English Works and from the Lives of Erasmus and Roper*, translated from the Latin by P.S. Allen, 1–9. Oxford: Clarendon Press, 1924.

Ames, Russel. *Citizen Thomas More and His Utopia*. Princeton, NJ: Princeton University Press, 1949.

Armytage, W. H. G. *Heavens Below: Utopian Experiments in England 1560–1960*. London: Routledge, 1961.

_____. "Utopias: the Technological and Educational Dimension." In *Utopias*, edited by Peter Alexander and Roger Gill, 85–94. London: Duckworth, 1984.

_____. *Yesterday's Tomorrows: A Historical Survey of Future Societies*. London: Routledge, 1968.

Ash, Brian. *Faces of the Future: The Lessons of Science Fiction*. New York: Taplinger, 1975.

Atkins, John. *Aldous Huxley: A Literary Study*. New York: Roy, 1956.

Attebery, Brian. "Fantasy as an Anti-Utopian Mode." In *Reflections on the Fantastic*, edited by Michael Collings, 3–8. Westport, CT: Greenwood Press, 1986.

Bailey, K. V. "H. G. Wells and C. S. Lewis: Two Sides of a Visionary Coin." In *H. G. Wells Under Revision: Proceedings of the International H. G. Wells Symposium, London, July 1986*, edited by Patrick Parrinder and Christopher Rolfe, 226–36. Cranbury, NJ, and London: Associated University Presses, 1990.

Baker, Robert S. *Brave New World: History, Science, and Dystopia*. Boston: Twayne, 1990.

Baker-Smith, Dominic. "The Escape from the Cave: Thomas More and the Vision of Utopia." In *Between Dream and Nature: Essays on Utopia and Dystopia*, edited by Dominic Baker-Smith and C.C. Barfoot. Amsterdam: Rodopi, 1987.

_____. *More's Utopia*. London and New York: HarperCollinsAcademic, 1991.

Barker, Arthur E. "*Clavis Moreana:* The Yale Edition of Thomas More." In *Essential Articles for the Study of Thomas More*, edited by R.S. Sylvester and Germain Marc'hadour, 215–28. Hamden, CT: Archon Books, 1977.

Batchelor, John. *H. G. Wells*. Cambridge: Cambridge University Press, 1985.

Beauchamp, Gorman. "Themes and Uses of Fictional Utopias: A Bibliography of Secondary Works in English." *Science Fiction Studies* 4 (1977): 55–63.

Bellamy, William. "Wells as Edwardian." In *H. G. Wells: A Collection of Critical Essays*, edited by Bernard Bergonzi, 83–109. Englewood Cliffs, NJ: Prentice-Hall, 1976 [1971].

Bergonzi, Bernard. *The Early H. G. Wells: A Study of the Scientific Romances*. Manchester: Manchester University Press, 1961.

Bloch, Ernst. *Das Prinzip Hoffnung*. Frankfurt am Main: Suhrkamp, 1980 [1959].

_____. *Geist der Utopie*. Frankfurt am Main: Suhrkamp, 1980 [1923].

Bloch-Lainé, François. "The Utility of Utopia for Reformers." In *Utopias and Utopian Thought*, edited by Frank E. Manuel, 201–18. London: Souvenir Press, 1973.

Boadt, Lawrence. *Reading the Old Testament: An Introduction*. New York: Paulist Press, 1984.

Bradshaw, David. "Open Conspirators: Huxley and H. G. Wells 1927–35." In *The Hidden Huxley*, edited by David Bradshaw, 31–41. London: Faber and Faber, 1994.

Brandon, William. *New Worlds for Old: Reports from the New World and Their Effect on the Development of Social Thought in Europe, 1500–1800*. Athens, OH: Ohio University Press, 1986.

Branham, R. Bracht. "Utopian Laughter: Lucian and Thomas More." In *Thomas More and the Classics*, edited by R. Keen and D. Kinney. *Moreana* 86 (July 1985): 3–43.

Bridgett, T. E. *Life and Writings of Blessed Thomas More, Lord Chancellor of England and Martyr Under Henry VIII*. London: Burns-Benzinger, 1904.

Brigg, Peter. "Three Styles of Arthur C. Clarke: The Projector, the Wit, and the Mystic." In *Arthur C. Clarke*, edited by Joseph D. Olander and Martin H. Greenberg, 15–51. Writers of the 21st Century Series. New York: Taplinger, 1977.

Briggs, Asa. *A Social History of England*. London: Penguin, 1991 [1983].

Brinton, Crane. "Utopia and Democracy." In *Utopias and Utopian Thought*, edited by Frank E. Manuel, 50–68. London: Souvenir Press, 1973.

Brockhaus, Heinrich. *Die Utopia-Schrift des Thomas Morus*. Leipzig: Teubner, 1929.

Campbell, W.E. *Erasmus, Tyndale and More*. London: Eyre and Spottiswoode, 1949.

Chambers, R. W. *Thomas More*. Harmondsworth: Penguin, 1963 [1935].

Chesterton, G. K. "Mr. H. G. Wells and the Giants." In *H. G. Wells: The Critical Heritage*, edited by Patrick Parrinder, 103–9. London: Routledge, 1972.

Churchill, R. C. "The Comedy of Ideas. Cross-currents in the Fiction and Drama of the Twentieth Century." In *The Pelican Guide to English Literature, Vol. 7: The Modern Age*, edited by Boris Ford, 236–45. London: Penguin, 1973.

Churchman, C. West. "The Design of a Perfect Society." In *Utopias*, edited by Peter Alexander and Roger Gill, 43–48. London: Duckworth, 1984.

Clarke, I.F. *The Pattern of Expectation, 1644–2001*. New York: Basic Books, 1979.

Clute, John, and Peter Nicholls, eds. *The Encyclopedia of Science Fiction*. New York: St. Martin's Griffin, 1995.

Cole, G.D.H. *Socialist Thought: The Forerunners 1789–1850*. London: Macmillan, 1962.

Coren, Michael. *The Invisible Man: The Life and Liberties of H. G. Wells*. Toronto: Vintage Books, 1993.

Costa, Richard Hauer. *H. G. Wells*. Revised edition. Boston: Twayne, 1985.

Cousins, A.D., and Damian Grace, eds. *More's Utopia and the Utopian Inheritance*. Lanham, MD, and London: University Press of America, 1995.

Croft, Pauline. *King James*. Basingstoke, Hampshire: Palgrave Macmillan, 2003.

Crossley, Robert. "Pure and Applied Fantasy, or From Faerie to Utopia." In *The Aesthetics of Fantasy Literature and Art*, edited by Roger C. Schlobin, 176–91. Notre Dame, IN: University of Notre Dame Press, 1982.

Csicsery-Ronay, Istvan, Jr. "Marxist Theory and Science Fiction." In *The Cambridge Companion to Science Fiction*, edited by Edward James and Farah Mendlesohn, 113–24. Cambridge: Cambridge University Press, 2003.

Daiches, David. *The Novel and the Modern World*. Chicago: University of Chicago Press, 1960.

Davis, J. C. "The History of Utopia: The Chronology of Nowhere." In *Utopias*, edited by Peter Alexander and Roger Gill, 1–17. London: Duckworth, 1984.

_____. *Utopia and the Ideal Society: A Study of English Utopian Writing 1516–1700*. Cambridge: Cambridge University Press, 1981.

Dawson, S. W. "Iris Murdoch: The Limits of Contrivance." In *The New Pelican Guide to English Literature, Vol. 8: From Orwell to Naipaul*, edited by Boris Ford, 214–21. London: Penguin, 1995.

Deery, June. "H. G. Wells's *A Modern Utopia* as a Work in Progress." In *Political Science Fiction*, edited by Donald M. Hassler and Clyde Wilcox, 26–42. Columbia, SC: University of South Carolina Press, 1997.

Derbyshire, John. "Huxley's Period Piece: Brave New World Turns 75." *National Review*, March 5, 2007. Available at: http://findarticles.com/p/articles/mi_m1282/is_3_59/ai_n19312005?tag=content;coll (accessed July 31, 2009).

Deutscher, Isaac. "'1984'—The Mysticism of Cruelty." In *Twentieth Century Interpretations of 1984*, edited by Samuel Hynes, 29–40. Englewood Cliffs, NJ: Prentice-Hall, 1971 [1955].

Dick, Philip K. "My Definition of Science Fiction." In *The Shifting Realities of Philip K. Dick. Selected Literary and Philosophical Writings*, edited by Lawrence Sutin. New York: Random House, Vintage Books, 1995 [1955].

Dickson, Lovat. *H. G. Wells: His Turbulent Life and Times*. Harmondsworth: Penguin, 1972 [1969].

Disch, Thomas M. *The Dreams Our Stuff Is Made Of: How Science Fiction Conquered the World*. New York: Touchstone, 2000.

Draper, Michael. *H. G. Wells*. London: Macmillan, 1987.

Dubos, René. *The Dreams of Reason: Science and Utopias*. New York: Columbia University Press, 1967.

Duhamel, P. Albert. "Medievalism in More's *Utopia*." In *Essential Articles for the Study of Thomas More*, edited by R.S. Sylvester and Germain Marc'hadour, 234–50. Hamden CT: Archon Books, 1977.

Edel, Leon, and Gordon N. Ray, eds. *Henry James and H. G. Wells*. Westport, CT: Greenwood Press, 1979 [1958].

Eliade, Mircea. "Paradise and Utopia: Mythical Geography and Eschatology." In *Utopias and Utopian Thought*, edited by Frank E. Manuel, 260–80. London: Souvenir Press, 1973.

Eliav-Feldon, Miriam. *Realistic Utopias: The Ideal Imaginary Societies of the Renaissance 1516–1630*. Oxford: Clarendon, 1982.

Elliott, Robert C. *The Shape of Utopia: Studies in a Literary Genre*. Chicago: University of Chicago Press, 1970.

Elton, G.R. "Thomas More, Councillor." In *St. Thomas More: Action and Contemplation. Proceedings of the Symposium Held at St. John's University, October 9–10, 1970*, edited by Richard S. Sylvester, 85–122. New Haven and London: Yale University Press for St. John's University, 1972.

Ferns, Chris. *Narrating Utopia: Ideology, Gender, Form in Utopian Literature.* Liverpool: Liverpool University Press, 1999.

Fink, Howard. "The Shadow of *Men Like Gods*: Orwell's *Coming Up for Air* as Parody." In *H. G. Wells and Modern Science Fiction*, edited by Darko Suvin and Robert M. Philmus, 144–58. Cranbury, NJ, and London: Associated University Presses, 1977.

Firchow, Peter. *Aldous Huxley: Satirist and Novelist.* Minneapolis: University of Minnesota Press, 1972.

Fishman, Robert. "Utopia in Three Dimensions: The Ideal City and the Origins of Modern Design." In *Utopias*, edited by Peter Alexander and Roger Gill, 95–107. London: Duckworth, 1984.

Fleisher, Martin. *Radical Reform and Political Persuasion in the Life and Writings of Thomas More.* Genève: Droz, 1973.

Fox, Alistair. *Thomas More: History and Providence.* New Haven: Yale University Press, 1983.

Freedman, Carl. *Critical Theory and Science Fiction.* Hanover, NH: Wesleyan University Press, 2000.

_____. "Science Fiction and Utopia: A Historico–Philosophical Overview." In *Learning from Other Worlds: Estrangement, Cognition, and the Politics of Science Fiction and Utopia*, edited by Patrick Parrinder, 72–97. Liverpool: Liverpool University Press, 2000.

Fromm, Gloria Glikin. "Through the Novelist's Looking-Glass." In *H. G. Wells. A Collection of Critical Essays*, edited by Bernard Bergonzi, 157–77. Englewood Cliffs, NJ: Prentice-Hall, 1976 [1969].

Frye, Northrop. *Anatomy of Criticism: Four Essays.* Princeton, NJ: Princeton University Press, 2000 [1957].

_____. "The Tempest." In *Northrop Frye on Shakespeare*, edited by Robert Sandler, 171–86. New Haven: Yale University Press, 1986.

_____. "Varieties of Literary Utopias." In *The Stubborn Structure: Essays on Criticism and Society*, 109–34. Ithaca, NY: Cornell University Press, 1970 [1965].

Gardiner, Michael. "Bakhtin's Carnival: Utopia as Critique." *Utopian Studies* 3, no. 2 (1992): 21–49.

Géher, István. *Shakespeare-olvasókönyv. Tükörképünk 37 darabban.* Budapest: Cserépfalvi-Szépirodalmi, 1991.

Gibson, R.W. *Sir Thomas More: A Preliminary Bibliography of His Works and of Moreana to the Year 1750.* New Haven: Yale University Press, 1961.

Gill, Roger. "In England's Green and Pleasant Land." In *Utopias*, edited by Peter Alexander and Roger Gill, 109–17. London: Duckworth, 1984.

Ginzburg, Carlo. "The Old World and the New Seen from Nowhere." In *No Island Is an Island: Four Glances at English Literature in a World Perspective*, 1–23. New York: Columbia University Press 2000.

Gogan, Brian. *The Common Corps of Christiandom: Ecclesiological Themes in the Writings of Thomas More.* Leiden: Brill, 1982.

Goodwin, Barbara. "Economic and Social Innovation in Utopia." In *Utopias*, edited by Peter Alexander and Roger Gill, 69–83. London: Duckworth, 1984.

Grace, Damian. "*Utopia* and Academic Scepticism." In *More's* Utopia *and the Utopian Inheritance*, edited by A.D. Cousins and Damian Grace, 1–21. Lanham, MD, and London: University Press of America, 1995.

Greenblatt, Stephen. "At the Table of the Great: More's Self-Fashioning and Self-Cancellation." In *Renaissance Self-Fashioning. From More to Shakespeare*, 11–73. Chicago: University of Chicago Press, 1980.

_____. "Introduction to *The Tempest*." In *The Norton* Shakespeare, edited by Stephen Greenblatt, 3047–53. New York: Norton, 1997.

_____. *Three Modern Satirists: Waugh, Orwell, and Huxley.* New Haven and London: Yale University Press, 1965.

Gueguen, John A. "Reading More's *Utopia* as a Criticism of Plato." In *Quincentennial Essays on St. Thomas More*, edited by Michael J. Moore, 43–54. Boone, NC: Appalachian State University Press, 1978.

Gunn, James, ed. *The New Encyclopedia of Science Fiction.* New York: Viking Penguin, 1988.

Guy, John. *Thomas More.* London: Arnold, 2000.

Hall, Peter. "Utopian Thought: A Framework for Social, Economic, and Physical Planning." In *Utopias*, edited by Peter Alexander and Roger Gill, 189–95. London: Duckworth, 1984.

Hammond, J. R. *H. G. Wells and the Short Story.* New York: St. Martin's Press, 1992.

Harrison, J.F.C. "Millennium and Utopia." In *Utopias*, edited by Peter Alexander and Roger Gill, 61–66. London: Duckworth, 1984.
_____. *Robert Owen and the Owenites in Britain and America. The Quest for the New Moral World.* London: Routledge, 1969.
Haynes, Roslynn D. *H. G. Wells, Discoverer of the Future: The Influence of Science on His Thought.* London: Macmillan, 1980.
Hexter, J.H. "The Composition of Utopia." In *The Complete Works of St. Thomas More: Volume 4, Utopia*, edited by S.J. Edward Surtz and J.H. Hexter. New Haven: Yale University Press, 1965.
_____. *More's Utopia: The Biography of an Idea.* New York: Harper and Row, 1965 [1952].
_____. "Thomas More and the Problem of Counsel." In *Quincentennial Essays on St. Thomas More*, edited by Michael J. Moore, 55–66. Boone, NC: Appalachian State University Press, 1978.
"H. G. Wells." *Contemporary Authors on CD DOS Version.* Gale Research, 1996.
Hillegas, Mark R. "The Construction of the Future: H. G. Wells and Utopian Fantasy." In *H. G. Wells, Reality and Beyond: A Collection of Critical Essays Prepared in Conjunction with the Exhibition and Symposium on H. G. Wells*, edited by Michael Mullin, 33–42. Champaign, IL: Champaign Public Library and Information Center, 1986.
_____. *The Future as Nightmare: H. G. Wells and the Anti-utopians.* Carbondale and Edwardsville: Southern Illinois University Press, 1967.
_____. "Introduction." H. G. Wells. *A Modern Utopia.* Lincoln and London: University of Nebraska Press, 1967.
Hollow, John. *Against the Night, the Stars: The Science Fiction of Arthur C. Clarke.* New York: Harcourt, 1983.
Holloway, Mark. "The Necessity of Utopia." In *Utopias*, edited by Peter Alexander and Roger Gill, 179–88. London: Duckworth, 1984.
Holquist, Michael. "How to Play Utopia: Some Brief Notes on the Distinctiveness of Utopian Fiction." In *Science Fiction: A Collection of Critical Essays*, edited by Mark Rose, 132–46. Englewood Cliffs, NJ: Prentice-Hall, 1976.
Hölscher, Lucian. "Der Begriff der Utopie als historische Kategorie." *Utopieforschung: interdisziplinäre Studien zur neuzeitlichen Utopie, Vol. I*, edited by Wilhelm Voßkamp, 402–18. Stuttgart: Metzler, 1982.
Hughes, David Y. "The Mood of *A Modern Utopia*." In *Critical Essays on H. G. Wells*, edited by John Huntington, 67–76. Boston: Hall, 1991 [1977].
Huizinga, Johan. *Homo Ludens. Kísérlet a kultúra játék-elemeinek meghatározására.* Szeged: Universum Kiadó, 1990 [1938].
Hume, Kathryn. *Fantasy and Mimesis: Responses to Reality in Western Literature.* London: Methuen, 1984.
Huntington, John. "H. G. Wells: Problems of an Amorous Utopian." In *Critical Essays on H. G. Wells*, edited by John Huntington, 136–47. Boston: Hall, 1991 [1987].
_____. *The Logic of Fantasy: H. G. Wells and Science Fiction.* New York: Columbia University Press, 1982.
_____. "Utopian and Anti-Utopian Logic: H. G. Wells and His Successors." *Science Fiction Studies* 9 (1982): 122–46.
James, Edward. "Before the *Novum*: The Prehistory of Science Fiction Criticism." In *Learning from Other Worlds: Estrangement, Cognition, and the Politics of Science Fiction and Utopia*, edited by Patrick Parrinder, 19–35. Liverpool: Liverpool University Press, 2000.
_____. "Utopias and Anti-Utopias." In *The Cambridge Companion to Science Fiction*, edited by Edward James and Farah Mendlesohn, 219–29. Cambridge: Cambridge University Press, 2003.
Jameson, Fredric. "The Dialectic of Utopia and Ideology." In *The Political Unconscious: Narrative as a Socially Symbolic Act*, 219–29. Ithaca, NY: Cornell University Press, 1981.
_____. "Progress versus Utopia; or, Can We Imagine the Future?" *Science Fiction Studies* 9 (1982): 147–58.
Johnson, Robbin S. *More's Utopia: Ideal and Illusion.* New Haven and London: Yale University Press, 1969.
Jones, Judith P. *Thomas More.* Boston: Twayne, 1979.
Jouvenel, Bertrand de. "Utopia for Practical Purposes." In *Utopias and Utopian Thought*, edited by Frank E. Manuel, 219–35. London: Souvenir Press, 1973.

Kateb, George. "Utopia and the Good Life." In *Utopias and Utopian Thought*, edited by Frank E. Manuel, 239–59. London: Souvenir Press, 1973.

Kautsky, Karl. *Thomas More und Seine Utopie*. Berlin: Verlag JHF Dietz, 1947 [1887].

Kermode, Frank. "Introduction to *The Tempest*." In *The Tempest*, edited by Frank Kermode, xi–xciii. London: Routledge, 1994.

Ketterer, David. "Utopian Fantasy as Millennial Motive and Science-fictional Motif." *Studies in the Literary Imagination* 6, no. 2 (1973): 79–104.

Kettler, David, Volker Meja, and Nico Stehr. "Mannheim Károly korai kultúraszociológiai írásai." In *A gondolkodás struktúrái. Kultúraszociológiai tanulmányok*, by Mannheim Károly, 335–59. Budapest: Atlantisz, 1995.

Knapp, Jeffrey. *An Empire Nowhere: England, America, and Literature from* Utopia *to* The Tempest. Berkeley and Los Angeles: University of California Press, 1992.

Knight, G. Wilson. "The Shakespearean Superman: A study of *The Tempest*." In *The Crown of Life: Essays in Interpretation of Shakespeare's Final Plays*, 203–55. Oxford: Oxford University Press, 1947.

Kumar, Krishan. "H. G. Wells and His Critics." In *A Modern Utopia*, edited by Krishan Kumar 244–61. London: Everyman, Dent, 1994.

_____. *Utopia and Anti-Utopia in Modern Times*. Oxford: Blackwell, 1987.

_____. "Wells and 'the So-Called Science of Sociology.'" In *H. G. Wells Under Revision: Proceedings of the International H. G. Wells Symposium, London, July 1986*, edited by Patrick Parrinder and Christopher Rolfe, 192–217. Cranbury NJ & London: Associated University Press, 1990.

Laozi. *Dao De Jing: The Book of the Way*. Translated with commentary by Moss Roberts. Berkeley and Los Angeles: University of California Press, 2001.

Leavis, F. R. *The Great Tradition*. Garden City, NY: Doubleday, 1954.

Levine, Joseph. M. "Thomas More and the English Renaissance: History and Fiction in *Utopia*." In *The Historical Imagination in Early Modern Britain: History, Rhetoric, and Fiction, 1500–1800*, edited by Donald R. Kelley and David Harris Sacks. Cambridge and New York: Woodrow Wilson Center Press and Cambridge University Press, 1997.

Levitas, Ruth. "Need, Nature and Nowhere." In *Utopias*, edited by Peter Alexander and Roger Gill, 19–30. London: Duckworth, 1984.

Lewis, C.S. "On Science Fiction." In *Science Fiction: A Collection of Critical Essays*, edited by Mark Rose, 103–15. Englewood Cliffs, NJ: Prentice-Hall, 1976 [1966].

_____. "Thomas More." *Essential Articles for the Study of Thomas More*, edited by R.S. Sylvester and Germain Marc'hadour, 388–401. Hamden CT: Archon Books, 1977 [1954].

Lichtheim, George. *The Origins of Socialism*. London: Weidenfeld and Nicholson, 1968.

Lockwood, Maren. "The Experimental Utopia in America." In *Utopias and Utopian Thought*, edited by Frank E. Manuel, 183–200. London: Souvenir Press, 1973.

Logan, George M. *The Meaning of More's Utopia*. Princeton NJ: Princeton University Press, 1983.

Lukes, Steven. "Marxism and Utopianism." In *Utopias*, edited by Peter Alexander and Roger Gill, 153–67. London: Duckworth, 1984.

Lundwall, Sam. *Holnap történt. Tanulmányok a science fiction világtörténetéből*. Budapest: Kozmosz könyvek, 1984.

Lurker, Manfred. *Dictionary of Gods and Goddesses, Devils and Demons*. London: Routledge, 1987.

Maár, Judit. *A fantasztikus irodalom*. Budapest: Osiris, 2001.

MacKenzie, Norman, and Jeanne MacKenzie. *H. G. Wells: A Biography*. New York: Simon & Schuster, 1973.

Manlove, C. N. *Science Fiction: Ten Explorations*. London: Macmillan, 1986.

Mannheim, Karl. *Ideologie und Utopie*. Frankfurt am Main: Klostermann, 1985 [1929].

_____. *Ideology and Utopia: An Introduction to the Sociology of Knowledge*. Translated by Louis Wirth and Edward Shils. London: Routledge, 1972 [1936].

Manuel, Frank E. "Toward a Psychological History of Utopias." In *Utopias and Utopian Thought*, edited by Frank E. Manuel, 69–98. London: Souvenir Press, 1973.

_____, and Fritzie P. Manuel. *Utopian Thought in the Western World*. Oxford: Blackwell, 1979.

Marc'hadour, Germain, ed. *Meliora Miscellanea de Mori Utopia*. Moreana 31–32 (November 1971).

Marcuse, Herbert. *One-Dimensional Man: Studies in the Ideology of Advanced Industrial Society*. Boston: Beacon Press, 1964.

Marius, Richard. *Thomas More*. New York: Knopf, 1984.

Martz, Louis. *Thomas More: The Search for the Inner Man*. New Haven: Yale University Press, 1990.

Marx, Karl. *A t_ke. A politikai gazdaságtan bírálata.* Vol. I. Budapest: Kossuth, 1978 [1867].
_____, and Friedrich Engels. *Manifesto of the Communist Party: Collected Works,* Vol. 6, 476–519.
    New York: International Publishers, 1976 [English translation 1888]. Available at: http://
    www.yclusa.org/readup/manread.html (accessed December 30, 2002).
McAleer, Neil. *Odyssey: The Authorized Biography of Arthur C. Clarke.* London: Victor Gollancz,
    1992.
McConnell, Frank. *The Science Fiction of H.G. Wells.* Oxford: Oxford University Press, 1981.
McCutcheon, Elizabeth. "Denying the Contrary: More's Use of Litotes in *Utopia.*" In *Essential
    Articles for the Study of Thomas More,* edited by R.S. Sylvester and Germain Marc'hadour,
    263–74. Hamden CT: Archon Books, 1977.
_____. *My Dear Peter: The Ars Poetica and Hermeneutics for More's Utopia.* Angers: Moreana, 1983.
_____. "More's *Utopia* and Cicero's *Paradoxa Stoicorum.*" In *Thomas More and the Classics,* edited
    by R. Keen and D. Kinney, 23–43. *Moreana* 86 (July 1985).
Meckier, Jerome. *Aldous Huxley: Satire and Structure.* London: Chatto & Windus, 1969.
_____. "Aldous Huxley's Americanization of the *Brave New World* typescript." *Twentieth Cen-
    tury Literature* (Winter 2002). Available at: http://findarticles.com/p/articles/mi_m0403/
    is_4_48/ai_108194336?tag=untagged (accessed July 31, 2009).
Molnar, Thomas. *Utopia: The Perennial Heresy.* New York: Sheed & Ward, 1967.
Morrison, Alasdair. "Uses of Utopia." In *Utopias,* edited by Peter Alexander and Roger Gill,
    139–51. London: Duckworth, 1984.
Morton, A.L. *The English Utopia.* London: Lawrence and Wishart, 1969 [1952].
Moskowitz, Sam. "Arthur C. Clarke." In *Seekers of Tomorrow: Masters of Modern Science Fiction,*
    2nd edition, 374–91. Westport, CT: Hyperion Press, 1974.
Moylan, Tom. *Demand the Impossible: Science Fiction and the Utopian Imagination.* New York
    and London: Methuen, 1986.
_____. "The Locus of Hope: Utopia Versus Ideology." *Science-Fiction Studies* 9 (1982): 159–66.
_____. "'Look into the Dark:' On Dystopia and the *Novum.*" In *Learning from Other Worlds:
    Estrangement, Cognition, and the Politics of Science Fiction and Utopia,* edited by Patrick Par-
    rinder, 51–71. Liverpool: Liverpool University Press, 2000.
_____. *Scraps of the Untainted Sky: Science Fiction, Utopia, Dystopia.* Boulder, CO, and Oxford:
    Westview Press, 2000.
Mumford, Lewis. *The Story of Utopias.* New York: The Viking Press, 1962 [1922].
_____. "Utopia, the City and the Machine." In *Utopias and Utopian Thought,* edited by Frank
    E. Manuel, 3–24. London: Souvenir Press, 1973.
Murray, Nicholas. *Aldous Huxley: An English Intellectual.* London: Little, Brown, 2002.
Nance, Guinevera A. *Aldous Huxley.* New York: Continuum, 1988.
Nelson, William ed. *Twentieth Century Interpretations of Utopia.* Englewood Cliffs, NJ: Prentice-
    Hall, 1968.
Németh, Andor. "Huxley 'Szép új világ'-a és az utópisztikus regény." *Nyugat* 2 no. 12–13 (1934):
    274–80.
Nicholls, Peter. "Arthur C. Clarke." *The Encyclopedia of Science Fiction,* edited by John Clute and
    Peter Nicholls, 229–32. New York: St. Martin's Press, 1995.
Norris, Christoph. "Utopian Deconstruction: Ernst Bloch, Paul de Man and the Politics of
    Music." In *Deconstruction and the Interests of Theory,* 29–58. London: Pinter, 1988.
Olander, Joseph D., and Martin H. Greenberg, eds. *Arthur C. Clarke.* Writers of the 21st Cen-
    tury Series. New York: Taplinger, 1977.
Paden, Roger. "Marx's Critique of the Utopian Socialists." *Utopian Studies* 13, no. 2 (2002):
    67–91.
Parks, George B. "More's *Utopia* and Geography." *Journal of English and Germanic Philology* 37
    (1938): 224–39.
Parrinder, Patrick. "Experiments in Prophecy." In *H. G. Wells: Reality and Beyond: A Collection
    of Critical Essays Prepared in Conjunction with the Exhibition and Symposium on H. G. Wells,*
    edited by Michael Mullin, 7–21. Champaign, IL: Champaign Public Library and Informa-
    tion Center, 1986.
_____. "Imagining the Future: Wells and Zamyatin." In *H. G. Wells and Modern Science Fiction,*
    edited by Darko Suvin and Robert M. Philmus, 126–43. Cranbury, NJ, and London: Asso-
    ciated University Press, 1977.
_____. "Introduction." In *H. G. Wells: The Critical Heritage,* 1–31. London: Routledge & Kegan
    Paul, 1972.

_____. "Revisiting Suvin's Poetics of Science Fiction." *Learning from Other Worlds: Estrangement, Cognition, and the Politics of Science Fiction and Utopia*, edited by Patrick Parrinder, 36–50. Liverpool: Liverpool University Press, 2000.

_____. *Science Fiction: Its Criticism and Teaching*. London: Methuen, 1980.

_____. "Science Fiction and the Scientific World-View." *Science Fiction: A Critical Guide*, edited by Patrick Parrinder, 67–88. New York: Longman, 1979.

_____. *Shadows of the Future: H. G. Wells, Science Fiction, and Prophesy*. Syracuse, NY: Syracuse University Press, 1995.

_____. "Utopia and Meta-Utopia in H. G. Wells." *Science Fiction Studies* 12 (1985): 115–28.

_____, and Robert M. Philmus, eds. *H. G. Wells's Literary Criticism*. Brighton: Harvester Press, 1980.

Parrington, Vernon Louis. *American Dreams: A Study of American Utopias*. Providence, RI: Brown University Press, 1947.

Pavkovic, Aleksandar. "Prosperity, Equality and Intellectual Needs in More's *Utopia*." In *More's Utopia and the Utopian Inheritance*, edited by A.D. Cousins and Damian Grace, 23–35. Lanham, MD, and London: University Press of America, 1995.

Perlette, John M. "Of Sites and Parasites: The Centrality of the Marginal Anecdote in Book 1 of More's *Utopia*." *ELH* 54 (1987): 231–52.

Pfaelzer, Jean. *The Utopian Novel in America 1886–1896: The Politics of Form*. Pittsburgh: University of Pittsburgh Press, 1984.

Philmus, Robert M. *Into the Unknown: The Evolution of Science Fiction from Francis Godwin to H.G. Wells*. Berkeley and Los Angeles: University of California Press, 1970.

_____. "The Language of Utopia." *Studies in the Literary Imagination* 6, no. 2 (1973): 61–78.

_____. "The Logic of 'Prophecy' in *The Time Machine*." In *H. G. Wells: A Collection of Critical Essays*, edited by Bernard Bergonzi, 56–68. Englewood Cliffs, NJ: Prentice-Hall, 1976 [1969].

_____, and David Y. Hughes, eds. *H. G. Wells: Early Writings in Science and Science Fiction*. Berkeley and Los Angeles: University of California Press, 1975.

Pintér, Károly. "A számkivetett Kalibán: Huxley *Szép új világa* Shakespeare *Vihar*ának fényében." In *Utópiák és ellenutópiák*, edited by Katalin Kroó and Tamás Bényei. Budapest: L'Harmattan, 2010.

Pitzer, Donald E. "Collectivism, Community and Commitment: America's Religious Communal Utopias from the Shakers to Jonestown." In *Utopias*, edited by Peter Alexander and Roger Gill, 119–35. London: Duckworth, 1984.

Plattel, Martin G. *Utopian and Critical Thinking*. Pittsburgh: Duquesne University Press, 1972.

Podmore, Frank. *Robert Owen: A Biography*. London: Allen & Unwin, 1906.

Polak, Frederik L. "Utopia and Cultural Renewal." In *Utopias and Utopian Thought*, edited by Frank E. Manuel, 281–95. London: Souvenir Press, 1973.

Popper, Karl. *The Open Society and Its Enemies*. London: Routledge, 1995 [1945].

Pritchett, V. S. "The Scientific Romances." In *H. G. Wells: A Collection of Critical Essays*, edited by Bernard Bergonzi, 32–38. Englewood Cliffs, NJ: Prentice-Hall, 1976 [1946].

Rabkin, Eric S. *Arthur C. Clarke*. Mercer Island, WA: Starmont House, 1980.

_____. "Fairy Tales and Science Fiction." In *Bridges to Science Fiction*, edited by George E. Slusser, George R. Guffey, and Mark Rose, 78–90. Carbondale IL: Southern Illinois University Press, 1980.

_____. "The Unconscious City." In *Hard Science Fiction*, edited by George E. Slusser and Eric S. Rabkin, 24–44. Carbondale IL: Southern Illinois University Press, 1986.

Raknem, Ingvald. *H. G. Wells and His Critics*. Norway: Universitetsforlaget, 1962.

Reid, Robin Anne. *Arthur C. Clarke: A Critical Companion*. Greenwood Companions to Popular Contemporary Writers. Westport, CT: Greenwood Press, 1997.

Reynolds, E.E. *Thomas More and Erasmus*. London: Burns & Oates, 1965.

Ricoeur, Paul. *Lectures on Ideology and Utopia*, edited by George H. Taylor. New York: Columbia University Press, 1986.

Ritter, Joachim et al., ed. *Historisches Wörterbuch Der Philosophie*. 11 vols. Basel: Schwabe, 1972–2001.

Roberts, Adam. *The History of Science Fiction*. Basingstoke: Palgrave Macmillan, 2005.

Robinet, Isabelle. *Taoism: Growth of a Religion*. Stanford, CA: Stanford University Press, 1997.

Rodden, John. *The Politics of Literary Reputation: The Making and Claiming of 'St. George' Orwell*. Oxford: Oxford University Press, 1989.

Roper, William. "Life of Sir Thomas More." *The "Utopia" and the History of Edward V., by Sir Thomas More. With Roper's Life*, edited by Maurice Adams, 1–61. London and Felling-on-Tyne: Walter Scott Publishing, 1890 [1626].

Ruddick, Nicholas. *Ultimate Island: On the Nature of British Science Fiction*. Westport, CT: Greenwood Press, 1993.

_____. "Clarke Crib Notes. Review of Reid's *Arthur C. Clarke: A Critical Companion*." *SF Studies* 25, no. 75, part 2 (July 1998). Available at: http://www.depauw.edu/sfs/birs/bir75.htm#e75 (accessed June 23, 2009).

Runcini, Romolo. "H. G. Wells and Futurity as the Only Creative Space in a Programmed Society." In *H. G. Wells Under Revision: Proceedings of the International H. G. Wells Symposium, London, July 1986*, edited by Patrick Parrinder and Christopher Rolfe, 153–61. Cranbury, NJ, and London: Associated University Press, 1990.

Sargent, Lyman Tower. *British and American Utopian Literature 1516–1975: An Annotated Bibliography*. Boston: Hall, 1979.

_____. "Utopianism." In *Routledge Encyclopedia of Philosophy*, vol. 9, edited by Edward Craig, 557–62. London: Routledge, 1998.

Scheick, William J., ed. *The Critical Response to H. G. Wells*. Westport, CT: Greenwood Press, 1995.

Schoeck, R.J. "'A Nursery of Correct and Useful Institutions:' On Reading More's *Utopia* as a Dialogue." In *Essential Articles for the Study of Thomas More*, edited by R.S. Sylvester and Germain Marc'hadour, 281–89. Hamden, CT: Archon Books, 1977.

Scholes, Robert. *Structural Fabulation: An Essay on Fiction of the Future*. Notre Dame, IN, and London: University of Notre Dame Press, 1975.

_____, and Eric Rabkin. *Science Fiction: History, Science, Vision*. New York: Oxford University Press, 1977.

Schulte Herbrüggen, Hubertus. "More's *Utopia* as a Paradigm." In *Essential Articles for the Study of Thomas More*, edited by R.S. Sylvester and Germain Marc'hadour, 251–62. Hamden, CT: Archon Books, 1977.

Sears, Paul B. "Utopia and the Living Landscape." In *Utopias and Utopian Thought*, edited by Frank E. Manuel, 137–49. London: Souvenir Press, 1973.

Seebohm, Frederic. *The Oxford Reformers: John Colet, Erasmus, and Thomas More. Being a History of Their Fellow-Work*. London: Longmans, Green, 1896 [1867].

Shakespeare, William. *The Tempest*. Edited by Frank Kermode. Arden Shakespeare Edition. London: Routledge, 1994.

Shklar, Judith. "The Political Theory of Utopia: From Melancholy to Nostalgia." In *Utopias and Utopian Thought*, edited by Frank E. Manuel, 101–15. London: Souvenir Press, 1973.

Sidney, Sir Philip. *Sidney's Apologie for Poetrie*. Edited by Churton Collins. Oxford: Clarendon, 1955.

Smith, David C. *H. G. Wells: Desperately Mortal*. New Haven: Yale University Press, 1986.

Smith, John Maynard. "Eugenics and Utopia." In *Utopias and Utopian Thought*, edited by Frank E. Manuel, 150–68. London: Souvenir Press, 1973.

Standley, Fred. "Ever 'More': Utopian and Dystopian Visions of the Future 1890–1990." In *More's Utopia and the Utopian Inheritance*, edited by A.D. Cousins and Damian Grace, 119–36. Lanham, MD, and London: University Press of America, 1995.

Starnes, Colin. *The New Republic: A Commentary on Book I of More's Utopia Showing Its Relation to Plato's Republic*. Waterloo, Ontario: Wilfrid Laurier University Press, 1990.

Strabón. *Geógraphika*. Budapest: Gondolat, 1977.

Suits, Bernard. "The Grasshopper: Posthumous Reflections on Utopia." In *Utopias*, edited by Peter Alexander and Roger Gill, 197–209. London: Duckworth, 1984.

Surtz, Edward, S.J. *The Praise of Pleasure: Philosophy, Education, and Communism in More's Utopia*. Cambridge MA: Harvard University Press, 1957.

_____. "St. Thomas More and His Utopian Embassy of 1515." *The Catholic Historical Review* 39 (1953): 272–98.

_____. "Utopia as a Work of Literary Art." In *The Complete Works of St. Thomas More: Volume 4, Utopia*, edited by S.J. Edward Surtz and J.H. Hexter. New Haven: Yale University Press, 1965.

Süssmuth, Hans. *Studien zur Utopia des Thomas Morus. Ein Beitrag zur Geistesgeschichte des 16. Jahrhunderts*. Münster Westfalen: Aschendorff, 1967.

Suvin, Darko. "Afterword: With Sober, Estranged Eyes." In *Learning from Other Worlds: Estrange-*

*ment, Cognition, and the Politics of Science Fiction and Utopia*, edited by Patrick Parrinder, 233–71. Liverpool: Liverpool University Press, 2000.

_____. *Metamorphoses of Science Fiction: On the Poetics and History of a Literary Genre*. New Haven, CT: Yale University Press, 1979.

Sylvester, R. S. "'Si Hythlodaeo Credimus': Vision and Revision in Thomas More's Utopia." *Essential Articles for the Study of Thomas More*, edited by R.S. Sylvester and Germain Marc'hadour, 290–301. Hamden CT: Archon Books, 1977.

Taylor, Keith. *The Political Ideas of the Utopian Socialists*. London: Cass, 1982.

Tillich, Paul. "Critique and Justification of Utopia." In *Utopias and Utopian Thought*, edited by Frank E. Manuel, 296–309. London: Souvenir Press, 1973.

Todorov, Tzvetan. *The Fantastic: A Structural Approach to a Literary Genre*. Ithaca, NY: Cornell University Press, 1975.

Ulam, Adam. "Socialism and Utopia." In *Utopias and Utopian Thought*, edited by Frank E. Manuel, 116–34. London: Souvenir Press, 1973.

Vaughan, Alden T., and Virginia Mason Vaughan. *Shakespeare's Caliban: A Cultural History*. Cambridge: Cambridge University Press, 1991.

Vespucci, Amerigo. *The First Four Voyages of Amerigo Vespucci*. Translated with an introduction by Stradanus. London: Bernard Quaritch, 1893.

"Vespucci, Amerigo." *Encyclopaedia Britannica: Micropaedia*, vol 12, 336–37. 15th edition.

Vogeler, Martha S. "Wells and Positivism." In *H. G. Wells Under Revision: Proceedings of the International H. G. Wells Symposium, London, July 1986*, edited by Patrick Parrinder and Christopher Rolfe, 181–91. Cranbury, NJ, and London: Associated University Press, 1990.

Wagar, W. Warren. "H. G. Wells and the Radicalism of Despair." *Studies in the Literary Imagination* 6, no. 2 (1973): 1–10.

_____. *H. G. Wells and the World State*. New Haven: Yale University Press, 1961.

_____. "Science and the World State: Education as Utopia in the Prophetic Vision of H. G. Wells." In *H. G. Wells Under Revision: Proceedings of the International H. G. Wells Symposium, London, July 1986*, edited by Patrick Parrinder and Christopher Rolfe, 40–53. Cranbury, NJ, and London: Associated University Press, 1990.

Walsh, Chad. *From Utopia to Nightmare*. London: Bles, 1962.

Watt, Donald, ed. *Aldous Huxley: The Critical Heritage*. London: Routledge, 1975.

Watts, Harold H. *Aldous Huxley*. New York: Twayne, 1969.

Weeks, Robert P. "Disentanglement as a Theme in H.G. Wells's Fiction." In *H. G. Wells: A Collection of Critical Essays*, edited by Bernard Bergonzi, 25–31. Englewood Cliffs, NJ: Prentice-Hall, 1976 [1954].

West, Anthony. *H. G. Wells: Aspects of a Life*. London: Hutchinson, 1984.

Westfahl, Gary. "'The Closely Reasoned Technological Story': The Critical History of Hard Science Fiction." *Science Fiction Studies* 20, no. 60, part 2 (July 1993). Available at: http://www.depauw.edu/sfs/backissues/60/westfahl60art.htm (accessed March 28, 2009).

Wilde, Oscar. *The Soul of Man Under Socialism*. London: Humphreys, 1912 [1891].

Williams, Raymond. *Keywords: A Vocabulary of Culture and Society*. London: Fontana/Croom Helm, 1976.

_____. "Utopia and Science Fiction." In *Science Fiction: A Critical Guide*, edited by Patrick Parrinder, 52–66. New York: Longman, 1979.

Wolfe, Gary K. "The Encounter with Fantasy." In *The Aesthetics of Fantasy Literature and Art*, edited by Roger C. Schlobin, 1–15. Notre Dame, IN: University of Notre Dame Press, 1982.

_____. "The Known and the Unknown: Structure and Image in Science Fiction." In *Many Futures Many Worlds: Theme and Form in Science Fiction*, edited by Thomas D. Clareson, 94–116. Kent, OH: Kent State University Press, 1977.

_____. *The Known and the Unknown: The Iconography of Science Fiction*. Kent, OH: Kent State University Press, 1979.

Woolf, Virginia. "Modern Fiction." *The Norton Anthology of English Literature*. 1921–1926 [1919].

# Index

absurdity 37, 68–69, 86, 91, 101, 137, 143, 152, 179
*Acts and Monuments* 50
Adams, Douglas 143; *Hitchhiker's Guide* series 143
Aeneas (epic hero) 58, 72, 75
*Aeneid* 74
*Against the Fall of Night* 174, 176–177, 179, 187
Albertz, Rainer 185
Aldiss, Brian 142
alienation 29, 118; *see also* cognitive estrangement; narrative estrangement
allegory 8, 31, 37, 54–55, 58, 101, 103, 128, 142, 153, 183
Allen, P.S. 55–56, 60
Alvin (fictional character in *The City and the Stars*) 176, 180, 182–187, 190
ambiguity 6–9, 16, 35, 37, 39–40, 47, 62–63, 67–68, 70–71, 86–88, 96, 100, 118, 132, 135, 138–139, 145–146, 173, 179, 183–184, 192, 194–195
anarchy 23–24, 123
anatomy (genre) 8, 35, 103–105, 118, 124
*Anatomy of Criticism* 24, 35–36, 104
*Anne Veronica* 100
*Anticipations* 99–101, 105, 118
anti-utopia 4, 21, 24, 133, 136–139, 141, 143–144, 147, 149, 170, 178, 195
apocalypse 101, 133, 135, 144, 188–189
*Apologie for Poetrie* 58
Arcadia 23, 181, 184
archetype 6–7, 137, 140, 155, 184
Aristophanes (ancient Greek dramatist) 94, 137; *The Birds* 137; *The Clouds* 137; *Ecclesiazusae* 137
Aristotle 36, 94–95
*As You Like It* 165
Asimov, Isaac 31, 171; *Foundation* series 31
Attebery, Brian 194
authorial intent 4, 16, 46, 67, 114, 139

Bacon, Francis (English dramatist and writer) 7, 21, 31; *New Atlantis* 7
Baker, Robert S. 150
Bakunin, Mikhail 145
Ballard, J.G. 144; *The Drowned World* 144
Barker, Arthur E. 55
Bellamy, Edward 21–22, 39, 136, 140, 155–156; *Looking Backward* 22, 39, 140, 155
Benford, Gregory 171, 174
Bennett, Arnold 98, 100, 104
Berdyaev, Nikolai 141
Bergonzi, Bernard 99, 101–102, 104, 108
Bernal, J.D. 176
*Beyond the the Fall of Night* 174
*The Birds* 137
Bloch, Ernst 5–6, 25–28, 35; *Das Prinzip Hoffnung* 5, 25
Bloch-Lainé, François 13
Boadt, Frederic 185
Bodin, Felix 20; *Le Roman de l'avenir* 20
Bolt, Robert 50; *A Man for All Seasons* 50
Boswell, James 118
Bradbury, Ray 144; *Fahrenheit 451* 144
Bradshaw, David 150
Brecht, Bertolt 29, 114
Brigg, Peter 173
*The Brothers Karamazov* 152
Budé, Guillaume 53–55, 64–65
Budrys, Algys 173
Burnet, Gilbert 50, 58
Busleyden, Jerome 53–55, 64–65
Butler, Samuel 7, 143; *Erewhon* 7, 143

Cabet, Étienne 21
Caliban (fictional character in *The Tempest*) 154, 158–167, 169
Campanella, Tommaso 21
Campbell, John W. 175; "Twilight" 175
*Candide* 106
*A Canticle for Leibowitz* 144
Cecil, William 56–57

227

Chamberlain, Joseph 117
Chambers, R.W. 59–61, 76
Charles, Prince of Castile (later Charles V of Germany) 53, 71
Che Guevara, Ernesto 145
Chesterton, G.K. 102
*Childhood's End* 146, 172, 174–175, 178, 189
Cicero, Marcus Tullius 49, 72
*The City and the Stars* 9, 146, 172, 174–191
Clarke, Arthur C. 9, 146, 171–191; *Against the Fall of Night* 174, 176–177, 179, 187; *Beyond the the Fall of Night* 174; *Childhood's End* 146, 172, 174–175, 178, 189; *The City and the Stars* 9, 146, 172, 174–191; *The Fountains of Paradise* 172; "The Nine Billion Names of God" 172; *Profiles of the Future* 172, 176–177; *Rendezvous with Rama* 172, 178; "Reverie" 175; "The Sentinel" 172; "The Star" 172; *2001: A Space Odyssey* 171–172, 174, 178, 189
Clarke, I.F. 34
*The Clouds* 137
cognition 28, 30–33; *see also* cognitive estrangement
cognitive estrangement 6, 8, 28, 31–34, 37, 39–40, 63, 111, 113, 115, 194–195; *see also* narrative estrangement
Cold War 27, 137, 145, 147–148
Columbus, Christopher 72, 75
Communist 19, 51, 148
Conrad, Joseph 100
consensus reality 30, 40
"The Contemporary Novel" 103
*Contrat Social* 12
Crane, Stephen 100
critical utopia 27–28, 145, 195
Croft, Pauline 154
Cyrano de Bergerac 38; *Voyage to the Moon* 38
Cyros (ancient Persian ruler) 58

*Daily Mail* 109
d'Alembert, Jean le Rond 103
Darwin, Charles 109–110
Davis, J.C. 11, 184
*De la Terre à la Lune* 142
decorum 49, 83
Deery, June 114–115, 119–120
Defoe, Daniel 4
Delany, Samuel R. 145, 194; *Triton* 145
Desmarez, Jean 64
deus ex machina 29, 101, 187
Deutscher, Isaac 148
Diaspar (fictional city in *The City and the Stars*) 175–190
Dick, Philip K. 130, 144; *Do Androids Dream of Electric Sheep?* 144; *The Man in the High Castle* 144

Dickens, Charles 4, 97
Dickson, Lovat 99–101, 105
*The Dispossessed* 145, 194
*Do Androids Dream of Electric Sheep?* 144
Dostoyevsky, Fyodor 152; *The Brothers Karamazov* 152
Draper, Michael 99
*The Drowned World* 144
Dunsany, Lord 175
dystopia 4, 6–9, 13, 24, 36, 44, 106–108, 136–153, 178, 193–194

*Ecclesiazusae* 137
Edel, Leon 102, 104
Edward VI (of England) 56–57
Edwardian (age) 97–98, 104, 109
Eliade, Mircea 13
Elliott, Robert C. 22–25, 29, 77, 83–84, 113, 136–138, 141
Elton, G.R. 49
Engels, Friedrich 5
Enlightenment 34, 140, 160
Erasmus, Desiderius 35, 46, 48–50, 53, 55–56, 60, 64–65
*Erewhon* 7, 143
Euripides (ancient Greek dramatist) 94
*Experiment in Autobiography* 102

Fabian Society 99, 101, 108
*Faerie Queene* 62
*Fahrenheit 451* 144
fantasy 4, 7, 15, 24, 28–34, 36, 38, 47, 63, 67, 116, 131–132, 166, 175, 177–178, 188
*Fantastic Voyage* 38
*The Female Man* 145
Firchow, Peter 152
*The First Men in the Moon* 144, 149
folktale 28, 30
*Food of the Gods* 101
Ford, Ford Madox *see* Hueffer, Ford Madox
Ford, Henry 150, 153, 168; *My Life and Work* 150
Forster, E.M. 144, 178; "The Machine Stops" 178
Fortunate Isles (of St. Brendan) 14, 54
*Foundation* series 31
*The Fountains of Paradise* 172
Fourier, Charles 21
Foxe, John 50; *Acts and Monuments* 50
Frederick, Elector Palatine (son-in-law of James I) 154
Freedman, Carl 25–27
French Revolution (of 1789) 18, 140
Freud, Sigmund 120, 145
Froben, Johann 55–56, 64
Frye, Northrop 6, 22–25, 29, 34–37, 102–104, 111, 184; *Anatomy of Criticism* 24, 35–36, 104; "Varieties of Literary Utopias" 22, 24, 34, 184

Galen (ancient Greek physician) 94
Galsworthy, John 98
Gandhi, Mahatma 145
Geldenhouwer, Gerhard 64
Gernsback, Hugo 141
Gibson, R.W. 52, 57
Giles, Peter 45, 55, 64–69, 71–73, 75, 77–78, 96
Gissing, George 100
Golden Age 12, 23–24, 154–155, 181
Greenberg, Martin H. 171, 174
Greenblatt, Stephen 153–154
Gulliver, Lemuel (fictional character) 112, 138, 187
*Gulliver's Travels* 7, 138
Guy, John 48–51

Haldane, Charlotte 152
Hall, Joseph 74, 139; *Mundus Alter et Idem* 139
*Hamlet* 163
Hardy, Thomas 4
Harrington, James 21; *Oceana* 21
Hegel, Georg Wilhelm Friedrich 29, 193
Henry VII (of England) 53, 78
Henry VIII (of England) 46, 49–50, 52, 57, 70
heresy 42, 50–51, 190
hermeneutic 6, 26–28, 35
Herodotus (ancient Greek historian) 94
Hertzka, Theodor 21
Herzl, Theodor 21
Hexter, J.H. 46, 60, 76–77, 83
Hillegas, Mark 119, 143–144
Hinduism 189
Hippocrates (ancient Greek physician) 94
*The History of Mr Polly* 100
*Hitchhiker's Guide* series 143
Hobbes, Thomas 12, 21; *Leviathan* 12, 21
Hollow, John 171, 176
Holquist, Michael 42–43
Hölscher, Lucian 17–19, 140
Homer 74, 94, 142; *Odyssey* 74–75, 142
Homo Ludens 41
Hueffer, Ford Madox 100, 102
Hughes, David Y. 109, 119, 128
Huizinga, Johan 6, 41; *Homo Ludens* 41
Hume, Kathryn 30, 37
Huntington, John 119, 138
Hutten, Ulrich von 48, 55–56, 60
Huxley, Aldous 7, 9, 141, 144, 146, 147–171, 181, 194; *Island* 149, 194
Hythloday, Raphael (fictional character in More's *Utopia*) 7, 45–47, 53–96

Ibsen, Henrik 109
*Ideologie und Utopie* 25
ideology 5–6, 19, 25, 27, 32–33, 35, 147–148

implied reader 31, 121, 124, 131
*In the Days of the Comet* 101
*L'Ingenu* 106, 152
intentional fallacy 7, 47
*The Invisible Man* 103
irony 4, 7–9, 17, 29, 36–37, 57, 63, 67–68, 70, 74, 76–77, 83, 85–87, 91, 94, 96, 112, 114, 116, 118–119, 122, 126, 130, 132, 135, 137, 146, 151–152, 160, 176
*Island* 149, 194

James I (of England) 154
James, Edward 33, 146, 174–175, 185
James, Henry 100, 102, 104
Jameson, Fredric 25, 27, 35
John the Savage (fictional character in *Brave New World*) 150–153, 156, 158–166, 169–170
Johnson, Robin S. 77, 83
Johnson, Samuel (Dr. Johnson) 118
Jouvenel, Bertrand de 13
*Julius Caesar* 165

*Das Kapital* 51
Kaufman, Moritz 20
Kautsky, Karl 51–52, 61, 63
Kermode, Frank 153–154
*King Lear* 164
*Kipps* 100
Knapp, Jeffrey 62
Kornbluth, Cyril M. 144; *The Space Merchants* 144
Kropotkin, Pyotr Alexeyevich 12; *Mutual Aid* 12
Kubrick, Stanley 171; *2001: A Space Odyssey* 171
Kumar, Krishan 106–107, 109, 136, 139, 147, 149, 192

*Last and First Men* 7, 173
Lawrence, D.H. 100, 151, 161; *The Plumed Serpent* 151
Leavis, F.R. 36
Le Guin, Ursula K. 145, 194; *The Dispossessed* 145, 194
*Leviathan* 12, 21
Lewis, C.S. 62
Littlewood, Derek 31
Logan, George M. 60
*Looking Backward* 22, 39, 140, 155
*Love and Mr Lewisham* 100
Lucian (ancient Greek author) 35, 38, 94, 142; *Fantastic Voyage* 38; *True History* 142
Lundwall, Sam 143
Lupset, Thomas 64
Lys (fictional country in *The City and the Stars*) 183–190

Macaulay, Lord 17
*Macbeth* 163
"The Machine Stops" 178
Magellan, Ferdinand 73
*A Man for All Seasons* 50
*The Man in the High Castle* 144
*Mankind in the Making* 101, 118
Manlove, C.N. 177–178
Mannheim, Karl 25; *Ideologie und Utopie* 25
Manuel, Frank 12–13, 17, 116, 136; *Utopias and Utopian Thought* 12
Manuel, Fritzie 12–13, 17, 116, 136; *Utopias and Utopian Thought* 12
Mao Zedong 145
Marx, Karl 5, 20, 29, 51, 145, 193; *see also* Marxism; *Das Kapital* 51
Marxism neo–Marxism 5–6, 25–30, 35, 51–52
Mary I (of England) 57
McAleer, Neil 171, 173–174
Meckier, Jerome 150–152
*Men Like Gods* 150
Mencken, H.L. 99
Menippean satire 35, 104, 106; *see also* anatomy; satire
Mercier, Louis-Sébastien 21
meta-utopia 8, 109, 123, 133–134, 192, 194
millenarian prophecy, millenarian vision 12, 133
Miller, Walter M. 144; *A Canticle for Leibowitz* 144
mimesis 4, 7, 28–29, 36–40, 47, 63, 67, 69–70, 76
*Mind at the End of Its Tether* 107
Miranda (fictional character in *The Tempest*) 151–152, 154, 156, 158–161, 163–164, 167
"Modern Fiction" 98
*A Modern Utopia* 101, 105, 108–135
Molnar, Thomas 190
Mond, Mustapha (fictional character in *Brave New World*) 156–161, 165, 170
More, Cresacre 48
More, Sir Thomas 3, 5–8, 13–15, 17–21, 26, 37, 39, 43, 45–96, 97, 137, 139, 142, 146, 155, 184, 192; *Utopia* 3, 6–8, 37, 39, 43, 51, 53–96, 139, 146
Morris, William 7, 21, 39, 122, 136, 140; *News from Nowhere* 7, 39, 140
Morton, John Cardinal 78–79, 81, 84
Moskowitz, Sam 172–173, 175
Moylan, Tom 25–27, 145, 174, 195
Mumford, Lewis 13, 21, 178; *The Story of Utopias* 21
*Mundus Alter et Idem* 139
*Mutual Aid* 12
*My Life and Work* 150
myth 22–24, 28, 30, 75, 93, 99, 102, 155, 177, 188

narrative estrangement 6, 8, 40, 43, 67, 69, 82, 84, 87, 109, 114–115, 118–120, 122–123, 126, 130, 134–135, 139, 146; *see also* cognitive estrangement
Nazism 147, 193
negative utopia 4, 137–138, 150
*New Atlantis* 7
*The New Machiavelli* 98, 100
Newnes, George 109
*News from Nowhere* 7, 39, 140
"The Nine Billion Names of God" 172
*Nineteen Eighty-Four* 7, 9, 144, 147–149
Northcliffe, Lord 109
Northumberland, Duke of 57
novum 6, 26, 28, 31–34, 39–40, 112, 141, 194

*Oceana* 21
*Odyssey* 74–75, 142
Olander, Joseph D. 171, 174
*The Open Conspiracy* 108, 150
*The Open Society and Its Enemies* 193
Orwell, George 7, 9, 97, 99, 144, 147–149; *Nineteen Eighty-Four* 7, 9, 144, 147–149
*The Outline of History* 98

Palinurus (epic hero) 71–72
paradise 13, 23; *see also* Golden Age
paradox 3, 11, 26, 37, 62, 106
parody 4, 38, 117, 122, 137, 144, 150–151
Parrinder, Patrick 30, 32–33, 97–102, 106, 108–109, 112, 130, 133, 142
pastoral 23, 28, 122, 138, 184
Patroclus (epic hero) 63
Peacock, Thomas Love 105, 118
Perlette, John M. 80
Philmus, Robert M. 32–33, 97, 109, 112
Piercy, Marge 145; *Woman on the Edge of Time* 145
Plato 4, 13, 21, 71–72, 82–83, 85–86, 88, 93–95, 137, 193; *Republic* 13, 82, 85, 88, 137
Plattel, Martin G. 17, 140
*Player Piano* 144
*The Plumed Serpent* 151
Plutarch (ancient Greek historian) 94
Poe, Edgar Allan 141
Pohl, Frederik 143–144, 174; *The Space Merchants* 144
Polak, Frederik L. 13
Popper, Karl 138, 193; *The Open Society and Its Enemies* 193
*Das Prinzip Hoffnung* 5, 25
private property 47, 51, 54–55, 87, 90, 156
*Profiles of the Future* 172, 176–177
Prospero (fictional character in *The Tempest*) 151, 153–163, 167–169

Rabelais, François 18, 35, 105
Rabkin, Eric 171, 173–174, 180, 182–183, 185

Raknem, Ingvald 99
Rastell, John 61
Ray, Gordon N. 102, 104
Reid, Robin Anne 171
*Rendezvous with Rama* 172, 178
*Republic* 13, 82, 85, 88, 137
"Reverie" 175
rhetorical strategy 33, 38–40
Ricoeur, Paul 22
ritual 22–24, 34, 161
Robbins, Amy Catherine 100
Roberts, Adam 142, 172, 174
Robinson, Ralph 52, 56–57
Rodden, John 147
*Le Roman de l'avenir* 20
romance 23, 28, 35, 100–103, 117, 121, 124–125, 131, 134, 195; *see also* scientific romance
*Romeo and Juliet* 163, 164
Roosevelt, Theodore 117
Roper, William 48, 52
Rousseau, Jean-Jacques 12, 122, 160; *Contrat Social* 12
Russ, Joanna 145; *The Female Man* 145

samurai 124, 128–129, 131, 133, 135
Sargent, Lyman Tower 11–12, 20, 138
satire 4, 7, 8, 16–17, 19, 23–24, 29, 31, 35–38, 61–63, 68, 77, 84, 103–106, 112, 117–118, 126, 135, 137–139, 140, 142–143, 146–147, 149–153, 156, 170
Saturnalia 23–24
Scholes, Robert 174
Schrijver, Cornelis de 64
science fiction, SF 5–6, 8–9, 27–35, 40, 44, 97, 102, 134, 136, 141, 141–146, 171–175, 177–178, 181, 185, 191, 194–195
*Science Fiction Studies* (journal) 171
scientific romance 8, 32, 97, 99, 103, 107–108, 112, 130, 142–144
Sears, Paul B. 13
Seebohm, Federic 61
Seneca, Lucius Annaeus 72
"The Sentinel" 172
Shakespeare, William 62, 146, 151–153, 160–163, 165, 170; *As You Like It* 165; *Hamlet* 163; *Julius Caesar* 165; *King Lear* 164; *Macbeth* 163; *Romeo and Juliet* 163, 164; *The Tempest* 62, 146, 151–153, 161, 164, 166, 168, 170; *Troilus and Cressida* 163
*The Shape of Things to Come* 108
Shaw, G.B. 101, 109
Sheckley, Robert 143; "A Ticket to Tranai" 143
Shklar, Judith 13
Sidney, Sir Philip 58; *Apologie for Poetrie* 58
Smith, Clark Ashton 175
Smith, David C. 100–101, 107
Smith, John Maynard 13

social contract 23, 41, 89, 183, 193–194
Socialism 5, 19, 51, 53, 101
Socrates (ancient Greek philosopher) 82
Sophocles (ancient Greek dramatist) 94
*The Space Merchants* 144
Spence, Thomas 21
Spenser, Edmund 62; *Faerie Queene* 62
Stalinism 147, 193
Stapledon, Olaf 7, 146, 173, 175–176; *Last and First Men* 7, 173
"The Star" 172
Starnes, Colin 83
status quo 26–27, 37, 140
Sterne, Laurence 35
"A Story of the Days to Come" 144, 178
*The Story of Utopias* 21
Surtz, Edward 77
Suvin, Darko 6, 25, 28–35, 36, 40, 111, 114–115, 141, 195
Swift, Jonathan 7, 35, 105, 112, 138, 143; *Gulliver's Travels* 7, 138
Sylvester, R.S. 84, 95

Taoism 189–190
telos 22, 29, 137
*The Tempest* 62, 146, 151–153, 161, 164, 166, 168, 170
Terence (ancient Roman author) 57
Themsecke, Georges de 71
Theophrastus (ancient Greek philosopher) 94
Thukydides (ancient Greek historian) 94
"A Ticket to Tranai" 143
Tillich, Paul 13
*The Time Machine* 103, 108, 130, 138, 176–177
*Tit-bits* 109
*Tono-Bungay* 100
topos 4, 137, 139, 155
*Triton* 145
*Troilus and Cressida* 163
*True History* 142
Tunstall, Cuthbert 71
"Twilight" 175
*2001: A Space Odyssey* 171–172, 174, 178, 189

Ulysses (epic hero) 65, 71–72, 74–75
*Utopia* 3, 6–8, 37, 39, 43, 51, 53–96, 139, 146
utopian community 11–12, 16, 38, 120, 123, 139, 184–185
utopian fiction 6, 11, 15, 19–20, 22, 27, 35, 120, 136, 140, 143, 192
utopian imagination 13, 108, 136–138, 142, 146, 194–195
utopian satire 4, 24, 138, 143
utopian Socialism 5
utopian studies 5–6, 11, 19, 25, 136
utopian thought 11–12, 15, 138

232      Index

utopian tradition 7, 11–12, 106, 118, 138, 149, 153
utopian vision 6, 111, 119, 121, 123, 137, 151, 175, 194
utopianism 12, 17, 19, 109, 135, 136, 138, 166, 170
*Utopias and Utopian Thought* 12
Utopus, King (fictional character) 93–95, 193

"Varieties of Literary Utopias" 22, 24, 34, 184
Verne, Jules 141–142; *De la Terre à la Lune* 142; *Vingt mille lieues sous les mers* 142; *Vingt mille lieues sous les mers* 142
Vespucci, Amerigo 65, 72, 74–75
Victorian (age) 109, 121
Virgil (ancient Latin poet) 58, 74; *Aeneid* 74
Voltaire 103, 105–106, 152; *Candide* 106; *L'Ingenu* 106, 152
Vonnegut, Kurt 144; *Player Piano* 144
*Voyage au centre de la terre* 142
*Voyage to the Moon* 38

Wagar, W. Warren 99, 102, 106–108
Wagner, Richard 109
Walsh, Chad 136
*The War of the Worlds* 103
Watt, Donald 148, 152
*We* 141, 151
Webb, Beatrice 101
Webb, Sidney 101
Wells, H.G. 6–9, 21, 32, 43–44, 97–135, 136, 138, 141–144, 146–147, 149–153, 156, 170, 175–178, 192, 194; *Anne Veronica* 100;

*Anticipations* 99–101, 105, 118; "The Contemporary Novel" 103; *Experiment in Autobiography* 102; *The First Men in the Moon* 144, 149; *Food of the Gods* 101; *The History of Mr Polly* 100; *In the Days of the Comet* 101; *The Invisible Man* 103; *Kipps* 100; *Love and Mr Lewisham* 100; *Mankind in the Making* 101, 118; *Men Like Gods* 150; *Mind at the End of Its Tether* 107; *A Modern Utopia* 101, 105, 108–135; *The New Machiavelli* 98, 100; *The Open Conspiracy* 108, 150; *The Outline of History* 98; *The Shape of Things to Come* 108; "A Story of the Days to Come" 144, 178; *The Time Machine* 103, 108, 130, 138, 176–177; *Tono-Bungay* 100; *The War of the Worlds* 103; *When the Sleeper Wakes* 144, 178; *The World of William Clissold* 98
West, Geoffrey 106
West, Rebecca 152
Westfahl, Gary 173
*When the Sleeper Wakes* 144, 178
Williams, Raymond 22
Wolfe, Gary K. 174, 178, 185–186
*Woman on the Edge of Time* 145
Woolf, Virginia 98; "Modern Fiction" 98
*The World of William Clissold* 98
world-1, world-2 30, 37–43, 92, 194–195
World State 8, 99, 103, 107–109, 123–124, 128–129, 146, 150, 152, 156–162, 166, 168–170, 181

Xenophon (ancient Greek historian) 58

Zamyatin, Yevgeniy 141, 144, 151; *We* 141, 151
Zola, Émile 109